FAIR TRADE

A New
Liaden Universe®
Novel

SHARON LEE &
STEVE MILLER

BAEN

A Baen Books Original

Baen Publishing Enterprises
P.O. Box 1403
Riverdale, NY 10471
www.baen.com

ISBN: 978-1-9821-9277-8

Cover art by David Mattingly

First printing, May 2022
First mass market printing, June 2023

Distributed by Simon & Schuster
1230 Avenue of the Americas
New York, NY 10020

Library of Congress Control Number: 2022003034

Printed in the United States of America

10 9 8 7 6 5 4 3 2 1

To Napa, California

The authors thank the following sharp-eyed
and stalwart persons who participated in
the Great *Fair Trade* Tyop Hunt of 2022

Kajsa Anderson, 'nother Mike, Deb Boyken, JC,
Millie Calistri-Yeh, Roseanne Girton, Gareth Griffiths,
Rich Hanson, Mallory Harper, Irene Harrison,
Julia Hart, Suzanne Hediger, Kathryn Kremer,
Mary Soon Lee, Evelyn Mellone, Judith Moffitt,
Bex O, Robert Parks, Marni Rachmiel,
Kate Reynolds, Lucian Stacy, Kathryn Sullivan,
Gordon G Wainwright, Sidney Whitaker, Anne Young

THE TRADER

＊＊＊＊＊✳＊＊＊＊＊

Frenol

THE TRADER

ONE

JETHRI GOBELYN VEN'DEELIN, SECOND TRADER ON *Elthoria*, out of Solcintra, Liad, felt the gravity change and the pressure shift in the same step. Frenol was efficient about such matters, supplying no more air nor gravity than required to incoming ships without being miserly about it. The walk through the portal allowed ship over-pressure to be expended, while at the same time inviting wandering particles from onboard to settle quickly to the lightly charged grids ramping into the station side.

Jethri was not alone leaving *Elthoria*; crew mates bustled around him on the ramp, rushing off to market shifts or to scout for prizes and bargains. If they were quick, they might shop before all the merchants registered that a new ship was arrived and raised prices for the occasion. The bargain-hunters hit the decking first, followed not too closely by knots of two, four, six—comrades with joint pleasure in their plans, eager, but not hasty.

They, too, achieved Frenol's deck before the second trader, who was walking alone, as he often did on port. There was, after all, no need to rush. His legs were long, and, if Protocol Master tel'Ondor was to be believed, there was his dignity to preserve.

3

He gained the first air well speedily enough, a space tall and wide, more formal than the dock sides and more crowded. He paused for a moment just aside the arch, to consider the signage and the traffic, and to consult the map in his head.

Elthoria was fresh in from Seybol, on the heavily Liaden front rim, where the new fashions from the homeworld itself had only just arrived. Since a trader must be seen to be prosperous *and* current, Jethri had new clothes, in the first stare of fashion.

In fact, he noticed that he was the recipient of actual stares from more than one passing pedestrian—which was not unusual in the Liaden markets, where he stood at least half a head taller than nearly anybody. Here on Frenol, it was more likely the clothes than the height.

Though there was the height, too, he thought wryly. The fashion whimsy of the season was that all footwear be given a rigorously measured big-toe of extra height, and the second trader had not been permitted to sidestep this.

So, with a plush purple stripe exactly the width of the tailor's math stick across the right shoulder of his new yellow coat, and added height for all that he was not short even among Terrans, Jethri *was* noticeable as he stood in a designated rest circle, overlooking what seemed to be a market day crowd at full-tide.

His experienced trader's eye noted this one and that moving casually toward himself, seeing a young, well-dressed, gormless, and inexperienced person just off a trade ship, who was likely full in the spending pocket as well. Time to get moving again, he thought. But there, the map in his head matched the signs, and he swung away from the wall and into the crowd. His stride was long, and strong for a ship-born ex-Looper, and Jethri soon put the hopeful pickpockets behind, as he headed not for the joys and pressures of a bedding station or souvenir parlor but for the business-as-usual comfort of one of the Trade Bars. He'd not been to Frenol before but the formal Liaden Trade Bar was not, as might be assumed from his position as second trader on a Liaden ship, first on his list. Today he sought news of kin and, truth be told, kind. The *Envidaria* was more than a minor part of his life these days, and he might as well see what the word was on the docks.

Frenol wasn't, exactly, a Liaden port, nor was it, exactly, a Terran port. It *was* closer to the big shipping lanes and farther from the usual routes of Loop ships. Loopers were for the most part Terran or equivalent mixed crew and their ships were, as Arin Gobelyn had known well, generally smaller and older than the Liaden tradeships dominating the main routes. And as the newer, larger Liaden ships needed the newer, larger berths, here on Frenol *Elthoria* was comfortably docked on the expansive New Market Wing of the station, while Practical Al's Trade Bar was on the far side of the Grande Esplanade, down in what was called Old Main Line, since it hadn't been main line for handfuls of decades.

The walk down-station did Jethri good, letting him stretch his legs with a will while seeing new sights—and the sights were worth seeing, though he doubted he'd be free to pursue any of them, given the fact that Master Trader Norn ven'Deelin, coincidentally his foster-mother, was to meet with Master Trader pin'Aker on the morrow. Given the general tendency of Master Trader ven'Deelin to orchestrate surprising situations, and use all of the pieces on her board, Jethri supposed he would be included—somehow.

He was approaching Frenol's more Terran district. Not only were the store fronts gaudier, and the come-on music louder, but the scents were different. That made his spacer's clean-air instincts leery—he'd spent far too much of his time on *Gobelyn's Market* doing Stinks to have this much odor poured at him without imagining what the filters must look like after a shift! He didn't doubt that the local merchants cheated on air exchange rules to flood the aisles and halls with the hints of oil and baked goods not usually found on the Liaden side, much less on long haul trade ships. Too, the under-scent near some locations openly hinted at *vya*, chocolate, and alcohol, all far too forward to be wafted about near the Grande Esplanade, where tender teas and fine pastries might be on offer.

The hall narrowed, narrowed again, kinked to the left, and opened into a space nearly as large as the Grande Esplanade, and three times as crowded. People were taller; their voices louder; their finery, while fine, tending more toward comfort than elegance.

Jethri kept moving in the crowd, squaring his shoulders so as to look bigger, which a Liaden would never do. Here, though, the trick worked; people stepped out of his way, when they could, and he was hardly jostled at all. He began to believe that his fancy new coat might survive this adventure.

Jethri had first heard about Practical Al's as the youngest and least-wanted mainline Gobelyn on the *Market*. His father had been trying to convince Captain

Iza to plot a course to Frenol, for some reason now lost to time. In the end, the captain had declined to deviate from the Loop, but before she had, Arin and Grig had plied her with data describing the station, and hinting at the profits to be made.

The file featuring Practical Al's Trade Bar had caught Jethri's young imagination, and he had promised himself right then that, when he was captain of his own ship, he'd take himself to Frenol and have a meal at Practical Al's, the oldest continuously run station-based Trade Bar in the Raifling Sector. The file had included pictures of the place—several of the ornate clock set over the wide entrance, which counted the Terran seconds, minutes, hours, days, and years that had passed since the bar's opening. The place itself—

Was right there; he recognized it immediately, though it was larger than he had imagined, reaching almost to the hall's vaulted roof. It had apparently caught the imagination of many beyond Jethri Gobelyn. The approach was surging with people. Looking around, Jethri saw that there was a *nerligig* dancing on a raised platform at what might be the entrance to the bar's business zone, which had drawn its own admiring crowd.

Practical Al's, Open All Hours Three Centuries and Counting read the sign above the clock.

Jethri scouted out a path around the *nerligig* and its adherents, hoping against fading hope that there might actually be a quiet table within the bar itself, a place to get a near-beer or a quiet glass of wine. A place to order food that was more in the Terran way, which he'd lately found himself missing, though no one could fault the food provided to *Elthoria*'s crew.

There! His eye traced a path taken by a number of people, which swept around the margin of the *nerligig*'s crowd, and snaked back toward the front entrance. Jethri was soon one of their number.

The line moved reasonably well, and the entrance was in sight, when the crowd bunched, separated, and swirled, perhaps because among the taller Terrans was a golden-haired Liaden doing an excellent job of not being stepped on by gawkers.

Within the confusion an elegant bow was swept, fine-tuned with nuance. No offense taken, no offense meant, please choose your route with . . .

While the finesse of the bow was perhaps lost on the pair of Terrans now detouring around the display with nods and semi-smiles, Jethri was all admiration, the moreso when he felt a jolt of recognition—

The polite Liaden, deserted by his partners in chaos, made no ill-timed straightening that might have been misread by someone glancing back, but finished the bow in detail as if all eyes were still on him, paused for a breath and—

"An excellent summation of the *melant'i* of the situation, all in good will!" Jethri called out, his use of Comrade mode in Liaden likely to mask his own Terran identity to those around.

A bland face turned toward him, rapidly recast to an acceptably pleased public face as he was recognized in turn.

They rushed together, careful of the march of other necessities about them, producing a playful series of bows as they closed the distance and finally clasped hands.

"But Tan Sim, how are you here, my partner?"

"To surprise, naturally. And you? Was *Elthoria* not to arrive tomorrow?"

Jethri broke into his Terran trader grin, pitching his voice lower as he leaned confidentially toward Tan Sim.

"That was the plan before it was decided that I should continue to amass board-time and the piloting of *Elthoria* was given to me. I got us here too quickly, and pleased everyone by arriving in one piece." He produced an entirely false expression of wondering regret.

"Who knew that *Elthoria* is not meant to Jump like a Scout ship?"

Tan Sim sputtered, and Jethri saw the laughter in him.

Their clasped hands were a warmth between them, and they were an awkward impediment to the swirl of the crowd.

"We should move," Tan Sim murmured.

"Before we're trampled," Jethri agreed.

Unclasping hands, they turned as one toward Practical Al's. There were several doors to choose from, the largest at deck level, another at the top of a ramp, and a third, three steps below the deck.

"We seem to be one mind in two bodies!" Jethri said lightly. "You choose the portal and the floor. I will choose the table and—" He looked up to the large sign spelling out Terran foodstuffs—"'the grub!'"

"I spoke in jest," admitted Tan Sim, "when I said we meant to surprise. What we *meant* to do was earn a bonus, due to my shrewd trading contacts." He smiled a nearly Terran smile. "Also, I wished to have a useful layover here. It happens that Frenol's yards are superior to those at our previous port. So, we have earned our bonus, for delivering in good time the package entrusted to us by Master Trader pin'Aker. In the meanwhile, the ship undergoes scheduled maintenance, while the trader goes about looking for goods that will draw favorable attention at the South Axis Congress. For I tell you with no shame, Jethri, I am much more skilled at trade than I am at lift-shifting."

Jethri grinned.

"I might have overstated my piloting skill," he admitted. "*Elthoria*'s departure from Seybol was clear from break-dock to Jump-point. This put us well ahead of schedule, with an uncomfortably early arrival at Frenol forecast.

"The pilots therefore decreed that I ought, in fact, be given an opportunity to gain board-time, as it appears to be the intention of everyone save myself to make me into a pilot. So I was put at the board and told to bring us to Frenol." He bestowed a droll glance upon Tan Sim.

"Come, Trader, you are ahead of me, are you not?"

"Not in the way of most business," Tan Sim said dryly. "This time, however, I venture to guess that the pilot-in-training did not Jump *Elthoria* as if she had no more mass than a Scout ship. Rather he fumbled his math, missed the entry point, and had to re-frame his equations twice."

"Three times," Jethri corrected. "I would not have you think me greater than I am."

They sat in a quiet corner—Practical Al's was all quiet corners, the interior cunningly partitioned—and if the portal Tan Sim had opened gave into the largest and noisiest floor, neither cared about the noise level, nor of the interest their joint arrival had occasioned. Clearly one or the other of them, if not both, were remarkable to the habitues; the nods in their directions were not from people they recognized but clearly from those people recognizing their right to be where they were and who hoped the traders would recall seeing *them*.

That they'd found a favored place was obvious: within moments of their settling into the space that provided views of three situation boards—one carrying trade updates and the other two showing port traffic in addition to an overhead speaker with table-side volume control—two other parties arrived seeking the same spot. Finding it occupied, both groups had smiled, and waved, and left in search of a less-favored corner.

Tan Sim's surprisingly animated face caught Jethri's appraisal: this was a confident man, well pleased with his life, certainly much improved in situation compared to their very first meeting when both had been not only younger, but in peculiar peril from Tan Sim's clan.

It was a confident man who waved Practical Al's server to their table side, using his chin to point toward Jethri.

"This trader will order for both," he said in confident Terran. "We are entirely at your mercy as we have neither one eaten for a ten-day!"

The waiter looked them over and smiled with Terran ease.

"Yes, I see all the signs of incipient starvation! Put your faith in me, Traders; I've completed many successful rescues in my career. First, of course, you'll be wanting drinks..."

Jethri ordered station-made ale for both, ran an

eye down the menu, and, heeding the promptings of what might have equally been nostalgia and honest hunger, ordered long-missed delicacies.

These he brought to Tan Sim's attention when the tray arrived—which it did with commendable speed.

"This," he murmured, indicating the plate of crispy logs in the very center of the tray, "is eaten with the fingers, so."

He reached for the condiment tray, and bestowed a generous amount of red paste onto his tray before reaching to the communal plate, plucking up a log in his naked fingers. He dipped it into the paste before conveying it to his mouth.

Flavor exploded in his mouth, and he sighed.

Tan Sim, however, was frowning. Liadens were fastidious eaters. A race that had produced a twenty-four piece formal setting as an improvement upon the work-a-day twelve piece, and which looked with horror, as he had been led to believe by Stafeli Maarilex, on the haphazard chaos of a six-piece setting that might serve at a working meeting between the traders on *Elthoria*—that race was in no way prepared for the informality of Terran dining.

"Is that grease?" Tan Sim asked, looking up, the frown more pronounced. "And eaten with one's fingers? You would not be *having me on*, Jethri?"

"Not a bit of it," Jethri assured him, dipping another log in the sauce.

Still Tan Sim hesitated, and Jethri felt that some encouragement was in order.

"A delicacy, on *Elthoria*'s honor."

Tan Sim half-laughed.

"Who am I to disregard such weighty assurance?"

He placed red sauce on his plate as Jethri had done, reached to the diminishing plate of logs, chose one, dipped it, and brought it to his mouth.

He chewed, his eyes grew wide; again he dipped and again he ate.

"Jethri."

"Tan Sim."

"This is very good. You must tell me what it is called so that I may demand it at every meal for the remainder of my life."

Jethri grinned and reached for another log.

"This is a taterlog," he said. "The sauce is crushed pomidor with spices." He dipped, ate, sighed.

"You have missed this food, from your former life," Tan Sim said gently.

"I have. Understand, it's not something we'd have every day, but when more than one family ship was together on port, or at *shivary*, for certain." He shook his head, feeling his mouth bend in a wry smile. "I haven't had the nerve to ask the kitchen on *Elthoria* to add it, even though they're perfectly capable, of course."

"Of course," Tan Sim said, without irony, which was really, Jethri thought, quite a trick. "There is the matter, too, of it being a true delicacy, meant to be served on premier occasions."

"Yes," Jethri admitted. He'd forgotten how perceptive Tan Sim was.

His partner helped himself to another taterlog, dunked it in the sauce like he'd been doing it all his life, and ate it with relish.

"Then there is the danger of this food spreading throughout the tradeships and coming at last to Liad. Only think of the horror."

"I don't see that," Jethri countered, "once they got past deciding whether to eat it with tongs or the small two-pronged fork." He cleaned his fingers on the napkin and leaned toward the tray.

"This, now, is a bun-burger."

"Let me guess. It is also eaten from the hand?"

"You're getting good at this," Jethri told him.

Tan Sim laughed a soft Liaden laugh, took a draft of his ale, and said, "Show me."

Their server had come by to collect the empty tray, supplied more ale at their request, and left without suggesting dessert.

"Though I suspect he will do," said Tan Sim, "when he comes back again to see to the ale."

Jethri nodded, sipped his ale, and leaned back, his body automatically adjusting itself into a more nuanced repose.

Across the table, Tan Sim noticed, and raised his eyebrows.

"It is fortunate that we met thus early," Jethri said in Liaden, "as it gives me the opportunity to arrive at information the master trader particularly requested I obtain, and to also ask if you had received my last letter."

Tan Sim sighed, had recourse to the ale, and likewise sat back. He had no need to realign his posture. Tan Sim's achievements in spoken Terran were admirable, but his body language was nothing other than Liaden.

"In fact, I did receive your last letter, and—well, what would you, Jeth Ree? I thought that it must be a jest."

"How so?" Jethri asked, noting with some amusement that the styling of his name had changed language, as well.

"You asked, an you recall it, if, in the face of my brother's death, Rinork was likely to name me *nadelm*, and, should that occur, what would be my answer."

"That was," Jethri admitted, "the information that the master trader requested I obtain for her."

"I cannot—" Tan Sim sighed, and raised his hand, showing palms. "Well, and she *is* a master trader, after all. She will wish to be certain which and how many coins she has to her hand. So."

He picked up his mug, and Jethri followed suit. When they were both refreshed, Tan Sim leaned forward.

"To be as clear as one might, saving the master trader's honor: No, I have no expectations of being raised to *nadelm*, and if I did, I should recuse myself, or if necessary, propose myself as general crew on an ore boat. Bar Jan dead and *I* the next *nadelm*? Well, you saw how it was, Jeth Ree—and he was the *favorite*! Only consider how it might be for one she holds in complete contempt—but not for very long, I beg. No, it will be best and easiest to simply get herself a new heir and begin immediately to shape the infant mind until it produces an adequate reflection of her own."

That was sobering, not to say horrifying. They both lifted mugs and drank what was left of their ales, each perhaps thinking of Infreya chel'Gaibin, who had thrown away two children.

"Another?" Jethri asked, when the empty mugs were back on the table.

"Of your kindness," Tan Sim said, bending a sorrowful look on the empty mug, before glancing up with a proper Liaden smile.

"And another order of taterlogs, if you will, Trader."

Jethri laughed.

"Well, I will!" he said, and raised a hand to summon their server, and placed the order.

"Now," he said, when the drinks had arrived—darker ale this time, on the server's suggestion. "Now, Trader, you will tell me everything about your schedule for the South Axis Congress. All my life, I've dreamed of attending an Axis Congress. I was too young for the East Axis Congress, and that set the route for *Gobelyn's Market* for ten years."

"Why weren't you allowed to attend?" Tan Sim asked, following him back into Terran.

"Well, I was the reason someone else had to stay on-board."

"As young as that! At least you have outgrown that excuse, Trader." He paused to sip ale. "Excellent!" He sighed, eyes closed.

"The congress?" Jethri prompted, when it seemed Tan Sim had forgotten him.

"Ah, yes." He opened his eyes. "As it happens, *this* young trader is bound for the South Axis Congress because *Genchi* is carrying three pods of set-up and specials for the trade fair and pre-conference."

"Three pods." Jethri leaned in close. "Say more, Trader, do."

JETHRI'S NEXT MORNING WAS FULL, THE LATE HOUR OF his arrival back at *Elthoria* translating into the necessity of apologetically answering via in-ship mail two celebratory invitations for the previous evening from interested bed partners, and then following up with a ship-side breakfast, where he believed that his mother and his master trader was not only well-pleased, but actually relieved to have news of Trader pen'Akla's whereabouts. Their plans for the day, made rather tipsily last evening, met with her enthusiastic approval.

"Surely such a day on-port will benefit both traders, and improve the partnership. Merely, I ask that your plans include your arrival at *Balent'i Chernubianda* at the local time thirteen bells. I have bespoken a table. You and Trader pen'Akla will do me the honor of being among my guests."

"The Galaxy of Desserts?"

Jethri raised an eyebrow. His mother bestowed upon him a gaze of wide delight. He held his breath.

"Your command of the Liaden language continues to impress, my son. Precisely the Galaxy of Desserts. I, who have been here previously as you have not, attest to the excellence of their desserts, as befits a bakery that grew into a Trade Bar." She paused to sip her tea before continuing, meditatively.

"Frenol has a tradition, I believe. Practical Al's began as a hardware shop, am I correct?"

Jethri didn't bite his lip. Not quite.

"Yes, ma'am," he murmured, as properly serious as he knew how. "Practical Al's Hardware and Supply."

"Indeed. A tradition." She put her cup aside.

"You should know, I think, that I have enjoyed our several recent conversations involving the upcoming trading season in the deep arm. You have given me much to think upon." She moved a hand. "But, there, you have plans! Go and fulfill them all! And do not fail to bring Trader pen'Akla with you to my table at the thirteenth bell."

By the time Jethri relayed the master trader's gracious invitation to Tan Sim, he'd thought it over five ways by fifty, as Uncle Paitor might have had it, and could see nothing but the signs of some secret agenda...which he also reported to his partner.

"She is no doubt up to something, my friend," he confessed, as they entered the textile hall. "And ahead of us, too, whatever it is!"

Tan Sim accorded him a small bow.

"If not actual mischief—which we must suppose it is not—then we may recall that she is a master trader. Therefore, I assume with you, my Jeth Ree, that she is *up to something*, and it is our sweet duty to be amazed by what she will reveal." He glanced up at Jethri, eyes glinting. "All will be made known in a few hours, and so our choice is clear. Do we spend those hours in a quake over what our parts may be in the master trader's plan? Or do we gird ourselves and do the proper work of traders on port?"

"Phrased thus," Jethri murmured, "the choice is clear. Onward!"

The trading on the day was gratifying to both. Though they returned to the topic of the master trader's intentions several times, they had reached no conclusions by the time they checked their persons for presentability as they risked not quite making the appointment on time.

The lack of a line at the entrance to the Galaxy of Desserts was the only thing between their being tardy and on time—it also helped that Master Trader ven'Deelin had achieved a private room on the first floor. They were escorted to the door, finding a server with floating tea cart barely ahead of them.

Jethri slid smoothly between door and cart, Tan Sim a half-step behind, going right as Jethri went left, in order to allow service to arrive.

"Our thanks," Master ven'Deelin said to the server who hesitated upon the threshold. "Please place the tray at table center. We shall do very well for ourselves."

"Ma'am." The server bowed, floated the tray forward and made the transfer.

"The main meal will arrive on the half-bell," she murmured, "unless there are new instructions."

"Again, my thanks, but no. Allow the meal to arrive on the half-bell. These our colleagues have been at the markets all day, and will be wishful of their dinners."

"Ma'am." The server bowed again and departed with the empty tray. The door closed behind her.

Standing out of the way, Jethri had been admiring

the quiet elegance of the room, so different from last evening's venue. There would be no extraneous sounds here, nor eager ears hoping to capture secrets.

"Now, did I not say, Rantel, that they would be with us, at precisely thirteen bells?" Master Trader ven'Deelin turned to the gentle sitting at her right hand, and Jethri recognized Master Trader Rantel pin'Aker Clan Midys, his dark brown hair shining in the room's lights, the lines on his pleasant face giving evidence that he was senior in age as well as in rank.

"They are struck speechless," Master pin'Aker observed gently.

Jethri felt his face heat even as he belatedly bowed respect to the masters. From the side of his eye, he saw Tan Sim perform a similar courtesy. When they had straightened, Tan Sim spoke, with a lightness that perfectly played off of Master pin'Aker's remark.

"But who would not be speechless in the presence of two such luminaries of trade?" he asked. "Master ven'Deelin, I am honored to be made a part of your arrangements. Master pin'Aker, I had hardly dared hope for another meeting so soon after our last."

It being Jethri's turn, he placed his hand over his heart, producing an effect of wide-eyed candor. "In my case, ma'am, I was speechless in truth, having run the length of the station when the time took me unaware."

"Well." Master ven'Deelin looked to the other master. "Rantel, what ought we to do with these scamps?"

"Surely, we ought to feed them," Master pin'Aker said. "To confess to having run the length of the station! That is no inconsiderable effort, Norn."

"Now, that is very true." Master Trader ven'Deelin

reached for the teapot. "Sit. Sit, both! And have your tea. Trader pen'Akla, by me, if you will. Jethri, my son, allow my good friend Rantel to support you."

Thus the tea was poured, and sampled, as Jethri considered the *melant'i* of the meeting. The masters had set the tone as casual, therefore, it was not a business meeting, nor was it merely a meeting of associates. Which only left a dozen or so other things it might be, *melant'i* being what it was.

Jethri's own *melant'i* was stretched in odd ways, here, he realized. Master ven'Deelin being the host, he was at present her son and potentially her second. However, he was in an equal partnership with Tan Sim, whose practical experience far surpassed his own, but who cruelly lacked funding, which Jethri could supply—and none of that even began to factor in the presence of Master pin'Aker, Master ven'Deelin's old friend, assuredly, but also an ally in who knew what schemes of trade or politics?

It was enough to make a trader's head ache.

Happily for his head, and possibly his *melant'i*, the masters took the conversational lead during the meal. The exigencies of travel each had overcome in order to raise Frenol at the appropriate time got them through the opening tea. During the meal, they chose to draw their juniors out about their day in the markets. Not that they inquired after the various trade opportunities they had encountered; that would have been too much like business. Rather, they asked about the people they had seen, the look of the station, and in particular, so it seemed to Jethri, the fashions.

And so it was about the fashions that he spoke,

when there came a lull in the conversation that was not, he judged, *wholly* about giving the dessert its due.

"Do you think, sir, that the Seybol fashions will find favor on Frenol, when they arrive?"

Jethri bowed slightly to *Barskalee*'s trader, offering him the conversational lead, if he wished it.

The trader did not lift his eyes from his dessert plate, which held one last bite.

"Indulge me, Trader. I fear that question hovers on the edge of business, and first I must decide if I am going to attempt to bribe the chef for this recipe." He forked the last bit into his mouth, and sighed. "Is it not fine?"

"It is, indeed," Master Trader ven'Deelin agreed. "Perhaps you will accept me as a partner in the matter of the bribe? I assure you, for this, I will go deep into my reserves!"

They all laughed lightly, and the juniors, understanding that the masters were ready to move into the meat of the evening, exchanged a politely bland glance that neither had the slightest difficulty interpreting as abject panic.

The sad empty dessert plates were cleared, and the tray arrived again, this time bearing several bottles of wine Jethri recognized as being from *Elthoria*'s own cellar.

"Excellent," Master ven'Deelin murmured. "There is no need to attend us while we tarry over the wine. We will call, should there be need."

The server bowed and departed. The door closed, and Jethri took a deep, quiet breath.

"Rantel, will you pour?" Master Trader ven'Deelin asked. "The sto'Helit first."

"Of course." The master trader rose and approached the wine tray. There came the sharp pop of a cork being drawn, the clink of glass against glass. He served Master Trader ven'Deelin first, then Jethri, which, he reminded himself, was *not* an error, since the second in precedence was in charge of the pour, then Tan Sim, and carried his glass with him back to the table.

"The sto'Helit," he murmured, lifting the glass and turning it so that the pale liquid shimmered against the light. "How many are left?"

"Only six now in the cellar. I hoped to recall us to happy endings, rather than bad beginnings."

"And yet we could not have achieved the second, had we not had the first," Master pin'Aker murmured.

"Very true."

Master ven'Deelin raised her glass, glancing round the table.

Jethri obediently lifted his glass, and Tan Sim his. "I suggest that we drink, then, to unlikely beginnings and triumphant results."

They touched glasses, all, and drank to the sentiment. It was a quiet wine, the sto'Helit. Jethri savored it, paying attention to what his taste buds were telling him. A fine wine, light, and slightly acerbic. He would know it again.

He held onto his glass a moment longer, but it appeared that Master pin'Aker would not be capping the toast, verifying that they had, in fact, crossed the threshold from pleasure into business.

Master Trader ven'Deelin placed her glass gently on the table, and allowed herself to leisurely consider the two junior members of the party.

"I am pleased to hear that your day on-port was

both profitable and pleasant," she said. "Truly is it said that successful trade is one fourth marketing, one fourth skill, and one half connections.

"You will be gratified to know that Master pin'Aker and I have also spent a fruitful day together." She inclined her head in what was clearly a cue to the other master.

"Indeed. A day spent with my good friend Norn is always a fine one—how could it be otherwise?" He tipped his glass to her gallantly, before turning his attention upon the breath-caught juniors.

"The theme of our day was the care of trade, which it often is, when masters meet. And so we come to you, Traders." He sipped and smiled before murmuring again, as if it were a refrain in a favorite song. "And so we come to you.

"I believe we shall come first to Trader ven'Deelin," he said, setting his glass down with a flourish. He held his hand, palm up, toward Jethri. "I wish to inspect your trade ring, sir."

Jethri felt a chill, but he flattered himself that he allowed none of the alarm he felt to reach his face. Carefully, he had the ring off, and gently placed it on Master pin'Aker's palm. Golden fingers folded over the token, hiding it from sight. Jethri put his hands together on the tabletop and tried to give the impression that he did not feel entirely naked.

"So."

Master pin'Aker raised his hand, showing what he held between thumb and forefinger: a silver ring with four channels at the head, each holding a baguette-cut stone. Neither the ring nor the stones were costly, nor even new. Yet, they were worth the whole of Jethri's future, representing his journey from 'prentice to full trader. The ring was designed so that the stones were replaceable. It had come to him with each channel holding a stone of crystal-clear quartz, which had been placed by Master ven'Deelin, each representing a port at which he had participated in trade. The next stones were topaz, signifying the manner of his trading, and the next after those garnet, which spoke to his acumen. From garnet, the stones progressed to amethyst, which referenced such traderly virtues as boldness, subtlety, and creativity.

"I see here," Master pin'Aker said to the table at large. "Three topaz and one garnet. Do you see them, also, Norn?"

Trader ven'Deelin admitted that she did, indeed, see three topaz and one garnet. Jethri breathed deep, riding down his rising temper. It wasn't as if he were the sole judge of when to replace a stone, after all! There were the guild rules to guide him, and his own master trader to inform him of any oversteps.

No, he told himself, look at the two of them! He thought Master ven'Deelin was up to something, and Tan Sim had agreed—only Master pin'Aker was in on it, too.

"Trader ven'Deelin," Master pin'Aker turned back to him. "How do you explain this ring?"

Jethri spread his hands. "Master, how else could I explain it, except to say that it maps my progress from 'prentice to full trader. I have taken part in trade on at least three ports, my style of trade has become refined to that level of—"

"Bah!" Master pin'Aker waved his unencumbered hand at Jethri, who took that as an order to desist, and turned again to Master ven'Deelin. "I wonder, Norn, if you have heard the full tale of this trader's endeavors at Tradedesk?"

Master Trader ven'Deelin spread her hands.

"I have had a report from Trader Jethri himself, as he attended the event at Tradedesk as *Elthoria*'s representative. In that, he was successful, having brought back with him several interesting contacts. The trader tells me that he became involved in a public challenge, and felt he had acquitted himself well there. Understand, my friend, Trader Jethri makes a habit of glossing his successes, possibly because he does not wish to put the rest of us to the blush. I believe, though this, I confess, is my own conjecture, rather than something I was told, that he was made a graceful welcome..."

Jethri felt his cheeks warm, for in fact he had enjoyed several graceful welcomes, the most demonstrative from Samay pin'Aker, the master's niece. Grandma Ricky had made him welcome, too, in her way, and a number of his useful new contacts were due to her kind attention to a fledgling trader.

Master ven'Deelin had stopped speaking and Master pin'Aker was silent, Jethri realized suddenly. Possibly he was waiting for her to tell him more of Tradedesk, but she merely lifted her glass and sipped the sto'Helit.

"I see how it is," Trader pin'Aker said, when she had put the glass aside once more. "You do not have the whole of it. In fact, this scamp of a Trader Jethri has withheld information from you. Well! You shall no longer reside in ignorance, for I will tell all!"

All?

Jethri dared a glance at Tan Sim, who was wearing

his blandest face, by which Jethri deduced that his partner was as dismayed and puzzled as he was himself. That, Jethri decided, was not reassuring.

Master pin'Aker had paused to refresh himself from his glass. After a moment, Jethri did the same. Whatever came of this discussion of *all*, it would not do to let so pleasing a vintage go unappreciated.

"Understand, Norn, that Tradedesk is a concept in process, born from a background rich in tradition, and a philosophy that allows traders to be peers. This philosophy makes Tradedesk a uniquity, for it aspires to be neither a Terran station nor a Liaden station, but a *trade station*."

He paused, and accorded Master ven'Deelin a seated bow.

"I know that this will resonate with you, for you have undertaken a similar project."

Master ven'Deelin making no reply to this—provocation, was it? Jethri wondered—he continued.

"Into this ongoing project born of long history, then, arrives Trader Jethri Gobelyn ven'Deelin. But, does he merely arrive, on tradeship, charter ship, or shuttle? Not he! Trader ven'Deelin is pleased to arrive aboard a Scout ship! Further, in a Scout ship which has the honor to list him as pilot-in-charge, with the redoubtable ter'Astin relegated to copilot!"

He held up a hand, though no one of his audience had any idea of interrupting, so far as Jethri could see.

"There is more," he said, shifting mode abruptly, and continuing as one speaking in utmost confidence. "The philosophies that govern Tradedesk are not alone in being a work in process. The station itself is yet somewhat under construction, and it was near to beginning the transition to its new and permanent orbit, though the Carresens' flagship was not yet fully mated for that move. To phrase it as poetically as possible, the station dances with the winds of space, only a very, very little."

He paused. Jethri was beginning to think that Master pin'Aker was enjoying himself.

"This situation with an unstable dock; it is one which might well give a Scout pause. Not so the pilot-in-charge of *Keravath*, bold Trader ven'Deelin, who live-docks with nary a fumble."

Master ven'Deelin drew a breath, and gazed at Jethri with wondering eyes.

"The Scout allowed me a few lessons at the board to lighten our travel," she said with a strong air of quoting someone.

Actually, as Jethri knew, she was quoting *him*. It had been Scout ter'Astin's whim to make him into a pilot and as such had seemed as off-topic in his report to the master trader as it had seemed in his life.

Still, he *had* docked at Tradedesk, and . . .

"I did note that Scout ter'Astin had awarded me a provisional Third Class, did I not, Mother?" That was slightly risky, in *melant'i* terms, but she allowed it.

"You did, my son; I recall it well. In fact, it was that admission which earned you piloting lessons on our own control deck. However, the difference between *piloting lessons*, and *live docking amid construction*, is, forgive me, considerable."

"Yes, ma'am," he said meekly, as one receiving instruction.

"Hah," said Master pin'Aker, taking up his tale again. "Allow me to inform you, Norn, that the trader's *piloting lessons* gained him attention at Tradedesk, notably from *Wynhael*, which produced its usual examples of misconstrued *melant'i*, while *Keravath* glides smoothly into dock, its pilot bearing both a Terran and a Liaden name, an elegant bow to the philosophies which formed the station and the conference."

Master pin'Aker paused for a sip, and the rest of the table followed suit. Tan Sim rose and stepped away, returning with the sto'Helit bottle, from which he refreshed their glasses.

"For myself, I was unfamiliar with Gobelyn, though I have since repaired my ignorance—but ven'Deelin? There was a name well-known to me. I directed my assistant—you recall Samay, Norn—to find who was this pilot-in-charge.

"Samay also became curious, having heard some talk here and there of a *new ven'Deelin*, and so, I gather, arranged to meet him. I ask not how, but meet him she did, and found him well enough."

Jethri recalled Samay's contrived meeting at *Keravath*'s lock, and thought he would like to talk with her again.

"When it came time for the traditional Trade-Off to occur—it is a charity event to fund various trade and spacer-in-distress accounts—Samay and Trader Jethri were called upon to stand as arbitrators, being new blood so to speak, and pleasant enough to look at. They did well in their roles, for all that they knew nothing of the tradition, and all present were pleased. Then came the main event, in which a trader is called at random to stand before the room, and raise money for the charities by trading—whatever they may.

"Understand, this is rarely the surprise it is made

to seem, unless random event favors a call to one who is new to the traditions. Such was Trader ven'Deelin, who had been played very nicely by Doricky DeNobli— what a pleasure it is to watch her work!

"Up Trader ven'Deelin went, onto the stage, wearing his fine coat, and this ring."

He held Jethri's ring up for all to see.

"This honest trader's ring he wore—and another, that one might wonder to find on the hand of an honest trader, or, indeed, anyone! A Triluxian shank finished with a firegem."

Master ven'Deelin gave a soft laugh. She reached across the table, and patted Jethri's hand.

"Go on, Rantel," she said.

"Certainly, I will go on! For I must tell you—with that piece of trumpery he ensorcelled a room of experienced traders, travelers, and merchants. For a moment, I thought Trader Auely might buy it from kindness to a new colleague, and to see the fund increased. One hundred bits, he called, and I thought the thing settled. Freely do I admit my error, for it had only just begun.

"Who should come to stand in the front lines, but our so-open and secretive rogue, Uncle—yes, well you may stare! Down the room came the Uncle, I was there; I saw it with my own eyes—indeed, I could not look away, nor could any other in the room! He asks and is given leave to examine this ring—Triluxian, recall it, and a firegem! Inspection made, he doubles Trader Auely's bid."

Trader pin'Aker sighed, and sipped his wine, absently turning Jethri's trade ring in his fingers.

"Well. It was a bidding war, for all it was quick,

Auely called in Sabemis, she called in some others, but the Uncle grew tired of the game, and closed it. One *cantra*, four hundred bits for the ring. For Trader Jethri, in a side deal, there came a request for a breakfast meeting, and a prepaid consultation fee for one Standard hour."

There was silence, as if they all had need of catching their breaths. It had been a performance on Master Trader pin'Aker's side, Jethri thought. A performance the like of which had been celebrated at Tradedesk in the name of the great trader, and given what Grandma Ricky had *not* said, even greater rogue, Sternako.

Master ven'Deelin cleared her throat.

"It sounds a very triumph."

"A triumph," Master Trader pin'Aker repeated. "Yes, a triumph. Achieved by the trader who wore *this*!" He held Jethri's trade ring high. "How do you account for that, Master Norn?"

She raised her eyebrows. "Jethri has his skills," she said mildly.

Master pin'Aker bent a stern gaze upon her. "Three topaz and a garnet. Do you *agree* with this, Master Trader?"

"Rantel, the child is my apprentice, and my son. We discussed each change of status as it was made, and if I thought him conservative, that is no fault in a young trader; nor did it approach deceit."

"In fact, an honest advantage. Yes, I have read Trader Jethri's records on file, and agree that more young traders ought embrace conservative action. Yet I sense that you are not astonished by this report that I make to you."

"Not at all. I had always believed Jethri capable

of greatness, even to the large amethyst." She moved her hand subtly, calling attention to her own amethyst, worn only by Guild-approved masters of trade.

"And that sooner rather than later, now that this *Envidaria* has been loosed upon us," Master pin'Aker murmured, gazing at her. "Will you or shall I?"

"Jethri is my son," Master ven'Deelin repeated calmly.

"So, so. It is plain. An objective master must address this pleasant understatement of *melant'i*. In addition, I adjure the young trader to be less modest in future and give to himself the same generosity he offers to his associates."

He fixed Jethri with a stern eye.

"Yes, Master pin'Aker," he murmured. He took a breath and added, as softly as he might, junior trader to master. "May I reclaim my ring, sir?"

"In good time, Trader. First, there is a lesson in how to count."

He placed the ring on the table, reached into the public pocket of his trade coat and brought out a small tapestry pouch, which he opened, spilling its contents to the table by the ring. Baguettes: yellow, red, purple, and crystal clear glittered under the soft room lights.

"So," said Master pin'Aker, picking up Jethri's ring once more. "Three topaz and a garnet. Before we discuss your Guild file, Trader Jethri, we must discuss something else. You hold a ten-year Combine key, I think?"

Jethri blinked; he had shown his Combine key to the rowdy audience at Tradedesk during the events Master pin'Aker had just finished describing. Still, a master trader had asked a question.

"Yes, sir. I hold a ten-year Combine key."

"I researched that key, and I learned that there are trades registered to it," Master pin'Aker said. He turned to Master ven'Deelin. "I wonder what color the stones were, when your 'prentice-come-junior received his ring from your hand, Master Norn?"

"Four clear," she said composedly.

"Hah. May one ask if you knew of the key and the trades recorded to it?"

"I did. If you will ask why I did not allow them to weigh with me in the matter of stones, I judged it best, given the number and kind of eyes upon *ven'Deelin's Terran* that it were wisest, at the beginning, to count...in Liaden, one might say."

She raised her glass and sipped, meditatively.

"I did this, knowing that there would be a rectification made, further along in Jethri's career."

"And we have arrived at *further along*. I understand." Master pin'Aker turned to Jethri, holding the ring up for him to see.

"Three topaz and a garnet," he murmured, and removed one of the topazes, replacing it with a garnet.

"The trades made prior to your certification as a junior trader, which were recorded to your ten-year Combine key, are now properly accounted," he said. "We now proceed to your Guild records. Those very records show that you are in a business partnership with a full trader, *not* as the junior partner, but an equal! That fact is not reflected here"—he thrust the ring toward Jethri—"*here* in the public record of your accomplishments!"

He paused, then asked, very gently, "Trader Jethri, was there a reason, such as your master's tender regard for the sensibilities of Liaden traders, why you did not wish to put your partnership with Trader pen'Akla forward?"

Jethri sat up a little straighter and took a deep breath. "I confess, sir, it never occurred to me that my arrangement with Trader pen'Akla had to do with *trade*. It was merely . . . an agreeable and convenient arrangement that benefited us."

Master pin'Aker withdrew his hand, fingers curled, and bent his head, as if recruiting himself to patience. A moment passed . . . two . . . three.

"We will rectify this," he said quietly. "Attend me, Trader."

He replaced a second topaz with a garnet.

"Thus, we account your agreeable and convenient *trade association* with Trader pen'Akla."

Jethri glanced at Tan Sim, who was giving all due attention to the master trader.

"Continuing," Master pin'Aker murmured, drawing Jethri's attention. "Your collaboration with Scout Senior Field Coordinator of Trade Relations, Captain Jan Rek ter'Astin, on a matter essential to the very foundation of trade."

Jethri blinked. "The very foundation of trade?" he repeated.

Master pin'Aker met his eye. "Trust, Trader Jethri. Surely you are aware." The third topaz was exchanged for a garnet.

Jethri bit his lip, and carefully released the breath he had been holding. Well, now he was schooled, and four garnets was no bad thing to wear.

"My thanks," he began, but Master pin'Aker showed him a palm.

"Be at peace, Trader, the lesson is only begun."

Jethri swallowed. "Yes, sir."

"Indeed. So, four garnets. You will say to yourself that this is no bad thing. Junior traders some years your senior wear four garnets and achieve good trading. However, of all the circumstances that might influence the colors shown on a trader's ring, age is not one of them.

"We therefore allow ourselves a moment to honor the garnets."

He showed the ring on his open palm around the table. Master ven'Deelin and Tan Sim both inclined their heads, as if greeting a colleague on-port.

"So," Master pin'Aker said. "We continue with the rectification."

He removed a garnet, and replaced it with an amethyst.

"This for the totality of your performance at Tradedesk. I include here your role with my niece as arbitrators of nonsense, your triumph with the Triluxian ring, and your other triumph with Grandma Ricky, who will treasure that earring, young Trader, mark me well, and the tales she will tell of your time together will do you no ill at all."

Jethri inclined his head, but said nothing. Master Trader pin'Aker smiled at him, and replaced another garnet with an amethyst.

"The *Envidaria*—its pursuit, capture, and the manner of its distribution, which reflects the philosophies we find at Tradedesk. These actions, performed by one who holds a ten-year Combine key, make a forceful statement, which any trader—Liaden or Terran as they might be—ignores at their very great peril."

Master pin'Aker raised his head and met Jethri's eyes.

"In addition to your responsibilties as second trader on a Liaden ship, you continue to be involved in the business of the *Envidaria*, and are an active participant in the Seventeen Worlds project developed by Terran traders to improve conditions in the face of the incursion of Rostov's Dust. This again demonstrates a commitment to the philosophies held at Tradedesk, and a matching commitment to better trade."

The third garnet was removed; an amethyst inserted.

He paused, holding the ring high so that the entire table might admire it: three amethyst and a garnet. Jethri felt a little gone in the head, and raised his glass for a careful sip of wine.

"So." Master Trader pin'Aker placed the ring on the table by the sparkling pool of stones, and turned aside. "Trader pen'Akla."

Tan Sim inclined his head. "Sir."

"You will be interested to know that our negotiations with Rinork progressed swiftly and smoothly. Our *qe'andra* was pleased to offer us an analysis, but you and I need go no further than to understand that *Genchi* and your contract were acquired as a package by Clan Midys, and we may now set about rectifying several regrettable errors."

Though Jethri would have said that he had been perfectly at ease, Tan Sim visibly relaxed. It was a startling breach of etiquette, Jethri thought, horrified on his friend's behalf. Then, he thought again, realizing that Tan Sim felt himself in trusted company, that he dared reveal so much.

"My thanks, Master Trader," Tan Sim whispered.

"Yes, by all means let us understand that you have

said everything that is proper. Now, Trader, attend me, for with success comes change. I propose to bring you aboard *Barskalee* as associate trader. You will trade for the ship, and also for yourself, as you are already in partnership. *Barskalee* will grant you a mounted pod—two!—but these are mere details, which you and I will discuss in depth tomorrow, before the contracts are drawn up, unless you disagree in principle, tonight."

"I have questions," Tan Sim said quietly.

"Of course you do," Master Trader pin'Aker said fondly. "Ask."

"Yes, sir. I wonder if associate trader might be, in fact, *junior* trader?"

Master pin'Aker blinked. He turned to Master ven'Deelin.

"Do you mark Infreya's hand just there, Norn?"

"I do, and seeing it I say, Rantel, that the trader does due diligence, and seeks to protect himself."

"So he does, and so would I do." He turned back to Tan Sim, who had been sitting outwardly calm, except, Jethri thought, that his lips were pressed just too tightly together.

"Trader, I guarantee that you will have all the range and more that you enjoyed on *Genchi*. I intend for you to work for yourself, as well as for *Barskalee*. You will accept training, to learn what *Barskalee* can do, and so that you may assist me in understanding how ships such as *Genchi* and her sisters may best support *Barskalee* as Rostov's Dust approaches and possibly engulfs many of our usual routes. It would not be appropriate to offer junior trader for the expertise these duties will require, thus I offer associate trader." He paused. "I expect that you and your partner will wish to discuss your necessities in detail, so that we may write a balanced contract. A balanced contract is my goal, I assure you, as I assured Master ven'Deelin this noon, when we discussed the matter." Another pause. "I hope this makes the matter clear to you, Trader."

Tan Sim inclined his head. "Master Trader, it does."

"So. Have you other questions, Trader?"

"Master, I do. It heartens me that you speak of *Genchi*'s role in assisting *Barskalee* through the arrival of the Dust. Allow me to represent her to you as an able ship. She is in need of upgrades, but her heart is large. You speak of bringing me to *Barskalee*, and gladly will I learn all that she can teach me, but *Genchi*—*Genchi* needs a trader worthy of her, sir. A bold trader, if I may say it, and creative, who will honor her for what she is, and know how best to build upon her worth."

Master pin'Aker glanced to Master ven'Deelin, and Jethri saw some communication pass between them, though he was not privy to the code shared by two old friends.

"We are in complete agreement, Trader, and may I say that your vehemence has reminded me of a task which I have left undone."

Once more, he took Jethri's ring in hand, deftly replacing the last garnet with an amethyst.

"With his master's agreement," he said, his eyes on the stones, "Trader ven'Deelin will stand as *Genchi*'s lead trader."

"I agree," Master ven'Deelin murmured, and gave Jethri what he knew for her true-smile. "*Ge'shada*, my son. This is a coup."

"Thank you, ma'am," Jethri managed, and offered his hand to Tan Sim. "I'll take care of her," he said.

"I know it," Tan Sim said, his grip hard and earnest. There were tears in his eyes, though he smiled. "Jeth Ree. You will be going to the South Axis Congress, after all!"

"Where better to send a man fully vested in the Liaden Trade Guild, who holds a ten-year Combine key, and who has also delivered the *Envidaria* to all trade-kind?" Master pin'Aker said gaily. He raised a finger.

"Now, Trader Jethri, attend me. As the master who has reviewed the record of your accomplishments, and witnessed you at trade, it is my honor to contact the Guild on your behalf. You should shortly receive from them an acknowledgment, listing your license number and codes, as well your responsibilities and privileges. Eventually, when you are on a port with a Guild office, you may claim your license card, but that is a formality. Have you questions?"

Jethri drew a careful breath.

"Not at the moment, I believe, Master. Thank you for . . . teaching me how to count. I will strive to be more accurate, in future."

"Excellent. Here, now, Trader—your ring."

Jethri blinked, and into that small hesitation leaned Master ven'Deelin, plucking the ring from Master pin'Aker's fingers.

"Allow me," she murmured. "Your hand, child."

Jethri blinked again, scrambling for his scattered wits—barely an hour it had taken them to upend his life and Tan Sim's, he thought rather wildly. Truly were the masters of trade said to be forces in the universe!

"Jethri?" Master ven'Deelin murmured.

He managed to extend his hand. The correct hand.

She steadied it with hers, and slipped his ring onto the proper finger. When it was done, she paused a moment, his hand pressed between both of hers, and she gazed full into his face.

"This is not the first time I have been proud on your behalf, my son, nor do I think it will be the last. You are, indeed, a marvel."

"Thank you, ma'am," he said then, feeling tears rising to his eyes. "For all that you have done for me."

"Silver-tongue," she murmured, and withdrew her hand.

"So!" Master pin'Aker said. "Tomorrow will be a full day for all of us. I suggest that we synchronize our schedules. Then, if my friend Norn is willing, I will open my bottle so that we may drink to the ascension of traders and the opportunities that await!"

· · · · · · · · ·

THREE

· · · · · · · ·

DESPITE A NIGHT VERY NEARLY AS LATE AS THE ONE PRE-
vious, two young traders met early for breakfast in a
private room bespoken by the elder of the two at the
Liaden Trade Bar in the New Main Line. Practical
Al's was closer to Tan Sim's lodgings, but as the same
elder trader argued compellingly, much of what they
would require to complete their business fell on the
Liaden side of the line.

There was also, as the younger of the two readily
acknowledged, Master pin'Aker's convenience to be
considered, as he would be joining their discussions
at midday, and *Barskalee* was absolutely berthed at
the new docks.

"When everything is completed," Jethri said, as
the door to their private room slid shut behind them,
"we should make both masters our guests for prime
at Practical Al's."

Tan Sim turned a gaze of wide wonder upon him.

"Be not *too* bold, my Jeth Ree. You must survive
to stand as poor *Genchi*'s trader."

"Oh, I'll survive," Jethri said blithely, placing his
bag on the long table bearing two screens, and above
it a mirror of the large trade screen from the room
below. "They need me as part of their grand scheme."

41

"Ah, but perhaps they do not. They are masters, recall it. Improvisation is not beyond them. Do you desire refreshment, Trader? I see that we are honored with a pot of Thunder Tea."

Jethri raised his eyebrows.

"Thunder Tea? Someone's shrewd."

"Or someone wishes us to keep our wits about us, and has paid catering to insure it."

Jethri grinned. "Let us not disappoint them," he said. "I will, indeed, have tea, if you will pour."

They paused for more tea and a revivifying pastry after an hour of heavy labor. Jethri was now fully informed with regard to *Genchi's* cargo, amended route, captain, and crew. Next order of business was a discussion of the necessities of their partnership, short-term and long.

Jethri finished his pastry and leaned back in the chair. He had some time ago shed his coat, and rolled the sleeves of his shirt. Tan Sim had also removed his jacket, but his sleeves remained fastened at his wrists.

"So," Jethri said, in wry Terran. "How many steps ahead of us were they?"

Tan Sim tipped his head.

"Do you suppose that we are now caught up?" he asked, seriously.

Jethri sighed.

"No, I'm not quite so much of a fool as that. I'm only wondering when they hatched this scheme between them. Yesterday, over tea? Or is this something pieced together over a longer timeline?"

"Ah! You seek a proximate event." Tan Sim sipped tea, fair brows drawn.

"I believe Master pin'Aker's thoughts began tending in our direction when we three met at Tradedesk."

"And he drew Master ven'Deelin in?"

"More likely she drew him in," Tan Sim said.

Jethri frowned.

"What makes you think so?"

Tan Sim stared. "Did you not hear her, Jethri? She means you to have the great amethyst on your finger, and soon. Sooner, if one may quote Master pin'Aker, rather than later."

Jethri stared in his turn.

"Master Trader—me?"

"I believe that the ven'Deelin's heir is her only other child, and has long had her own ship and routes."

Jethri took a deep breath.

"She's—I'm not Liaden."

"Observably," Tan Sim agreed. "However, you have achieved the rank of full trader, according to Guild rule, and you do not offend those Liadens who put trade before lineage. Among the Terran traders, you possess both lineage and a Combine key. Thus, you are acceptable to both sides of the table, and Trade-desk's ideal made flesh." He put his cup down. "*That* is what drew Master pin'Aker's interest."

Jethri tried again.

"There are no Terran master traders."

"Clearly Master Trader ven'Deelin feels that this is an error."

"And Master pin'Aker agrees with her."

"Master pin'Aker was at Tradedesk and it was not his first conference there. Master ven'Deelin was invited, but found it convenient to send her second and her son to be the face of the ship."

Jethri closed his eyes. It was as Tan Sim had said, he admitted. The duty of master traders was to the advancement of trade. A master trader who could bargain equally with Terran and Liaden traders? That would serve both trade, and the Liaden idea of Balance.

Gods.

He opened his eyes to find Tan Sim watching him with interest.

"They're sending me to the South Axis Congress," he said.

"They are," his partner agreed. "What is the Terran equivalent of a master trader, Jeth Ree?"

"No exact equivalency. Commissioner'd be nearest," he said. He paused, suddenly breathless, remembering his conversation on Port Chavvy with Sector Commissioner Brabham DeNobli, and Freza, his assistant, though he'd bet she was closer to junior commissioner.

"Do they want me to be a commissioner?"

"Will it serve trade?" Tan Sim asked. "I believe that is the measuring stick we must apply to such questions. As do the master traders."

It was, a voice murmured in the back of Jethri's head, the next logical step, after all. His father had been a commissioner, and there *was* the *Envidaria*. Surely, becoming a commissioner would serve trade. The question remaining was—could a man stand up under the combined weight of master trader *and* commissioner?

Jethri doubted he could, frankly.

"For the nonce, my Jeth Ree," Tan Sim said, slipping back into Liaden, and tipping his head toward the screen. "*We* are called to serve trade. What are our necessities? To make money, surely, and increase our legend, but else?"

Jethri took another deep breath, and resolutely put master traders and their machinations aside.

"*Else* proceeds from *has*," he quoted. "Here is what we *have*." He leaned forward and opened the inventory file on the screen. "Your advantage, Trader, is that *Barskalee* has a route. What of our goods will you have?"

Jethri arrived early at *Genchi*'s maintenance site, though he rather expected Tan Sim to be late. His partner had been called to *Barskalee* to wait upon Master Trader pin'Aker, and while the master trader would of course be prompt, and respectful of another trader's commitments, there was the travel time from the new docks to the old to be added to the equation.

He was therefore surprised—and then agreeably surprised—to see Tan Sim round the corner, accompanied by—

"Samay pin'Aker," Jethri murmured, sweeping a bow of pleased recognition. "I am happy to see you again."

"Jethri ven'Deelin," she answered, answering his bow precisely, graceful despite the case she held in her left hand. "How pleasant it is to see you again, Trader, and so soon."

"Accountant pin'Aker graciously offers her skills to us as we do a walk-through of *Genchi*. We are to note all those items which are less than perfectly operable."

"Also, I will wish a copy of the estimate of repairs which have been undertaken, Trader pen'Akla," Samay murmured. "The master trader..."

She hesitated. Jethri exchanged a grin with Tan Sim.

"Please, say no more. We have both lately come under the master trader's scrutiny."

Samay's dimples appeared briefly, and Jethri managed not to sigh. He quite admired Samay's dimples.

"Then we all understand each other," she said solemnly. "That is good. Trader pen'Akla, if you would—?"

"Certainly," said Tan Sim, taking the lead. "I warn you that the interior is somewhat less spacious than *Barskalee*."

"Nor does she require the number of servants that *Barskalee* holds as her due," Samay said, following, with Jethri last in their train. "I am certain she is everything that is admirable."

Some time later, having completed a most thorough walk-through—even the crotchety old tea maker was marked for replacement!—the three of them stopped at the office. Samay was introduced to the yard's accountant, and handed her a letter of credit.

"*Barskalee* will pay for necessary repairs now underway," she told the openly astonished accountant. "Additional repairs may also be requested. To whom would those requests best be forwarded?"

"Yard boss," the woman behind the desk said, her voice slightly slow from, Jethri assumed, the shock. She recovered quickly, however, and added, in a firmer tone. "Copy to me, if you would, too. Just to make sure there aren't any mistakes. Here, let me give you names and codes."

This was quickly accomplished, and the three of them found themselves at the edge of the yard, somewhat disheveled, and momentarily at a loss.

"Tea?" Tan Sim said, somewhat faintly.

"Lunch!" Jethri countered, looking about them. He smiled, and turned to Samay.

"I wonder if you will join us for a meal, ma'am? There is a place that Trader pin'Aker and I have a fondness for, only a few halls over."

"Lunch would be very welcome," Samay returned. "But I insist that it be among friends. For I will not tolerate *ma'am* over my meal, Jethri."

"You make hard terms—Samay," Jethri said, and glanced at Tan Sim, who was staring.

"Practical Al's?" he asked, tentatively, glancing at Samay.

"Do you prefer something farther away?" Jethri countered.

Tan Sim's lips bent. "Put that way..."

"Right," Jethri said, and nodded to the left. "Just down this way, friends."

·······
FOUR
·······

"I WONDER ABOUT THIS CLAUSE HERE," JETHRI SAID, highlighting it on the screen.

Master pin'Aker glanced at the screen, then Jethri's face.

"This is the clause that names you as *Genchi*'s lead trader for a period of three Standard years, under my auspices," he said. "It seems extremely clear to me, Trader Jethri. Unless you feel that three Standard years is too short a time?"

Jethri took a careful breath. That he was negotiating *personally* with Master Trader pin'Aker was something out of the ordinary way. He had expected to be dealing with *Barskalee*'s *qe'andra*, only seeing Master pin'Aker when it was time for the lines to be signed—and possibly not even then. Surely, a master trader on-port had more important matters to tend to than sitting beside a new-made trader in a rented office within the Liaden-side Trade Bar, going over a personal services contract, clause by clause.

"I find three Standards to be wholly reasonable," Jethri said. "As *Genchi*'s trader, I will be exploring possibilities so that I may suggest a new route—or several—to the master trader. Three Standards will provide sufficient time to find if I am suited to the task and to *Genchi*, and if *Genchi* is suited to me. There is the standard language covering early termination, and contract extensions. I am content with everything here, save one thing."

"You have me enthralled, Trader Jethri. What is this one thing?"

"The date," Jethri said, "the *specific* date on which I am acknowledged as *Genchi's* trader, able to accept goods, order repairs, reassign crew—"

He stopped. He hadn't meant to mention that last, but his recent conversation with Tan Sim regarding *Genchi* and, specifically, her crew was still fresh in his memory—"Every one of the under crew is excellent, Jethri, as you will have seen during our tours. Captain sea'Kera, though—is of a fixed temperament. The traders before me were content to allow him to set the route, the result of which you have heard me lament. He deplored a system where the trader guided the route, and my changes were by necessity modest. The projected scope of *Genchi's* new duties—it may be more than he can bear. Be aware of this."

Jethri'd blinked.

"I recall your lamentations, but—what ought I to look for? Is it likely that he will—damage the ship?" The thought of that was enough to cramp Jethri's stomach.

Tan Sim gripped his shoulder.

"No, gods, nothing so dire! Only, he may become obdurate, which I have seen happen, and this will disturb the others, and you will need harmony among your crew."

Tan Sim sighed. "I had spoken to Master pin'Aker

of the matter, so he is aware. I wished to do the same service for my partner. Once on Meldyne—even Captain sea'Kera cannot find fault with our delivery arrangements at Meldyne!—you may wish to visit the job fair, and take on a first mate. Right now, the captain is prime pilot, and dea'Lan—both as engineering and cargo master—is his back-up."

Jethri sighed. "Personnel..." he muttered, and Tan Sim laughed.

"Indeed! And yet one cannot run a ship without personnel!"

"Yes," Master pin'Aker said in the here and now. "I quite see your point, Trader Jethri. As you are aware, Trader Tan Sim is today relocating to his quarters on *Barskalee*. How if we make your date today, as well? *Genchi* need not languish without a trader for even an hour."

Jethri drew a careful breath. "That is acceptable," he said, and did not add, "Thank you," which would have weakened his bargaining position.

"Very good," said Master pin'Aker making the change, and affixing his initials. He handed the stylus so that Jethri might do the same. When that was done, he sat back in his chair and tipped his head at the screen.

"Is there anything else, Trader Jethri?"

"Two more things, sir." Jethri flipped the screen to the appropriate page. "This sentence here..."

The contract had been signed. Master pin'Aker had poured them each a glass of wine so that they might seal the contract with goodwill, and now they sat together in a windowed alcove overlooking the trade floor.

Jethri sipped his wine carefully, and resisted the lure of the extremely comfortable lounge chair.

"I wonder if you might give me a little more of your time, Trader Jethri. I wish to discuss a . . . personal matter."

Personal? Jethri was inclined to be unnerved, but there—not only was he a master trader, but Rantel pin'Aker stood as his sponsor to the Guild. In either *melant'i*, he might well have something to say to a new trader about to stand up as lead trader for the first time. And Jethri would do well to listen closely to everything the master wished to say.

"Certainly, sir," he murmured, at a loss for a more graceful phrase.

Master pin'Aker inclined his head.

"I know you for a modest young man, Trader Jethri, and I will therefore exert myself to spare your blushes. Merely know that I unreservedly admire your accomplishments, your wit, your geniality, and most of all, your intelligence."

He paused to sip his wine.

"In fact, you are so accomplished, so good-natured, and so very intelligent, that you may have led your elders into error."

Jethri blinked.

"Sir, if by any fault of mine, you—"

Master pin'Aker raised a hand.

"Please, Trader Jethri. There is no fault. There is merely—how best to say this? Custom? No! *Culture*. You have been taught—well. And you have learned— surpassingly well. One could almost forget that you were not Liaden from your cradle—and there lies our error. I speak for myself and for Master Norn, who has learned so much while overseeing your education that she believes you to have access to information and nuance that you *cannot* have."

"Because at core, I am Terran-born," Jethri said, quietly.

Master pin'Aker shot him a sharp look.

"Do not repine, Trader Jethri. You have heard my opinions on the core philosophy of Tradedesk. To be clear, I approve. As I approve of you. Plainly you are not a Liaden trader, though you have been taught to trade in the Liaden mode. Turnabout, I am not a Terran trader, and much less apt than yourself, yet I have been able to carry trade to Terran markets."

He leaned forward slightly, looking directly into Jethri's eyes, which wasn't the Liaden way. Jethri held his gaze, and Master pin'Aker smiled.

"I am a master trader. My duty is to the betterment of trade. I take this to mean *all trade*, as does my good friend Norn. There are those of our colleagues who consider that we are unnecessarily broad in our understanding of duty." He leaned back, smiling still. "And those others, who consider that we are dangerously deranged."

Jethri managed to stifle the laugh as he inclined his head.

"Yes," Master pin'Aker murmured. "Exactly."

"You will be pleased to learn that we are approaching my topic," Master pin'Aker said after a moment. "I must ask you, Trader Jethri, if you understand—if you *entirely* understand—what we two masters are about on behalf of trade."

Jethri tipped his head, looking down at his hand, at his trade ring. Three purples. Full trader. Yet there were those within the Liaden Trade Guild who were opposed to admitting a Terran to the guild, no matter how well he might trade. It could be, Jethri thought—it could *well* be—that Master pin'Aker's sponsorship of "ven'Deelin's Terran" had been—rebuffed.

And the master was waiting for his answer.

"I understand," Jethri said slowly, "that you are the objective master who has certified my status as a full trader, under Guild rule," he said slowly. "I understand that, though you have reviewed my files, rectified the accounting, and certified my worth, the Guild may still not accept me as a full trader."

"Ah."

It was a soft exhalation. Jethri looked up.

"I had feared it," Master pin'Aker said. "Well, indeed, that I asked. Trader Jethri, attend me, I beg, while I repair my error."

He raised a finger.

"Firstly, you need have no fear that you will be denied your earned rights as a full trader within the Guild. The guiding documents are written to mean that anyone who has satisfied the requirements set out by the Guild and approved by the membership may stand up as a trader. This proposition was tested several times in the past, when politics arose, and the result is that the Guild is most wonderfully firm on this principle. Anyone who has satisfied the requirements may—indeed, must!—stand up as a trader in the Guild.

"You will in good time receive your acknowledgment from the Guild. You will be accorded your rights and be held to your responsibilities. This is not in doubt."

He paused to sip his wine.

"Even should the Guild rewrite the charter—which was tried during those times of politics that I mentioned—Even then, those who had fulfilled the former requirements would qualify, until the new requirements were set into place."

Well, that was certainly clear. Jethri inclined his head.

"If that is the case, Master," he admitted, "then I am—uninformed regarding your efforts on behalf of trade, which involve myself."

"I will enlighten you," Master pin'Aker promised him. "It is really quite simple, Trader Jethri. As anyone who fulfills the Guild's requirements may stand up as a full trader, so must anyone who fulfills a further set of requirements stand up as a master."

Master pin'Aker tipped his head.

"You do not appear shocked, Trader Jethri."

"If I do not, it is because Trader pen'Akla had speculated regarding your intentions and shared his thoughts with me, his partner." Jethri smiled. "Which makes your point, sir."

"Regarding culture—yes. Having failed to shock you, I must yet inform you of the process. I promise that we are almost through, for I know the markets are calling."

Jethri inclined his head.

"I hear," he said formally.

"Excellent. Once you are established as a full trader in the Guild, I will propose you as a candidate for the amethyst. This is a simple application, signed by myself and two other masters of like mind.

"Very rarely, a master trader is certified upon application. The last time this happened was, I believe, seventy-six Standards ago. You must therefore be prepared to receive a denial from the Guild. Do not allow it to distract you. Everyone is denied upon application. It is expected."

"I understand," Jethri said.

"Good. The next step requires your sponsor to appeal, and to produce evidence of widespread support of your candidacy. All of the effort of this falls to me. There is nothing for you to do, save go about your business. I have sponsored five worthy traders to the amethyst, and I am confident that you will be the sixth.

"Once in receipt of the evidence of support, the Guild has two options—one is to accept the expanded application, which is not *so* rare, and we may hope that you will also enjoy victory at this point."

He raised his hand.

"However, there is another option. The Guild may declare itself swayed, but not won over, and allocate the final determination to itself. In this case, there will be a test.

"Such tests are crafted by the Guild Masters; we cannot know what form it will take. All I may do is explain the procedure, which is this—

"The candidate will be called to a particular guild-hall at a particular date and hour. Twelve masters of trade will witness. If you pass the test, you will be certified as a master. If you fail the test, you may make another application six Standards after the first was filed. Failure to arrive at the testing site will mean the same to the masters—you will have failed the test. In such an event, you are permitted to re-apply for testing twice more—in total, three times."

He paused.

"Do you understand this procedure, Trader Jethri?"

"Yes, sir, I do," Jethri said. "May I ask a question?"

"I insist upon it."

"Why me?"

"Because, as you sit there you are proof of the assertion made by Tradedesk—that trade falls outside the lines of culture, and that traders must come together *as traders*, to learn from and assist each other—thus improving trade for all."

"So, I'm a symbol," Jethri said.

Master pin'Aker sighed.

"Trader Jethri, that is not worthy of you," he said, gently chiding. "I fear that my long prosing has dulled your sharp wits. Go! Go out into the markets and practice our art to the best of your considerable ability! *That* is the tonic that will revive you!"

Jethri hesitated.

Master pin'Aker rose and bowed his permission to go.

And that was a hint blatant enough for even a dull-witted trader.

Jethri rose, and bowed in return—gratitude to the elder.

"Sir," he said, and left to seek the markets.

FIVE

IT HAD BEEN TWO DAYS SINCE JETHRI AND TAN SIM HAD been in the same space. Despite the grand plans of the masters of trade, there was mundane business to accomplish, as well. Jethri still being, on this port, *Elthoria*'s second trader, had all his usual duties to handle, including attending two soirees given by Norn ven'Deelin for what seemed to be Frenol's entire population, or at least the two-thirds of it which partook of trade.

He had taken tea with Samay once, a hurried affair by Liaden standards, at a chanced-by pastry shop, but most of his time and energy had been consumed by business until it was, suddenly, and seemingly without warning, time for *Barskalee* to depart, taking Tan Sim and Samay with it, and *Elthoria* due to leave dock not many hours after.

That they might part without a proper leave-taking was something that Jethri found himself unable to support.

He sent out his invitations; the time was rather earlier than Liaden fashion approved, but this was not, so he told himself, a Liaden gathering. It was a gathering of friends, comrades, kin, and fellow conspirators, hosted by a man who was both Liaden and Terran—or neither.

By the time he had contacted his venue of choice, arranged for a private room, ordered several of the house's specialties, as well as a tray to be brought in, he had heard back from his guests, each professing themselves pleased to attend.

There only remained the matter of gifts, and there his imagination almost failed him, until he recalled the sto'Helit.

Practical Al's was—not empty, nor quiet. Say rather, the crowd was less pressing, and the ambient noise somewhat decreased.

Jethri had of course arrived earlier than his guests, though not by so very much. He had scarcely satisfied himself regarding the refreshments, especially the tray from *Balent'i Chernubianda*, when the door was opened, and the server bowed in Masters ven'Deelin and pin'Aker, looking very grand and very Liaden in their best trade coats.

"Traders," Jethri said, stepping forward, and sweeping the bow of host to honored guests. "Welcome to my small gathering. It is my very great pleasure to see you this morning."

"Trader, it is an honor to be invited," Master Trader ven'Deelin murmured, while Master pin'Aker gazed around the room in frank curiosity.

"So this is the place! Samay waxes poetic. Though, I confess to you, Trader, I had expected something more...persuasive, shall we say? In terms of sound."

"It is early, sir, as the station keeps time."

"So it is, so it is! Well. I shall make it a point, when

next we are at Frenol, to come here at the loudest hour, in order to sample the full effect."

The door opened again, admitting Samay and Tan Sim. Jethri smiled.

"Welcome, both," he said, beginning the bow—only to be snatched out of it by Tan Sim's hand on his arm, pulling him upright and into a hug, like a Looper born.

"Jethri, that you thought of this!" he exclaimed in Terran. "I should have done, and yet—" He turned once about, and arrived at his starting point, smiling broadly. "I could not have achieved anything so grand!"

"You haven't seen the trays, yet!" Jethri protested.

"I don't need to see the trays!" Tan Sim declared.

Jethri turned to Samay, who held up a hand.

"Please do not bow, Jethri. We are friends, are we not? In the Terran way?"

Friends in the Terran way? Jethri managed not to blink, and instead showed her a Terran smile.

"We are friends, yes. I'm glad that you came, so that we can share one more memory, and properly say *volent'a serapeyz*."

"Indeed, indeed," said Master pin'Aker from the wine tray. "Let us drink together, friends, if our host will allow me to serve, and recall that we will meet again, as the trade allows."

"A splendid gather! My felicitations to the host!"

Master pin'Aker stood, his wine glass raised, and the rest of the table followed, leaving Jethri seated alone and feeling slightly foolish.

"To the host!" Master ven'Deelin echoed.

"To my partner, and my friend!" Tan Sim said, smiling down at Jethri with open fondness.

"To my friend, Jethri, who taught me much." Samay smiled too, and Jethri felt his ears heat, even as he came to his feet and lifted his own glass.

"To all of us," he proposed.

"To all of us!" came the affirmation, and they drank together.

"Now," said Master pin'Aker, putting his glass aside. "We have some unfinished business, Trader Jethri. Your ring, please."

He held out his hand.

Jethri blinked, set his glass aside, and drew his trade ring off, placing it in the outstretched palm.

Master pin'Aker considered it, and sighed.

"No," he said, "it will *not* do. It is, you understand, a perfectly good ring of its kind. It informs, but it does not serve notice. Very nearly, it misleads."

He slipped the ring away into his pocket.

"Now, this," he continued, bringing his hand forward again, "serves notice that the trader who wears it is something out of the common way."

He opened his fingers.

Four fine, faceted amethysts adorned a gleaming shaft of—

"Is that Triluxian?" Jethri cried, reaching for the ring, and holding it up to the light.

"What else?" asked Master pin'Aker. "We must remember our triumphs, Trader."

Jethri gasped a laugh, slid the ring onto his finger. It fit—well, of course it fit! It had been made for him, after all.

"Master Trader," he bowed, simple gratitude.

"It is my pleasure to give it," Master pin'Aker said,

and reached out to grip Jethri's arm. "Wear it well, Trader Jethri. And now, I regret, but duty calls."

"Yes, of course."

Jethri became the host again, seeing his guests to the door, bestowing on each a bottle of Blusharie, "So that we will have something worthy to share our adventures over, the next time we meet."

Three of his guests gone, Jethri turned back to Master ven'Deelin, who was standing, seemingly at a loss, gazing at the remains of the small feast.

"Mother?" he asked, moving to her side. "Is all well?"

She looked up at him, her eyes bright, and put her hand on his arm. The great amethyst in her master trader's ring gave the room's lights back in flashes of deep purple.

"All is well and more than well, my son. Come, bring your great self down here, so that I may give you a proper leave-taking."

He dropped lightly to one knee, which put them on more equal terms.

"Hah," his mother said softly, and leaned close to kiss his cheek.

SIX

. . . .

GENCHI WAS QUEUED FOR DEPARTURE IN EIGHT HOURS.

The ship was a-buzz with workers finishing upgrades, and cleaning up. Captain sea'Kera had ceded oversight of these final comfort and cosmetic details to the trader, as he readied *Genchi* for departure.

Samay had been generous with suggestions and permissions, so that Jethri's efforts mostly consisted of insuring that the workers cleared ship soonest. He had just signed off on his stateroom/office, leaving the contractor to pack up her tools, when Captain sea'Kera's voice came over the all-ship.

"Trader, your attention, please!" The captain sounded peeved, his Liaden clipped in the mode of Authority.

Jethri frowned, wondering if he'd missed a call. The captain did like prompt attention to such details, so that his board was free of clutter.

"Trader Jethri ven'Deelin, you are required immediately at the deck-lock to personally sign for a delivery!"

Liaden phraseology carried an extra *melant'i* burden on the "personal" side of things, so Jethri reversed course, arriving at the lock to find a pair of well-groomed Terrans in messenger service livery patiently awaiting his arrival. Each carried a parcel so small that either might have carried both without breathing hard.

The livery bore the name of the service in Terran—Quicksilver—the ID badges showed Terran above the Trade and Liaden transliterations. Jethri nodded, and spoke in Terran.

"I'm Trader Jethri ven'Deelin. I understand you have need of my signature?"

The messengers showed surprise. She attempted a bow while he nodded and held his parcel—a signing pad with video scan and touch pads—toward Jethri.

"Sir," she said. "We received a package with an eight-hour delivery limit but we saw your ship listed for departure in eight hours, so we thought we'd best hurry it. I need to confirm. Are you LTG Trader Jethri ven'Deelin?"

"Yes," he said, feeling his pulse quicken. "That's me. The only Trader Jethri ven'Deelin on Frenol."

"Excellent, very good."

She held up her packet, showing him the intact seal, turning it so that he could see his name ornately inscribed on one side, the delivery label on another, before she offered it to him across her palms, ornate side up.

He took it, glancing down to read the name of the sender as *Trade Guild, Frenol*, the Guild crest bright beside it. His pulse kicked up a notch.

The man stepped forward, holding the screen out.

"Please confirm by voice that you have accepted this package in good condition, sir."

Jethri did so.

"Thank you. Now, if you will touch the fingertip reader?"

"Delivery accomplished, sir," he said, after Jethri had done this, too. "And sir, may I say it is a pleasure.

We at Quicksilver are pleased to be permitted to serve the messaging needs of a Liaden trader!"

"Sir, should we wait for a reply?" asked his partner.

He glanced down at the packet again, produced a pleased Terran smile and bestowed it upon the messengers.

"Thank you—there's no reply."

He realized he was on deck with no cash to hand for a gratuity—though he did have a card. An out of date card, now, but a card with his name.

"May I have your card?" he asked.

This was given with alacrity, and Jethri handed his card over, bowing.

He watched them off the deck, then closed the hatch, and leaned against the wall, staring at the packet in his hand.

It's here, he thought, and shook himself.

"Verify, Trader," he said aloud. "Might be documents to sign, after all, and no license at all."

He went to his office, finding the worker gone. Closing the door, he broke the seal, fingered out the certificate with its dependent ribbons and seal, and placed it on the desk. The license, he considered closely, then, with memories of past guildhalls, and comments referencing *ven'Deelin's Terran* to guide him, he bent to his comm, and brought up the trade feed.

Barskalee was barely out of Frenol's local traffic control zone, the time delay for a simple telecom negligible.

Master pin'Aker took the call with evident pleasure.

"Trader Jethri! How may I be pleased to serve you?"

Jethri inclined his head.

"By displaying your usual good-humor and allowing

me to tell you that my license and certificate are in my hands."

Master pin'Aker paused—or it could have been the lag, the silence was so short.

"So quickly! I am gratified to hear this news, indeed! Tell me, Trader Jethri—who gave themselves the honor of signing your card?"

Trust a master trader, Jethri thought, as he admitted. "The card is unsigned, sir."

"Ah. An oversight, perhaps. Who sat down with you at the banquet?"

Banquet?

Jethri inclined his head again. "There was no banquet, sir. But, as you know, *Genchi* is in line for departure. The decision must have been made to bring my license to my hand before departure, even if it meant the banquet be omitted."

"In some cases of imminent departure, the banquet has come down to tea and cakes, but doubtless you are correct, Trader Jethri. They did not wish you to depart without holding that which you have fairly earned. Who from the Frenol Hall brought the packet to you?"

"It was delivered very timely by Quicksilver Messenger Service, sir," Jethri said. "They are Terran-side. I will be sure to use them, when next I'm on Frenol."

"I shall engage them as well, on your recommendation."

Master pin'Aker was looking—stern.

Jethri took a breath.

"Sir, perhaps you will be pleased to know that I used my card and my account to purchase a break-pack of tea—and sold it to the buyer for *Balent'i*

Chernubianda. Both transactions cleared immediately."

"Wisely done, Trader. It is always good to be certain of one's tools and connections. On that topic, I see your name in the Trade Register, updated scarcely an hour ago. LTG Jethri Gobelyn ven'Deelin, properly listed as lead trader on *Genchi*, and *at large*. This means that Frenol Hall has not claimed you for its own, and leaves you free to attach yourself to a Hall of your choosing—eventually. There is no need to choose hastily. *At large* has been good enough for quite a number of us."

Noise interrupted Jethri's concentration, and he sought the status board. Pressure tests completed. All seals good. Excellent news.

He glanced back to Master pin'Aker.

"Trader Jethri, I thank you for calling to share your triumph with me. Have you informed your mother?"

"It is my intention to write to her next," Jethri said. "I saw that *Barskalee* was still within reach, and thought you would wish to have the news from me, as my sponsor."

"Beautifully mannered. Yes. I am informed. You have your ring, your license, your certifications, and your ship. Go forth and serve trade, Trader Jethri! After, of course, you write to Norn."

"I will, sir. Thank you—for all that you have done on my behalf."

Master pin'Aker smiled.

"But I have not finished, yet, Trader Jethri. Until soon."

"Until soon, Master," Jethri said, and the screen went dark.

* * *

His letter written and dispatched, the ship clear of workers, Jethri went for a walk, eventually entering a Trade Bar on the Liaden side.

He took a table with a good view of Arrivals and Departures, and asked for light wine when the server came to inquire.

"Trader ven'Deelin," a rich voice murmured from near at hand. "May I intrude?"

The face was as unfamiliar as the voice—but no, Jethri thought, looking again. The face was . . . very nearly familiar. Brown hair, brown eyes, a general impression of pleased goodwill, even as the face was held properly still. He wore a well-used leather jacket over a sweater and work-a-day pants. A duffel was slung over one shoulder by a strap.

"You have the advantage of me, sir."

"I had feared as much," the pilot said wryly. "He cannot resist his little surprises. But at least he gave me this, so that I might prove myself."

His free hand vanished into a pocket and appeared again, holding a card between thumb and forefinger. He offered it with a slight incline in Jethri's direction.

Carefully, Jethri received the card, feeling the fineness of the stock, and the embossing on the back. *Rantel pin'Aker, Master at Trade* the text ran, in formal Liaden script, Barskalee, *Solcintra Liad*, followed by a 'beam code. Beneath the same message repeated in Trade.

Jethri flipped the card over to smile at the star with three rings, the sign of Clan Midys. It was precisely Master pin'Aker's card; twin to the one in his possession.

"Will you sit, Pilot?" he said politely, placing the

card in the center of the table. "I've called for wine. If you would care for something more, or a meal—?"

"All that is gracious," the pilot murmured, taking the seat opposite, with his back to the boards. "I will be pleased to share wine with you, Trader."

His name was Bry Sen yo'Endoth Clan Midys, yo'Endoth being the secondary Line, as the pilot explained briefly, and himself honored to be *a'thodelm*.

"For our purpose, Trader, first class Jump will interest you more. Trained on small ships, large, and all those that fall between. My father would not see his heir a pilot, so I am also trained in diplomacy, and ought to have gone to *Barskalee* as culture officer, but there was one more able ahead of me, which I did not mourn, for that meant I could pursue the stars."

"You are sent to me as a pilot?"

Bry Sen yo'Endoth once again showed wry.

"The master trader sends me to you, Trader, as one who will ascend to the office now held by Captain sea'Kera, who will be re-assigned soon, as I am allowed to understand. I am also sent because of that training in diplomacy—which I did attend to, somewhat—the master trader having arrived at the belief that you would welcome back-up at the South Axis Congress."

Jethri raised his eyebrows.

"Did he?"

Bry Sen raised his wine glass, and turned his free hand palm-up.

"I cannot say where master traders find their beliefs, Trader."

"No, nor can any of us," Jethri said, soothingly. "An able pilot must be welcomed, and so I welcome you."

He thought briefly of Captain sea'Kera, whose ideas were set, often to *Genchi's* dismay. Tan Sim had been able to force some expansion in the captain's ideas, but a younger, more flexible captain would benefit both ship and trade. That line of thought, Jethri was fairly certain, had at least been part of Master Trader pin'Aker's reasoning. As for the belief that he would require back-up from someone trained as a culture officer for a tradeship . . . from one side, it was a piece of high-handed meddling that took the breath.

From the other side, however, it was extremely well-thought. Politics were going to be rife at the congress, if he was to believe Freza's letters, and he did. The release of the *Envidaria* had generated high feelings, as had the information that the agent of that release had been Arin Gobelyn's son, Jethri. Arin had been a trade commissioner, and one who had pushed hard in the direction of change, which made him popular with some, and—just the opposite with others.

"Of this other thing," Pilot yo'Endoth said softly. "We might—"

Jethri held up a hand.

"Of this other thing—you will appreciate, Pilot, that I have been trained by a master trader, and while I do not know where they find their beliefs, I have learned that it is well to examine the actions that resolve from those beliefs. In the case, I think that Master pin'Aker is correct at root. It is always wise to carry a back-up, though it never leaves the holster."

The pilot's face eased into a quiet smile.

"Then we are in Balance, Trader?"

"Almost," Jethri said, switching languages. "How's your palaver?"

"I have standard Terran, of course," Bry Sen said, following him. "My palaver, shipmate, could use some workin' on, but I'm willing to try for shine."

Jethri grinned, full Terran, and received a Terran smile and a wink in return.

"Perfect," he said. "We can work on that shine in transit."

"Deal," said the pilot, and put his glass on the table. "The other thing we can work on in transit, Trader, is your piloting. I've got my teaching certs, and it never hurts to have two skills on your belt."

Jethri eyed him. "In case I'm stranded on port and need to make my way as a pilot?"

Bry Sen looked earnest.

"Stranger things have happened, Trader. Stranger things by far."

DULCIMER'S NEW VOYAGE

•••••••❖•••••••

At Chantor's Way Station Number 9

. . . .

ONE

. . . .

THE MATH WAS BEAUTIFUL, EVEN IF THE JUMP HAD BEEN completed several days ago—they'd been in port for more than a whole day now!—but Squithy looked over the equations again, and sighed happily.

It was good to see the math, to *feel* the math, that had moved *Dulcimer* between star systems, the math that could show her what made the universe work, if she could just have enough of it at once. She didn't often get a chance to see actual Jump equations, having no need, and the family of the opinion that she'd be wasting her time looking. Klay, though, would share with her, so long as there wasn't a matter of pilot confidence, or ship safety, and he'd answer her questions when she had them, instead of only telling her not to bother herself. Sometimes, he'd even ask her questions, and that was best of all.

Right now, she couldn't give all of her attention to the numbers, because she was waiting to be called into the meeting. Still, there'd been something in *this* equation that made her particularly happy and helped her forget that maybe she should be nervous. Numbers always helped calm her, and it wasn't like she was counting by sixes, which was what had made

Ma call her stupid, and a burden to the ship. Tranh said she worked as hard for the ship as anybody else, and Tranh was captain now. And so that's why she was waiting for her turn to join the negotiations.

Squithen Patel wasn't usually in on negotiations, or trade deals, and neither was Klay, but her and him together were responsible for the norbears as far as *Dulcimer* was concerned, insofar as anyone could be responsible for norbears except norbears. They hadn't asked for the job, they'd been *given* it, because none of the rest of the crew was the same kind of comfortable with the creatures, and on account of that, they couldn't give good information to their "contact" from Crystal Logistics.

There'd been a lot of talk between the seniors about that "contact" and about Crystal Logistics. Seems the company wasn't quite as up-market as Tranh wanted them to go. Tranh was of an ambition to leave all of the former captain and trader's "contacts" alone, those "contacts" being, as Rusko put it, only slightly blacker than space itself.

So, they'd argued about Crystal Logistics, some, forgetting she was there, like mostly everybody did. Crystal, said Tranh, was grey, and nobody'd argued that, only Rusko pointing out that they wanted to clear the holds of *kajets*, and also that they were short of cash to do needed upgrades.

"Better to sell 'em, if we got a taker," he'd finished, and Tranh, after some hard thinking, and a frown, agreed that grey was better than black.

"Squith?"

She closed the tablet and looked up.

Klay was standing in the door to the galley, which

was also the meeting room, where the seniors and pilots had been talking to their "contact" from Crystal Logistics this while, telling her to wait 'til she was called in. That was right, she wasn't senior crew, but her and Klay, they had to talk for the norbears.

"We need you at the meeting, now," Klay said, serious, because this *was* a serious business, she knew that. She nodded and stood up, leaving the tablet behind, and followed Klay into the meeting.

Everybody around the meeting table was serious, she thought—but, no, the "contact" from Crystal, who was named Dulsey Omron, and wearing a pilot's jacket, she was *trying* to be serious. Squithy could tell, though, that she was amused by the norbears, and especially by Synbe and Rutaren, who had set up right in front of her on the table, and were patting her hands, and showing her faces and places inside her head, and asking questions. That was why so many of *Dulcimer*'s crew wanted them off-ship, and didn't want to talk to them. Which was why there was so much excitement among the norbears, now, Squithy thought, trying to sit calm and not dance in her chair.

She real quick looked at Klay, sitting next to her. He was wearing a serious face, like he did when he was piloting, but she could tell he was feeling the excitement, too.

Oki strolled up the table and sat down in front of Dulsey Omron, bumping Synbe aside, and putting a hand on the pilot's wrist. Oki was the oldest norbear, and didn't usually put herself to the front. She'd sit way back in the corner-most parts of the room, so the seniors forgot she was there, like they forgot Squithy was there, and Oki would listen, serious, and have long private talks with the other norbears.

Pilot Dulsey, though, she bowed her head a little, like Oki was the equal of a pilot and said, very softly, "Ma'am. I'm honored."

The traders were being *very* serious, and Tranh's purpose was clear—he wanted *all* of the norbears off the ship, preferably a port or two ago, and the pilot, who was clearly the most interesting person anybody on *Dulcimer* had ever met, wanted to *know* the norbears, but had made it plain that she was unwilling to *buy* them or even consider them as purchasable. She wanted to have norbear company for a while, and was willing to host one or all of them, but she wanted guarantees that *Dulcimer* would take them back, and Squithy could see that Tranh wasn't happy at all about that.

The conversation being in Tranh's court, Klay leaned over and whispered in her ear.

"Squith, I'm getting face flashes like Pilot Dulsey's been visiting every port there is and was these last hunnert years, and they keep dragging more faces out of her memory than she knows she knew!"

Squithy nodded, watching in her head as people's faces flowed by in a steady stream, like Pilot Dulsey was having a good time sharing. Of a sudden there was a pause in that flow, like the pilot and Oki had both had an idea—maybe even the same idea—that they were considering close between themselves. Meanwhile, Squithy got the notion that Synbe was feeding Oki a side argument, and Rutaren had left the table, and was over near the counter with Mitsy and Ditsy.

Something was up, she thought. It felt something like a crew vote, or—

"Tranh." That was Klay, interrupting the captain, which wasn't done except in 'mergencies, and even then, at a risk. Not that Tranh was as strict about rank as Da—the old captain—had been, but—

"Tranh," Klay said again, "you gotta hear this before you make an agreement you can't keep."

Tranh lifted his hand, and nodded to Pilot Dulsey. "A minute, Pilot," he said, and looked to Klay. "Talk."

"You can't agree without they agree," Klay said, "the norbears, that is. You might have a preferred outcome, but they're still negotiating, trading something among themselves. I'm hearing that they're trying to decide who wants to go and who wants to stay, if any of them go. That's not our decision."

"Indeed." Pilot Dulsey looked up from her conversation with Oki. "That is my opinion, as well. I learn from my friend here just now that the group has an—obligation, perhaps to the ship, perhaps to Squithy and Klay." She frowned slightly, head tipped. "There is also a sense that some of the group have acquired a taste for adventure, and may wish to go..."

"Best would be to let them all go!" Tranh said sharply, and sighed, opening his hands to show Pilot Dulsey empty palms. "We're not set up for animals. They'd be better some place other."

"With all respect, Captain, that is for them to decide. They are *able* to decide. Or so it seems to me. Also, it appears that they wish to trade. I may not have that precisely. Perhaps they believe the ship has something of value to offer, if—ah."

Squithy caught it, too, a sudden flow of faces, from Oki, maybe familiar, but being fed so fast, until—

"Hey!" Squithy gasped. "I know who that is!"

The flow stopped in mid-share, accompanied by a feeling like maybe Oki had patted her approvingly on the wrist. Then, slower, the same face, from several angles, matching her memories of a grim youth throwing a hammer at a wine keg, and blood on his face, and—and then another image, which must have been from Dulsey, the same face, the same man, but dressed up in party clothes, serious and smiling by turns, and then Squithy's memory again, standing by the tool rack on Port Chavvy, and the hammer again, thrown this time at a person—one of the faces that had gone by too fast, Squithy realized, but she was caught up in the flow—and then pulled out of it, when warm fingers touched her hand.

"Who do you think that person is?" Dulsey asked.

Squithy took a hard breath, ordering her thoughts, feeling that the norbears were excited, but there wasn't any danger, and no need to start counting, only to look and to remember, and answer the question.

"Arin Gobelyn's boy, is what they said," she answered, looking into Dulsey's eyes. "The one they call Jethri ven'Deelin. He's a trader, Old Name Looper on his ma's side—the Gobelyns, that's what the crew off *Nubella Run* said. A Liaden prince challenged him to a duel at Port Chavvy, right on our dock, practically. He came to us to borrow hammers, so they could fight even, and the prince got mad and shot at him. Everybody said it was an accident, a real bad accident, everybody did say, that being better than what really happened, and—"

Squithy took another breath, seeing the Liaden prince who'd pulled the gun, and how he'd been pretty in a way and then ugly and all wrong—and then huddled in his own blood.

More images of Jethri, from Dulsey it must be—holding a ring high, smiling at a pretty woman, sipping a glass of wine...

Some of the norbears were echoing the fight scenes Squithy had remembered while others were echoing Dulsey's more peaceful images.

Another face came out from the cloud then, as if the trader's image triggered it, a strong face, with quick eyes—

"Jethri's Scout," said Dulsey.

"That's right," Klay said, who must've been seeing it all in his head, too.

Two images slid side-by-side into Squithy's head: the Scout as viewed from *Dulcimer*'s dockside cameras and in some big room crowded with people, where it must have been Dulsey had seen him.

"We got the whole thing—the fight—on the dockside cameras," Klay said, and Squithy heard Tranh sigh.

"We do," he agreed. "Nobody official asked for it—like Squith said, the story outta *Nubella Run* was it'd been an accident. No sense making an argument when everybody was all agreed."

"I see," said Dulsey, sitting back, and slipping her wrist out from under Oki's paw. "I—which is to say, Crystal Logistics—will buy a copy of your Port Chavvy external vids. I will also buy the whole story of how you acquired these—norbears." She paused, frowning slightly. "Who named them? Or did they name themselves?"

"Squithy named them," Klay said. "We didn't know what they were, and there wasn't anybody around to tell us, except them, and all they were to themselves was *us*."

Dulsey nodded, and looked back to Tranh. "I will double my price if you give me the coords for the place where you found them. I guarantee absolute confidentiality—everyone knows Crystal is good for quiet."

She paused, then nodded to herself.

"The topic that brought us together was *kajets*," she said slowly. "I will be pleased to evaluate what you have. We offer competitive prices."

Tranh's eyes got wide—Squithy saw him change his posture, and knew why for once. It was the *kajets* that had to go, even more than the norbears. The *kajets* made the ship vulnerable. It was, Squithy had heard Tranh say to Rusko, the *kajets* that put *Dulcimer* and all her crew in danger.

Squithy felt eyes on her, and turned her head; Dulsey was watching *her* instead of Tranh or even Klay, and one of the norbears had noticed, and let it slip out into the wider thinkings.

Squithy felt that the norbears were interested in Dulsey. She was a challenge to them: Not Terran, not Liaden; not old, but somehow not young. Her connections were crowded, but neat—much neater than Tranh's or even Klay's. More, Squithy realized, like hers *now*, though her thinking hadn't been *any* kind of neat before . . . before Klay had killed the monster and saved the norbear troop.

"Yes," Tranh said. "We'll walk with you that way; show you what we got, and you make an offer. Some of what we got was hard to come by, some of it's been with us a port or two so's to not—" He broke off and turned his head.

"Squith, can you set out a lunch here for us all—maybe you and Klay both? No reason to keep the whole ship on this, if you know what I mean."

And she did know what he meant. Whatever they had, Tranh didn't want either Klay or her knowing exactly what it was, didn't want them able to tell somebody else, or even be able to recognize it.

That was good. These days she still felt like she was getting herself sorted out, and since she was afraid that the *kajets* might have been the reason for the firefight that had killed...

"Lunch!" she grabbed the word out of the sentence so she wouldn't go into the loop of too many what-ifs and might haves, and so Tranh wouldn't think she was falling back into counting or something.

"I can put out lunch, and Klay can help, 'cause he knows what the stations serve."

She smiled at Klay, hoping he understood that it wasn't just Tranh wanting them out of the meeting, but that she really did want him to help her. He nodded back and gave her a smile, which made her feel fine.

Squith and Klay oversaw a quiet lunch. Tranh had a port side appointment, and Falmer'd been put to going through the dockside vids from Port Chavvy, while Rusko and Susrim went back into the cargo section. Even the norbears were elsewhere, having retired to their made-over grain-bin.

Dulsey chatted about some of the goings-on of interest to indie traders and small Loopers, especially news of that Jethri, who'd been all of a sudden talking about his pa's *Envidaria* and Rostov's Dust. She talked to Klay specifically about the Dust, after he'd said as how it wasn't any news to the Looper ships, like *Dulcimer*.

"It's been out there," he said, "just we've been

piloting around it. Not something the big ships can do, with all they got to move in and out of Jump. Might give us some advantage, is what I'm reading in the *Envidaria*, if the Dust thickens up, specially round the Seventeen Worlds." He shrugged. "Might just be wishful thinking, but I'd like there to be something throws an advantage to us."

There was a little more of that, with Squithy paying attention to what was being said, but not having much to add, not being a pilot, or having read the *Envidaria*, though it came to her that Klay might send a copy to her tablet, so she could read it. She was about to ask him, when Dulsey turned to her.

"I wonder, Squithy, how do you like the port? Does it seem very noisy to you?"

"I don't know," she admitted. "I haven't been out. I don't go out on ports, just right on our dock, sometimes. I mean, ports are dangerous, Tranh says, and I need to stay close. I'm not sure what there'd be to do."

"I see." Dulsey nodded, and turned her head again. "And you, Klay?"

"This one's not too loud, I guess, and not really all that dangerous. I can see why Tranh might've said that to Squith, though. If you look at the old port lists, you see quick that the captains before favored some pretty rough dockings. That was before I came on board. We—well, really Tranh and Rusko—are looking to design a new route for us, a proper Loop. The old captains didn't favor being tied to a schedule, which made sorta sense, given their dockings, like I said. Anyhow, they took venture jobs, mostly, and one-offs."

"Something to be said for security," Dulsey agreed. "Have you been here at Chantor before?"

Klay shook his head. "When I was fresh born, the records say, but there's no memory there. This is my first real crew visit. I had a quick walk-around yesterday evening."

He nibbled on a cheese biscuit, realized the conversation was still his, and smiled at Squithy and Dulsey both.

"I like the bakeshops—found three of them—and I walked the view ring twice, 'cause they have a decent gravity track with star view, so there's people-watching. I hit the veggie shops, to see what was there, and so I could talk to Squith about what the norbears might like to have. That's for later, though. What with getting in, I'm behind on Stinks. Ought to catch up this shift."

Dulsey finished her 'toot and looked at the table for a long minute, like she was counting, Squithy thought, but that wasn't likely, Dulsey being a pilot and—

She looked up.

"Well, here's an idea I have," she said brightly, turning to Squithy. "If Klay needs to do Stinks, and the rest of the crew's busy like they are—and unless you've got your own orders—would you like to walk out with me? I'd like some company, and you could find out how you like the port."

Squithy felt a distant flutter of a familiar touch, that conveyed excitement, sleepiness, and a warning to be careful.

"Well..."

She opened her eyes.

"This is kind of my watch with the norbears—not ship schedule, just something we do after we eat. But Bebyear's just told me that the young ones are all asleep, and Oki, too. So I could—I mean, I'd have to ask permission. To leave the ship."

Dulsey smiled.

"My question stands—would you like to walk out with me? Perhaps we can see if there's a fashion-bag or two and see who's walking on the tracks! If you'd like it, I'd like it, too."

There was a flutter in her stomach that she knew was her and not a norbear listening in. To just *walk out* on port? *Could* she do that? Did she *want* to?

She felt something else—Klay's concentration, she realized. That was something that had come with the norbears, that her and Klay could feel each other, like they were norbears, too. She'd asked Ebling about it, and had come away with the impression that her and Klay had been adopted.

Right now, though, Klay was feeling serious, concerned, and undecided.

She looked at him, and saw that he was watching her hands. Looking down, she saw them clenched, which she did to hold back a fit of counting, or worse, one of her Big Silences. The only thing was that she didn't feel like counting, and instead of getting quiet, she wanted to talk! She had so many questions!

"Not to tell stories, Pilot," Klay said carefully, "but sometimes Squith gets the worries on pretty hard—kind of loses her breath and concentration. Not sure when the last time was she went walking with someone not crew, I mean by herself."

That was fair, Squithy thought, and Klay was right to give warning. He couldn't know how she'd be, going out on the docks with Pilot Dulsey—how could he when she didn't know herself?

"You could check the logbooks, Klay, but I can save you the trouble and count it out right now. Never.

I *never* been out on dock or port by myself alone. Never, without family, and hardly ever, then."

Dulsey nodded, and Squithy saw she was studying both of their faces.

"This might be a good time to try it out. The station's not rough, and I'm known here. It's healthy to get off ship; gives you a shot of new air to work on robusting your resistances, while seeing new things and getting used to what docks are like. If there's an emergency, and you have to go out by yourself, you'll need to know that. And, maybe you'd just want to go out and get treats or surprises for the ship."

Dulsey smiled right *at* her.

"Please, walk with me. I'll put it to the captain, if you like."

"He's not here," Squithy began, but Klay interrupted.

"That all makes good sense, Squith. I'd take you myself if it wasn't for Stinks being overdue. People do know the Crystal folks, and they might as well get used to seeing *Dulcimer* crew in their halls. Tranh's due back soon, I think, but if you want to go now, Rusko can give permission. Just be sure to wear your crew jacket."

"I don't have a crew jacket, Klay. Never had one, remember?"

He blinked, then nodded.

"You hold right there, and I'll get my ship scarf. You wear that, and nobody'll mistake you for anything but *Dulcimer* crew. Won't be a sec."

He turned, and nearly collided with Tranh at the door. The captain was carrying a red and white striped box with a blue comet across the stripes. The box smelled of bread and sweets...

"Brought back some stuff to share," he began, but Squithy blurted out—

"Tranh, I want to go on port with Pilot Dulsey. She asked me to!"

Dulsey nodded at him, "It's true. It's good for a young woman to get a port tour—a shopping tour— from another woman. She may have needs she doesn't see in the catalogs."

Tranh shook his head, a frown between his brows.

"That's real obliging of you, Pilot, but see, Squith doesn't really need shopping. She stays on the ship, and—"

Klay stepped up, and Tranh turned to look at him.

"We all get to shop, Tranh, even if it isn't a long liberty. I'm on Stinks, or I'd take her. But crew gets to shop—part of the rules, I think. She don't *have* to shop if she don't want to—but if she *wants to*, Tranh . . ."

He left the sentence undone, and in the quiet Tranh sighed.

"I take your point, I do. I really do. But Squithy doesn't know—"

Dulsey stood forward then.

"If Squithen doesn't know, she should. Crew needs to be flexible, crew needs to be able to be autonomous at times. So, I have an eighth-shift I can share, and I'd be pleased to have Squithen's company. She's already agreed, but properly said that she needed to ask permission of the captain. If the captain is withholding his permission, that is of course his right."

"I—dammit." Tranh looked goaded. He turned and put his box on the table, then turned back to Dulsey. "Squithy's a special case, see, Pilot? Sometimes she gets to counting, and don't pay attention to anything else. We don't know how she'll react to going out on port. Suppose she just starts counting out there and won't pay attention? That's something that happened, and it's not dangerous of itself, but she's a handful to get back when she's like that."

"I want to go," Squithy said then, looking straight into Tranh's eyes. "If the captain will give permission. I won't start counting. I haven't been, Tranh, you know it. I want to shop for a crew jacket, so when I go out at another port, everybody will know I'm on *Dulcimer*."

Tranh stared at her.

"Another port?" he said faintly, but Squithy was still talking.

"Can I borrow one of the ship's figurators, so the logo's right on my jacket?"

"A figurator," Klay said, tapping her lightly on the shoulder. "That's a great idea, Squith. Listen, I could use a new wallet. Will you get one for me?"

Klay was asking her to shop for him. She smiled, and touched his hand.

"I'll do my best. What should it look like?"

"Something plain, ship colors, right?" He pulled his old wallet out of his pocket. "Here, I like this style. Six windows would be good, ship-sign on it. This one's frayed, and 'sides, it's my old ship's logo there, see? I want people to know I'm with *Dulcimer*. You're taking the figurator, so you can have them put *Dulcimer*'s sign right on it. Plain colors, now—nothing bright and glittery, hear me?"

"All right," she agreed, watching as Klay took a credit chip from his wallet. He held it out, and she hesitated before she realized what he was offering, and pressed her thumb against the nearest corner.

Klay nodded, pressing his thumb against another corner, and then putting the chip in her hand. "All right, you're on this card for the next day cycle. Don't spend it all in one place, but get yourself a good jacket. *Dulcimer* crew's gotta be proud, right? The wallet—ought to be able to find something decent for under ten kais, down to crew zones. And, buy yourself a bisgot an' tea or something, on me!"

"Thank you, Klay!" She put the chip carefully into her pocket, and sealed it before she turned to Tranh.

"*Can* I go, Captain? *And* can I borrow a figurator, so Klay's got our logo right on his new wallet?"

Tranh threw up his hand, which he did when somebody had out-argued him. Squithy had never out-argued Tranh, nor nobody else. She wasn't sure how she felt about that, but there was a little giggly feeling at the back of her head that told her Mitsy and Ditsy were happy with the outcome.

"All fine, all fine," Tranh said, and looked at Klay. "Have we seen a figurator since...events?"

Klay frowned.

"Even if they both had one on them, there should still be the 'mergency figurator. I'll check the inventory. If we're down to one, it'd be good to get a couple more, while we're on-port..."

He moved to the screen across the room, and touched it.

"It's cooler on port than it is in-ship," Dulsey said, and Squithy turned to look at her. "I'll be comfortable in my jacket, but if you have a sweater, it might be good to have it."

"I will!" Squithy said, her stomach a little unsettled as she realized that this was going to happen. "I'll get it. Just a sec, please!" And she flew down the corridor, half-afraid that Dulsey would leave without her, and half-afraid that she wouldn't.

Klay located two figurators, and one was signed out to the girl, who had bundled on a grey sweater that was too big for her. Dulsey sighed, wondering if anybody had ever put themselves out for Squithen Patel. Young Klay was inclined to look out for her, but Klay was new crew, himself, and Squithy needed to look out for herself, from herself.

Which was going to be hard, even with an ally, when the rest of the crew seemed to consider her as something between a child and a doll, without a ship-share—or at least without a credit chip. That she had a rapport with the norbears only made the rest of her family think she was odder, since none of the rest of them cared for the creatures—with the exception, again, of Klay.

Dulsey sighed again, telling herself that it wasn't her problem to solve. She would do what she could while she could for Squithen, but it *wasn't* her problem, and Yuri would deliver an observation on the sins of meddling when she made her report. As if he didn't do the same.

"I'm ready," Squithy said, having checked her pockets for the third time. Dulsey believed she had been memorizing the contents of each, and no one could say that was a foolish precaution, even on a relatively tame port. The less passersby knew of the state of one's pockets, the more peace there was in the universe.

"Then, please, lead us to the appropriate hatch."

Squithy turned right, and suddenly there were norbears, filling the hall with furry bodies, and the head
with demands to be brought along, and well-wishes
for Squithy, and warnings about something large and
toothy and altogether unpleasant.

Squithy stopped, hands on hips, glaring at the mob
surrounding them.

"No, you can't go on port. I don't know if there are
any of those outside. Pilot Dulsey an' me're gonna go
look and see is it safe. We'll bring back lots of faces,
but not if you don't let us go!"

The mind-pictures that Squithy produced to accom-
pany this were astonishingly robust. The uproar around
them faded somewhat. Dulsey had the impression
that the more boisterous were somewhat cowed. The
grizzled norbear she had been sharing memories with
prior to lunch seemed to be delivering herself of a
stern lecture, which, Dulsey noted with interest, she
could *almost* understand.

"C'mon, now, no crowding the hall, you know better!" That was Klay, coming down the hall with another
grizzled norbear in his train. "Back here, now, clear
the hatch! I'm just getting ready to put out some extra
greens, but I can't do that if I gotta carry all of you
back to your room!"

Klay's mental communication was also strong, sending
pictures of norbears obediently turning back toward a
cozy nest, and piles of greens so fresh Dulsey felt her
own mouth water.

One by one, the norbears ceded to the force of
Klay's argument, and moved back down the hall.
Squithy took a step, checked, and stared down at a
small shadow, standing upright on two feet by the wall.

"Synbe," she said, and a feeling of sadness flowed from her.

The norbear hesitated for a bare heartbeat, then dropped to four feet and waddled hurriedly back up the hall.

"That's all of them, now," Squithy said, moving quickly toward the side hatch, and all the wonders of Chantor's Way Station, Dulsey in train.

Squithy shivered as the hatch sealed, and Dulsey saw resolve build in her and the girl strode purposefully forward, toward the station proper. They were one of two ships on the tube, so there was only one direction to go. Dulsey listened hard to the girl's breathing, listened hard to her walk. She could measure to some extent how fast Squithy's heart must be beating . . . so she took a gentle, conversational tone when she spoke.

"When we reach the pressure door ahead, we can turn right immediately. There'll be a 'fresh station a little ahead, and a snack counter. We can stop and plan there. Best to check real-time with each other and make sure of comm codes and such."

"Yes, good," Squithy said, sounding more determined than breathless. "I don't need to count the steps; I know the elphbets and numbers, and I know we're at K7L. That means I can find us on the left side of the K Tube any time I want!"

Squithy looked back briefly when they exited the K7 Tube, as if memorizing the spot, then she was striding forward again, to Dulsey's eye more eager than apprehensive.

"Exactly right about the tube address, and here we are on the Level 7 mezzanine," Dulsey said. "The mezzanines are the best place to find the verticals. Let's look at the station guide around the corner—do you know how to read a map? If you touch here you can ask it for directions to a particular location—say 'open med clinic' or 'closest bar.'"

She demonstrated those, watching Squithy's face, and seeing something very familiar.

"Do you do that, too, Squithy? Sub-vocalize to remember?"

Squithy frowned. "What do you mean?"

"Do you tell yourself the directions again a few times, saying the words in your head or in your mouth without saying them out loud? A lot of people learn that way."

The frown cleared, replaced by a pleased expression.

"Yeah, I do that! Sometimes, when I read, too. Ma told me that I needed to do better if I ever wanted to be—"

Squithy stopped herself with a gasp, closed her eyes, and opened them again.

"Ma and Da, they both said I was slow and stupid." Another deep breath. "Not useful enough to draw a share."

Dulsey nodded. She'd heard more than enough about Rorik Smith, Jenfer Patel, and their various failures. Desperate for a fortune, they had denigrated and dismissed the wealth they did have. The best thing they'd done for their children had been to die in one of Choody's pointless arranged violences. But of course, she couldn't say any of that to Squithen Patel, standing tight-faced before her.

"People learn differently," Dulsey said. "When I was in my first learning, the teachers tried different ways to teach me and my cousins, and no one thing was good for everybody. I practiced reading and more reading, and got good at it, but nobody can know all the words in the universe. I still try unfamiliar words out, try to hear them in my head even if I don't say them out loud. We all learn different, but none of us are born knowing everything. So practice is good, even in later learning."

She stopped for a moment, reckoned she'd said enough and smiled, pointing at the station map.

"Since you've got an errand, let's look for an outfitter. Some places they're called outfitters, some places they're shareshops—I'm assuming you want new, not recycled, for this?"

"New," Squithy agreed. "Klay wants a new wallet, he said that. And I want a new jacket, so I can put my name on it, and *Dulcimer*'s, without having to patch them on. I like your jacket, but I think I should have one with a hood, so I can wear it on a planet—in weather, I mean."

"Good; that's think-ahead. My jacket has a hidden hood, it was made for me exactly—do you want a shop that can print exactly to measure?"

Squithy glanced over Dulsey's shoulder, an absent expression on her face. Thinking, Dulsey thought, and waited, not turning around.

"Exact measure's not so important," Squithy said a moment later. "Important is that it fits. I might still get some growth, Falmer says, so it might be best if there was room for me to grow into it."

"That's sensible," Dulsey said, and turned again to the map. "Let's check the directory."

*   *   *

There were five outfitters to choose from on-station, one each on levels F though J—

"What's on A?" Squithy asked abruptly, pointing at the uninformative green blobs on the map.

"Admin, and residences for station crew and staffers."

"Can we go there? To A? So I know what's there?"

The girl had a sense of adventure, Dulsey thought with approval. She nodded, and tapped the map for more information.

"There are tours," she said, standing back so that Squithy could read the screen, too. "The timing doesn't favor us today, but we might be able to take one during our next port-time together."

While she waited for Squithy's reaction, she thought about this offered second outing. It made sense, since it appeared she had decided to broaden Squithy's experiences, and, Dulsey thought, she'd like to see the girl's reactions to the admin level.

"I'd like that," Squithy said, slowly. "Do you really mean you want to come out with me again?"

"I do really mean that," said Dulsey. "So we're settled. Now, how should we look for an outfitter?"

Squithy opted for starting at F Level and moving up, so she could see what each shop offered before she made a decision. Dulsey nodded, and stepped back to let her lead the way, so it was a good thing, Squithy thought, that she'd memorized the map.

The outfitter at F Level shop carried new things, and Squithy walked among the displays quietly. They *looked* good, but they didn't *feel* like proper shipside clothes.

She felt one pair of supposed work trousers, wrinkled

her nose—and wasn't quite sure what Dulsey's silence meant. That lady touched some items, too, and turned toward the door, which gave Squithy the idea that she hadn't been wrong about the clothes. That heartened her, and she gave the clerk a smile and a "thank you," as they left.

On G Level, the items were more practical, though the prices were higher—Squithy could imagine working in the clothes on offer. The port jackets, though, were flimsy to her way of thinking. The catalog promised better in the fab-to-order line, but Squithy wanted to touch the jacket before she bought one. Dulsey nodded over her reservations, her expression serious—and Squithy suddenly realized that she was watching for Dulsey's expressions, and trying to read them. The norbears did that; their faces would change when they considered things, or when they were having a discussion with her or Klay. The norbears thought she was interesting and reasonable, and not unfit to be crew, and here was Dulsey listening to her, and her decisions as if she was reasonable, and—competent.

So often, she'd seen complaint, concern—and worse, contempt—on the faces of people waiting for her to make a decision, or struggling to understand what things meant. She'd heard them talking, like she wasn't there sometimes, impatient with her counting or weighing what was best: "No, don't *ask* her; *tell* her what to do if you think she can handle it without making a mess. If you ask, she'll be three weeks figuring it out, and I ain't got the time!"

Klay'd been different when he came on-board. He had, Squithy realized now, the same thing Dulsey had—watchful eyes, that saw how things were, but not like she was wrong, not like he expected her to just stand there—*like a dummy*, Ma said—not like he was looking for faults, just like he was looking.

They left the G Level store, too, without buying anything, and found a bench to sit and rest, in front of a window where two people were spinning flat breads in their hands, and tossing them high in the air, catching, spinning, and throwing again. Squithy caught her breath, being afraid that the bread would be tossed too high, but the bakers had a keen sense of just where their ceiling was. At least, they did now.

Squithy pointed up.

"Those marks—are they real?" she asked.

Dulsey grinned. "The apprentices must make a mistake now and then when they start, what do you think?"

Squithy nodded, concerned for the bakers learning the craft—which these two were not. Their arms were corded with muscle, their concentration cool and confident.

"Will you share a snack with me?" Dulsey asked. "They sell sweet, spicy, and savory. Do you have a choice?"

"Sweet!" Squithy said before she even thought what it meant—sharing a snack, and then Dulsey was gone, crossing to the little window to the left of the big one where the dough was being thrown, and was back just that quick, with a box in one hand.

Dulsey sat, putting the box on the bench between them before she reached inside and broke the dough into pieces, offering one to Squithy bare-fingered.

She hesitated, thinking about all the rules she'd been given, don't dos, the must dos, and the never tries.

"They told me," she said finally, "that I need to be careful of food from the stations."

Dulsey nodded.

"Indeed, I can understand why you might be taught that. Yet we watched these bakers at work, and I— and you, I warrant—have seen nothing amiss in the way they work, in their process, or demeanor. Also, there is something else you might consider in your decision—look here!"

The bread nestled in a striped box with a blue comet—

Squithy thought back, made connections—

"This must be the bakery Tranh came to!"

Dulsey spread her hands wide.

"Yes, it would appear this is the same location. I, for one, am prepared to have my snack. I hope you will decide to have some, too. It smells delicious!"

Hesitantly, Squithy reached out and accepted the piece of bread Dulsey offered. She admired the color and shine of the sugars and nearly started to count the colors. She looked up and watched Dulsey casually lift a piece of bread to her mouth with no hesitation or concern.

And there, she thought; if she needed to, she could look at the colors in her head, but she didn't need to count them—not now. *Now* she wanted to taste the delightful smells that were already loading her senses.

She closed her eyes, not to be distracted, took a bite, and chewed, letting flavors cover her tongue and fill her mouth. She swallowed, felt the aftertastes had a sense still of breads, began to note where each flavor settled on her palate ...

"Squithen?"

Startled, Squithy opened her eyes then, saw Dulsey's concern flash away into a smile.

"Savoring?" she asked, and Squithy nodded.

"It's very good. Tell me what kind it is and I'll take some to *Dulcimer* myself!"

••••••

Klay was feeling put upon—that's how his old shipmates would have rated this problem—right there at *put upon*, which was a step down from *overwhelmed*. *Overwhelmed* was what happened when he'd been out-voted by everyone else on *Bon's Bodega*, and that had happened enough, even with him being a pilot, because he was the youngest by a few years and pretty tired of taking jokes as *the kid*, when he wasn't one.

Worse, he'd been showing signs of being the *best* pilot in some situations, and that hadn't made the old guard happy at all—well, no, they were happy *for him*, but *not* happy *for them*, which was what counted, the ship going pretty well by time-in-grade when it came around to making assignments and getting paid.

So, when *Dulcimer*'d come up in big trouble and the call went out to family, he'd been kind of voted off one ship and on to another by acclaim. That is, everybody'd known it was the best solution, even him, though he knew nothing in his life would be the same again, for all that he'd been chaffed on *Bodega*.

The funerals were over by the time Bon got the ship to Lorimer, and after a couple days of papers and book balancing and contract jawing he'd been cashed out of *Bodega* and invested in *Dulcimer*, with guarantees that his training and testing would be check-pointed with the Pilot's Guild, as possible.

Benin Rusko and Tranh Smith—his uncles, officially—
were senior pilot and captain, and they were trader and
senior trader. Given the youth of everyone else on the
ship they were senior and standard everything else on
the ship, from 'ponocists and medicos to tech and cooks
and the cousins—Cousin Susrim and Cousin Falmer
and Cousin Squithy—they were all general crew, which
happened sometimes on family ships.

And since Klay was a pilot ready to test from First
Class to First Class Plus, and since Uncle Rusko was
First Class Plus, but not a Master Pilot, he couldn't do
anything more in that regard but name Klay an equal.
The chance of Klay getting time on a big ship to go
for actual Master rating, that was going to be hard, all
things considered. And at the moment he was back-up
everything despite being a hardly known outside cousin
to the general crew who were ship-born and lived on
Dulcimer all their lives.

Everybody but Tranh was too young to be what
they were, the ship having come to them after a
really stupid firefight on Trask-Romo took out Tranh's
Da and Ma, who were Squithy, Susrim, and Falmer's
parents too.

Susrim was studied to be cook and arms, and was
up to a local class three back-up pilot rating any day
now according to the sims, but he didn't have the
credits from a recognized school or committee yet.
Susrim wasn't all that pleased with the norbears,
finding them too nosy, as he put it.

Falmer was one cycle behind Susrim in age and
ought to have been head cook a while back, but Susrim
was studied and she wasn't. Falmer had some medico
stuff; when Klay had come on board Falmer'd been in

charge of Squithy when Tranh wasn't, which it turned out had been most of the time, and Squithy being treated like a no-wit or a minor on account of being an uncertain kind of person. Now? Now Falmer'd been trying to put Squithy on Klay's schedule, but he wasn't seeing that she needed to be on anybody's schedule but hers. True, she wasn't like everybody, and she sometimes took frights or started in to counting, but there'd been less of that since the norbears, and even before the norbears, in his opinion, she'd been bright and thoughtful whenever anybody gave her the time she needed to get everything lined up in her head.

Well, that wasn't neither Jump nor local. The problem wasn't Squithy, or any individual, the problem was what the past had left them to sort out, and what future they was going to pilot to.

Captain Tranh was where he was because he took the warguilt payoff the bar came up with on account of the bloodshed and boom, he brought in pretty Uncle Rusko, who'd not been a fit on *his* home ship despite his top grade piloting, on account of that ship, *Proud Plenty*, was looking for blood-heirs, and that meant *Groton* needed a Patel or a Smith, and when it all filtered down through a Standard of people-trades from ship to ship—Klay'd ended up here, on a ship where neither the captain nor the senior pilot had ever run a crew meeting from the top, and where the crew, aside from Klay and Rusko, had never *been* in a real crew meeting on account of the *Dulcimer*'s previous, now departed, owners hadn't run a genuine crew-share ship.

Just at this present, Susrim was the one pushing to make Klay feel put upon—and he said it again, same phrase, which was as good a way to get on Klay's nerves as there was.

"The animals gotta go. They got us in trouble before, and here it's lucky somebody wants 'em. So the animals gotta go. You can send them off with Crystal Dulsey for a few bits—heck, she might have a *cantra* for us with everything Tranh's trying to do. But them animals have *all* gotta go."

Right then, Tranh limped into the mess room, still not quite over the bad news from their landing before Port Chavvy and shook his head at Susrim.

"Heard that, and you ought to know better. That's badgering, and you know it. You might be able to dock this ship but you're not taking her into Jump in the next three Standards, is my guess, so don't badger the pilot that got us through to Port Chavvy and has been taking lead since Rusko's been dealing with the tech stuff. Don't want to get all rankish here, but if we have to, you're a couple steps down, got that?"

"But *you* want the things gone, too!"

"I do. Seems like there's a couple considerations going on, and one of them is that Crystal might be paying for us take some of them somewhere to be studied, and Crystal's got an in at some yards that can do us some reconfigure to get us all up to true. Crystal's already in for taking every bit of what was left over from the old runs—and the reconfigure'll find out if there's anything else hidden that Ma and Da didn't bother to tell us about. Don't push 'til we see what's left on deck when we Jump out of here."

"They make me shiver," Susrim said with heat— "reaching inside and wanting to know who I know.

They gotta go! Then Squithy can go back to permanent on Stinks and clean-up, and the rest of us could . . ."

"Susrim," came a clear voice from the piloting chamber—"Susrim, I do believe I wish *not* to hear whatever else it was you were going to say. We've already agreed in crew-meeting that we'll explore Crystal's offers, and most of *us* think that having Squithy a step up is good for the ship."

With that Rusko appeared, a warm smile for Tranh, a pleasant nod and smile for Klay, and a thin-lipped glance at Susrim's clenched hands and grim face.

"I think me and Falmer have enough cause to ask for another meeting soon."

Susrim's threat was quieter than his complaint had been. Klay frowned, thinking he might—his timer went off right then, buzzing and vibrating on his belt.

"Back to Stinks for me," he muttered, heading toward 'ponics to clear the green vents, but Rusko held up his hand.

"Just another minute, if you can, Klay. We gotta make sure all four of us are clear on some details." He glanced at Tranh, who nodded.

"Best to get it out now, while we're all in one place," he said.

"Right, then. Here's what we got."

He turned. "Klay, I'd like it if you'd step up to second seat, now. No reason to hold off; we all seen what you can do with a ship." Rusko glanced at Susrim, thought better of something, and put his gaze back on Klay. "If you're agreeable, I'll do up the paperwork, and file it with the office here, so it's done and finished."

He paused, and Klay realized he was being asked, not told.

"I'm agreeable," he said, and tried not to see Susrim's glare.

Rusko nodded. "Soon's you're finished with Stinks, come see me. There'll be papers for you to sign, and I'll be wanting you to have a look at those Dust maps I been collecting. We're gonna have to run some sims, is my thought, so be thinking about how you want to get that set up. Priority is setting up good routes, now we won't be using the whimsy engine."

That was cutting real close to a complaint about how Tranh's Ma and Da had done what they called *bidness*. Klay cut a glance sideways, but Tranh wasn't showing anything near a frown. He nodded with clear approval.

"That's all got my okay," he said. "Good approach to planning, and going forward with getting us regularized and clean on duty-lines. Like you say, no need for Klay to prove anything more in the pilot's room. Second chair'll look good on him. You need me for anything, on that, or otherwise?"

Rusko shook his head.

"Then I'll leave you to it, Pilots. I got the trade feed to study on, so you know where to find me if the local office needs captain's assurances or whatever. After dinner, let's the three of us sit, look at what we got—routes, Dust, and trade—and see what matches up." He looked at Rusko, at Klay, and pointedly did not look at Susrim.

"All good on approach?" he asked.

"All good," Rusko said, with a nod.

"All good," Klay affirmed, thinking, *the three of us*. He dared a glance at Susrim, and saw his face close when he realized *he* was *four*.

• • • • 🟊 • • • •

H Level was different from the Levels above; it was newer, brighter, and much less crowded. There was a display in the center of the hall that explained how there'd been a collision decades before, and H Level had been rebuilt according to an "open plan."

That meant that, instead of being a shop, with a few real items on display, and most things available through catalog order, Level H Outfitters and Supply occupied a space that was a former hangar deck, and it had real goods on display, in different colors, sizes, styles, and prices. Squithy heard another shopper say that she was sure the other shops were getting their catalog orders and next-day goods from this one, enormous shop.

Squithy stopped just inside the big doors, staring around at all the things, all the people, all the . . .

"Well," Dulsey said next to her, "isn't this an eye-opener?"

Squithy half-laughed, and looked at her.

"It is!" she said. "I'm—there's a lot of things here, aren't there?"

"There are," Dulsey agreed, looking out over the space all hung with racks and displays, and the people moving around, talking to each other, handling the goods . . .

"It's a good thing," Dulsey said, "that you know what you're shopping for. You can start with those first."

Squithy took a deep breath. That was right. She did have things to shop for. Klay wanted a new wallet, and she needed a crew jacket.

She turned back, looking with a purpose, now, and right there—*there* was a rack of port jackets, right there!

✳   ✳   ✳

These jackets felt much better in her hands than the ones in the first and second shops! And there was one that was just about a perfect match for *Dulcimer*'s colors.

"Want to try it on?" Dulsey asked from beside her. "I can help, if you need."

"Yes," said Squithy and between them both, she got the jacket on. It was a little too big, but not so big that people would think she was wearing a lend-me, or a hand-down from a bigger crew member. It felt good on her shoulders, too, not too heavy, and there was a hood zipped into the collar.

"Help you, gentles?" asked a new voice.

Squithy turned to see a woman in station clothes, wearing a bright green vest with H Level Supply Associate stitched on the left shoulder.

"I want to buy this," Squithy said, and touched the pre-sized spots on the breast and sleeve, where ship name and logo would go on a proper crew jacket. "Can you use my figurator for these?"

The Supply Associate nodded. "Oh, no problem with any of that," she said. "I'm afraid we're a little backed up, though..."

Squithy sighed, ready for disappointment, when the associate noticed Dulsey, standing quietly by the rack, and gave her a nod. "Is she with you, Lady Dulsey?"

"I'm with her, actually; she's buying for herself and other members of her ship, not mine."

"I understand."

The salesperson pulled a tablet out of a vest pocket, ran her eye down, and turned back to Squithy.

"We'll be able to get to you in half-an-hour. If you're sure you want this jacket, I can start a pile for you. You can shop for other items, and add them to your pile, so you won't lose your place in line. Will that be acceptable?"

"Yes!" Squithy said, giving the jacket into her waiting arms. "Thank you!"

The wallets were—fascinating. Squithy decided on Klay's first, hand-worked from recycled space leather, made by a retired engineer who had his own booth in a corner of the outfitters. After inspecting it closely— and noting how nice it felt in her fingers—Squithy decided that she would have one, too.

"I don't have anything to keep in a wallet right now," she told Dulsey. "But maybe I will, later."

"Your crew card?" Dulsey asked, and Squithy blinked.

"I didn't think of that! I'll put it in first. And Klay's chip, too, though I'll have to give that back."

"Do you draw a line?" Dulsey asked, which Susrim would say was none of her business, but Susrim didn't like anybody but him knowing things, and Dulsey had already helped her understand so much . . .

"I don't have a share, or a line. Ma and Da thought I'd spend all my time counting my credits, if they gave me a chip, and really I only did Stinks and kitchen scut, nothing worth the ship paying for. I been upgraded since, though, so maybe Tranh will think about giving me a line."

"Maybe he will," Dulsey said, dryly.

They took the wallets to the booth, and watched the engineer take his own readings from the figurator and cut an overlay, all the while explaining what he was doing.

"See, this press here will take the wallets and give us about a ocean-bottom's worth of pressure on a touch of genyouwine Clutch glue . . . won't come apart for nothin', guaranteed, and it's the same sealing glue and substrate they use on the jackets. Not quite Jump jackets, but pretty darn tough. See if this wallet don't get handed down to your great-grand-kids when you turn over your log books, Captain Squithen . . . I can just see it now!"

Squithy blushed, because it sounded like being made fun of—but Dulsey gave the man a sharp look.

"Can you, Engineer?" Dulsey asked. "*Can* you see it?"

The engineer looked startled, then turned his attention to watching the press work its wonders. When the plate lifted, he used long tongs to pick the wallet up and sprayed it.

"This here will cool the leather right down, so you can put it in your pocket," he said. "We'll let this one rest while we do the next . . ."

Once again, he took readings, cut the overlay, and aligned the wallet.

It was while the press was working that he looked back to Dulsey.

"Your question doesn't have a hard answer, Pilot," he said, talking quiet, like he didn't want anybody but Dulsey to hear. "When it comes blurting out like it did, then it seems like I'm right a lot more than I'm wrong. You can look at me and see I'm not propping up a Banbury story here." He smiled slightly. "I'm an engineer, you know; it's kind of embarrassing."

Dulsey was silent for a long moment, and Squithy wondered if she *could* see for sure if someone was having a Sight. She knew some people did—Liadens mostly, Ma'd said, which was another reason not to trust Liadens.

Dulsey bowed a small, gentle bow.

"Perhaps I will be able to provide empirical data in the case, to ease your embarrassment. In the meanwhile, it is good to know you're on port."

The press released, then, and he turned back to his work, removing the wallet, dousing it, and setting it aside to cool while he picked up the first and buffed it with a soft rag.

"Here you go," he said, handing it to Squithy. "Touch that imprint, now—not going anywhere!"

Squithy took the wallet, admiring how smooth it was, how fine, looking at her name pressed there, and *Dulcimer*'s own sigil.

She sighed. It was the finest thing she'd ever owned. She opened it, and looked up quickly.

"But, there are funds in here!" she said, feeling panic. What if it was a trick, and he said she'd stolen from him? Da had said those kind of things happened on stations, and—

"Them's yours," said the engineer. "It's bad luck to buy an empty wallet, that's what they say here on Chantor Station. So we figure it into the cost that each wallet has dated scrip included. Those are only good for the station month, so spend 'em before you leave. They won't be money the next time you're on Chantor."

Dulsey shifted slightly, and the engineer cleared his throat, reaching for Klay's wallet to give it the final buff before handing it up to Squithy to inspect. There was station scrip in it, too, which soothed her.

"Thank you," she said to the engineer. "They're both beautiful."

"You're welcome," he said. "You come back and see me, the next time your ship's in. Luck to you, now—and luck to the good ship *Dulcimer*!"

TWO

"AND YOU HAVE TO SPEND THE STATION SCRIP BEFORE WE leave, because there's a good-through date," Squithy finished, while Klay turned his new wallet over in his hands, looking at the windows and rubbing his fingers over *Dulcimer*'s sigil and his name.

"That's fine," he said, and looked up at her with a smile. "That's real fine, Squith, thank you."

"I liked doing it," she said. "And getting you a wallet made it seem think-forward to get one for me, too, for when I have something to put in it." She pulled hers out, and opened it, showing him the first window. "Besides my crew card, I mean."

"You ought to get a draw, Squith," Klay said slowly.

"Dulsey said maybe Tranh will think of that, now I've been upgraded."

He kind of half-smiled.

"If Dulsey said that, I'm pretty sure Tranh's going to remember real soon. In the meantime, here—" He reached into his pocket and pulled out the chip he'd let her use today. "Let's get this transferred over to you, yourself, so you got something to keep your crew card company. Bad luck for a wallet to be empty, wasn't that it?"

109

"Bad luck to *buy* an empty wallet," Squithy said, remembering the engineer with his maybe-Sight.

"Well, the theory holds," Klay said. "When your good-through money ages out, your wallet'll be empty. Can't risk that. Here, put your thumb right there in the center."

Squithy hesitated, because that would make her the owner of the chip and the credits on it, but Klay wanted her to do it; she could tell it would make him happy if she did, and it would, she thought, be something to have real credit of her own.

She reached out and pushed her thumb in the center of the chip.

"That's it!" Klay sounded glad. "Next time you go out on port, you can spend your own."

Squithy smiled, picked up her wallet and put the chip carefully away in a window.

"Dulsey and me're gonna take the tour of A Level," she told Klay. "I'll buy my own ticket."

"And a snack for you and Dulsey, if you want," Klay said.

She hadn't thought of that, either, but it would be right, she told herself, to buy Dulsey a treat, and... fun to share it with her.

It had been fun to bring the striped box of dough squares back to *Dulcimer* and put it in the galley for everybody to find and choose one. Some of the squares were sweet, and some were savory, and some were spicy. Falmer'd been surprised by her first taste of a spicy square, and she'd been careful to choose one with sugar on top for her second.

She'd been worried that there wouldn't be any left for Klay, and there'd only been three left when he came into the galley—one of each.

"Those are for you," she'd told him, when he sat down at the table with her.

"Yeah? Don't you want any?"

"I already had mine," she said, and he'd nodded and tried the savory one first, and while he ate it, she'd told him about the shopping trip, and when he'd done, she'd given him his new wallet, and the credit chip.

Now, he took a bite out of the spicy square, his eyebrows going up, and the tips of his ears getting red.

"That's—something," he said, his voice whispery. "Might go good with some water."

"I'll get it," Squithy said, and jumped up, getting water for both of them and coming back to the table.

"I didn't like the spicy ones much, either," she said.

"They take some getting used to, is all," Klay answered, and finished the rest of the square, followed by a big swallow of water.

"So, Squith, you gotta know this. There's gonna be a meeting after dinner. That'll be the captain and the traders and the first classes. That's you and Falmer and Susrim left out. It's a security thing, and the word comes from the captain and both traders."

Squithy got cold.

"They're deciding about the norbears," she said, breathless, and feeling like maybe she should start counting—but no, this was important. If they were going to decide about the norbears *without* her . . .

She felt them, then, as if from a distance; a sense of sorrow and determination fading even as she felt them.

"Is Dulsey going to be at the meeting?" she demanded. Klay shook his head.

"Crew meeting, and anyhow Dulsey's gone. Saw her out the hatch myself just before I came in to find you."

She bit her lip.

"Klay—"

"Squith, I'll be in the meeting, right? If there's anything where you're needed to translate for them, I'll push for them to call you. But, see, it's not just norbears we'll be talking about—and they're talking themselves, you felt it, didn't you?"

"I did," she said quietly, and took a deep breath. "I just don't like not *knowing*."

"Won't be much knowing at first," Klay said. "There's a ladder of things that have to happen. First, we got to all agree that we've got a good offer from Crystal, and if we don't, what could we ask for to make it good. Now, me, I think we've got a good offer, best we'll get, considering, and I'll vote that way. The norbears—well, you know Tranh wants them gone. They amuse Rusko, but not so much he'll go against Tranh to keep 'em. Thing is that the norbears are themselves, like Dulsey says, so they get to decide do *they* want to come to terms with Crystal, and if they do, will they all go, or some stay? They're coming back to us, once Crystal's finished with their project, Dulsey's not moving on that, though Tranh might try once more. Problem is, we're not even. *Dulcimer* needs Crystal more than Crystal needs *Dulcimer*." He paused, and looked into the box.

"I'm not sure I can eat that one all by myself. Share?"

Squithy smiled. "Sure."

He picked up the square and broke it in half, giving her one.

"Crystal don't even need the norbears, is my reading, though Dulsey thinks they might be *useful* for whatever it is. Big difference between useful and necessary, and if Tranh pushes too hard, she can just as easy leave them on the table, like they say. And if the norbears decide to stay with *Dulcimer*, then that's what'll happen, no questions there."

Squithy chewed the sweet dough thoughtfully.

"Do you think they're going to turn it down—the norbears?"

He shrugged.

"Hard to know what to think, there. I'm getting that they don't want to go away from what's known and safe and at the same time, they want to see new things." He grinned. "We're not the only ones going to be talking long tonight."

She finished her sweet and took a drink of water.

"You said you think Dulsey's deal is good," she said. "What's everybody else think?"

"That's why we gotta talk. There's two sides to every trade, see. Crystal's made their offers, and now *Dulcimer's* got to decide if it's good, or if we want something other than what's offered, or more of it, or less. Then Dulsey's got to think about is it worth it to Crystal to alter the original offer. What I think..." He paused. "I think nobody—Crystal, us, or the norbears—will get exactly what they want, but close enough to agree. And that'll be a problem, sort of."

She'd nodded him on and his smile was honest, like his voice. He wasn't trying to fool her, or make her think things were better or different than they were.

"So, what I'm getting from the norbears is that some'll stay with *Dulcimer*, and some'll go. They gotta decide who goes, who stays. Whoever stays, and I think Tranh might stick at this, and Susrim won't like it one bit, will be alt-crew, that's the third side of the trade, but if they're themselves, then they can't be passengers; gotta be crew. And whoever goes, we'll be missing friends, but the ones who stay, they'll be missing *family*."

"But we'll be here."

"Thing is, as much as they live with us, we're not their family and they're not yours or mine. Patel wouldn't take that for real anyway, and you know that's true. Me and you . . . we got different connections to them, warm, but not family."

Squithy sipped her water.

"I tried to explain crew rank to Mitsy, and I'm not sure it got through," she said slowly. "And there's something else, Klay. I'm worried . . ."

She stopped, wondering if she should tell him, but it was Klay, and he wouldn't laugh at her.

"What's worrying you?" he asked.

She took a deep breath and met his eyes.

"I'm worried, with the norbears gone, that I'll—I'll go back to how I was, counting to not be confused; slow, and a trouble for everybody." She felt her eyes filling with tears. "I don't want that."

"Hey." Klay touched her hand where it was on the table. "We'll still have some norbears, remember? And you know what I think?"

She blinked at him.

"What?"

"I think you was out of true, and the norbears got you on-course, however they did, and you won't drift, now."

She caught her breath.

"You really think that?"

"I do," said Klay stoutly. "You ask Oki what she thinks. And there's another thing I think, too."

His voice sounded different, sad, maybe, but his eyes didn't look sad, and he didn't move his hand from hers. It felt nice, so she didn't pull away.

"I think that you and me, we're maybe working our way into something special. I'm glad of it, but there might be problems, too."

So, it just wasn't her feeling warm about Klay? He felt it, too? That made her feel warmer, somehow, and she thought she ought to tell him, but instead, she said, "If I think about you, or if I say your name, Mitsy shows me your face, but there's mine right there with you, and when she shows me feeding them, there's this . . . echo that's you, right with me. They know it, what you said, about us being special. And, you know what else? If Mitsy thinks of Tranh, there's Rusko right there with him, the same way, and Rusko echoes Tranh."

"I've seen it, all of it," Klay said. "That's how they work, the norbears. They connect to each other, and they have lists, or lines of support. I see me in there, and you, and Mitsy and Ditsy, and some of the rest. So, that's something we're part of that we gotta watch."

She nodded, and thought she might lean forward, just a little, and put her lips against his cheek. He'd like that, she thought—

"Crew meeting, one half hour," Rusko's voice came out of the comm. "Crew meeting, one half hour."

Klay sighed, and took his hand off of hers.

"Well, that's me. Listen, Squith, when there's time— maybe when Susrim takes his liberty tomorrow, we can talk more, 'kay?"

She nodded. People didn't always remember when they promised to talk to her, but that was changed now, and it was especially changed with Klay.

"I'll like that," she said, "to talk more."

"Good." He stood up and smiled down at her.

"It was a good thing you brought those tasties back. It's gonna be a long meeting, and we'll be running on paste 'n crackers and 'mite."

Then he was gone.

Squithy sighed, and finished off her water, then kept sitting at the table, thinking. Thinking about Klay, and how she'd almost put her lips against his cheek, and how he'd glanced back at her as he left the galley, as if he knew what she'd almost done. That was good, she told herself. That was better than good, it was *fine*.

She got up, and put the cups to be washed, cleaned the table, folded up the box and put it in the recycler, paying close attention to what she was doing, and wiping the table twice. Definitely, she was not counting, or *fixating*; she was doing things that needed to be done, and making sure they were done right.

Definitely, she was not thinking about all the decisions that were about to be made without her being a part of the deciding, when whatever was decided might change everything . . .

Just when everything had gotten so much better than it ever had been.

THREE

SQUITHY WOKE KNOWING, IN THE WAY THAT BEING IN touch with a norbear let you know things, that the meeting had been a disappointment. Real quick after that thought, there came a faint quiver, also typical of norbear communication, and she realized that she had misunderstood the message.

Some things had been decided, but everything *hadn't* been decided. So there would be another meeting. Well, that was all right, sometimes deciding things took time, she knew that better'n almost anybody. She got the impression that the norbears themselves were still undecided. There was another idea inside that one that she wasn't sure about, but when she thought specifically about the norbears having another meeting, she didn't get the you-misunderstood quiver, so mostly she must've got it right.

A glance at the clock established that she was awake ahead of schedule, which mostly she always was. She didn't need so much sleep. Ma had said that was because she didn't have as much to recharge as—

Squithy straightened up in her bunk, and *stopped that thought*. It was hard; she thought about counting to make it easier, but, no. She didn't count anymore.

And she didn't have to think about what Ma had said about her that was wrong.

Ma had been wrong, she thought deliberately, and felt some one of the norbears—she thought it was Oki—suddenly right there with her, rumbling a little like they did for each other, sometimes. It was a comfortable thing, there inside her head, and it made her less scared about what she'd just thought, *which was true*, she told herself forcefully, and felt the rumble get deeper, like Oki agreed with her.

She sat there for a minute, while the rumbling quietened off into nothing. She felt something like a pat on the wrist, only it was inside her head, and she smiled, and thought of herself patting Oki's paw, then got up to get dressed.

It was early, but Susrim was in the galley, working the breakfast shift like mad, and dressed like he was going portside. He was shivering, like he was cold, or maybe really excited about getting off the ship. Squithy smelled *vya*, which was against rules to wear on-ship, but it was faint, and she was sensitive, so it was prolly a sealed wipe in his pocket, and *that* was all right.

"Popovers," Susrim was muttering when she walked in. He pulled the pre-mades out of the coldbox, moving real quick, and cutting through her standing-space so close she had to go back a step.

"Will there be a working breakfast?" she asked, remembering that not everything had got decided last shift. There were vague norbearish nibblings in the back of her head—some of them were having early breakfast, too.

Susrim turned his head to glare at her, then looked at the chronometer, which meant he was mad because she was there. But she was *always* early for breakfast, and always had been—well, almost always. She took a deep breath, and deliberately refused to think of the times she *hadn't* been early, and why, because that was even worse than counting.

"No business of yours or mine if there is, is it?" Susrim said now, and his voice was shaking, too. "Not *senior crew*, either of us."

The oven pinged. Susrim snatched out a tray of hot handwiches, and clattered it to the counter. Squithy blinked. The handwiches were pre-mades, like the popovers. She moved to the board, intending to catch up with the supply check, which Susrim was always light about, and using two pre-mades in one breakfast, that wasn't to meal regs. If they'd run out of—

Susrim banged the oven shut, snatched up one of the handwiches, swearing when it was too hot against his fingers, and dumping the rest with no care at all into a keeper. He bit into the handwich he'd taken, and bits fell on the floor, but he didn't even look down.

"My leave started about the time I got up," he said, not looking at her. "Since you're up and busy, you might as well finish what needs done." He crammed the rest of the handwich into his mouth. "I'm signing my cards, and I'm out. Got my figurator, too!"

Squithy bit her lip so she wouldn't say that it wasn't *his* figurator; it was the *ship's* second figurator, but that would've only made him madder, and he might stay to fight, and what she wanted right now, she thought very clearly, feeling a touch of norbear approval as she formed the thought—what she *really wanted right now* was for Susrim to take his excitement and his chancy mood out of the kitchen and off of the ship.

"I can finish making breakfast," she said, quiet and calm. "You go on."

"Right you are!" He slapped the screen up and pressed his finger to it. "Got an eight hour meet-up through Port-catch, shoulda been there ten minutes ago. Don't forget Tranh's damn vegetables, hear me?"

"Yes, Susrim," she said, still quiet. One of the norbears—she thought it was Ebling—did the patting-wrist thought, and she smiled a little.

Susrim opened the keeper, grabbed another handwich and was gone, almost running to the hatch.

Squithy walked over to the screen. Susrim had signed himself morning chef, so he'd get her points, not that it would've mattered if he'd given her the half-shift with her not having a line. It just would've been . . . better if he'd told the truth.

She tapped the screen, calling up ship systems, making sure Susrim had sealed the hatch behind him, then she turned back to the kitchen.

The oven pinged, and she crossed to it, taking out the popovers and putting them in the keeper next to the handwiches in the buffet. That done, she started the 'toot dripping into the hotpot, and mixed up some 'mite. Klay liked to have some 'mite now and then during the day, so it was all right to make a whole hotpot full. Rusko drank 'toot the same way, and sometimes Tranh wanted an extra cup.

Falmer never drank 'mite, though Squithy liked it. Not as much as Klay, she thought, but enough to have a mug during the day, most days.

Her eye fell on the fallen bit of handwich and

she cleaned that up, put the trays in the washer, and went into the coldbox to assemble the pieces of Tranh's medical drink. That was veggies and special antioxidants all mixed together with juice. It was supposed to be made fresh right before drinking, but it didn't hurt to measure it all together ahead of time and keep it on freeze so it could get put in the splitterator and whizzed altogether when Tranh was ready for it. Mixed together, it was a pretty green color that Squithy admired profusely, while Susrim would shake his head and mutter, "Damn grass for breakfast," like he was the one had to drink it.

Ingredients assembled, she paused with her hands on her hips, wondering what else she should do. Susrim having put up handwiches *and* popovers, it didn't seem like she should be making any batter for waffles.

Maybe just some of the fruits Falmer had brought back from the port market, she thought, instead of waffles or a sweet.

She moved across the galley to the fresh safe.

The 'toot and the 'mite were both done, steaming gently in the hotpots, and she had just finished putting the fruits in a bowl in the center of the table, where everybody could reach it, and it looked nice.

Squithy frowned. If there was going to be a working meal in the galley, then her and Falmer would need trays. She turned to the cabinet, and had just taken them down, when she heard a step in the hall, and felt a purr of norbear happiness alongside her own.

Klay stepped into the galley, looking fine and fresh, with a smile on his face, *for her*, she thought, and the norbear keeping her company thought so, too.

"Hey, Squith," he said, his smile fading a little and he looked around. "Susrim here?"

"He was late for a meet-up," she said, feeling her own smile wide on her face. "I was up early, and he gave finish-up to me."

"Nice of him," Klay said, sounding dry, like he did when he said the opposite of what he thought.

"'Mite's ready," she offered, and that fetched his smile back.

"That's good. I'm wondering, with Susrim gone and us both early, maybe we could have that talk now?"

Her stomach clenched, and she almost said she was too busy right now, but that wasn't true, and Klay had remembered his promise to talk with her, so she took a breath and nodded.

"That would be good."

"Yeah," Klay said, and then didn't say anything more, like he didn't know where to start, or how.

Squithy bit her lip, and did *not* count, and Klay leaned forward kind of slow and careful and took her hand in his.

"All right, now, see I'm new at this, and so are you. But what I was starting to say, about us working our way into something special with each other—well, I don't think that's only because we can both hear the norbears. I think the norbears made it easier for us to be together."

"Yes, they did," said Squithy. "Without the norbears, I was counting, and drifty, and not worth my air."

Klay jerked, his fingers tightening on hers.

"Who said that to you?"

"Ma," she answered, and saw his face relax, because Ma wasn't going to be saying anything at all, anymore.

"Well, she was wrong. Even when you were counting, you saw things, and you figured things out. I'd've died on Thakaran if you hadn't been there to help. So, I think this special thing, it would have happened, regardless of norbears."

So Klay thought Ma'd been wrong, too; that made her feel even warmer than she already was. Squithy wasn't so sure about the rest of it, but she didn't argue. Klay was going in a direction, and she should let him finish what he had to say.

"I'm wondering if you'd like to go out walking with me on the port while we're here. Ought to be able to align our shifts for a couple hours, and make it happen. If you'd like it, I'll talk to Tranh."

"I'd like it," she said, breathless with wanting it. "Dulsey and me were going to go walking again. I'm not sure Tranh'll give me permission for all that."

"Only way to find out is to ask him," Klay said, sounding cheerful. "Want me to ask?"

"Yes!" she said firmly, and smiled, holding his hand tight, and thinking—

Thinking that she needed to eat, and there wasn't enough. Seeing faces turned toward her—furry faces, and big sad eyes. The norbears, all of them hungry at once.

Klay said something under his breath. Squithy turned toward the hallway that led to the norbears' pod, pulling Klay along by their linked hands.

All nine norbears were bunched together near a dwindling pile of greens. When Squithy and Klay got there, Mitsy was at the pile, being very careful with choosing this leaf, and that group of grasses, and that other leaf. Paws full, Mitsy turned toward the ones who were waiting and offered each a portion until they were all served. They cuddled close in and ate.

When the eating was done, they combed their whiskers and their fronts with careful paws, and settled back. After a minute, Holdhand got up and approached the dwindling pile of greens.

Squithy frowned, but the sounds she was hearing, and the pictures she was seeing in her head didn't mean anything to her. There was a feeling of solemn determination, as if they were working on a difficult task together.

"They're still thinking," Klay said. "Not decided yet. Or maybe they decided and now they're thinking twice. I'm not getting any—"

And suddenly, as if the norbears had admitted them to their deliberations, they *were* getting something. Norbear faces, looking subtly different than they did when she looked at them with her eyes. Then there was her face, also different, with a kind of glow that she didn't see in the mirror, and Klay's face, glowing, too. Rusko's face and Falmer's were distant—neutral, thought Squithy—Tranh's face was dim, Susrim's was dark, and Dulsey's was one moment bright, one moment dim, distant in a way none of *Dulcimer's* crew was.

"They're measuring what's best, change or safety," Klay whispered. "Tough choice. Always a tough choice."

Holdhand brought over the chosen greens and began to distribute them among the group. Squithy felt a nudge inside her head, and looked up to see Oki standing next to a very small pile.

"They're almost out of thieves clover," she said to Klay. "I'll get it."

She ducked into the storeroom, grabbed a small bale, and took it to the norbears. Oki patted her arm as she put the bale down, and she felt what she called the thank-you feeling inside her head as she stepped back to Klay's side.

"I think they're feeding each other up, Klay, to make sure they're well fed before changes happen. And you can see who seems to be getting the most attention—I'd say Mitsy and Ditsy are treating Ebling and Oki special somehow. And they're all crowding around pretty hard. Holdhand's being real serious too!"

The new bale to hand, the norbears grew more careful of their choices, it seemed to Squithy, and taking more and more time to lean against each other, to groom faces carefully... and then Oki stood at Squithy's feet, yawning, all of them yawning, leaning on each other, looking at Squithy as they yawned...

"They want to sleep on it," she said, watching the heavy eating fade into bare nibbles. "They fed themselves up and look at 'em all pile together. They need to sleep on this, maybe dream on it together!"

Klay silently nodded his agreement, not seeing her glance, standing away from the norbears and from her, entranced. Watching them curl in next to each other, cuddling, grooming. It'd be fine, real fine to feed Squithy a good meal, and then the two of them curl up together...

"Klay!"

He blinked back to himself, not certain if he'd been thinking his own thoughts or channeling sleeping norbear suggestions.

"Sorry," he said, as Squithy tugged his hand, pulling him back to the hall.

"This is their time," she said. "They got themselves stuffed with food and need to dream it off! Best we treat them like crew on this, isn't it? Like they can have their off time to decide things?"

Klay nodded. He tossed a salute to the curled-in norbears, getting sleepy murbles in return, then Squithy took his hand, and pulled him away.

The galley was full of people when they got back. Rusko was exploring the keepers on the buffet, and Tranh was sitting at the table, watching Falmer, who had just added the ingredients for his special drink into the splitterator, and hit the button, mixing it all with a loud zziizzz-zzzizz—zzizz!

Squithy swallowed and dropped Klay's hand—*tried* to drop Klay's hand, but he held on tight, so they came into the galley together. Falmer saw them first, as she turned to pour Tranh's drink into a mug. Her eyebrows rose, but she didn't say anything, which was good because Rusko was exclaiming loudly over the breakfast choices.

"No waffles for us, Tranh," he said, "but our choice of popovers or handwiches. Or maybe one of each!"

"Thank you," Tranh said to Falmer when she set the drink by his hand, and to Rusko, "Handwiches *and* popovers?" He looked at Falmer.

"Did you make breakfast today?"

Falmer shook her head. "It was all set up when I got here, and nobody in sight. The ingredients for your drink were all together in one bag in the front of the freeze, like Squithy usually does it..."

Klay moved forward, bringing Squithy with him, still holding her hand.

"Morning," he said easily, nodding to the room in general.

"Morning," Rusko said, as Falmer moved to the hotpot and drew herself a mug of 'toot.

"Morning," Tranh said, sipping his drink. He put the mug down. "You make breakfast, Squith?"

"Card's signed by Susrim," Rusko said from the screen. "Chef, breakfast shift."

Tranh lifted his mug and swallowed some more of his drink.

"That right? Where's Susrim, then?"

Squithy took a hard breath, felt Klay's fingers briefly tighten around hers.

"He's on leave," she said. "I was up early, and he'd already done the handwiches, and put the popovers in. Said he was late for a meet-up, and so long as I was up, I could do finish-up. He signed out and left."

She looked around the galley.

"I took the popovers out when they were done, put Tranh's mix together, like Falmer said, and started the 'toot and the 'mite. Figured with two pre-mades we didn't need waffles, though I can make waffles, Uncle Rusko, if you want some."

"Thank you, Squithy, but there's no need. I agree with your reasoning; we have plenty, and doesn't the fruit look good! Your idea?"

"Well, I mean, Falmer bought them at the port-market yesterday. I just thought it might be nice, a piece of fruit, since there wouldn't be waffles."

"Excellent. Tranh, can I give you a popover and a handwich?"

"Thanks," Tranh said, finishing his drink and pushing the mug to one side. He looked at her hard, and if it had been Da, she might've started counting, but it was Tranh, and Tranh, she reminded herself, was *not* Da.

"So, Squith, looks to me like you made half of breakfast. How come you didn't claim it on the schedule?"

"Susrim'd already signed for the shift," she said.

"That's right, he had—thanks," he said to Rusko, as a plate landed in front of him. He kept his eyes on Squithy.

"I guess Susrim got ahead of himself, is all. I'll fix it for him—half-shift for you, half for him."

She took a quiet breath, not wanting any part of Susrim's moods, and when he found out he'd been "shorted" a whole half-shift—

"Right," said Tranh, picking up his handwich. "I tell you what, Squith, if you see Susrim get ahead of himself like that again, you let me know, and I'll have a talk with him."

The breath this time was deeper, and she gripped Klay's hand hard.

"Tranh," she began, but he waved his hand.

"You don't worry about Susrim getting mad at you. I asked you to do it, and I'll make that clear when we talk, right?"

Klay squeezed her fingers.

"All right," she said. "Thank you, Tranh."

He nodded, looked at the handwich, and put it back on the plate.

"While we're talking about talks, why don't you come see me in my office before lunch? I been looking over the pay-lines, and come to see that you and the ship need to get caught up. Be best if you come sit with me so we can go over it together."

Squithy glanced sideways at Klay, who wasn't really

grinning, though his eyes were dancing. Dulsey must've had that word with Tranh, she thought, and smiled herself as she turned back to the captain.

"Yes, Tranh. Thank you."

"Part of trying to make the ship reg'lar, like we all said we wanted. Get yourself some breakfast, now, you and Klay—Falmer, you, too—and sit down."

Squithy hesitated. "I thought there was going to be a working meal. I got out trays for Falmer and me—"

"We can have that meeting later," Tranh said. "Right now, let's just share the meal together, and get caught up." He looked around.

"Falmer, can you come back to the office with me after breakfast? Got a couple things for you, too."

"Sure," she said, and moved to the buffet.

"The norbears all had a good meal together just now," Squithy said, not just to Tranh. "It seemed to make them happy."

"Now we know where Tranh got the idea," Rusko said, and Tranh looked up fast, like maybe he was going to snap—but grinned instead.

"Sure I did," he said.

"Gimme ten, then come by," Tranh told Falmer when the meal was done. It hadn't been a meeting at all. Rusko had asked Falmer about the port market, and she'd brightened right up like Falmer hardly ever did, and talked about what had been on offer, and how she wished she could get studied more on food prep, so she'd know better what to do with the freshies when they had them.

Then Uncle Rusko thanked Squithy for bringing the treat back for her crewmates, and asked about the rest of her "port tour." She was happy to tell him about the various outfitters, and the H Level shop and how the ship's logo had gotten pressed into Klay's wallet—and hers—and about the plan to tour A Level, and—

"This was good," Tranh said, when everybody'd finished their meal, and gotten up from the table. "Oughta do this more often, I think. Not a meeting, but a catch-up."

"If it works for the norbears," Rusko said, drawing himself a take-away mug of 'toot, "it oughta work for us."

He nodded and followed Tranh out of the galley.

"Well—" Klay started, but Falmer turned to him, not smiling.

"Klay, you got a sec? I need advice 'bout what to tell Tranh."

Klay frowned. "Tell Tranh?" he repeated.

"About Susrim," she said rapidly. "Tranh's gonna ask, and do I tell it?"

"Tell what?" asked Klay sensibly. Squithy bit her lip, and Falmer looked just as unhappy as she'd been happy, talking about the market.

"Susrim's not cleaning the greens tubes as reg'lar as he ought to—when I took the turn last I needed to double-scrub. Not sure but what he's been accepting stuff that's under par a percent or few. He said I worry too much about what's none of my business."

She took a breath and glanced at Squithy.

"I'm sorry, Squith, but he says it's not fair that his shifts got changed around because of you doing other stuff. We all of us know that's not the why—all the shifts got changed because everything else changed!

New pilot, new trader, new captain... two dead... it all *changed* and Susrim wants it back like it was, like there was never a shoot-up and Ma and Da—"

Falmer gasped, blinking—just this side of crying, Squithy thought. That scared her because crying pushed her into counting sometimes... and she didn't want to be doing that, not ever again— She felt something warm on her hand, and looked down, not really surprised to see Klay's hand there on top of hers.

She looked up and smiled, and then Falmer was back with them, talking with some more energy.

"Point is, his shifts aren't getting covered right, and he wants me to make it up, but only by me doing the work, and him getting the hours. Some work's not getting done at all—I'm talking basics, here, 'cause he says it's not his schedule, on account of he's *chef.*"

Falmer threw her hands in the air.

"There's details, but that's the outline."

"You haven't talked to Tranh about any of this?" Klay asked.

She shook her head. "Kept thinking I'd find Susrim reasonable one day, and get it worked out, but he's stuck on counting his grievances. Keeps saying that he oughta be senior crew, and going on about the cargo-shares Da promised him, which *I* never heard about, and it wasn't much like Da to promise out shares to nobody, never mind *senior crew.* Only body senior to Da was Ma, and then not always."

Falmer got up and went over to the hotpot to draw more 'toot, and turned back, holding the mug in both hands in front of her chest.

"If I tell Tranh all this—"

"Absolutely, you tell Tranh," Klay said, sounding

serious and maybe a little stern. "He's the captain, and it's the captain's job to care for the ship. That means making sure needed work is done, and the crew's running tight with each other."

Falmer bit her lip. Klay shook his head.

"No *if*, Falmer." He paused and added, less stern. "You said you wanted my advice."

"Yeah, I did. I do. But, see—Susrim's got the idea fixed that he's being punished—I don't understand it, myself. Thought he shoulda been made pilot 'stead of bringing you onboard—and he don't got the certs, which we all know, him included. Anyhow, he's blaming everybody for everything they got that he doesn't—you and Squithy for the norbears, Squith for stepping up a level, Tranh and Rusko for having each other, me for not doing his work and—hey! What're you two doing?"

Startled, Squithy looked to the aisle coming from the transport area . . . where Ditsy and Mitsy stood, shoulder to shoulder, and looking at them.

Klay rose. "Good thing the boy's not here, he don't like you to come down this way."

There was, perhaps, a murble. Maybe two.

Squithy felt a gentle touch inside her head, half between a complaint and a request. Falmer was in it, and so was Susrim, but with a touch of what might have been the *tobor* standing behind him, then an image of the rest of the norbears resting, wanting something, the door to their room, an image of Klay . . .

Squithy felt her eyes go wide, even as Klay shook his head.

"That's too much, don't you think?" he said to Mitsy and Ditsy.

Falmer looked at Squithy.

"What's happening?"

"They're making an important decision and they want Klay to sleep across their door, so they aren't disturbed. Also, we're all noisy in the head right now, and it would be good if we could give them room to think."

Falmer took a couple deep breaths. "Susrim says they gotta get off the ship. He says they get in our heads."

"Yeah," Klay said without looking around, "Susrim says a lot. Talks big. Says he'd just space them, and maybe *he* would, but *we* can't."

He gave Mitsy and Ditsy another hard stare, and Squithy felt—but it was gone, and the norbears were gone, too, back down the hall.

"Right," Klay said, turning back to them. "So, Falmer, it's getting time for you to talk to Tranh. My advice, tell him all of it. Squith—I guess we'll talk later. Right now, I've got some piloting lessons to catch up on. I'll take my tablet and sit up against their door for a while. Pilot lessons oughta be quiet enough, and they'll know I'm there."

Squithy nodded. "I've got clean up here. Falmer, do you want me to scrub the tubes?"

Falmer shook her head.

"No, leave 'em. If I'm gonna tell Tranh all of it, he'll maybe want to see."

She took a deep breath, and pulled herself up tall.

"Time," she said, and walked out of the galley, heading for Tranh's office.

Klay sighed, and came back to the table, holding out his hand.

"Hey," he said.

Squithy put her hand in his.

"Thank you, Klay."

He frowned.

"What for?"

"For helping me be brave."

He snorted. "Says the woman stood between guns and norbears. We'll talk some more, right, Squith?"

"Right," she said.

He squeezed her fingers, and then let go, down the hall to get his lessons and guard the norbears.

Sighing, Squithy began to clear the table.

FOUR

KLAY WAS DEEP INSIDE HIS 'QUATIONS WHEN HE HEARD a step in the hall leading to the norbears' quarters. He looked up as Tranh appeared, carrying two mugs, and walking careful on his almost-healed leg.

"Studying in the hall to get some peace, my friend?"

Klay grinned, and stretched, letting some of the tension in his shoulders go. Truth was, he'd been feeling an overflow through the door he was leaning against, had seen vague visions of himself and Squith, sometimes of Dulsey and Tranh—those were easy enough to mostly ignore, and the mentions of Falmer and Rusko were so distant, he barely noticed them at all. What had been hard were the images of Susrim, which carried a weight of—well, he didn't really know. Caution? Dislike? Both? Neither? Then, there was someone else in there, not Susrim, but—adjacent? It might, Klay had thought, taking a break from his work to consider it, have been Choody, or one of his crew, and an occasional light touch along the fight at Port Chavvy dockside.

Right now, as he stretched, he was getting norbears, like they were talking about each other like crew does, figuring who would be best at what. There was some overlay there of the planet of norbears and *tobors*, a kind of wistful feeling, like family being missed.

Klay brought his arms down. He wasn't going to get into what he'd been hearing with Tranh, that wasn't his to share, so he let the grin fade with the stretch and looked down at his tablet, rueful.

"Funny thing—sometimes I had to study this way on my old ship, catch a spot with a mug of 'mite, and my tablet, and stay out of the way. It's not like that, here. I was specifically requested to guard the door while they're making their decision. They know Pilot Dulsey wants some of their company for a while, and they're not in general against it, but there's factors, and they need some time to sort it all out."

"Can't blame 'em for that," Tranh said surprisingly. "Not like we haven't been doing the same thing ourselves."

He bent a little, offering a mug. "'Mite?"

"Thanks."

Klay took the mug, and watched Tranh slide down the opposite wall, holding his own mug in two hands.

"Squith and Falmer are doing kitchen inventory," he said, like he was continuing a conversation they'd been having. "That's 'ponics and the kitchen lab, too, so Falmer's putting out box lunches on the buffet. You pick one up when the bosses in there give you a break."

Humor, Klay thought. He hadn't known Tranh had a sense of humor. He took a sip of 'mite. Well, maybe Rusko was helping him grow one.

"So, first thing: Far's I can know, every bit of black and grey, Old Tech, jumblestuff, and just plain trash is outta every single smuggle hidey on this ship. We got it in a lock-pod at the edge of our docking here, and sent Dulsey the combination. She'll come by and do an eval, prolly alt-shift, so she sent, and send an offer. Prelim offer is that she'll take all we got, subtracting disposal costs from trade-worth, to find her number."

He gave a wry smile. "So now all we gotta do is hope we don't wind up owing her disposal fees."

"Not likely, is it?"

Tranh shook his head. "Truth? It's not. Choody ran reals, *kajets* and Old Tech. Da didn't have much of an eye, but Ma surely did. There's not much outright trash, to my eye, being studied on our cargoes like I was, though it's nothing I want *Dulcimer* to be shipping."

He sighed.

"Transfer already come through for the Port Chavvy vids. Crystal pays good, and they pay fast, grey as they are. Your ears and mine, Choody was so far into black, Crystal looks near white." He shook his head. "If they get something special out of the Port Chavvy vids I don't know what it might be unless they're hunting Liadens, but see, I'll sell them info from here to infinity to get the ship clean. I don't think info is grey if it isn't stole, do you?"

Klay belatedly realized that this had been an actual question and he readily agreed that information that came to hand, no, that wasn't grey.

"Now, since you're senior crew, you gotta know that Crystal's paying us a stipend for information from wherever we go. Putting you on that so Rusko and I can handle the other trade stuff. I'll give you a list of what they're watching for."

"Can't they just subscribe to the trade news?" Klay tried to keep his face bland. It wasn't like he had anything against knowing stuff, but sometimes keeping your nose out of people's business and looking away felt like the best policy.

"We can send mood reports and gossip and the trade news can't, if you know what I mean. Not that you'll be making up rumors or sharing secrets. But we got ears, and we'll all be on ports now, so it's an income-stream and I want you in charge. You got a compelling no, shout it out now."

"No," Klay said, and then laughed slightly. "What I mean to say, Captain, is yes, I'll take care of the info-trade."

"Good," Tranh said, and had a drink—'toot, according to Klay's nose—and put the mug on the deck by his knee.

"Talked to Falmer," he said. "Bottom line, she wants to get studied in kitchen-keeping. Feels like there's more to it than the same ten-days-and-repeat we been doing since before any of us were born. Previous captain and mate didn't care what they ate, focused as they was on other things. Susrim got studied because he wasn't me, and older'n Falmer. He might've figured it made him important, but he didn't choose it, if you take me. Falmer *wants* the kitchen, and she wants to do better for us."

Tranh paused, apparently waiting to hear what Klay thought about that.

"Let her go with it, then," Klay said cautiously.

Tranh nodded. "My thought, zackly. I figured you'd want to know how it went, there, since you advised her to tell me everything out straight." He sipped. "Good advice. Captain can't fix what he don't know's broke."

"My thought, too," Klay said, and had a swallow of 'mite.

"So, here's the rest of my thoughts, and you let me know yours, if you will. Falmer'll go down a level, ship-wise, while she's doing her study-work. So that's Stinks and general cleaning on her, and her studies. Stinks comes off you, cleaning comes off Squith. The two of you will be our norbear handlers, so long's we got norbears, but losing general cleaning leaves Squith free to do kitchen back-up..."

Klay stiffened, and Tranh paused.

"Seen a problem? Go ahead and say it out."

"If Susrim thinks he's being slighted—like Falmer's getting studied up so she can step into his spot, he's gonna bear down hard on Squithy."

"And that ship won't fly while you're at the board, is that it? You'll be pleased to hear Rusko feels the same."

"'Course," Klay heard himself continue, "that won't be anything like what'll come outta Susrim when Squith starts studying for pilot."

Silence.

If it could have been possible, Klay would have stared at himself just like Tranh was staring at him, but he saw it in a flash, and it was obvious, it was *right*.

"Pilot," Tranh said, real neutral.

"She's got the math, or most of it. Mind, it's not in any kind of order, but she *sees* it—you know what I'm talking about."

"I do. And you know this how, zackly?"

Klay felt his face heat, but he kept his eyes steady on Tranh's.

"She asked to see the Jump numbers, so I showed her. Figured it couldn't do any harm, and anyhow she'd be bored real quick. Only she wasn't. Asked how they were different from the coming-into-station numbers, so I showed her them, too. She had some questions— they were *good* questions, pilot-think questions, Tranh. I think she can do it, and I'm not talking third class. I think she can take it all the way to Jump, if she gets to study on it."

Tranh sat sipping from his mug, eyes on a point in the floor between them.

"I was supposed to be talking to Squith after lunch. Now that we're on serve-ourselves, I'll grab her off inventory after I leave you. I'll see where her understanding is, about piloting. If she's eager, Rusko'll give her an aptitude screen. If she's good for it *and* apt, then we let her go with it, same like Falmer. Piloting self-studies, we got; couple dummy boards, if it comes to that. If she can't learn it from the tapes, though ..."

"I'll teach her," Klay heard himself say, unsurprised.

Tranh nodded. "You got it."

"Good." Klay finished his 'mite and put the mug aside. "So, Susrim," he began, but Tranh held up a hand.

"We let Susrim go one step at a time. First, we see how he takes the news that Falmer's studying with an eye to becoming a nutritionist-chef." Tranh paused and gave Klay a narrow look. "That's what she told me. Been reading up, she said. So, we get Susrim 'round that corner, and give him what lessons he might need to have, including in manners, and plain shipside rules. Rusko and me'll take point on that."

He finished off what was in his mug and put it on the floor.

"I'm gonna be needed up front in a few, so let me just say the rest of this real quick, and we'll talk again, soon."

He held up his forefinger.

"One. I'm still in favor of whatever you and Squith are working out between you. It's looking good on both sides, and that's as far as I'll go, captain and cousin."

Second finger.

"I want you working with Rusko on putting together a list of haven-spots for us. The old ones were all Choody's friends—hard getting in and a lot harder getting out. We're done with that.

"Other thing, with the Dust coming in, we need to work out which ports are gonna be hard for the Liadens and the big ships to get into. We'll be looking to make a couple Loops with those ports as anchors. We won't be the first to be figuring out our advantage, but maybe not the last. You give me a whole catalog—twenty, even thirty—so I can run the trade analysis." He paused, looking thoughtful. "Might be we can hook up with some short Loopers and do an intersection Loop. Nothing's off the table, is what I'm saying. I want us thinking wide."

"Got it," Klay said. "Wide and deep."

"Right. Now—"

"Tranh?"

Rusko's voice came out of Tranh's beltcom, calm and soothing. That was Rusko, thought Klay—especially when he talked to Tranh.

"Go ahead," Tranh said.

"Dulsey's arranged for a transport crew to be on our dock early tomorrow. She'll be providing transfer boxing, mini-pods and bins, so she can shift some of that freight direct, instead of carting it through the port. Also, she wants to pay upfront for the *kajets* she's already seen, as a separate transaction. I think you might want to talk to her on this, so we're all clear."

"On my way."

Tranh sighed, and Klay rose to help his captain rise, having seen the unsteadiness as the other man tried to get his feet under him.

"Thanks." Tranh smiled, and tapped lightly on the door of the norbears' compartment.

"You get news from this department, you tell me on the instant. I want to get this settled."

"Right," Klay said. "I'll take the mugs back when I go."

"Thanks," Tranh said again, and left him.

Klay was doing the math for a triple Jump to Skander from Port Chavvy. He didn't hear footsteps so much as he noticed a part of his attention caught by a sense of welcome presence.

He glanced up from the screen, and Squithy smiled at him, holding two meal boxes.

"You forgot to pick up your lunch," she said, holding one out to him.

He took it with a smile. "Looks like I'm not the only one. Let me save this..."

He put the box on the deck, and saved his place before putting the tablet down.

"I was having that meeting with Tranh," Squithy said, and he was caught by how bright her eyes were, and how her cheeks glowed. "He said I could eat while we met, but I was afraid I'd miss something, so I decided to wait." She looked doubtful. "I told Falmer I'd be back with her on the inventory, but then I saw your box sitting there, so—"

"I 'preciate you bringing it to me. Since you gotta eat anyway, you mind eating here?"

"Here? With you?"

She smiled like he'd offered her a treat, and settled down on the decking beside him.

"There," she said, smile widening. "That's good."

"Glad you could join me," he said solemnly, opening his box. Coofu on fresh bake bread, a fresh fruit from the port market, and a sealed pack of soy milk. A reasonable lunch, no flash, no attitude on display in the form of crumpled napkins or broken bread.

"They're still dreaming, is what I'm getting," Squithy said softly, picking up her handwich.

"What I'm getting, too. Trying not to think at 'em direct, in case I interrupt something." Klay opened the soy milk and took a sip.

"Everything work out okay with Tranh?"

Squithy sat up straight, her handwich forgotten in her hand.

"Klay, Tranh says he's gonna ask Uncle Rusko to give me a screening to see if I'm apt—if I have the aptitude to be a pilot! A pilot! He says you told him I was innerested in the 'quations and that I asked good questions, and—I'd only have the test if I wanted it, and I said yes I wanted it, so that'll be happening, when Rusko has a break in his schedule. Might not be until we're underway again, said Tranh, but later I saw Uncle Rusko and he said if we both get up early the next time we're on the same shift, it can get done then, and I checked the schedule to be sure, and that's two days from now!"

"That's great!" Klay said. "Good opportunity for you, Squith. I'm glad you decided to take the test."

"Well, I have to, don't I? So I'll *know*?"

Klay bit his lip, suddenly struck by an aspect he hadn't considered before.

"Say, Squith, if the screening don't suggest you go on to study, you know that's just—"

"It's a fact," Squithy said, raising her handwich again. "Not everybody's a pilot. I know *that*." She took a bite and chewed meditatively. "Still, I *should* know, right?"

"Right," he said, relieved.

They ate in silence for a few minutes. Klay wondered if he should ask, but before he could, Squithy spoke.

"The important thing is, I got a ship-line, like you and Dulsey thought I should have. Turns out Stinks carries a draw, only it didn't ever transfer on account of I wasn't allowed to hold a chip card. We figured out the back-shifts owing, and Tranh's gonna give me another chip, all loaded, so I can give yours back, Klay, if—"

"You keep that," he interrupted. "I got plenty."

Squithy nodded, slowly. "All right, then. Thank you, Klay."

"So's Tranh got a going-forward?" Klay asked, blatantly changing the subject.

"He does, and wait'll you hear! Going forward— that's starting with today's breakfast shift—Tranh says I'm gonna draw at Falmer's level, on account I'm being jumped up to fill her spot while she's studying for her chef certs. That means I'll be Susrim's back-up, which Tranh says previous orders're in force. If Susrim gets ahead of himself, or speaks contrary to ship standards, I'm to tell Tranh, who'll be working with Susrim, he says, to bring him level to his level." She paused to have a sip of soy milk.

"I'm s'posed to read over the ship standards, as a refresh."

"That's not a bad idea for me, too," Klay said. "A lot's happened since the last time I read 'em."

Squithy smiled. "You're right, a lot has happened."

"We never finished our talk," Klay began before his voice and his thoughts were overwhelmed by a kind of mind-heard music so resonant with joy that he felt tears start to his eyes even as he came to his feet. Squithy was pressed against his side, their fingers entwined.

"They've decided," Squithy whispered, which it appeared they had, though what they were witnessing went far beyond simple agreement, or mere decision. This was a declaration of intent, a pledge of commitment, and a celebration of brave friends about to embark on the next stage of the adventure they had found together.

Klay's head was thrumming, not painfully, but with a reflected joy, as he beheld them, one by one, then all together. He was suffused with strength, of purpose, of connection.

The air thrummed with pride, even as rapid footsteps sounded down the corridor, and here was Falmer and Rusko, their faces holding wonder, and Tranh behind them, looking puzzled.

"We having a celebration?" he asked, looking first to Squithy, then Klay.

"Didn't you hear it?" Falmer gasped. "I—it was this big . . . noise in my head! I even *saw* something!"

Tranh shrugged. "I was deep into catalogs and star maps. Heard a disturbance; thought Susrim might be back. Then Rusko came and grabbed me. Said we were wanted here."

"Yes," said Squithy. "It's a celebration, Tranh! They're all of them brave scouts!"

"That's it," Klay said, seeing or only sensing the man

Dulsey had called "Jethri's Scout," in the warp of the norbears' thoughts. He looked to Tranh. "They made their decision, and they're celebrating it and themselves."

"They're all going with Dulsey?" Tranh's voice was hopeful.

"I don't think—"

Squithy stepped forward and touched the plate. The door opened, and there before them were Mitsy and Ditsy, projecting joy at having found harmony, and also a picture of themselves with *Dulcimer*'s crew, with Dulsey in a pivotal point beyond them, across the lanes of companionship.

"Mitsy and Ditsy are staying with us," Squithy said. "The rest will travel with Dulsey. All will have adventures and be true, bold scouts, valuing their connections with each other, until they are together again."

It sounded like she was repeating what the norbears had given her to say, only norbears didn't think in words. Still, Klay thought, it summed the thing up neat enough.

"I see," Tranh said, and stepped forward to look down at the two proud creatures in the door.

"Staying, are you?" he said seriously. "If you stay, you're crew, and I'll expect you to act like crew, and work like crew. Can you do that?"

Their assent was so firm that the inside of Klay's head rang, and it apparently got through to Tranh.

"I heard a *yes*," he said, looked to Klay.

"That's right, Captain," Klay confirmed.

"All right, then," said Rusko. "Glad that's settled."

"Me, too," Tranh said, and turned away, accepting Rusko's arm. "I'll call Dulsey and give her the happy news."

. . . . . .

FIVE

. . . . . .

SUSRIM WASN'T LATE GETTING BACK FROM LEAVE, NOT *exactly* late. But he wasn't anywhere near early.

Squithy was on hatch, on account of Tranh was out on the dock with Dulsey; Klay and Rusko were ear-deep in star maps, according to Rusko; and Falmer was on tight-message with the certs office on-port, figuring out where she should start, and what modules she'd need, and how she'd certify for her levels, there not being a certified chef aboard.

That left Squithy on the hatch, knowing that crew was due in. That meant she was right there to open it when the request light flashed, and Susrim pushed in, barely waiting for there to be enough room, and jostling her against the wall in his rush to be inside.

The inner hatch wasn't open, though, and he had to stop while she cycled down the outer hatch, and made sure of the seal.

"Open the hatch!" Susrim snarled. Squithy turned, and he did, too, and she could see that his hair was mussed, and one eye was swollen shut, and he wasn't wearing his jacket. He smelled, too, of *vya*, and chocolate, and something unfamiliar and sweet. One hand clutched a bag to his middle; the other hand was fisted at his side.

"Open the hatch!" he said, and he was madder than Squithy had ever seen him, well beyond one of his moods. She took a deep breath that clogged her nose with the mix of odors and she felt like she couldn't breathe, and then the outer hatch beeped, and the inner hatch opened, and Susrim was gone, walking fast, head down, and his boots making a racket on the decking.

Squithy blew out her breath, and went through the hatch, heading for the galley, and maybe, she thought, a mug of 'mite.

She'd finished her 'mite and was thinking about what she should put out for working snacks when a tone sounded, which was the main hatch letting her know that somebody wanted to be let in. But there wasn't anybody else, she thought. Tranh had gone out the side hatch, and would let himself in when he was done with Dulsey, so—

The tone sounded again and she went over to the screen to look.

Two people, both wearing official Port jackets and caps, one plain, and one fancy. The one wearing the plain cap and the wide belt was carrying a bag over his shoulder. The one wearing the fancy cap was carrying a case.

Squithy touched the comm switch.

"*Dulcimer* crew here," she said. "State your business."

"Thank you, *Dulcimer* crew," said the fancy cap and case. "I am Sebi Irom, inspector with the port Health and Safety Office. My colleague is Bailiff Pars of Port Security." She reached into a public pocket and withdrew what looked to be a crew card, which she held up to the camera.

Chantor's Way Station, Health and Safety
Sebi Irom, Liaison Inspector

Squithy read the card, her stomach unsteady. Port security. Ma and Da had told them about port security, and how they should never let anybody from port security, or anybody from the port who hadn't been specifically invited by Da and Ma onto the ship, and—

She swallowed.

"I need to go up a level," she said into the comm. "Please wait, Inspector."

Then she tapped the hatch comm off, and opened the line to the piloting chamber.

"Uncle Rusko," she said sounding breathless in her own ears. "There's an inspector and port security at the hatch and they want to come in."

"Are there?" Rusko sounded faintly amused. "Thank you, Squithy, I'll take care of it."

"Susrim just got back," she blurted, so Rusko would know where all the crew was.

"Did he? That's good to know. Rusko out."

"I am sent by the port council to investigate a matter of extreme delicacy involving Susrim Smith of *Dulcimer* and a member of the vice president of council's immediate family. This matter is my highest priority and I have been instructed to treat it confidentially, and to insure that there are no indiscretions."

Inspector Irom paused, sighed, added.

"No *further* indiscretions, I should say."

The inspector and bailiff stood in the galley, and all the crew, including Dulsey, who wasn't, but nobody said so, and anyway she was being quiet and almost invisible over in the corner near the oven, besides having come in with Tranh, so Squithy didn't say anything and tried not to look at her. Klay was standing with Rusko, next to Tranh, and one step back. Susrim wasn't anywhere that Squithy could see him; Falmer was standing next to her, and the norbears were a great, solemn, listening presence inside her head.

"In order to pursue my duty," Inspector Irom was saying, "I must speak in absolute privacy with the captain of this vessel, and with Susrim Smith. If I am refused, I have been instructed to lock this vessel down, and place all crew members into the custody of port security."

Tranh's face was smooth; he didn't look angry, or scared, or even very much concerned. He nodded at the inspector.

"You may take the fact that you are standing on our decks as assurance that *Dulcimer* and her crew will cooperate fully with your confidential investigation, Inspector. I am Captain Tranh Smith. Susrim Smith is in his quarters. He is indisposed, but has told me that he is willing to answer questions."

"Very good. I appreciate your willingness, and will note it in my report." She held out a hand, and the bailiff slipped the bag off his shoulder and handed it to her. She picked up her case with the other hand, and nodded at Tranh.

"Please, Captain, let us go at once to speak with Susrim Smith."

Rusko and Klay had gone back to the piloting chamber, leaving Falmer and Squithy, and Dulsey— well, no. Dulsey was gone, too, Squithy saw. So that was her and Falmer and Bailiff Pars in the galley, together. Squithy bit her lip and wondered what they were supposed to do with him.

The bailiff was easily the largest person Squithy had ever seen, by height and width. This close, she could see the things hanging from loops and clips on his wide belt, though the only thing she could identify for sure was a stun-wand. She guessed the rest were weapons, too, and that made her feel both nervous and a little mad. You weren't supposed to have weapons on deck, unless the captain had declared an emergency.

"We were just getting ready to set up work snacks," Falmer said, brisk and cool. "Can we get you anything to ease your wait, Bailiff? 'toot? 'mite? Piece of fruit or a sweet?"

"'Preciate that offer, so I do, but the answer's gotta be 'no.' On duty with the inspector like I am, that means not ingesting anything that don't come straight from port supplies—sealed at that. If I even took a mug of 'toot, I'd be released from my position."

He glanced around the galley, and nodded at the bench. "I'll just have a seat there, and stay outta your way while you work. The inspector'll call if she wants me, and then I'll have to attend her. Otherwise, I've got my tablet here to keep me company."

"That's all right, then," Falmer said. "You sit wherever you want. Squithy, you go ahead and make another pot of 'toot and some 'mite, too, and take fresh mugs to Rusko and Klay. I'll get the snacks together."

Squithy nodded, and started by pulling the in-use carafes and putting them to be washed. Then she started the 'toot. She usually made 'mite in the small pot, but it was starting to look like being a long shift for everybody, so she pulled out another large pot and made double the usual 'mite, working around the big bailiff, who was so absorbed by what was on his tablet that he didn't look up even when Falmer clattered some pots together.

It was while she was measuring the 'mite into the pot that she got a sudden and vivid mind picture: all nine of the norbears crowded around Dulsey, who was sitting cross-legged on the decking by a pile of clover. They looked like a bunch of littles listening to a story from one of the olders at a meet-up, Squithy thought, and smiled a little to herself.

Tranh walked the inspector and bailiff to the hatch, came back to the galley and drew a cup of 'toot before he walked over to the comm and flipped the switch.

"General crew meeting right now in the galley, that's everybody 'cept Susrim, who's got alternate orders."

Klay and Rusko came in so quick they might've been waiting at the door, Klay stepping close to Squithy's side. She slipped her hand into his, and smiled when he gave her fingers a little squeeze.

"All right," Tranh said. "Crew meeting. Nothing we say in here goes out there. Now—"

Someone cleared their throat, and Tranh spun to stare at Dulsey, standing in the door of the galley.

"Got it all confirmed and clear with the seven who'll be traveling with me for a while, Cap'n Tranh," she said. "If somebody'll let me out, I'll see how my crew's doing on the side dock."

"I'll do it," Rusko said. "Tranh, sit down, you're not doing that leg any favors." He nodded at Dulsey. "Pilot. Right this way."

He left at a brisk pace, Dulsey following, and Tranh staring at the spot where she'd been, only lower.

"What are you two doing here?" he demanded, and not like he was real pleased.

"They're crew!" Squithy said. "Tranh, that's Mitsy and Ditsy. You said it yourself that they're crew!"

Tranh turned his gaze on her. He looked tired, Squithy thought, and wondered what kind of trouble Susrim had brought onto the ship.

"I did, didn't I?" Tranh closed his eyes and had a sip of 'toot. When he opened his eyes, he didn't look any less tired, but he didn't look mad, either.

"All right, crew members, get in here and be prepared to listen hard."

"Coming!" Rusko said, slipping back into the galley. He grabbed the mug of 'toot Falmer held out to him and slid onto the bench next to Klay. Mitsy and Ditsy marched into the room with great solemnity and settled themselves by Squithy's feet.

Tranh walked over to the table and propped a hip against it, not really sitting down, but taking some of the weight off his leg.

"None of this goes outside the ship. Inspector Irom is firm about that. We keep everything confidential, and there's a bonus in it for us when we clear dock. There's other conditions I don't like as well, but it was pretty clear that 'yes' was the only answer that kept crew outta jail and *Dulcimer* in the hands of the family."

He sipped, and put the mug on the table beside him.

"According to the inspector, Susrim's at risk of short-term physical and behavioral modifications, because of the inadvertent misuse of some drugs that were given to him without his knowledge."

Tranh met Rusko's eyes.

"Real insistent on that *inadvertent*, was the inspector."

Rusko nodded. "Inspector's gotta live here," he said.

"So she does. Anyhoot, the inspector's a medic. She took samples, gave Susrim a preventative shot which'll help clean his system. This time tomorrow, Bailiff Pars or one like him will come and escort Susrim to a med office for a resample."

Falmer started to say something, and Tranh held up his hand.

"I'll go with him. I'm his captain and that's port rules in reg'lar ports—captain goes with crew to any port-mandated hearings or interviews. In the meanwhile, some other port office is doing damage control. They don't want it out that a vice president's family member is within three Jumps of what happened to Susrim. That means any calls that might come in for Susrim, from now 'til we clear dock, come to me. Any queries of any kind, if it's not a known contact, those come to me."

He picked up his mug and drained it.

"Now those conditions I don't like—crew on dock is strictly limited. The inspector would like to see us in lock-down, and I'm inclined to let her have her way, *not*—"

He looked at each of them one-by-one, even Mitsy and Ditsy.

"Not because I can't trust you to keep confidence, but because this thing that happened to Susrim, it means the station isn't as safe as we thought. We're warned, and I'm not risking anybody else. Same reasoning, we're closed to off-port supply. We'll place our orders with the warehouses, but nothing off the docks—that includes the fresh market, Falmer."

"Right," said Falmer.

"That's it." He gave her a faint smile. "Next port."

"Next port I'll know better what I'm doing," Falmer agreed. "No worries, Tranh."

"Squith, I know you was going walkabout with Dulsey again, but you'll have to catch up with each other at another port, too."

Squithy sighed, and squeezed Klay's fingers before she nodded.

"I understand, Tranh."

"I know you do," he said, and looked to Rusko.

"There's some trading to be done, and appointments already made that have got to be kept, unless we want to quit dock empty. When I go out, Rusko or Klay will be my second. When Rusko goes out, he'll have me or Klay as back-up."

He shifted against the table.

"Bottom line is we want crew *safe*. Everybody got that?"

"Yes, Tranh," echoed in the galley, Mitsy and Ditsy adding a mind-picture of norbears snuggled into a pile of grass, which even Tranh must've caught, because he smiled.

"One last thing, then we'll get back on-shift," he said. "We will respect Susrim's privacy. Nobody'll ask him about this, or blame him for what happened. If he opens up to one of you, listen quiet, for however long he wants to talk. We're crew and we look out for each other."

He paused.

"Questions?"

Squithy stirred, and he looked at her.

"Go."

"Susrim wasn't wearing his jacket when he came back aboard," she said slowly. "Should we—"

"The inspector brought Susrim's jacket back with her," Tranh said, and shifted his gaze to meet Rusko's eyes. "Also one of the figurators."

Rusko sighed. "I'll take a look at it."

"Thanks. Other questions?"

There weren't any, and Tranh straightened up.

"Then let's get back on course."

THE TRADER

. . . . . . ✦ . . . . . .

Meldyne Station

BECAUSE THEY WERE CARRYING SHOWROOM SET-UPS AND conference supplies, *Genchi* had arrived well before the South Axis Combine Trade Congress officially opened, and a few days before the beginning of the so-called pre-congress.

Once he knew that he was bound for Meldyne and the congress, he'd sent the news to Freza. Despite he had loosed the *Envidaria* into an unsuspecting and largely unwilling universe, Freza and Brabham DeNobli had for years been fronting the Seventeen Worlds Initiative, trying to pull Loopers together, and get Combine assistance in the face of the movement of Rostov's Dust. They were going to be at the congress—had to be—and the news that Jethri's schedule had suddenly resolved in their favor had been greeted with real enthusiasm.

> *Jeth, that's great news all around! We can finally get together in the same room, share info, strategize, get you set up with meeting people, and selling the Envidaria. I'll set it up. Balrog will be coming in early, too—pre-pre-congress, so we can hit the decks running during the pre-congress,*

and have all our motions ready to go, once the congress opens.

Speaking on my own behalf, I'm looking forward to seeing you again, soon.

Until soon—

Freza

Jethri had reasons to be looking forward to seeing Freza; reasons that had nothing to do with the *Envidaria*. Which was why, the instant station feed was available, he was checking the incoming ships file.

This being the pre-pre-congress, Meldyne was still thin of company.

Among those not yet listed as in-system, was *Balrog*. Which, Jethri told himself, was not only just as well, but perfectly reasonable. Unless *Balrog* was carrying set-up supplies, too, there was no reason for them to be *this* early to the event. He'd personally been hoping for an early arrival, so that he and Freza could resolve themselves before business, including the *Envidaria*, sucked down every available bit of time, and the air supply, too.

Given the addenda to her last three notes, he was pretty sure Freza had intentions toward sharing—*real* sharing, not a grab-a-hug, or even a bundle. As for himself, hadn't he been daydreaming of her in his arms off and on since about the time his arms had let her go the first time?

Still, he was worried, a little, knowing *Balrog* was older even than *Gobelyn's Market*, and her schedules had gone from desultory to frenetic as a result of his unleashing the *Envidaria* at what was definitely short notice to the still-forming Seventeen Worlds Consortium. Also, *Balrog* had a history of arriving a dozen or so shifts ahead of schedule, and here she wasn't in at seven ahead. The fact gave rise to unwelcome thoughts, particularly with Brabham himself looking more than a little frail at their last meeting. It came to him that there might be more than one reason why he'd been hearing more from Freza than from Brabham, and that it was Freza's name he was seeing attached to the detail-stuff that would eventually be in the as-yet unfleshed SeventeenW Coordination Office.

The duties of that office had been agreed on in ship meetings across the Dust Zone but the staffing, the paying for, the . . . details! All needed to come together for what the ship-chat had as *Sactizzy*—which was an attempt to make the mouthful of "South Axis Combine Trade Congress" into something more manageable in conversation.

He felt *Genchi* make an adjustment as they approached their assigned docking. Bry Sen was PIC on this, with Captain sea'Kera sitting second. It was Bry Sen's opinion, as teacher and Class One Jump, that Jethri could easily earn a second class piloting license, but he had excused Jethri from the bridge for docking. Not only was there no need to impress Sactizzy with his prowess as a trader and a pilot—a combination that was fairly common among Loopers and Terran small-ship handlers—but it was assumed that Trader ven'Deelin would have "trade business" to deal with.

Which, in fact, he did.

Congress information was already hitting his queue—trade room hours, agenda for delegates, official conference social events, an ack for the reception room they'd rented for the duration including the hour they might take occupancy—and more piling in.

Right, Jethri thought.

The ship stopped moving. Jethri looked up from his screen.

"We're in," Bry Sen announced on the all-ship.

Less than a minute later, there was a ping directly to his comm.

"Breakfast is set up in the galley, Trader," said Kal Bin, *Genchi's* cook and back-up engineer. "Will you be wishing to tour the docks?"

Jethri grinned. The crew knew him. He stood, making sure of his pockets and placements—comm, gun, back-up, Terran coins, his "lucky" fractin. He'd wear the ring he had been given by Master pin'Aker. It was remarkable, but not recognizably anything to do with trade. His father's commissioners ring . . . that he would leave here on the ship until he had to stand formal. For right now, he wanted *not* to be formal, to be neither Jethri ven'Deelin, nor Jethri Gobelyn, but just anonymous crew, touring the port before the big doin's began.

"Thank you," he said into the speaker. "A quick breakfast for me, and a port-ramble. Hold any messages until I return."

It being a ramble and nothing official, Jethri stepped off *Genchi* wearing a crew jacket and a cap. The cap served double—keeping his head warm on the cool docks, and hiding his obviously Liaden—or, at least, obviously not Looper—hair. As a concession to the venue and his eventual place in the conference, he had his South Axis Combine Trade Congress official ID hung round his neck, hidden inside the collar of his jacket. The *Genchi* crew card hung on its own lanyard, outside the jacket.

He took a deep breath of cold air and set out, flashing a casual salute to the customs agent sitting beside a portable scanning rig nearly at the end of *Genchi's* ramp. The agent nodded as he approached and held up the crew card for her to see. He didn't set off any alarms, and she'd seen he was first off a ship just in. First off could be anybody, really, and it wasn't her job to know who or what, just that he wasn't carrying anything against regs, and he had his tags on.

"Calm shift?" he asked and she laughed, shaking her head.

"It'll get busier, real soon," she said. "Make sure you plan for crowds, if you're out more'n a couple hours."

"Shouldn't be that long," Jethri told her. "Just a walkabout."

"Enjoy it," she told him, and he walked on, smiling, and warmed. It *was* good, sometimes, to be just crew.

He glanced about, getting his bearings, seeing that aside from the agent and himself the docks were quiet.

The starboard slot next to *Genchi* was empty, but the docking to portside was occupied by *DelYWare Deposes*, the screen showing a departure in three hours, dock bustling with crew moving last minute cargo bins into position, which explained the agent's position. Nobody paid him any mind, nor should they.

After *Elthoria's* departure from Frenol, Jethri had made a modest study of the way he was received when he wore crew jacket and working boots, compared to how he was received wearing trade clothes, stylish boots, and a cloak. He had suspected that regular crew didn't get half the scrutiny offered even a junior trader. If he dressed as crew, but left his ring on, that might change the equation, but many Terran spacers wore rings; they weren't the status markers they were on slim Liaden hands.

Right now, wearing what had been his best boots when he'd been *Market*'s crew, he might catch eyes for reasons other than trade, or his business connections. Jethri-the-spacer might be someone up for a quick bedding, or a game of skill or chance; someone looking for a job, or who knew where a job might be found. Who knew, but that a Terran-looking spacer off *Genchi* might not be willing to front a drink or two for the local scuttlebutt, and maybe breakfast too?

Ahead of him, next dock up from the empty, was *Elsvair*. As he approached, a pair dressed in somber black and greys slipped down the ramp. Dressed simply, even to their shoes, little more than heavy-weight ship mocs... Maybe people like him, people needing some quiet time away from the ship before crowds became the rule everywhere? Else spacers who kept their own schedule wherever they were: he was afraid that given his own ship in truth he might go that way—why put a body through all the trouble of relearning time at each port?

Past *Elsvair*'s mooring, he turned to look back. There was no one behind him, nobody out on *Genchi*'s dock. Just ahead, the pair from *Elsvair* had stopped to consult each other. Something about them drew his attention, some vague recognition despite their ship's name was unfamiliar to him. At this distance, they might be any of a thousand people he'd seen in a port bar or trade hall.

As he considered, the pair reached an end of their consultation, and moved on. He was aware of a faint tingle from his pocket, a sensation he had felt often as a child, less so as he grew older. His fractin—a *real* fractin, not one those produced in quantity, and much more recently—his fractin was...interested.

Maybe, he thought, one of *Elsvair*'s crew also carried a lucky fractin.

There were eight more moorings between him and the gateway, some with ships attached and several without. They were out on the outer rim where *Genchi's* three pods of set-up and showroom specials would be unlocked and moved by tug to the conference access dock.

Two docks in from the gate the sign bore a legend in dark green: ARRIVAL DUE: BALROG.

So close! So near! Jethri didn't even try to contain his grin. Freza...and Brabham, too—arriving soon. He felt suddenly energized, and passed through the gate with a positive spring in his step, his fractin pleasantly warm in his pocket.

The first thing he noticed when he rolled out of the lift on the second level was the aroma of baked goods. He should, he told himself virtuously, remember to bring back a treat for the crew, and he followed his nose down a slightly lower-overhead side-hall off the main ramp leading to the conference halls.

As he paced deliberately toward his goal, he caught a reflection in a shop window. The pair from *Elsvair* was close behind him, and he thought for a moment that they, too, had been seduced by the scent of hot dough—but no. They'd stopped, and were staring into the window of an outfitting shop. He turned his head slightly to get a better look. They were much alike, perhaps young, though spacer ages were hard even

for spacers to parse. His cousin Dyk might pronounce
them *comely*, even—high praise—*interesting*.

His *fractin* had warmed again, but he did not reach
into his pocket. Instead, he inhaled that delightful scent
and followed his nose again, down the hallway, toward
a bright yellow sign that read LONG DOCK BAKERY.

He reached the door and stepped back to allow a
laughing trio in red mechanics overalls to exit. The
shortest one grinned at him and gave her head a toss.

"Best brumberry muffins in known space!" she
told him.

"I'll be sure to try them," he said, matching the grin.

The tallest laughed.

"That'll be tomorrow, spacer, 'less we beat you
here again!"

The middle one added, "You only brought one pair
of hands—bad mistake!"

"Maybe not," said the short one. "Could be it isn't
his payday."

The others conceded this point with another burst
of laughter, and then they were away down the hall,
passing *Elsvair*'s crew without giving them a glance.
Jethri paused another minute, watching them go,
pleased by the contact, and wondering, just there
beneath the pleasure, if they would have treated him
with the same casual good cheer, if he had been in
his trading clothes, rings and fashion forward.

He moved his shoulders under *Genchi*'s jacket and
slipped into the bakery, eager to see—and taste!—the
delights within.

"Good shift to you!" said the man behind the counter. "Anything you're wanting direct to go?"

"Intend to buy for my shipmates, soon's I find what's here," Jethri answered, and grinned. "An' after I fortify myself."

The man laughed. "Gotta fortify, an' that's a plain fact. Wouldn't do to collapse under the weight of ship treats before ever you got back." He swept out a hand. "Go 'head, have a look about. I'll just be getting these empties into the back, and bringing out some more."

"Brumberry muffins?" Jethri asked, having developed a lively curiosity about that particular treat.

The counterman looked regretful.

"No, them three cleaned me out. Always do, their payday. You go 'head and see if you can find something to console yourself with. I'll be right back."

He pulled three empty trays from the case and vanished through a door, leaving Jethri alone with the delicious odors, enticing sights.

There were three counters of fresh bake bread, trays of binets, handcakes, coldcross buns, grumble-toes, pearl slices, cookies, fruit toast; more trays of savories—the cheese buns and spice popups particularly caught Jethri's eye, as did the curiosity of four trays of recognizable *chernubia*, soft and tempting.

He pointed them out to the counterman.

"We always offer some Liaden sweeties. The baker, she likes to keep her hand in, and sometimes an' another we'll get in some Liaden spacers. This is more than we usually put out, but there's word this confer-ence is going to draw a good number of Liaden ships."

"Really?" Jethri said, trying to decide between binet and grumbletoes for his fortification. "Word say why?"

"Couple things—this *Envidaria* you'll have heard about? S'got everybody in a swivet far's I hear it, despite it was put together by a famous commissioner. Dead now, poor soul, but it's his son's going to argue for it. That's for one thing. T'other is there's a trader said to be coming in who's Terran—"

He held up a hand. "Terran, mind, but trades Liaden, *as* Liaden, which I'm told is quite the trick, aside upsetting some Terrans and some Liadens so much it's practically a bond between 'em."

Jethri laughed. He couldn't help it, and the counterman nodded.

"That was the baker's take, too. 'Anything that makes peace,' that's what she said. 'Even a common enemy.'"

"Something to that," Jethri said, and pointed into the case. "I'll have a grumbletoe and a cup of 'toot to eat here," he said. "Now, let me just pick out some specials for my mates."

"That'll be a box, then?" the man asked, reaching behind the counter.

"At least," Jethri said.

In the end, it was two boxes, a careful mix of Liaden and Terran delicacies.

"My mates're always after new tastes," he told the counterman as he paid for the treats.

"Good on 'em, then. You be sure to let me know how those *chernubias* go, next time you're back. The baker likes to hear about her art—all her art, now, but those in particular."

"I will," Jethri promised.

Replete and glowing, he picked up the sack his boxes had been packed into and exited the bakery.

He'd formed a plan while he'd enjoyed his sweet and 'toot. Once *Balrog* was in, he'd bring Freza here.

He wanted to watch her face when she saw all the treats, and the bread, and—yes, he promised himself; no matter how tight time was, he *would* bring Freza to the Long Dock Bakery.

As for the present, it was time to head back to *Genchi*. He hadn't done as much exploring as he had hoped to do, but he couldn't regret his time at the bakery, either. He stopped at the kiosk at the top of the side hall and consulted the map.

Right. He could cut across this level's plaza area to a lift that would take him down to *Genchi*'s docking section. That way, he'd be able to take in some of the sights, even if he had to hurry.

He entered the wide avenue to the plaza at a brisk walk, taking note of the increased traffic. Many of the people he passed now were wearing station colors, or shop-clothes. It must, he thought, be station day-shift, and people starting to work.

The crowd wasn't so plentiful that he couldn't keep to a brisk walk, and he was able to chart a course close enough to the shops to window-shop. It was an interesting mix, this close to the far docks: every third storefront was a restaurant, about half sit-down-with-your-party-and-take-some-time, and half quick-bites: noodle shops, bun-burger stalls, kiosks offering ices, handcakes, cookies, 'toot, and tea.

The shops offered clothes—station clothes, ship clothes, *shivary* clothes—jewelry, supposed ship supplies, which any spacer who bought ship supplies from a retail store in a shopping district—

A recently familiar figure exited just such a supplier's shop ahead of him, cutting their push past him so close their elbows touched.

Jethri felt a sharp thrill, turned, saw the *Elsvair* crewman striding away at a good pace, and here came the second of the pair, exiting the shop displaying *shivary* clothes in its window, also moving with a will, as if there were things to do and people to meet.

Jethri turned . . . and followed them, his fractin vibrating with such urgency that he knew they had to be carrying a piece of Old Tech that any Scout would confiscate on sight—and the owners, too, if it could be shown that they were somehow *using* it.

It occurred to him that his Uncle Yuri might like to know about such a potent piece of Old Tech, and—

Ahead of him, the foremost of the pair from *Elsvair* swept into a jewelry store, while the other strode on, seemingly oblivious.

Jethri came level with the jewelry store's window and looked into the shop where a slim, dark-clad back was presented to him, as the *Elsvair* crew leaned over the display cases. Jethri caught a reflection—only the side of the face, and realized that they were using the cases to watch behind them, even as they went deeper into the store, where the more expensive items would be kept.

Suddenly aware of his own visibility, Jethri reached into his bag, plucking a sweet at random from the top box and bringing it to his mouth—becoming, so he hoped, a spacer at leave, enjoying his treat and the pretties on display in the window.

Inside the shop, well away from his dark-clad quarry, at the counter furthest from the door, a small top-counter display moved—and moved again, suddenly sliding down the angled glass front, to the floor, the small bright items that had depended from it scattering.

There was confusion in the shop as the counter-woman, who had gone deeper into the store with her customer, raced to the front. The dark-clad figure moved, with great deliberation and displaying not the least confusion, toward the door and out, slipping something that sparkled in the depths of the dark jacket.

They turned back toward the plaza, and Jethri followed. It was more difficult now that the work-day crowd was out in full force. His fractin was warm in his pocket . . . alert. He *knew* that it sensed his interest in the piece of Old Tech *Elsvair*'s crew carried. He'd had this feeling before, with the weather machine back on Irikwae, and then when the fractin had been stolen, he'd felt its presence, *knew* it for his. No question it was attuned to him, and he to it.

There, there went his target, down another port alley, this one leading, according to the signage, to the cross vent system.

But as he turned down the same alley in some hurry, here came the crewman or his double, pulling his tunic straight—his *pale blue* tunic! Which matched his pale blue shoes. He now carried a shopping bag from one of the shops they had recently passed. No one would confuse this person with the dark-clad, brusque person from the jewelry store.

Jethri, however, was not fooled, nor was the fractin warmer as they closed on the prey—yes, prey, since he had determined that he needed to talk with this person, to—

The blue-clad figure walked past him with no sign of recognition, and went on to the plaza, Jethri following.

And there, coming down the row of shops, was the crewman's companion, also wearing pale blue—cap and shoes, the jacket carelessly slung over one shoulder, as if the exercise of a walk on port required thermal adjustment.

They nodded each to the other, the bag exchanged for the jacket as they laughed together, and walked on past Jethri and down to the next intersection, where they clasped hands, and parted.

Jethri wondered if he should be following the package or the person, but there, the fractin was clearly interested in the one who now had charge of the jacket, moving among the crowd without a care in the universe, glancing into the shop windows and coming at last into the spacious plaza. Jethri barely spared a glance at the multileveled shops and walkways, scarcely noticed the trees with their arching flexible branches with pale flowers showing dainty among dark green leaves.

The course they followed was a wandering one. They were slowly, Jethri realized, closing back on their earlier walk and heading for the docks. In that case . . . he brought to mind the station map he had studied aboard ship. Yes. He could outflank the merry wanderer and meet one—or, as he suspected, both—on *Elsvair*'s very dock.

Jethri moved to a stairlift, rushing now, where he could not be seen, turning the corner and . . .

"*Kohno?*"

The one in front of him was the second of the *Elsvair* pair, blocking his access to the lift in part with the package he still carried.

Jethri bowed an acknowledgment, ignored the word he did not know, and moved to go around.

"No," came the quiet voice. "I am interested

to know why you follow my sister so long. One is permitted to be concerned for one's sister in a strange port."

"We are from the same dockside," Jethri said, careful of his tone, "and I'm returning to my ship."

"Yes, I see this. In fact it appears you intended to intercept my sister, *Kohno*. Perhaps in a single quiet place to...do what?"

Jethri felt the warm fractin in his pocket, *thrum* against his skin. The second crewman—crew woman, he corrected himself—the one who had taken charge of the bag and the Old Tech item—she was closing with them.

"I believe I might have some business with your sister," Jethri managed, feeling slightly off balance. That he remedied, knowing the one he faced saw the move and understood it. "I believe that she—"

"What do you believe of me? How would you even see me to think you might believe something of me... of business? Do you expect me to be for sale?"

Jethri didn't take his eyes off the man in front of him, set his feet carefully so that he might glance at her with neutral eyes, while maintaining a defensible front to the other one, should such be required.

She closed with him—he could feel the vibration in his pocket.

He chanced a quarter turn in her direction, alert in ways his arms master would be proud to see, and tried not to stare into that sharp face, compelling eyes so brown they were nearly black. They widened, those eyes, as if she saw something unexpected in his face. As if, in fact, she recognized him.

He managed a Terran shrug.

"You brushed by me earlier, and it struck me then that you might be carrying an object that would be better sold quickly, than impounded by a Scout—an object of some peculiar manufacture, or perhaps of some peculiar purpose."

"Odd, odd that our *kohno* would be so interested in a passing *Nomahda*, I think, and then I say it is odder, since I have seen your face recently. It takes comparing memories to find it, for I have not seen you close in person. But there, with that hat you look so ordinary, and instead, you are not ordinary at all."

She turned toward her brother, allowing Jethri to give over looking at her eyes, and catch the shape of her face, the determined chin, the firm, decisive mouth; and see that the clothes had hidden a leanness that was perhaps informed by a diet not over rich in extras.

"Vally, do you see who has taken an interest in me? Under the cap he wears like a mask, it is the *magiestro* of the Dust. We should welcome him, should we not? One does not come face to face with such power very often."

There was a note of mockery in the voice, and a note of—perhaps apprehension.

Vally rounded to stand beside his sister, and perhaps there was enough of a similarity in their faces to call them kin, though Jethri thought not brother and sister. They were of a height, Vally's eyes more grey than brown, his hair lighter than hers, who had brows that mirrored her dark eyes.

"It may be so," he said, "that this person is *magiestro*, the *komercisto* who will save the small ships. His face looks like a familiar spacer face, and he stands like a spacer. Does he seek you for his pleasure like some ordinary rude man?"

Jethri'd never had his motives questioned in this particular way, though his male kin on *Gobelyn's Market*, Paitor, Dyk, and particularly Grig, had warned him of scams and traps that were set for the unwary and the naive on strange ports.

For all that their faces had his attention, so did the fractin in his pocket. He was certain that there were multiple devices involved. They had moved away from the head of the lift as they spoke, and people were going past them in a steady stream.

He felt another sensation entirely; the watch on his wrist shook, reminding him that it was time to return to *Genchi*, and yet—there was a trade to be closed, here. He *knew* it.

"I am Jethri Gobelyn," he admitted, using the half bow, half nod he'd become easy using with non-Liadens as a reason to move himself another quarter step back from them for safety's sake.

"My interest is as I say. I saw you on the docks and noted when you went by that you may be carrying what Scouts call contraband, though I don't know how this port deals with such."

They had also moved, subtly; not a threat, but not a weak or giving stance, either.

"Huh!" The woman's frown flickered into a short grin, and she rounded on her supposed brother.

"On the docks, he said. That means he knows where we are bunking, Vally. Look at his face, does it not remind you of someone, someone with credits enough to get by a day without risking a *fleez*? Maybe he can buy us a meal and we can talk to him in some quiet place. Perhaps he has seen others of our heptad, lost without us on this giant place."

Vally grimaced, appearing taken aback.

"La, Malu, we only have suppositions of this man, do not trade our security..."

She wrinkled her nose at him, making a *fuffing* noise through thin lips at the same time she turned her head to take another hard look at Jethri.

"We must deal with him in some fashion, Vally—he had concerns and he has an address we cannot easily deny. Likely he is a man with resources."

She switched then to a language Jethri did not know... finishing with something like *"Fisco kya Onklo, vero? Miyage revoj!"*

Vally frowned, and she turned back to Jethri smiling with piercing sweetness.

"I told him you have a trustworthy face, Jethri Gobelyn. Buy us breakfast, and maybe we will discuss this Scout thing you mention."

Jethri nodded. Malu turned and marched off, apparently in search of breakfast.

The pair across from him actually smiled when they realized what the problem was once they found a place to eat—*none* of them wished to sit with their back to the door and *none* of them wanted to be in the first available booth, closest to the door.

So they waited an extra few minutes, but not *too* long. Jethri tugged his dockside blue-topped lead trader ID from beneath his jacket "accidentally" as he searched his pockets for something he didn't need. Poof. The delay they'd experienced vanished and a clean but unserved booth well to the back was suddenly noticed by the roving eye of the staff-leader, who ushered them to it with a genteel, "Please, follow me, Trader, gentles..."

Jethri took coffee and 'mite with his order. Vally, after a thoughtful look, added the same to his already extensive order. Malu went with tea as her drink, and ordered more carefully than Vally, whether because she was less hungry or less willing to be beholden, Jethri didn't know. His companions were not willing to share their food with talk, and ate with quiet efficiency. Meals finished, then it was time to talk. He insisted on buying another round of beverages to keep the table active, and leaned back in his chair, waiting.

"So," Malu said, "you think we carry contraband? That is hardly a polite thing to say to a neighbor at dock. And why you should think so is to be wondered at. I carry nothing revealing, not even jewelry!"

Likely, she *did* have jewelry, Jethri thought, or Vally did. But his concerns were elsewhere.

He finished a sip of 'mite, and held up his hand, forestalling any more denials.

"I have experience of Old Tech, gentles. I have handled some—these hands—" he showed them, palms up. "I have had to deal with Scouts who took portions of cargoes I had purchased in sealed bid lots. I have had to deal with Scouts who were honest and some who were not so honest. This place, at this time, will soon be crowded with traders and dealers of all kinds. Curiosities will doubtless change hands. Things like fractins—"

Brother and sister both laughed loudly; Jethri saw that there was that about Malu's face that wanted to fascinate him. Her eyes were sharp and trained and she seemed to lean a little toward him from her safe distance when she saw him measure her face as compared to her brother's.

Her smile at least felt genuine, if her brother's less so. Perhaps it was merely brotherly care he saw there, or perhaps he saw enough difference in the faces that he thought them maybe cousins rather than siblings.

"Fractins are contraband? What would be dangerous of them, or valuable? Which game do you like to play with them, Trader? Do you use them as counters, so you may keep your cash to wallet until you need to pay? Do you build walls, making them stand as tall as they might? Or lines, and then knock them down? Some old places are so full of fractins that they are shoveled into 'crete as filler, and the pretty ones are used as jewelry by children. How could you know if we carried dozens? Why would you care?"

Jethri held up his hand, nodding.

"I'm from Looper stock, lady, and I've seen piles of fractins sorted on a deck, and played in a pile. If you're ship born you know that many fractins you come across are fake. Why they were made, I have no understanding. Those that aren't fake? Most of them are duds that had long ago lost whatever powers they had. The same with . . . old, well let us say *odd* tech. Most of it doesn't do anything now, if it ever did."

He sipped his 'mite, pleased with the mouth feel of it—so many non-Loopers tried to stretch it to tea, or strain it to smooth. This had enough body from the yeast to remind of his home ship's cooking.

He looked at them, offering each a glance that watched their pupils as he said again. "I recognize Old Tech. I have been able to recognize live fractins, in a muddle of deaders and fakes."

He sighed, waved his hands in a spacer's sign for *some good, some bad*.

A trader's pause; he let them fill it.

"This is improbable," Vally said. "We have heard rumors of such a skill, but only some very few might have it, only some with a reason..."

Jethri shrugged, sipped again.

"In the meanwhile," he finally said, "can you tell me that you are not interested in relieving yourself of the burden of such a thing before proctors track you down for the confusions you have caused?"

They tensed, two pair of dark eyes on his face.

"We should not talk to you of this," Malu's voice was barely above a mutter. "I have bad luck, you see, bad, bad luck. I am awkward. Things fall near me, they break, they..."

They were stalling. Jethri pushed his mug aside.

"Yes, things fall," he agreed. And stood.

They continued to stare at him, but neither made a move to bring him down to his chair again.

"My card, gentles."

He handed one to Malu, a second to Vally.

"These are updated to this port. I will be extremely busy sooner than later; once our pods are offloaded, and become busier during the pre-congress, and job fair. Once the congress is brought to order, I will not have time for side-trades. It will be easier for me to find time to speak to you today or this evening than it will be tomorrow, or tomorrow evening, and easier by far tomorrow than the next ten days. As I have missions, I also have budgets, and in the ordinary way of things as my missions go forth I expect so will my budgets and time to deal with...oddities and old things."

Still they stared, cards in hand. Still they made no other move.

Jethri nodded gently.

"Good shift to you. It was pleasant to share a meal."

He was aware of them behind him during his return trip to *Genchi*, a meandering return to a walkabout that had expanded in time and scope. He reached dockside, finding it busier than it had been. A service jitney bearing the Meldyne Station logo and "Courier" raced past him as he cleared the gate. Another jitney was making a looping turn out of *Genchi*'s dock, and another, just entering the dock three places past.

There was nothing and no one on *Elsvair*'s dock, the end-of-ramp sign stating ship name, and homeport; the captain's name, length of stay, and departure all shrouded in mystery.

At the empty docking between *Elsvair* and *Genchi*, a tech was working on the sign. Jethri gave her a nod, which she returned distractedly, as she closed the hatch, and hit a button. A test pattern glowed bright. She grinned, saluted, and stuffed the rag into her back pocket.

"'Bout damn time," she muttered, apparently not to Jethri, though he chose to believe elsewise.

"Equipment failure?" he asked, feeling . . . something . . . in the air. A shiver, *almost* like a live fractin, only . . . bigger, more . . . dispersed; a cloud as opposed to a pinpoint.

"Equipment's lazy, you ask me. Shoulda been an easy button-push, but all the comm feeds on this dock were scrambled up overnight. Thing here hasn't been right since the overload back when *Elsvair* docked, three shifts ago. This here shoulda been done an hour ago, y'know?"

He didn't know, but he nodded and said, "'Preciate you keeping things working right. I'm right here, on—"

He stopped, staring at the sign, which now read: "BALROG DOCKING TODAY."

He felt the smile hit his face, broad and Looper, and that was okay; he was a Looper right at this very minute. A pleased and excited Looper, at that.

"Here?" he asked. "I saw their sign downline, earlier."

"Sure. There're signs all over the place for ships due in—big, long list of ships due in. Lot of 'em are fill-spaced 'cause Admin wanted to be sure wasn't nobody left out. Now, ships is popping in, and who knows? Could be someone paid extra not to sit next to *Elsvair*, or felt like it would be buddy-do-good to sit next to the only actual Liaden ship on this level. Liaden ships gotta reputation for some of the best wine and vittles there is—who wouldn't want to see if they couldn't wrangle an invite? Anyhow, might be that this *Balrog* is left-ported and ought to sit this end up for gravity. Hard to tell about Loopers, but you might know that, Trader."

He didn't miss the nod at his chest, and Jethri glanced down, saw his trader tags still sitting outside his jacket, so he smiled, nodding.

"When can we expect these neighbors?"

A shrug, a glance at the carried comm.

"My orders to fix it came just 'bout an hour, so I'd guess this shift or next."

The fractin in his pocket warmed, and Jethri sighed to himself. If he understood how these things worked, Malu, Vally and whatever Old Tech they carried were close by. He turned his head.

They *were* close, standing to one side of the dock, heads angled to read the sign.

"So now, Malu, the crowds will be everywhere, the port will fill up!" Jethri heard Vally, who nodded agreeably at him, but the next words he spoke were low, and in their private language.

Whatever he had said, Malu either accepted or discarded it with a shrug of her shoulders.

"We have your card, *Kohno*," she said to him. "Consider that we consider."

TWO

······

HE'D BEEN AWAY TOO LONG.

Unlike *Elsvair*, *Genchi*'s captain had sent all pertinent news to the public screen at the end of their dock.

GENCHI CHONSELTA LIAD
PAR SYN SEA'KERA CAPTAIN PILOT
BRY SEN YO'ENDOTH FIRST MATE PILOT
JETHRI GOBELYN VEN'DEELIN SENIOR
TRADER
DOCKING LENGTH OF CONGRESS

Nodding his satisfaction, Jethri proceeded to the main hatch, where he took receipt of his error.

The screen in the tiny vestibule just beyond the main hatch, that served as foyer, lobby, and waiting room on those occasions when there were more than five visitors—that screen displayed, under *Welcome Notes for the Trader* a scrolling list of eighteen names. By the time he had read those eighteen, two more had been added to the list and Jethri was feeling a little weak in the knees.

Some of the names, he knew—Looper ships from past *shivaries*; from his father's port gathers, and

183

Paitor's. The others were vaguely familiar from trade boards, except those that weren't familiar at all.

The scroll had started again, another name having been added to the top, when a slight rustle alerted him to the approach of a large floral display attached to Bry Sen yo'Endoth.

"Pilot," he said, warily.

"Trader." The reply was gentle, and told him nothing.

"What is this?"

"Flowers, Trader. The newest of the dozen delivered so far. Indeed, I am pleased you have returned to us so timely. I hope you will be able to give me guidance of the placement of these same dozen arrangements." He paused, and peered around a particularly large yellow bloom.

"Unless it was the welcome board? I had thought it best, Trader, that you knew the comms had been busy for you, since approximately the moment you left us."

"I thank you," Jethri said, "but I was inquiring into the reason for the flowers—a dozen, you say?"

"So far. The first arrived soon after the first comm call, directed to you personally, another arriving before the first was properly received. We placed those in the crew lounge. We scarcely had enough time to congratulate ourselves on a clever recover when three more displays arrived, those for *Genchi*, and joined the others in the lounge. Two additional displays arrived for you, and one directed to Trader pen'Akla. There was no more room in the lounge by this point, but we moved the flowers intended for *Genchi* into the piloting chamber, reasoning that this was both respectful and practical, as the pilots will not be required for some time."

Jethri said nothing. Bry Sen swayed a slight bow. The flower display rustled.

"We of course have all the names so that proper acknowledgments may be sent, however, we have advance warning of at least four more displays bound for us."

"Put them in the passenger cabins," Jethri said.

Bry Sen looked regretful.

"Alas, Trader, the first is nearly full with gift baskets, and boxes, and the second—"

"Why is this happening?" Jethri interrupted. A stateroom nearly full with gift baskets? He'd received no more than six port welcome baskets in all the time he had traded from *Elthoria*.

Bry Sen bowed.

"We are both an opportunity and a curiosity. You are a ship-born Looper who holds a ten-year Terran Combine trade key and a Liaden-trained trader. Who would not wish to meet such a marvel, especially here at the great congress of Terran traders? More, you have liberated a trade document that is likely to change how business is done among the very traders who form this congress."

"I—" Jethri began. Bry Sen raised his hand.

"And then there is *Genchi*, no larger than a modern Loop ship, and a joint venture between the Rabbit and the Star with Three Rings—both of whom trade at Terran and hybrid ports. And the trader they pick to represent their venture, to one of the premier Terran trade conferences, is—"

"The trader with two heads," Jethri interrupted.

Bry Sen frowned.

"If a comrade may say so, your *melant'i* in this is

key. Those who curry favor with traders, who seek alliance with the new and exciting—they have goals that may stretch for generations. You stand to benefit, in your *melant'i* as *Genchi's* representative trader, in your *melant'i* as a Loop-wise trader, in your *melant'i* as the liberator of the *Envidaria*. Not only this, you stand to bring benefit to Ixin and to Midys, and to trade as a whole. Did you think the master traders sent you here at whim?"

Jethri laughed, and threw up his hand, fingers forming *I yield*.

"Of the few things I *do* know," he said, "is that I am not sent here *at whim*."

Bry Sen gave him a Terran smile, sympathetic and warm.

"They are masters of trade, Trader."

"Indeed they are, and I honor them both. Now, though, my friend—these flowers and other things—"

A low musical tone sounded, and Bry Sen touched his ear set.

"The captain reports more flowers at the door, Trader, and a few boxes of wine and specialty cheeses, all called Welcome Bounty..."

Jethri closed his eyes, reached into his pocket and felt the soothing smooth surfaces and gentle warmth of his lucky fractin, considering—feeling questions come together with potential answers as he meditated on the relic.

He opened his eyes, glanced down at the ring born of Master pin'Aker's genius. The four amethysts made a statement that was hard to argue with on the hand of a ship's senior trader, even if it hadn't been backed up by the ten-year key around his neck—six years left on that key, and the details of every single one of his trades saved to it. He was not an *oddity*, he was an *experienced trader*—two cultures that agreed on very little, agreed on this.

He lifted his eyes to Bry Sen, waiting patiently behind the flowers, and looked to the message board—forty-five names now. He watched them scroll, seeing this name and another that he recalled from a group docking; another he had seen once, at a distant *shivary* . . .

He looked back to Bry Sen.

"We are not on a Liaden port, or at a Liaden event," he said slowly, working it out even as he spoke. He used his chin to point at the board. "I see two Liaden names among those; the rest are Terran, and most of them are Loopers. Our dock is our own. We will share the joy we have received with everyone who passes by. The flowers may reside there in perfect propriety."

He stopped, realizing that he was speaking Liaden, even though the custom was Looper . . .

Bry Sen's face brightened. "I see. Yes, excellent. We share our joy, and so is joy increased. I will see it done, Trader. And—the gifts?"

"Continue to gather the names and the particulars of each. When our reception room is ready, we will have the wines, cheeses, and other treats taken there. The same principal applies—to share joy as widely as we may."

"Trader." Bry Sen swayed, the flowers rustling around him. "It will be done as you say."

"Good," Jethri said, and looked again at the screen—sixty now. "I see that I have fallen behind in answering my messages, and there are a number I must read soon, if I am to leave the ship before the congress is history!"

Jethri carried a cup of work tea with him to his quarters, took off his jacket and sat down at the flat surface that was both table and desk. He opened the screen and accessed his messages, which were arranged in order of receipt.

At the top of the list was a letter from Tan Sim. Jethri smiled and opened it.

My dearest of Jeth Rees, receive, I pray, my salutations and admiration.

Recall that I was trained on Wynhael, a tradeship of some note, if troubled in its melant'i. Recall also that I was raised as a child of a house both High and high in the instep.

In brief, I considered myself the equal of Barskalee.

I confess to you now, sweet youth, that I was wrong.

Wynhael is a tradeship; Barskalee is a great ship. Not merely a master trader's vessel, but a diplomatic mission, driven by a desire to refine trade and relations between traders into a state of purity that I, in my ignorance, can scarcely grasp.

To say that I have much to learn is laughable. I feel as if I have everything to learn, save the language.

I recently had reason to recall the occasion of our meeting—I, angry and in my cups, chancing across a lad practicing his bows in a back

*hallway. A Terran lad, that was, and I say to
you now, my Jethri, that you are an amazement.
To master the intricacies of trade, the operations
of mighty Elthoria, the language, and the bows?
You are beyond me, on my honor.*

*You will by now be all blushes, I know, so
I will end my praises here, though I beg that
you will believe them sincere.*

*The rest of my news is quickly told. Master
pin'Aker is busy on your behalf. You must not
lose faith—he bade me assure you of this, when
I wrote, so there is that duty done.*

*I am kept busy learning my duties as asso-
ciate trader, and also by relieving the master
of those things I am competent to attend to
on his behalf, so that he may do his work on
your behalf. Despite this, I have found time to
scout the trade lists for those items you and I
discussed, and I hope to have more concrete
news for you very soon.*

*You must write to me—see how I recall you
to your duty!—and tell me how you have gotten on thus far with Genchi. I fear she must
still be in some disarray from her recent hasty
upgrades, and Captain sea'Kera is never one to
be easy with change. Still I know that you will
carry all before you, as always and ever.*

*I have been instructed to forward fond good
wishes from Samay, and to those I add my own.*

Until soon, my Jethri.

*From: Tan Sim pen'Akla, Barskalee
sent via pinbeam*

Jethri sipped his tea and read the letter a second time. Tan Sim was settling into his new role. More, he was feeling valued and safe. That was good, and he felt warmly toward Master pin'Aker for stepping up and making right what had been beyond Jethri to fix.

He moved the letter to his action file, so that he would remember to answer it, and went back to his message list.

The welcome messages from the Looper ships were automated, sent whenever a ship from a particular list docked. He scanned and filed them—there was no need to answer.

The message from the trade center was of a different order, being sent specifically to him, as lead trader. Apparently *Genchi* was not alone in being inundated with flowers, foodstuffs, and other gifts. The reception hall had been accepting more of the same. Each logged arrival carried an asterisk, indicating that a receiving fee had been added to the reception room's bill.

"Cost of doing bidness, Jeth," he said aloud, in plain Looper Terran.

He sent an ack to the facility and moved on, scrolling quickly—and abruptly stopped.

There were five messages from *Balrog*, sent one right after the other, forming a solid block in his message list.

He smiled, and felt some deeper stirring as well, as if he was coming home. He opened the first, and it was Freza's voice, matter-of-factly reporting:

We're in and got traffic's attention, they're being right nice to us, which is fine. Sending messages multibounce so I'm not bothering with 'crypts.

Don't forget we're kind of ambassadors here, and so are you.

... Balrog's got a slot number now; looks like we can finagle it to be right next to you if Brabham says pretty words to somebody, which I know he will, but like I say, they're being nice, though they seem to be taking their time, when there's dozens of ships incoming ... Looks like customs is going through some algorithm; doing random checks. Got folks complaining to us, like we got any influence here. Anyhow, we've got a lot to talk about and a lot to do. I hope we can fit in some quiet times too, even if Brabham thinks we'll need to run to Terra itself to get any peace out of all this.

My direct comm code is set—we're using the Seventeen Worlds account, and you can too, I'll send you the codes. I got a bunch of business stuff to send after this, but I want you to know I'm thinking I owe you some touches, after you had to get out so quick from Port Chavvy, an' after I already'd put you off the time before. Hope you got some for me, too. 'member, we got help here, and we got plans. You don't have to think you're doing this all alone, 'cause you're not.

Brabham's standing here behind me with all kinds of official business so I'll just say you'll like what I plan.

Freza

Jethri smiled, his face heating a little as he considered what Freza's *plans* might entail, remembering his earlier gentle plan to bring her to the bakery—gods, the bakery felt like a week of hard trading in the past! And the thought of Freza offering touches, a bare neck, and her lips—yes, that was energizing, but it wasn't moving his message queue, so he hit *reply* and offered:

> *I have your first note; remember Genchi's got a suite on port and I have a good size spot right here for over-nighting if the suite doesn't. Soon. Jeth*

He considered Freza again, and *Balrog*, thinking she'd probably be operating everything out of the ship's small control room and that the multibounce was true, so really, no need to get explicit about plans with so many eyes possible, anyway. He let the message go and opened the next from *Balrog*.

It was from Brabham: straightforward and not a little upsetting.

> *Jethri, I am prepared to back you as far as I can, but my energy levels are low these last hundred shifts and not looking to get much higher. If necessary, I will make a motion at general session to seat someone in my place; you'll recognize them if it comes to that. I've got some message I got in 'crypt that I'll hand carry for you; this will be a busy session and likely nights aren't going to be big on sleep or fun. Usual rules apply, boy, all the usual rules!*

The last sentence, with the emphasis, gave Jethri more pause. Not only was Brabham sounding as if he felt on the down-spin, but also like he thought Sactizzy was going to be...*dangerous*.

Well, yeah, he had to admit he'd carried weapons when he went for his walkabout, with an extra and a back-up extra, and that he'd been careful even when following Malu and Vally. He hadn't known about the deck's comm problems—and that was a failing of vigilance which would have gotten him a sigh from Pen Rel, and a gently sarcastic remark about children growing out of thoughtlessness, if they could be persuaded to survive long enough. He surely should have been alert to the fact that he wasn't connected to his ship; that he'd been without any kind of back-up on a strange dock. And now here was Brabham, *stressing* the usual rules.

He remembered Arin, Paitor, and Grig trying to explain to the ship's youngers exactly what the *usual rules* were, trying to give them an edge for dealing with situations where strangers were involved. And there, more to the point, were defining moments of his life, things that happened because he might not have been as up on following the usual rules as he ought to be.

First off had been Jethri's encounter with Sirge Milton, a Terran grifter whose fast-talking scheme had, however inadvertently, brought Jethri into contact with his Liaden adoptive ship and family. Milton's desperation at being cornered resulted in his suicide, and in the long run, in Jethri being on *Genchi*.

But there, the *usual rules*—arrived at among the three elders and imparted before docking on a port whose name Jethri'd forgotten—were not exactly clear, after all, but depended on circumstance. They'd spun down to something like this: always know your life is more important than your money. Always carry an extra weapon. Don't ever trust somebody just because they seem to belong to a particular faction or family. Always mind who's at your back and which way is out. Always know which ship you can run to if you can't get to yours. Always...

And that right there was the problem. *Always* didn't work if you had to apply all the rules at once. Dyk had prolly summed that training up best: "Just be careful, kids, that's all. Be careful. And if you can't be careful for you, be careful for your ship."

Jethri sighed. He had a drink named after him on one space station, celebrating an instance of having *not* been careful. And then there was the fiasco on Port Chavvy, for which he still had great regrets that blood had been spilled. He'd nearly killed a man outright and he could have avoided being in that spot, he could have been careful...

Brabham though... Jethri saved the message. The next three messages were from Brabham, these more official, naming names he needed to know, pointing out sessions he ought to be at, and sessions he ought *not* to be at, too.

He saved them all and moved down the queue. Not much of substance; just first contacts—in a few cases, reminder contacts—the opening moves in the game of networking. All could be answered quickly, with an apt phrase, and, thanks to his protocol master, and to Master ven'Deelin, he had an abundance of apt phrases to hand.

Within the next bunch of messages were two more from Freza, giving more of the same—background on sessions, background on who was compiling reports unfavorable to the *Envidaria*.

That group was surprisingly large—and growing larger. In addition to old Loopers who ought to know *some*thing by now, Freza named TerraTrade councilors and Combine commissioners who warned of the dangers the *Envidaria* brought to Loopers...

Jethri took a deep breath, and despite he didn't care to include fools in his contacts lists, he saved the names, and Freza's information, in a folder all their own.

Next were invitations from three traders he didn't know, desiring him to join them at a dinner-reception to be held in his honor on the evening before Sactizzy officially opened. It was instinct to accept; meeting people and extending one's net of acquaintance was precisely what trade was about—and he caught himself with his finger on the send button. He considered the invites—three different names, three different addresses, almost identical phrasing. None of the names appeared on the list provided by Freza, which proved neither friend nor foe. And the *usual rules* would have him forget that trade was contacts.

No, he corrected himself, the *usual rules* would have him acknowledge that *Elthoria* was considerably more in the way of backup than *Genchi* was and to act with proper prudence.

He sighed, did a relaxing pilot's exercise Scout ter'Astin had taught him, closed his eyes and said out loud, "The usual rules apply."

He let his thoughts drift to Freza for a long moment, opened his eyes, and deleted his first, instinctive reply. So. Apt phrases. As it happened, he had appropriately apt phrases directly at his fingertips. He applied them to the three unknown traders, doing them the honor of providing to each their own phrase.

The next message was from *Elthoria*.

Jethri felt his face relax as he opened it.

My son, allow a mother her fond greetings.

As you embark upon the next stage of your career, I write to you with news of home.

Elthoria continues upon her scheduled business, as do we all. I must, however, report that your absence is noted among crew and friends, though all of us honor your commitment to clan and duty, which requires that you continue to widen your scope, and build your influence. Though you are sorely missed, be assured that Elthoria in whole recalls your modesty, gentleness, and determination, and does not begrudge you the challenges of your new estate, nor Genchi's fortune, in having gained you as senior trader.

For myself—you have given me a wealth of memories, my son, and I belatedly express my gratitude for so handsome a gift.

There. That is quite enough, I think. You are, after all, busy at your new life.

I beg you write a line or two, as duty allows, and in the meanwhile, believe me to be

Your fond mother

From: Norn ven'Deelin, Elthoria

via pinbeam

It hit him in the chest, that letter, and he closed his eyes against a rush of pure homesickness. He'd missed *Gobelyn's Market* when he'd first come on to *Elthoria*, but nothing like this sudden assault of loneliness. Of course, he'd been kept busy from the start—by both design and necessity. And while he'd missed Seeli, Khat, and the rest, the truth was that his mother was on *Elthoria*, and Captain Iza Gobelyn nothing but a relief to have out of his life.

He opened his eyes, and saved the letter to his permanent file.

Then he moved on to the next in-queue.

The last message had been answered, and Jethri had accepted Bry Sen's invitation to sit second on the flight deck, as *Balrog* made her final approach. She came in under her own power, without the aid of tugs. Most Loopers rejected tugs, preferring to "hole the ring our ownselves," as he'd once overhead his cousin Grig tell it, and *Balrog* had shaken off the suggestion that she wait hours for an assist when the docking station was clear.

Jethri glanced at his screens, noting that all the berths in their section were accounted for now, and most were filled. None of their berth mates were of the largest—those needed far more room to maneuver and had special maintenance and service loading requirements in any case.

And here at last, *Balrog* came into view. Jethri sighed as he saw her. She looked her age, showing the dings and lost shine of something used hard, and then used hard some more. The pod mounts were firm, well maintained, and two generations younger than the ship herself.

Jethri had been aboard *Balrog*, and knew it for a

cramped little ship; *Genchi* loomed large in comparison, and, thanks to her recent upgrades, sprightly. In comparison, *Balrog* was tired, and approached the dock carefully, with gentle use of jets, and frequent pauses.

A glance at the side screen brought Jethri the startling news that the pilot in charge was *3C Brabham D600*. He blinked. 3C Brabham? Brabham was third class, like he was? That was ridiculous. Brabham was...

Then he recalled Brabham's note, leaned in and upped the comm on the ship-band, caught the chatter, and leaned back.

"Six hundred?" came the stunned question from a ship at dock. "Are those numbers off, Jac?"

"Numbers are good," came the answer. "Pilot's been there and done that."

"*Six hundred* and not a port jockey?"

And here was the rest of it, coming in from the ships awaiting tugs, or clearance, all watching that careful approach.

"Six hundred. You children watch close, now. This is number *six hundred*. Ol' Brabham's got *Balrog*, yes he does, and if you're lucky, children, you'll be able to tell your children you saw it, 'cause ain't none of *you* getting to six hundred dockings."

Balrog's progress, already slow, slowed even more, and she seemed to be drifting a bit as she nosed in between *Genchi* and *Elsvair*.

"Can we lose half that chat and let the pilot work?" came the sharp suggestion from the traffic controller. Jethri frowned, hearing strain.

"*Balrog*, that maglink's not matching," the controller went on, her voice light now. "You got the poles on backwards again?"

That was a joke, but the essential thing was that *Balrog* was just slightly off-center in the cradle, slightly too far away, slightly . . .

"We have a sensor reading we're checking on, *Balrog*. Even up and we can give you two more minutes here, but there's a crowd behind, sir."

"That was gently said," Bry Sen murmured. "He could have been waved off twice already . . . but—his six hundredth docking?"

Jethri nodded wordlessly, as Brabham's voice came through the comm.

"Just a little interference coming off a ship at dock, Traffic. I'm pretty sure we got this pegged now. Give me the six digits on station motion one more time."

"Coming, to your reference, sir. Forty seconds from my last number."

The numbers came, Brabham answered, "Hear ya," and *Balrog* moved in crisply, orientation precise, lined up proper now, and Traffic was on it.

"Straight on the lead link, damp that vibration, zero out, and you're in, *Balrog*. Good show, PIC Brabham."

"Twelve seconds left?" Brabham queried. "Think o'that. Twelve seconds. Thanks much, Traffic, and that'll be a surrender. In eight seconds, I'm a tourist. Tell you what, Traffic, come on out to celebrate, on your off-shift. I owe you a dinner."

"In," someone said in plain awe. "He's in."

Somebody else said, "I got me two hundred ninety docks and they think I've pushed it!"

And then the echo, going from ship to ship, as the lag found them. "Brabham on *Balrog* surrenders at six hundred even."

"Did I tell you?" Brabham said conversationally

across the wide-open band. "My Number One live dock was at an axis congress, so here's Loop-end for me!"

Jethri sighed, heard an echoing sigh from the pilot's chair.

He glanced over, and caught a Terran smile and a seated Liaden bow.

"You keep company with those of excellent *melant'i*, Trader. A ship of distinction, with pilots the same. I would hope to meet that pilot before we undock, if you might arrange it for me."

Jethri returned the smile and the bow.

"Yes. I will do my utmost. He is a remarkable person, quite aside the six hundred. I believe you would enjoy each other." He glanced again at the screen; at *Balrog*, comfortable at dock. "If the ship does not require me, I have—"

Bry Sen waved a hand, fingers shaping the pilot sign for *go*!

"Your overriding *melant'i* here is trader. This, the ship understands."

Jethri rose, checking his hair in the reflection of a dark screen, knowing that Freza would not mind if he did not come in the full force of his trade cloak and boots.

The comm on his belt buzzed. He snatched it free, glancing at the screen—*not* any of the codes given him by Freza. He feared he knew which code it was.

"ven'Deelin," he said, crisply.

"This is Vally, Trader. Malu and I wish to speak with you in person, here on *Elsvair*, as soon as possible. This concerns our earlier most pleasant conversation. The captain has granted us the conference room in a quarter shift in order that we may do business together."

Of course it would be now, Jethri thought, and was of half a mind to claim a previous engagement—not a complete untruth—but there was Uncle Paitor in the back of his head, a remembered lesson in trade etiquette and how to get what you wanted.

"There's an old, old saying, used by gamblers, I think, but also by traders, and it comes to keeping your face with folks you're trading a little pushy with. Pushy ain't always the best way, but sometimes it's the only way, and if you got yourself into that spot you got to either put up or shut up. Show the money or the contract, be able to finish what you started, be able to be specific, and willing to shake hands or knock elbows on the deal. You ain't absolutely certain you want the deal, then don't push."

Jethri sighed inwardly.

"I'll be there," he said into the comm.

THREE

· · · · · · · ·

SO IT WAS THAT JETHRI'S FIRST GLIMPSE OF *BALROG'S* crew at this docking was barely more than that. He was first at the ship's flag, felt the slight over-pressure as the hatch slid aside, and a moment later felt Freza's hands on his as she dragged him laughing into the tiny entranceway and pushed him briefly against the nearest wall with a crushing hug, the scent of her perfume to him.

Their mouths almost collided as they both tried to take the same side for a fast kiss, while behind Brabham chided them with an undercurrent of laughter.

"Let the man in, Freza, so we can all see how good he looks, right? I might need to steal him away from you..."

They managed the kiss anyway, Jethri barely avoiding getting tangled in Freza's ear-com, and after a very few suggestive touches, she dragged him into the crew lounge where Brabham was pulling drinks to the table.

"I had to come," he told them, "but I can only stay a few breaths. Got a 'pointment next ship over, *Elsvair*. Not sure how long it'll take."

Still holding Jethri's hand, Freza shook her head, and wrinkled her nose.

"Traders are like that, I hear, always on the lookout and gotta do it now. Date on the books or no!"

She laughed, sounding as giddy as he felt just looking at her. This—

"Oh, look at the ring!"

She held his hand high, showing pin'Aker's gift to the room. Jethri did his best to ignore that, ceding his hand to her use, as he caught Brabham's eye.

"Heard you come in, sir," he said, nodding and bowing both. "I guess that's congratulations. Always good to get safe to the end of the Loop, is how I hear it!"

Brabham's face shone; his smile shy. "Yeah, but I hadda do it, so these fine folks know where I stand and where I don't. Pilots can't get by on quarter-shift snatches, and I was a bit loose, even at that. That *Elsvair* you're going to, there's some transmissions or emissions coming off her, I dunno. Not like me to bobble that way—never has been—but there, they was giving off some kind of interference that ghosted the close radar and jiggled the vid sensors. Just as well I won't be on deck to take us past 'em on the way out. But hey, don't look too hard, this is a big port and a big party, so the usual rules apply and we better all get the good rum while we're here!"

"*Genchi*'s pilot admired your docking, too, and asked could he meet you. All good if I bring him along to one of those parties?"

"You do that," Brabham said with a nod. "Be happy to know him."

"Tell us about the ring, Jeth?" Freza said.

"When there's time—long story, really it is. I'm due down the row, but I wanted to be first in, so I can brag on that when the stories get told!"

Freza raised his hand, holding tight, kissed his knuckles, then pushed his shoulder harder than maybe playful called for.

"Go on 'way then, Trader, and get yourself back here when you're done. That's an order!"

"Yes'm! Soon's I can, I'll be back through. *Just* as soon!"

He'd decided not to go to full dress for this dockside visit—his contacts had seen him in his casual outfit as he'd seen theirs, and now he'd be on their deck at their invitation. And the quick visit to *Balrog* had been a necessity.

There was an orange *at-home* flag on display at the end of *Elsvair*'s dock, but the sign was dark. Might be the electronic wooblies weren't done with this end of the dock. There was a welcome sign on the hatch, but it, too, was dark.

The tell-tales admitted to there being pressure on the other side of the hatch, but didn't show unlocked, as many on port would. Despite, Jethri presented himself to the camera, stating his name, and showing his palm to the lens. Then he waited, practicing patience, while the auto-answer got someone inside to come take a look.

If he hadn't already informed Bry Sen of his destination and made sure the comm set was working before putting it to silent he might have checked it . . . but showing signs of impatience wasn't a good look for a trader come to deal.

Since he assumed he was on video he kept his hands well away from the pocket holding his lucky fractin, though he felt its warmth, as well as a faint tremble, as if it were anticipating this meeting.

The hatch itself showed *Elsvair*'s name, and Tokeo as her home port. There was no captain's plate, and none for the owner, though the Carresens shipyard plate was there and obvious, putting the ship's keel at thirty-seven Standards and odd tenths, so while it wasn't the newest ship on port it was by far not the oldest.

While he waited, Jethri memorized the ship serial numbers for something to do. He'd decided that he needed eyeball information on what ships were here, their capacity, their age, condition, and crew—all data that would weigh on how the *Envidaria* was implemented. He couldn't facilitate markets and routes for lower mass ships if he didn't have a feel for what that meant in person, and across a wide range of ships, not just Loopers like *Balrog* and *Gobelyn's Market*.

Elsvair, now—*Elsvair* was running light on pods, according to the docking specs he'd seen, and her ports of record did not suggest that she was a proper Looper. Rather, there'd been a lot of opportunity ports, ranging from high end to low, and from one end of the arm to the other. Maybe he could get them to discuss cargo types, and cost-of-runs. A not-old, not-new ship in good repair—they had to be earning money somehow...

The hatch lights brightened, and Jethri thought he heard the hum of motion just before the hatch rolled away with a hiss that released warmth and tantalizing odors that suggested highly spiced meals and a ship kept above usual Looper temps.

Vally faced him from within, dressed in simple shipwear, mocs and light form-fitting shirt and pants. The warmth might make such more reasonable than a heavier uniform, especially if Vally was not on the ship's ordinary duty roster but was a passenger.

His host bowed, very slightly, showing hands, palm-up and empty.

"Trader, we give thanks for your time," he said in clear Terran, with no hint of the accent Jethri had marked earlier. "Please, follow."

He stepped into the ship, standing aside while the hatch closed and sealed, and then followed Vally down a main hall. The fractin in Jethri's pocket was warm, but not excited now. Maybe it was waiting.

The ship's layout reminded him of a family ship, though the lighting was much lower than that of any Looper he knew. He understood why the warmth of air had been so evident, with a strong vent moving the atmosphere with some alacrity. Vally, whose slight form moved with a certain sinuosity here on his home decks, was silent as he led the way deep into the ship, past sealed doors and dim passages and finally to a compartment close to the size of *Genchi*'s break room, a function this space might have performed in a past life.

It seemed clear that the room was not as it had been—built-ins had been removed, with mountings left behind. Extra vents suggested that food might have been prepared here. As always, Jethri evaluated the access points he could see—that is, access to the filters and air-moving equipment that must be...there... and...there, and which *might* be *there*...

Toward the rear of the area, to one side of a pair of fine kermandel panels, was a table and chairs. There Malu stood by a chair, her form not so different from Vally's in ship attire, a little taller, perhaps, and her shoulders not quite as wide. Another woman was standing by a second chair, her hair dark and her eyes serious. Her features were like enough the other two that she might have been an aunt, or cousin. All three were slim, the older woman more so, as if, despite the savory odors of recent cooking, she ate more lightly than most Loopers.

Vally walked to the table, turned and stopped. Jethri, following, stopped within polite Looper distance, which put him closer to all three than Liaden custom permitted, nodded, and waited. The fractin in his pocket was vibrating, just a little.

Vally moved a hand toward the older woman.

"Trader Jethri Gobelyn ven'Deelin, I bring you to the attention of Minsha. Minsha is the ship's . . . trade advisor. Each of us trades independently, but in cases of complexity she advises us by agreement. She has experience with the rules of contracts, delivery specifics, and the like, which we individually cannot match. You must understand that we travel independently and that we each trade independently in this."

Vally paused. Clearly, Jethri was supposed to say something. He inclined his head politely and said, "I understand."

"Good," Vally said, turning toward the woman.

"Minsha, Trader ven'Deelin of *Genchi* is brought to your attention."

"I see Trader ven'Deelin," Minsha said, her voice deep and firm.

Jethri bowed to her, as to an equal, and produced another bow for Malu and Vally, acknowledging previous acquaintance.

"Thank you. We should all be clear that I seek a

private transaction, where I represent myself only, the ship's partnerships are not involved. Further clarity—I will pay cash, if I buy. Any deal that we agree upon between us will be a private dockside transfer of personal property. Trades of this kind go unreported. Again, none of my partners or associates is in any way involved, nor will they learn of my trade sources, since all traders are expected to have and give confidences."

For all that it was true, it needed be said: if something went out of true only Jethri was responsible, just as the trade advisor's guidance to Vally or Malu was only advice, and not the trading of the ship.

He bowed again, in conclusion, allowing a little humor to be seen.

"Having now established clarity, I thank you for your invitation and welcome."

"It is well," Minsha said. "Malu and Vally, you will offer tea."

They left the room together, and appeared a moment later, each burdened with a tray. Minsha sat, and indicated with a wave her hand that Jethri do the same. The chairs put him across from the three of them, with Minsha's chair drawn a little apart from the other two.

Vally placed cloth mats that were clearly hand-made at each place, and then saucers. Malu poured, and placed the cups in the saucers. Jethri, the guest, was served first. Vally placed a plate of small savories in the center of the table, Malu kept the teapot to hand. When all was seemly, and Vally and Malu had taken their chairs, they all four raised their cups and sampled the beverage.

The blend was not familiar to him, though it had

many notes he knew. He suspected that it was a custom blend, and complimented it, and the antique service as well. A Liaden service, he saw, which was not particularly surprising of itself. What did surprise was the fact that it was in use for the ship. But, perhaps his hosts didn't know that such a set—old, intact, but obviously well-used—would bring a good sum at Liaden-side auction.

The whole time he'd been seated at the plain table overlaid by hand-stitched place mats he'd struggled to keep his hand away from the fractin; its vibrations had increased while they politely drank tea, so much that he was astonished not to hear a buzz. If it called to local Old Tech or something called to it, he didn't know.

When the pot was done, Malu rose, taking up the cups, removing the textiles, and placing them on the tray Vally held ready. When it was full, he carried it away, returning quickly.

"We will work here," Malu said. "Vally will bring things. And you, Trader, let me move the table this way so that your light will be better."

Jethri rose, nodding, stepping away so the table and seats might be moved appropriately. Minsha gave a half bow, and moved her chair away from the table, making it clear that she was there in an advisory role, and not as a party to the trade.

Jethri considered the new placement of his chair, noting that Minsha's angle would allow her to watch him, and note his reactions.

He smiled, a trader's pleasant, meaningless smile, and she solemnly inclined her head, acknowledging his understanding. Well, and that was trade—all information from all possible sources was gathered, weighed, and crafted into the offer or asking price.

He turned to Malu.

"I will ask you to show me your items one by one, in any order you like, assuming we're not talking dozens—or hundreds."

Malu's face, already bland, went blander, still.

He sighed.

"Fractins, yes," he said. "If you have piles of fractins, those I will see in cartons if need be. And if you have frames, it makes sense to bring those together, or in groups of six. Larger items, however, I'd like to see one by one, and perhaps a good way to start would be with the larger ones."

Vally looked to Malu; Malu looked to Minsha. Minsha smiled at all three of them.

"Surely the trader must see what is offered. This seems an equitable method."

Wordlessly, Vally turned and left them, vanishing behind the kermandels. Jethri admired them—portable folding screens useful for hiding ugly piles of things at an auction, or on a ship. Unfolded, they could change the mood and the dimensions of a room. Again, there was information here; and like the tea service these were well-used, possibly also old and rare, though he would have to make a closer inspection to be certain.

Jethri heard the first item trundling from the back, well before he saw it and when it emerged from behind the beautiful screens there was no beauty in it. At first glance, it looked like a lump of solid metal, but as it came closer, Jethri could see layers and details. There were modules, pins, connectors, all of a uniform gritty color. The size of one opening reminded him of a ship's pump, or maybe...

The fractin in his pocket cooled somewhat, though it still vibrated. This item did not excite it, which was, Jethri thought, just as well. Vally wheeled the thing to Jethri's chair, and indeed it was easier to look at it from there than it would have been standing.

He withdrew a magnifier from his pocket.

"It is permitted that I touch? That I look closely?"

"Yes, of course," said Vally.

Jethri was guessing the majority of the thing was metallic-ceramic hybrid, and as he peered he began to touch, and to probe it with his fingers.

He rose, moved his chair to another angle, sat again, and peered some more. Finally, he looked up, first to Vally, then to Malu.

"I see by the numbers and letters here that this has a Terran history. It is not something I am familiar with, though I feel that it is old... Yes. Old. Forgive me, but unless there is another part that goes to this, I have no interest. I can guess that it's a portion of a mechanical system, perhaps part of a weapons system from the Terran wars. There are collectors of all sorts for this kind of thing, and it may be quite valuable, but it is not my interest. Old is not enough."

The other three exchanged glances.

"There is another part," Vally said quietly.

"I will look," Jethri allowed, "but I do not expect to buy."

The second part came out in a few moments, also trundled, though it was smaller. One symbol—Jethri took a deep breath, and examined this new section more closely, trying to see where a connection between the pieces might be made, and relieved when he discovered none.

He sat back.

"Not this, gentles. This item here, whatever it is, requires a module, and then they attach elsewhere. You do *not* have the third module?"

Vally shrank a little where he stood, and shook his head glumly.

"If there was more to it, Trader, we did not see it."

"It's likely just as well. These markings—" he pointed to them, not to the mark that had made him gasp, "suggests that this requires a timonium power supply. I have no interest. Someone may—there are people who collect such things, as I said."

The pieces were removed from the trading zone, Vally promising to return with something else that would surely interest the trader more. When he was gone, Malu leaned forward across the table, pulling from her hip pouch a delicate stylus, enamel and maybe even gems inlaid. Jethri felt his breath go; it was simply that beautiful. The fractin warmed somewhat, and cooled when Malu put the piece on the table before him.

"I may touch to examine?" he asked.

She nodded, but he looked first with the magnifier, not touching. It appeared to be nothing more or less than a stylus, though an unusually valuable stylus, given the apparent handwork, the colors, meant to attract the eye. He was careful not to let the frown reach his lips, as he mulled that over. Meant to attract? Some Old Tech was deliberately attractive; inviting a touch, and more.

When he touched the thing his fractin warmed

gently, as if in acceptance, and stayed warm. He sat back, and looked to Malu.

"Does this write on any surface you've tried it on?"

A rueful smile. "We are not even sure what kind of an instrument it might be, Trader."

"So you do not have instructions for it, a hint at what it does?"

"Nothing."

"May I hold it—manipulate it?"

Glances between Malu and the advisor. A slight nod from the elder yielded permission from the younger.

Jethri picked the stylus up, the warmth in his pocket growing and a feeling of familiarity stealing over him. The enamel work, the feel of the object against his skin, reminded him of...something, some object he had handled, though not recently. He couldn't bring this previous object to mind, but this one was very familiar to his hand. If it *was* a writing instrument, there would be an extendable point.

Carefully, he twisted the barrel, and found no motion that way, though a portion of the enamel-work glowed faintly blue. He pushed that section, gently, and was rewarded with a *snick*. His pocket warmed again, and he was sure, now, that the stylus was...active. The upper half of the barrel glowed ivory beneath the enamel, and he recalled in that moment why its feel against his fingers was so familiar.

It felt like the weather machine he had held on Irikwae, even though it had been a larger item, less elegant, heavier. But the feel against his skin, as if there was a field around the object that made the air plush—that was all too familiar.

He looked at Malu, who was watching him intently.

"You do *not* have hundreds of these?"

Malu smiled, shook her head—and gasped, a look of horror on her face.

"No, Trader," she said, and Jethri could see that she *didn't* want to speak. "This, it came from the same crash site as the weapon parts Isaddon found, attached to an abandoned uniform jacket. It was not close to the remains of the others..."

She slapped her hand over her mouth.

Jethri looked at her in amaze.

Minsha hissed, her face suddenly red and grim. Vally, who had returned during Jethri's examination, was staring at her, his face gone pale, the objects in his hands forgotten.

"Bayilta, what—" he began, and stopped, teeth locked, jaw hard.

Jethri looked down at the beautiful stylus, with its glowing enamel work, and pressed his finger against the blue-lit section.

The pearly glow faded.

Vally, or Isaddon, said something harsh under his breath in that language Jethri didn't know.

Jethri caught a movement from the side of his eye, looked up in time to see Minsha lean back in her chair, her hands empty. She returned his look grimly, and he inclined his head.

"I suppose you do have some familiarity with the *oltick*," Vally said, then, slurring what Jethri thought might have been Old Tech. "We had guessed that object had a use, but for three Standards could do no more with it than scratch a line on soft plastic. While you—you snatch our masks off in thirty seconds."

"Old Tech is unpredictable and dangerous," Jethri

said. "That's why the Scouts collect it and destroy it. It seems wasteful, to us, and an infringement on trade. But they do have a point."

He nodded at the stylus, careful not to touch it. "I will place this in the pile of items I want to purchase," he said. "It's inactive now, and I would like something to wrap it in."

"You will buy after only one test?" Vally asked. "Should we not test it on you?"

Vally looked more petulant than disturbed, challenging Jethri with the set of his shoulders.

"I think," Jethri said carefully, "that one test is sufficient to the day. My need to test something more than once nearly leveled the winery of an ally several years ago, and if there was more to learn of that device I'm glad I didn't. I gather that at times the devices act for their own goals, and I don't want to push what luck I've had so far."

Jethri glanced to the advisor, who glanced at Malu, who nodded to Vally.

"Is there more?"

"There are these," Vally said, bringing forward a transparent box of some unfamiliar material. Inside were five objects, each partitioned from the others. At first glance, and second, they appeared to be nothing more than simple wooden puzzles. It was with another sense entirely that he felt them vibrating. He flinched, the fractin going cold in his pocket. These things, he thought, are *hungry*!

He looked up at Vally.

"Have you had these in the same box all along?"

Vally bit his lip.

"They were each in their own box, but I thought

to bring them to you together, and there was this other . . ."

Jethri shook his hand, raised his hand and pushed at the air.

"Take them away; they're yours. I want nothing to do with them. If it was my choice, I'd leave them anonymously for some Scout on the way out system, each in their own box, the boxes not close together. I hope you know which box each came from. I advise you to separate them immediately, return them to their own particular boxes, and keep them as far apart as possible until you find a way to get them out of your inventory."

"You will not want them?"

This from Minsha, who was looking at him sharply.

Jethri shook his head. "I swear, if you *paid me* to remove them from your ship I would follow my own advice. If I turn the stylus on, I'd say the same. I think Scouts may carry stasis boxes and blankets, which would calm these . . . things. I won't have them on *my* ship."

Malu's face was stiff, Vally's showing a little anger. Jethri waved his hand at the box and the snarling things inside of it.

"If you have more like this, please don't bring them to me. I don't want to know about them; I don't want to be known as a source for them. You decide if you want to be known for these."

"If not here, if not you—who are we to sell them to?" Malu demanded. "You thrust yourself upon us. You said you knew Old Tech."

Jethri closed his eyes briefly, supposing he should bow contrition, because she was right, he had forced himself—but his body did not soften into the bow. Rather, it firmed, and he was sitting taller in the chair, feeling his mouth tight, because—she was *not* right, and not only that, *she* didn't think she was right. It was a trade tactic—and a crude one. Make him feel guilty, cast him as an abuser of innocence, so he would buy anything, out of remorse. *That* was the game.

And he was *not* playing games.

He opened his eyes, and looked to Malu. Her eyes widened. Beyond her, Minsha bent her head, but not before he had seen the corner of her mouth lift slightly.

"I suggested that you were carrying Old Tech and that you might do well to be rid of it. I also thought you were playing a dangerous game, employing at least one of those devices on the port. You are, according to my...senses...carrying at least one device that is sufficiently powerful to cause problems with authorities, even here, if it's detected. You must know this. Maybe you want trouble with the port authorities. I think you don't, or you wouldn't have called me over here—*to trade*. We're not at the moment trading, in fact, you're coming very close to wasting my time. The devices that brought you to my attention—may I see them, or do we agree that we can't do business?"

There was a quiet pause, the silence filling with the tension of waiting, the kind of pause that Jethri sometimes found difficult to deal with as a trader. Here, with *Balrog* a few hundred paces away and Freza waiting...here he was afraid his patience would fall out of orbit pretty quickly.

"You feel it *obvious*?" Minsha asked, pointedly.

"Yes. I feel it obvious. Vally and Malu at least were carrying devices that were active, if they knew it or not. And active Old Tech devices—they can surprise." He nodded at the stylus. "We've just seen that."

The three exchanged glances again. Minsha flicked a finger. Malu rose.

"I return," she said, her voice full of the strange accent that hinted at a language nothing like Looper Terran. She nodded to Vally.

"I, too, will return," Vally said, and walked with her down the room, and past the screens.

Jethri turned to Minsha, who was looking somewhere between stern and amused.

"Ma'am?" he said politely. "Do you have something to say to me?"

"In fact and indeed. I have something to say to you, Jethri Gobelyn ven'Deelin." She leaned forward, moving a hand toward the screens, or maybe past the screens, to wherever Vally and Malu had gone.

"Is this wise, do you think? As you know, eventually the useless and the useful divide themselves. We make delivery of the useful as we can. There ought to be no need to check our work, or our methods."

Jethri stared at her.

"Make delivery? You didn't start out to bring those to me, did you? How would you know I'd be here? I barely knew myself until recently."

It was Minsha's turn to stare, which she did for what felt like a Standard year, her gaze tracing his features, his hair, his eyes.

Finally, she sighed.

"You *are not* the Uncle, this I know. Clearly, you are an instance. I mean to say, a brother."

"I'm not *an instance* of anybody." Jethri heard the heat in voice, and took a hard breath, hearing Master ven'Deelin inside his head, gently chiding: *Fire eaters catch cold at the trade table, young Jethri.*

Another breath, before he said, speaking slowly, giving each word its own space.

"My name is Jethri Gobelyn ven'Deelin. I'm the adoptive son of Norn ven'Deelin Clan Ixin, son of Arin Gobelyn of *Gobelyn's Market*. I'm a Looper born, 'prenticed to Master Trader ven'Deelin of *Elthoria*. I hold a Combine ten year key. The way I hear it, the person called 'Uncle' *is* my uncle—I mean to say, my father's brother. I'm here for Sactizzy, as a representative of the Seventeen Worlds. I also represent Arin, my father, who drafted the *Envidaria*, and which I released."

Another breath, his gaze locked with Minsha's.

"I'm not here to take delivery of—anything. I'm not here to check your methods or the quality of your work, whatever it is. I'm here to *trade*. If you're expecting anything other than that from me, your expectations are getting in the way of trade."

Minsha was silent, holding his gaze, still, her face smooth once again. Calm. Whatever was going on in her head, and Jethri was sure it was *some*thing, she gave no outward hints.

Eventually, she nodded.

"Yes, it is precisely this that I see," she said, her voice as calm as her face. "You are young enough to be Arin's son; old enough and forward enough, too. But this ability to read Old Tech by walking by, or looking at it—that is no ordinary thing, Looper, Liaden, or elsewise. And that you should see members of a forming heptad before the Chafurma—well. We shall have to admire your extraordinary eyes, Trader, and say no more on that topic."

She paused, maybe waiting for him to say something. He didn't.

She inclined her head.

"As I honor the brother of your father Arin, I will tell you that your tasks here will not be easily accomplished. This *Envidaria* you and your father together have proclaimed—it has enemies. I have heard them chattering through their radios. Those two of this ship who you have met, wandered here a seven-day, looking for others of their heptad and finding the early comers for this congress—and among the earliest they find those who wish nothing more than to see you fail."

She seemed to be earnest. Jethri shook his head.

"If there is no plan—and the *Envidaria* is a good plan—planets—whole systems!—would be left without trade—isolated until the Dust moves on, however long that might be. It would kill people, I believe it!"

"I believe it, too, son of Arin. I believe too that you will do what you will do, and the universe will be patient with you, for surely you will not be patient with it."

Minsha tipped her head, gaze distant, as if she contemplated the wall, or the galaxies beyond it. She stirred, her expression gentle, now, one hand raised, as if to soothe him.

"I am glad we have had this moment to speak. I see now my mistake," she said. "You are no one but yourself, Jethri Gobelyn ven'Deelin."

She shook herself and smiled, edged, and slightly mocking.

"Now, let us call those two back in, and have some proper trading."

✳   ✳   ✳

Jethri's fractin warmed slightly when Malu and Vally returned. He had the impression that the same energy that had alerted him to them on-port was in play.

Malu approached first, and placed a delicate blue-linked chain on the table before him. Depending from the chain was an equally delicate flower. He didn't need the fractin's increased excitement to note that the flower was made of the same sort of ceramic the real fractins were cast from. He also knew, by what process he couldn't have said, that the artifact was active, and—malicious.

Vally came forward and placed a bulkier item beside the necklace—it looked electronic, but again, cast from fractin material. This was not aware in the way the necklace was, but Jethri felt the hairs rise on his arms, and spared a thought for the safety of the comm on his belt.

Head bent, he considered the two items for a little longer than he required, wanting to maximize the effect of the tension.

Finally, he looked up, and met their eyes, first Malu, then Vally.

"Do you know what these items do?" he asked, keeping his voice merely curious. "You were using them on-port this morning. They were active, and I think you had the results you expected."

Malu looked hard to Minsha who kept a bland face, though her shoulders moved, just a fraction.

Vally broke the quiet.

"We have not had formal training; but these came to us with notes. One of them lets you push something with your thought. Not hard, not very violently, but push anyway. The other one," he looked at Malu, "the other interferes with video transmission or reception, or the operation, it is not really clear, there's no science about why in the papers...but it can be useful if you wish someone to not see you where you stand, assuming they use video rather than eyes to see with."

"You have practical uses for this, then?"

"It is in the nature of what we can do for the ship while we search for others who have the need to be elsewhere, soon, who can use a ship with an unclear destination."

Jethri nodded.

"Yes, I can see that you might find such people here, at the congress, people with changed futures and pasts that need forgetting."

Malu's quiet voice was wistful.

"More than on most ports, *magiestro*, because you try to make large waves in what will happen. Someone living ten years to move up to a berth on a large trade ship in this arm, only to find the ship moved to another? Someone who was about to sell off a factory ship running skimpy in a three-way Loop and now they find they may be the only ship able to cover the need with the Dust coming? What of the crew already warned to find a new berth, what of them? But you, *you* are responsible for all these unhappinesses and more!"

Jethri's ears heated, and he felt his shoulders tighten.

"I'm bringing a solution," he snapped. "*I* didn't make the Dust."

He spoke more loudly than he had intended. He took a breath and made a small, seated bow to all.

"Forgive me," he said, and not *I'm sorry*, because he had nothing to be sorry for!

He waved a hand over the objects on the table.

"I'll trade for these items you offer, which you should offer to me now if you want them gone. If you don't, then take them off the table now."

Vally's mouth set. Malu's fingers twitched toward the pretty necklace, but she met Jethri's eyes, and shook her head.

He nodded slightly.

"Sometimes, the Old Tech . . . forms an attachment," Jethri said, softly.

Malu's eyes lifted to his face, and she shook her head once, hard.

"Make an offer, Trader."

"I will, yes. In addition to the objects, I will want the notes Vally mentioned, what you have learned, as users; and to be shown how to activate and deactivate them. If there is a special bag or box in which they should be stored, I will want those." He looked at Vally. "If you have such, bring them now."

Vally shook his head. "There is nothing, Trader. The necklace came wrapped in a piece of silk, long lost. The . . . device came to hand as you see it. We have kept notes. I will get them and the information that came with them."

He turned and vanished behind the screens.

Jethri looked at Minsha and Malu.

"My offer is good for this meeting, right now. If I leave without them, they are your problems, and I advise again that they will very likely be sought by authorities, and that this will not be pleasant or useful for you or your ship."

Minsha inclined her head. Malu nodded.

"We are selling now, Trader," she said somberly. "I must ask—you will take the fractins?"

"If you have fractins worth having, I'll offer on them. I must see and count before I can make an offer on all of what I agree to buy. I need to satisfy my wallet and my storage space."

"If we trade for the fractins, I think we must trade for all of them, *magiestro*," Malu said, not bothering to glance at Minsha. "We, too, can use the storage space."

There were many large sealed cases of fractins, each requiring a trundle cart or two men to carry; and in them were thousands of the ceramic things and a dozen or more racks to hold them. Jethri's fractin was quiet until the seal on the first case was released.

Jethri was afraid his pocket might burst, so energetic was the reaction of his one fractin.

He looked into the case, the grey squares seeming identical to a quick glance at a distance, though several were obvious fakes. He ran his fingers through them, stirring them, letting them cascade . . . and there, right there, vibrating among the junk, appearing to slough off the grey imitations around it, a fractin vibrating in time to the one in his pocket.

He ran his hands through another part of the collection, and . . . felt another vibration from the far side of the case, and a third, deeper in the mass.

"Yes," he said, "I'll take this case."

There'd been seventeen bags and cases, and Jethri'd taken them all, with the stylus, necklace, and the jamming device. Then, of course, he had to move them.

Minsha had kindly allowed him the use of *Elsvair's* trundle and he'd made two trips to *Genchi*, passing *Balrog's* dock and the hatch open and welcome, and feeling free to call himself all kinds of an idiot in the privacy of his own head.

He paused after he got the second case stowed, to catch his breath and embroider on his theme before he grabbed the trundle's handle and—

"We can take it from here, Jeth, if you got more," came an all-too-familiar voice from behind. "Saw the first two go by."

He turned, his grin something shamefaced.

We was Freza, dressed semi-fancy it seemed to him and looking really good, both paler and taller than he remembered after all his time living among Liadens—and a taller Terran-looking man dressed semi-fancy himself, with *Balrog*'s logo on his suit cuff, and looking DeNobli in the face, though Jethri didn't think he'd seen him before.

The unknown was handling a trundle sturdier and bigger, and more automated than the one on loan from *Elsvair*, and Jethri looked at it with real longing.

"It's not *Genchi*'s cargo," he told them; "it's mine. I'm taking delivery personally to get it aboard."

Freza looked at her companion.

"Now, wasn't that just like I told you?" she asked him, and shook her head. "I bet he has help waiting behind that hatch, but he's crossing thresholds and all."

"Trader's gonna trade," the companion said, with a nod and a smile at Jethri.

Freza waved a casual hand at him.

"Jeth, this is cousin Chiv. He's DeNobli-side with a touch of Wilde somewhere, we're pretty sure, almost. Been studying ship systems with us. If he don't get snapped up at the trade fair, he'll be sitting second on *Balrog*."

"Trader." Cousin Chiv's voice was pleasant and low; he touched his forehead in a brief salute. "I've heard a lot about you."

"And we're standing here on the dock with goods to shift," Freza said. "C'mon, let's get this thing moving. The longer we're out here the longer he's not sitting comfortably on my deck!"

"*My* cargo," Jethri said again, not wanting her to make a mistake, and be part of his mess if *Elsvair* decided to play more games. Since it was *his* cargo, *Genchi* would likewise be exempt from that kind of trouble.

Freza looked at him reprovingly.

"Now, I know Liadens care about kin, so it must be you *forgot* about us being cousins."

"Cousins" was what Loopers from different ships were on ports where one or all had gotten into trouble with Ground authorities. Jethri gave Freza a grin.

"Never forget that," he assured her, and looked to the other part of their kin-circle.

"Cousin Chiv, been a while. I'd appreciate your hand on this, and that's a fact."

"Let's go, then," his new cousin said agreeably, and they turned back to *Elsvair*, trundles trundling, and Freza walking beside.

There were quick introductions at *Elsvair*'s dock— ships and call-names. Jethri took delivery of the last bagged items while Chiv got four containers onto his bigger trundle, and the last onto Jethri's. Jethri settled the bags securely, and they were for *Genchi* again.

Glancing back, he noticed that Malu and Vally had lingered, apparently to admire Freza's progress down-dock.

"Jeez, Jeth," she said quietly, leaning in to him. "What'd you do? Buy a pod-load of fractins?"

He laughed. "What can I say? Everybody knows I'm a fool for fractins."

She stopped and put her hand on his arm.

"Jethri Gobelyn, you ain't a fool, and don't think you can tell me you are, even for a laugh. Now, I'm lookin' forward to you showing me this ship of yours—the one you're *senior trader* for? The ship that outpods the *Market* by twice or more and *Balrog* by six, if I seen it right. Why, I'm betting a ship that big has a lot of dark spaces where we can listen for ghosts."

Loading in to *Genchi* went quick, with Chiv's help, and Jethri sighed in mingled relief, hope, and thankfulness, Jethri's quietest smile breaking out a couple times with the understanding that "looking for ghosts" was a well-known Looper excuse for finding a private space to bundle in.

"Cousin," he said. "I 'preciate your help. Take a tour, and have a brew?" He nodded at *Genchi*'s hatch.

"That's an agreeable thought," Chiv said, with a fair semblance of regret. "I'm on deck soonest, though. Let me take a look later, when we both got some time. Deal?"

"Deal," Jethri agreed.

Chiv turned to Freza.

"I'll just get this back to *Elsvair*—send another cousin over from *Balrog* to pick up ours when I go by."

"Sounds the best plan," she said.

"Cousin," Chiv said to Jethri. "Word of notice—you're gonna be hearing a whole lot about traders having no respect for personal free time, if you let that woman onto your decks."

"Out!" Freza yelled, moving toward him. "I'm on my own time, and you're spending it!"

Laughing, he spun, trundle in hand, escaping Freza's half-hearted kick at his backside.

"Cousins," she muttered, and turned back to Jethri.

"You off-shift, Trader?"

He nodded and wiped his brow, embarrassed at his overheated state. Freza—

"You look fine," he told her, and drew a breath, sweeping a hand toward *Genchi*'s hatch in a gesture that was partly a Liaden bow of welcome.

"Like a tour?"

"It's why I came. I'm on my own time, like the cousin said, and I'm in for the whole tour, if you are."

His breath caught, and then he caught her hand.

"The whole tour," he said. "Sure, I'm in for that."

FOUR

....

LAST NIGHT, THEY'D BEEN TIRED BUT WILLING, THEN more willing than tired and it had become a bold and joyous sharing of pleasure, 'til they'd fallen asleep in each other's arms, waking again to another sharing, another nap, another waking—

And the start of Jethri's shift.

Freza took first shower, while Jethri arranged for breakfast to be delivered by the time he was showered and mostly dressed. The chime sounded just as he finished with his cuffs, and Kel Bin eyl'Fassa announced, "I bring the tray, Trader."

It had been a festive tray, with a pot of Gentle Rising tea, plates of Kel Bin's special *chernubia*, vegetable muffins, cheeses, biscuits, and jam.

If they lingered over such a meal in the afterglow of pleasure, who could blame them? But it was Freza who sighed as she put her empty cup down.

"Duty-time, Trader."

"So soon?" he asked, though he knew she was right.

"Always that way, ain't it?" She leaned in to kiss his cheek before rising.

"Let me get my coat, and I'll walk you over to *Balrog*," he said, moving to the closet.

The comm pinged just as he was finishing up with

the buttons, and it was Freza's quiet, "Jeth," that brought his head around.

The urgent light was lit.

"I'll be a second," he told Freza, crossing the room, and tapping up the comm.

The crest of the Liaden Traders Guild flashed on to the screen. Below, was a letter, very brief, signed by the "Review Board."

Jethri blinked.

"Bad news?" Freza asked.

He turned to look at her.

"Not ... exactly," he said. "I sorta expected it—in fact, I was told to expect it! I just didn't expect it so ... soon."

"If you don't mind sharing, what's 'it'?"

"Denial of my sponsor's application to elevate my standing in the guild from full trader to master trader," Jethri said. He raised his hand, showing her the ring Master pin'Aker had made for him.

"I'm a full trader in the Liaden Trade Guild, like I wrote you. This—my sponsor, Master pin'Aker—he's got it in his head that I'll be a dandy master trader. So, he applied to the guild on my behalf. And they just refused the application."

Freza put her hand on his arm.

"Jeth, I'm sorry."

"No—no. Nothing to be sorry about. Way it was explained to me was that everybody gets rejected on the first application." He gave her a brief smile. "In fact, I was told not to let the rejection bother me, to tend my bidness while Master pin'Aker tends his. It's only—"

He hesitated, frowning at the letter; at the date of the letter.

"Only?" Freza prompted.

"It's awful *fast*," he said. "When he said he was going to propose me for master after I was established as a trader, I was thinking more on the order of a couple *years*, not a couple *weeks*."

He reached to the screen, filed the letter with a couple of quick finger-taps, and crossed the room to get his coat.

"What happens now?" Freza asked.

"Now?" He shrugged. "Nothing. Eventually, there'll be a test. That's standard procedure, too. The guild sets the time and place; my job is to appear. If I don't appear, I fail by default. If I *do* appear—then I'll find out what the test is."

"That likely to happen—soon?" Freza asked. Jethri shook his head.

"I don't think so. It's in their favor to stall, and put it out as far as they can, within the rules. How long d'you think it'd take TerraTrade to put together something like that? Nothing to worry our schedule here, for sure."

Freza smiled—and jumped when the comm chimed.

"My pardons, Trader, but Cousin Chiv is here to escort Cousin Freza to *Balrog*."

Freza muttered something that sounded like, "Mud," before raising her voice for Bry Sen's hearing.

"Tell Cousin Chiv I'm on my way, please, Pilot." She looked up at him.

"Jeth—"

"I know," he soothed, and offered his arm.

"Let me escort you down to Cousin Chiv."

Chiv was just settling in to *Genchi*'s lounge when they arrived, glowing, maybe. At least Jethri felt like he was glowing, and Freza was as bright as a new ring.

He looked up, and something complicated happened

to his face, but it ended up in a smile, and Jethri couldn't blame the man for being dazzled.

"Cousins," he said, raising the glass of juice he'd accepted as *Genchi*'s hospitality.

"What's the news?" Jethri asked.

"Our section's full, Loopers and small haulers. Welcome signs're lighting up, and we're seeing some casual bidness being done. There's a crowd o'station dwellers— security, catering, techs by the whole-pod. Decking's up in a few places. Guess they're not used to this section being quite so full. Putting a strain on the systems."

He paused and drank off his juice, then rose, holding a sealed box out to Jethri.

"To keep his hand in, Trader, our Brabham made you some of these maize buttons!"

The box was warm, the contents warmer, and Jethri longed to be able to return to his room and share them with Freza. Still—maize buttons. Jethri smiled. Brabham hadn't forgotten.

"Also sent this along."

Chiv offered a spare handful of hardcopy. Jethri flipped pages, seeing lists of names, lists of topics, times blocked in—meetings, he realized. When Freza'd said they were going to be sharing info, he hadn't realized the extent of the info, nor how many needed to be brought up to date on happenings and plans.

If he and Freza hadn't already made their plans to spend the night together again, he might have wilted on the spot.

"Time to get this part started, so we can get the next part done." Freza leaned over to kiss his cheek. "There's a jitney on the way. I gotta grab some things off *Balrog*, then we can all of us go down to the suite together."

She gave a playful tug on his hair. "I like this," she said, which she'd also said last night. "You keep it nice and long."

Ears burning, he walked her and Chiv to the hatch and saw them to the end of the dock.

Then, he returned to the lounge and picked up the pile of hardcopy, going over it more carefully.

"I'm going to have to hire a co-trader just to keep me moving," he said to the empty air.

He turned just as Bry Sen arrived, holding a pair of small comms.

"Trader, there you are; I had been concerned that you had left us already. Here."

He handed Jethri one of the units.

"This comm, with the blue button, you see—this comm interfaces with local station systems."

"This comm—yellow button—has been upgraded. It is not dependent on station systems and will be available to you, should those systems become overloaded, or fail. Codes are loaded for *Genchi*, for *Balrog*, for myself, and Captain sea'Kera."

"Thank you," Jethri said, taking the comms and slipping them onto his belt.

A light flashed at the edge of his vision, and he looked to the screen.

"There's the jitney," he said, and glanced at Bry Sen again.

"By the looks of things—" he waved the hardcopy. "I'll be back late."

"Your crew anticipates your return with delight," Bry Sen assured him, in dulcet Liaden.

Jethri laughed and headed for the hatch.

DULCIMER'S NEW VOYAGE

Departing Chantor Way Station Number 9

ONE

DULSEY ARRIVED MID-SHIFT, BEARING SEVERAL RED, white, and comet boxes, which she put on the table in the galley before turning to look fully at Squithy.

"I'm riding some bad news and some good news for the ship, the crew, and you. Since we're together, might I begin with you?"

Squithy considered her.

"Tranh's here," she said slowly. "I mean, I can call him. He's the captain, and speaks for the ship and crew."

"So he is," Dulsey said, "but you and I made a private arrangement. I'd like to talk to you about that, if you're free."

"Oh," Squithy said, with a sinking feeling. "I can talk now. Would you like a cup of 'toot? Or 'mite?"

"I'd welcome a mug of 'toot," Dulsey said, opening up one of the boxes. "Will you share a snack with me?"

"Yes!" Squithy said, catching the scent of warm bread and sugar.

She returned to the table with two mugs of 'toot, and two snack plates.

"Here," she said, putting a mug and a plate by Dulsey, and sitting down across from her.

"I have some bad news of my own," she said, after they had each chosen a treat from the box. "That inspector who came by yesterday to—well. She wanted *Dulcimer* on tight lock-down, but Tranh talked her out of that, on account of there's ship's business to do. So what it is now, is senior crew can go out on port to tend ship's business. The rest of us, though, we're ship-bound. Tranh says the port's not as safe as we thought it was, on account of what happened to—"

She bit her lip, not wanting to violate Susrim's privacy, though she was pretty sure Dulsey knew more about what had happened to him than Tranh, or maybe even Susrim himself.

She took a breath, and met Dulsey's gaze.

"So, that means we can't tour A Level, like we planned. I'm sorry."

Dulsey nodded.

"I'm sorry, too," she said, putting her mug down. "I was looking forward to spending more time with you, and—" her lips quirked, "deepening our association."

Squithy laughed.

"Like we're norbears!"

"Yes, exactly like that." Dulsey broke off a corner of her dough. "They're not wrong, you know. Everyone needs associations, allies." She nodded at Squithy. "Friends."

Squithy picked up her dough and looked at Dulsey.

"I hope," she said seriously, "that we'll be able to deepen our association at another port when we're together."

"We share a hope," Dulsey said, and popped the dough-bit into her mouth.

Squithy took a bite, and let the flavors spread over

her tongue. Sighing, she sipped some 'toot, and looked over to Dulsey.

"So, that's my bad news. What's yours?"

"Firstly, that we would have to postpone our next outing until we meet again at another port," Dulsey said, picking up her mug. "There's an expanded version, which I'll be giving to the captain, but I'll share it here and now, with you, if you don't mind. There's no reason to rush through our snack, unless your duty presses."

Squithy looked at the chronometer.

"Clean-up's finished. The norbears are next on my schedule, but Bebyear says they're in no rush."

"Well, then, we have some time to ourselves. I agree with the captain's decision to keep general crew and youngers aboard. Not because the port has suddenly become more dangerous, but because *Dulcimer* has become *interesting*."

Squithy stared at her.

"Interesting? But that inspector, she said—she wanted us in tight lock-down because she didn't want any word of what—of Susrim—to get out on the dock!"

"That's because Susrim's adventure, let's call it, involved a person in the near family of one of the station's administrators. It's the inspector's job to make sure there are no scandals attached to the administrators or their kin. She can't stop rumor, and she knows that. A port this size is full of people who know people, and secrets shout themselves off the walls as soon as they're sealed to silence. *Dulcimer's* logo is by this time well-known on port, and anyone wearing a crew jacket will certainly be approached."

"But—" Squithy began, but Dulsey held up a hand, asking for more time.

Squithy picked up her mug and drank some 'toot. Dulsey smiled.

"There are unscrupulous people everywhere, and I've never heard of a station administrator who lacked enemies. The inspector can't stop rumor, but she *can* stop corroboration. That's why she wanted a tight lock-down."

She picked up her mug, and gave Squithy a smile over the rim.

"The captain let her have a lock-down for all but senior crew because he knows that *Dulcimer* crew will be approached, badgered, and possibly even threatened on-port by people who want information which may damage the administrator. It's safer for crew to stay with the ship."

Squithy frowned.

"That's bad," she said. "It would violate Susrim's privacy and the privacy of, of that other person."

"That would be bad, yes; but it's best to keep in mind that Susrim has been *very* lucky in his adventure. There are some ports where he would have been disappeared for his involvement with a high-ranking person. *Dulcimer* would never have known what had happened to him. His mates and family would think that he'd jumped ship."

Squithy put her mug on the table, feeling a little uncertain in her stomach. In her head, she felt the norbears as a single presence, listening hard. She caught a whisper of the *tobor* shape from—one of the youngers, she thought. Oki sent a sharp thought and the shadow was gone.

"Given all of this interest, I think it will be better not to transfer the norbears into my care here," Dulsey continued. Squithy braced herself for norbear protest, but none came, only the continued impression of hard listening. She listened hard, too, as Dulsey continued.

"I'll be making arrangements with Tranh so that the transfer can be made at another port, or perhaps we will do a rendezvous transfer. We will consider together what will be best and safest for all."

She smiled again.

"I do intend to honor our arrangement. They have chosen brave scouts to stay and brave scouts to go—all of them are now brave scouts, you see, having studied the incidents from your dockside videos and decided that Jethri's Scout is the most remarkable human they have met since they met Klay, who ranks with you as the humans who help keep order in the universe."

Squithy spluttered. "They can't think that! They know what I was like when we found them! They must have seen people who are..."

She stopped, uncertain, but Dulsey finished the sentence for her.

"People who are well-intentioned and honorable?" she asked, and shook her head lightly. "They had little direct personal experience with humans before you and Klay discovered their tragedy, and since then they have had second-, third-, and more hand experience through you and your contacts. It is quite amazing to witness in action and to watch the patterns grow. You, Squithy, are an anchor point to those who plan to stay with *Dulcimer* and to those who will be taking their *side tour*, as they see it. Those who stay will be *farshlogging* on their *memtrek*, that they can all share later. They have a very clear idea about the passage of time, so later is something they understand."

"But I'm not a good example of *any*thing," Squithy

protested. Jethri's Scout, she thought, was a worthy model for norbears, but Squithen Patel?

Dulsey was still speaking.

"You are a good example of yourself, and that is exactly what the norbears need. How you deal with your next Standard or two as you grow and mature, and the way in which you have already dealt with the universe, the choices you have made—all of these things interest the norbears, greatly. To them, you are both interesting and a center point."

She raised her mug. "More 'toot?"

Squithy took both mugs, refilled, and brought them back to the table. Dulsey had another piece of sweet bread on her snack plate. After a moment, Squithy took a second piece, too.

"Thank you," Dulsey said. "There is one more thing I would like to talk to you about. We may come close to the edges of Susrim's privacy, but I think we may avoid a violation, and this is information that you should have. May I continue?"

Squithy swallowed her bite of bread, and took a sip of 'toot.

"Yes, please," she said to Dulsey.

"First, then a question—do you *know* what happened with Susrim?"

"Tranh talked to me, and—Susrim used the social boards to make an appointment with somebody. The boards are run by port admin, so everybody thinks they're safe, only Tranh said they're not safe so much as less risky than making a hook-up at a portside bar where you don't know anybody, and everybody else is friends. The problem being that the—the person Susrim hooked up with was using the system for themselves, which they could do because of who their cousin is. Tranh said that's why really we should only make hook-ups with ships we know, or at *shivary*, though I haven't ever been to a *shivary*. Tranh says now that we're reg'lar—" She stopped herself, feeling her cheeks heat.

"I'm explaining too much."

"Sometimes people explain too much when they're worried or upset," Dulsey said, pulling a smaller piece off of her bread. "We all do it. What else did Tranh say?"

"Well, he said that we should all be careful, and he gave me database cites for the drugs, so I could read about the short- and long-term effects, and delivery methods."

"Did you read them?" Dulsey asked. "Do you have any questions?"

"Yes," Squithy said, surprising herself. "How can you know if somebody intends to take advantage of you, and put you in the way of harm? I did read the long-term effects. If the inspector hadn't given Susrim that shot, he could've died. Not right away, but within the Standard, maybe, if his immune system hadn't been able to clear itself."

"It was very bad, what was done to Susrim. As I said, he has been extremely lucky in this encounter. As to how you can tell if someone intends to hurt you..."

Dulsey shook her head with a smile that seemed sad.

"I watch what people do, and I listen to what they say. If there is a discrepancy—bearing in mind that there is *always* a discrepancy—then I watch harder. As a broad general rule, believe what you see, not what you hear."

She sipped her 'toot, and sighed as she put the mug down and met Squithy's eyes.

"There's no way I've ever found to know in advance,

if someone intends you harm. The best you can do to protect yourself is to be advertent. Tranh's suggestion regarding known companions is not without merit, though of course you, like norbears, will want to widen your circle of acquaintance, which means meeting new people. Be careful of food and beverage offered by strangers. Make certain that your drink and theirs is from the same bottle; that they have a slice from the same piece of cake. If you're uncertain, don't drink, though that can be difficult, since our social rules tell us to drink what's offered—do you know why we have that particular social rule?"

Squithy frowned, and paused in the act of shaking her head.

"To show trust," she said, and it wasn't a guess, though she didn't know where the answer had exactly come from.

"That's right." Dulsey nodded. "One thing I have learned is that, if someone gets angry with you for refusing refreshment, and presses you hard to drink or eat—that's often a sign that there's something out of true, and it would be best to disengage."

"Susrim went to his meeting carrying *vya*," Squithy said, which was maybe a privacy violation, or—

Dulsey nodded. "Expectations can get people into trouble. It's human to have expectations, but if you can train yourself to step back and take a good, hard look at what's factually in front of you, that'll give you an edge over trouble, too."

Squithy frowned. Inside her head, she could feel Oki listening, and saw a shadow-picture of a dim path, and a norbear at the side, scenting, and listening, and waiting before stepping forward.

"What was that, do you think?" Dulsey asked.

"Caution," Squithy said. "Oki's old, so she must have learned to be careful."

"That's my guess, too."

The door opened and Tranh came in, mug in hand, headed for the hot pot. He stopped when he saw Dulsey.

"Pilot. Looking for me?"

Dulsey smiled at him. "Now that Squithy and I have settled our business, yes, Captain, I am looking for you. Do you have time?"

"Let me grab a refill, and—is that sweet dough?"

"Dulsey brought it," Squithy said, getting up and crossing to the cabinet. "I'll get you a snack plate, Tranh."

Tablet in hand, Squithy sat on a bale of greens, norbears lounging more or less at her feet.

Inside her head, they were busy having questions, and being excited. She got the impression that, since they had finally made their decisions, they were impatient with any more delays. Silver in particular was ready to go with Dulsey when she was done her business with Tranh, and was pushing a little at how much danger could there be? They weren't silly cubs, they were brave scouts, and—

Oki, who was sitting next to Silver, shifted, bumped the other norbear forcefully with her rump, and Ebling produced a sharp picture of Silver tangled in a thorn bush. That got a sharp denial, as Silver got up on hind legs, apparently willing to have an argument right here, right now.

"Everybody stand down!" Squithy said, which Ma used to say when there was an argument. Inside *her* head she made a picture of calm norbears tucked up among the leaves and grasses, listening quietly.

Bebyear—she thought it was Bebyear—made an amused thought-noise, that sounded like Uncle Rusko when he didn't quite want to laugh out loud. Squithy grinned, but the norbears did settle again, and there eventually came that feeling of intense listening.

"All right," she said, glancing down at her tablet. She'd made a list, a *short* list, so she wouldn't forget anything.

"You all heard that this port's gotten dangerous," she began, saying the words out loud while she thought about crowds of shadows on the port, looming and threatening.

Her image was overridden by an image of Susrim when he'd come back to the ship after his appointment. There was the whisper of *tobor* there, and she wasn't clear if that was meant to be Susrim or what had happened to him.

Before she could agree, another picture formed—of Dulsey standing tall in her leather jacket, and the shadow-*tobor* slinking away.

"Yes, Dulsey is very brave, and she would scare the *tobor* away. But there are a lot of *tobors* and only one Dulsey." She concentrated and managed to produce several *tobors* and Dulsey standing between them and the norbears.

This brought silence. Thoughtful silence. No one disputed the image; *many tobors* was clearly too much for anyone to handle by themselves, no matter how well-connected and brave.

The image had everyone's attention, then, slowly, it began to change. There was Klay with his gun standing next to Dulsey. The sense of *many tobors* eased a little, and there was a general feeling of acceptance of this solution. Surely even *many tobors* could not stand against two such brave scouts.

Squithy took a breath, wondering how she was going to explain—but there! The image had changed again! Now there were three protectors and the sense of *many tobors* faded away, leaving the norbears safe with Dulsey, Klay—and her.

One of the norbears hummed in satisfaction of a fine solution to their problem.

"But wouldn't it be better if there were no *tobors* at all?" Squithy asked, picturing Dulsey and the norbears walking together down an empty ramp to a quiet dock.

More thought, followed by agreement.

"Well, that's what Dulsey and Tranh are talking about now," Squithy said. "Prolly, we'll meet Dulsey in a place where there aren't *any tobors*, and you can cross over to her ship, quiet and calm."

She changed the image of Dulsey and the norbears, showing the group entering another ship.

Yes, came the feeling. Yes, this idea was better.

"That means you're going to all be alt-crew for a while longer," Squithy said. "Since we're going to be moving, Tranh wants crew—that's *all* crew—to review emergency protocols."

That got some argument. She and Klay had already told them *that*. They didn't need to be told again. The images flowed to her in precise order.

In emergency, norbears were to go to the pile of back-up grass bales in the storage closet and curl themselves into the corners until they were called out safe.

The last image hung inside her head until she admitted that, yes, that was exactly right.

The image faded though something like a smug, *so you didn't need to remind us, did you?* lingered.

Squithy sighed, stood up, looked at her tablet,

turned it off and shoved it into the thigh pocket of her pants. Then she settled back onto the bale and started again, this time going over the rest of the crew and pointing out that each had things to do and things to back up, and talking to herself as she thought of them, partly telling them how things used to be and how they were now and what she thought they'd be with the changes coming.

"But until the new plan's made, you're crew, and crew has duties. When you're with Dulsey, you'll have to work out with her what you are, if you're crew and have duties, or you're passengers, or—"

Her head rang with their approval, and a lot of echoes, as if the norbears had one and all *studied* Dulsey's sharing of faces. Oki and Ebling, and surprisingly Bebyear, who was often the least sharing of the full adults, had between them ranked the faces: there, always, the serious human face that showed over and over again, older and younger, greyed and not, a serious face no matter what age, full of what Squithy thought of as *thought wrinkles* around the mouth and eye-corners, aging the space between the nose and eyebrows... They were at once the same person and someone else, one seemed to be exactly that Jethri from Port Chavvy, but so very close to several others who looked almost exactly the same but who had different shading—mental shading!—that meant they were *not* the same person.

Dismayed, Squithy struggled to separate herself from the torrent of faces that were *almost* the same face. She'd explained it wrong, she thought, and now they were back to believing they were leaving with Dulsey right now.

"The new plan—" she began again—and paused.

The pictures in her head slowed, and she understood that the norbears were sharing important information now, while there was time.

The pictures sped up again—Dulsey, her faces, and the echoes of strange places—restaurants, a vast and almost empty plain with three spaceships settled nearby, images of ports and people.

Squithy gasped for breath, remembering what Klay had said, that Dulsey'd been visiting every port there was over the last hunnert years, and it seemed likely, given what the norbears were showing her.

There was a touch against her leg. She looked down to see that Oki had settled against her left ankle, and Ebling and Bebyear were settling against her right, all leaning into her the way she'd seen the youngers leaning in to them in what Klay called cuddle-piles, saying they reminded him of not quite adult Loopers starting a bundling session. In the midst of her thinking it felt like there was some kind of a meeting going on, and soon Mitsy and Ditsy joined in by settling on the other side of Oki.

Squithy had studied enough to know about circuits and that's what it felt like—like she was part of a circuit of images and ideas, and that what she was feeling was something they'd gathered, bits of things getting clearer the longer they sat together.

Yes, it was clear that Mitsy and Ditsy were volunteers— the feeling came that while they both admired Dulsey as a well-formed person with lots of attachments, they also admired Klay and Squithy, who they were sure had saved all of their lives back on Thakaran: upstanding, brave, true, strong, and such a beautiful pair-to-be who'd soon snuggle and . . .

Squithy knew what blushing felt like; this felt like a blush times three as the norbears apparently were looking forward to Klay and her acting with wild abandon really soon now, even if they hadn't yet chosen their time, hadn't got the right time and the right weather and the best sun spot all at once, but soon, soon. There was, somewhere, maybe from Silver who was still not part of the pile, a snarky feeling that maybe *his*—and here came an image of a scowling Susrim walking into the norbear den throwing grass like he was mad at it—or them—bad times were going to make Squithy run off and never touch anyone.

Unbidden came Squithy's thought about holding Klay, kissing him, and she blushed even deeper, while Oki, Ebling, and Bebyear all sent approvals and Mitsy and Ditsy leaned harder on each other.

The circuit, if it was a circuit, certainly felt warmer than it had, and Squithy felt the familiar request to share, and realized that, with all the important decision-making going on, she hadn't given them her port-walk.

Slowly, she began to visualize, starting with the norbears in the hallway, eager to come with, which got a round of unashamed norbear-chuckles that faded as she remembered the walk down the tube, and identifying their access number.

She showed the map, and how it had looked to her, and noticed a soft overlay, in which she saw herself studying, as if she was—as if she was watching herself from the outside.

It was Dulsey, she realized then. Dulsey had shared the port-walk from her perspective, and the norbears were matching up their viewpoints.

By the time she had shown them the first outfitters

shop, she had stopped being distracted by the double vision.

Until she got to the dough-throwing. There was a ripple of amusement through the circuit, and there was Dulsey's viewpoint again, seeing things Squithy hadn't noticed at all. There was someone inside watching the dough-throwers, looking like a supervisor, frowning as the spinning got faster, and the tosses higher, and—

Squithy felt herself blush again, as Dulsey's viewpoint showed her that the dough-throwers, and some others inside the shop had been watching *her*, jostling each other to peer around a work table she'd hardly noticed—and there, there was a strange view, as some motion of the front 'prentice had caught Squithy's eyes and Dulsey's, so the scene was somehow all around her, in three dimensions.

There was, Squithy realized suddenly, *a lot* going on in the circuit. She got several more glimpses of that strange world in 3D, with her standing against the other *Dulcimer* crew demanding that they put their guns away. Klay's voice again, and hers, and a feeling of proud tenderness, and she was trying to *not* blush when somebody fed in another scene that might, she understood now, actually be true. She was between the norbears and the guns, and there—it was Klay's viewpoint, Klay's admiration of her in the midst of the confusion, seeing her so clearly as exactly who he needed to be there, full of pride and wonder.

Amusement spread through the circuit, then, accompanying another vision of Klay, but this time in this room and—Silver murbled, the sight echoed and reinforced by Synbe and Rutaren, who were still munching grass against the wall.

Squithy shook herself out of the circuit, and looked up, blinking.

There in the doorway were Tranh and Klay, quiet, respectful of the meeting and her concentration.

Her eyes met Klay's, and he turned to Tranh, saying something very quiet before he met Squithy's gaze, his cheeks flushed and his eyes widening as Silver fed his viewpoint into the circuit while he was standing right there, showing him looking intently at her face, and her lips, as if she were something delicious...

"Sorry to interrupt," Tranh said then, his voice breaking the circuit. Squithy bit her lip as the images went flat, lost depth, and dissipated.

"There's a crew meeting in one hour. Alt-crew can listen in, which I gather they'll do anyway; everybody else in the galley. One hour, right, Squith? We'll need snacks and fresh 'toot."

She nodded and stood up, feeling the norbears moving away from her ankles, and sad to lose their touch.

"One hour in the galley," she said. "I'll do the set-up, Tranh."

"Good." He turned—"Take a minute to make sure things are clear here, would you, Klay?"—and was gone.

Klay came further into the room, the norbears making room for him to get next to Squithy.

"That was...amazing," he said.

"You heard it?" Squithy asked, which—of course Klay had heard it; Klay had heard the norbears from the first.

"I did." He was close now, and he was smiling, kind of, with one side of his mouth, his eyes wide, and his cheeks still flushed.

"So, the right weather, and the right sun spot, and the right things to eat, did I hear that right?"

"It sounds like what I heard," Squithy admitted.

"Well, I'm glad they agree. I've been looking for the right conditions, but with everything so busy..."

He extended a hand and touched his fingertips to her cheek.

"Warm," he said, which made it seem right for her to put her fingers against his cheek.

"You, too," she said, and leaned forward, and Klay did, too, bending some because he was just that much taller than her. Their lips met, and that was fine, Squithy feeling Klay's hand slip down to her shoulder, and it was more than fine—and then Klay gently pulled away.

"I could do a lot more of that," he said, breathing hard. "How about you?"

"Yes," she said. "A lot more. Please."

He grinned.

"I'll make that a priority." His grin twisted a bit, which was him having humor. "Right after the crew meeting." He leaned down again, and kissed her forehead.

"See you soon," he said.

With that he was gone, and murbles and small chitters grew around Squithy, the norbears delightedly having taken to mimicking Klay, kissing each other on the forehead while trading replays. Squithy stood as if rooted, her mind accepting the various long-angle visions of their kiss, decided that, yes, she wanted a lot more of that.

TWO

"SO, THE FIRST PIECE OF NEWS IS GOOD: CRYSTAL'S ACCOUNT-ing came through and looks like the previous seniors had better instincts than I knew. We're in good shape to get those upgrades Rusko's been wantin'."

Tranh paused to take a slow look around the table, making sure he connected with each of them, and they understood what he'd said. Connection took a little time with Susrim, who was studying on his piece of sweet dough, but he finally looked up, met Tranh's eyes, and nodded.

"Now, when I say the accounting's in, that's a direct transfer, Crystal's account to ours. And that's all the grey and questionables off our decks. *Dulcimer*'s clean for the first time in *my* life."

He sighed, lifted his mug, and put it down with a sigh.

"That's a weight. A big weight off me," he said. "Been wantin' to go reg'lar for a long, long time."

"And you did it, Captain," Rusko said, quiet and firm. "We're clean and ready to fly."

Tranh smiled faintly.

"Which brings up the next item—*where* do we go? Pilots and traders've been working on that late into their sleep shifts, and the plain telling is that there's no easy door into reg'lar on the trade side. Previous admin didn't want to be tied into a Loop. Reg'lar ships got reg'lar ports, reg'lar goods, and we don't have that—not yet, we don't have it."

"We got contacts, though," Susrim said, his voice sharp. "Da and Ma had plenty contacts."

Tranh turned to him.

"We're done with those contacts. All else aside, those contacts set Da and Ma up for getting killed."

Susrim frowned. "That's going a bit, Tranh. Not sayin' that they didn't take risks. 'course they did—any ship does spec-n-special takes risks. But to say Choody pointed them into dying—"

"And yet," Rusko said, "we have the log entries. Captain Patel was keeping a second log book, not meant for the eyes of inspectors, should an inspection be impossible to avoid. We found it in a bin with the private cargo. Turns out previous admin'd been skimming, and it seems they got found out when they skimmed a little too deep and didn't turn over an item that was particularly wanted."

Susrim stared. "I got your word," he said after a long pause. "Lemme read it for myself."

"It's gone," Tranh said, briskly. "I'll vouch for it having been here, and the account being just what Rusko's said. Believe us or don't, that's an aside. Our route—*none* of our routes—will take us through, by, or near Choody nor any other of previous admin's contacts. We're reg'lar now, Susrim, unnerstan' it?"

Tranh wasn't just stern, Squithy thought, sitting next to Klay on the opposite end of the table from Susrim. Tranh was mad. More particularly, *Rusko* was mad, and Squithy didn't think she'd ever seen that.

She bit her lip, and thought hard at Susrim to be quiet, while the norbears listened with interest.

"How reg'lar can we be, when the traders can't find us bidness, nor the pilots any route?"

Squithy clenched her stomach, waiting for Tranh to yell, but he only nodded and raised his mug at Susrim.

"Now, that's the point, see? It's been worrying us just as much as I see it's been worrying you—how're we gonna pay our way?"

Tranh paused and looked around the table. Lifted his mug, saw it was empty and put it back down.

Squithy got up and took it over to the hotpot for a refill. Rusko and Falmer held their mugs up, too, and she made those refills.

"Klay?" she asked, when she got back to the table, and though she didn't want to—"Susrim?"

"I'm good," Klay told her with a smile. Susrim didn't even look at her.

"Thanks, Squith," Tranh said, smiling up at her before he looked at them all again, one by one, and finally coming to rest on Susrim.

"Comes about, we're lucky in our timing. The South Axis Congress and Trade Fair's about to get started at Meldyne Station. The congress is where the commissioners hear bidness from the Loopers trading the South Axis; the trade fair is just that. We can pick up connections there, meet other reg'lar ships and form associations. I'm told there's traders who'll sit down and design a Loop for a ship—lot of call for that, just right now, with the Dust moving like it is. Seventeen Worlds might be where we need to start. It's looking promising."

"*Told*," Susrim repeated. "Who *told* you about this, Tranh?"

"Pilot Dulsey," Tranh said. "Rusko's determined that there ain't anything that woman don't know, and I'm inclined to agree."

"So," Susrim said, "I think I'm unnerstanding this. We're trading Choody for Crystal, is that your way of going reg'lar?"

Tranh's shoulder's stiffened, and it was Rusko who answered.

"Our way of going reg'lar is listening to well-met advice when it's offered and doing our research. That's been my part while Klay's been considering routes. We could do worse than showing up at that conference. *Dulcimer*'s got a lot to offer; we just need another head or three on how to do best for ourselves."

"That's it," said Tranh, with a brisk nod. "So, we'll be setting course for Meldyne Station."

"After," Klay said quietly, "we make rendezvous with *Alkovo Alvokita* and get the norbears who're going with her safe aboard."

"Aren't they *all* going?" Susrim's voice was sharp as he stared down the table at Klay. "You an' me, we talked about this."

"*You* talked about it," Klay said. "If you remember, the points are: the norbears aren't *animals*, they get to decide which, if any, of them goes with Dulsey, and which, if any, stay with *Dulcimer*. Then there's the unnerstanding shared by Squithy, senior crew, norbears, and Dulsey, which is that the ones who travel with her, are coming back to *Dulcimer* when they've finished their tour."

"Oh, Squithy's got an unnerstanding, does she?" Susrim said, "An' it weighs more with senior crew than what sensible people think."

It was like a slap against her mind. Squithy gasped, thoughts flickering—and there were Ditsy and Mitsy with her, projecting the wrist-patting sensation, and she realized she was holding Klay's hand too tight, and tried to ease her grip, only then understanding that it was Klay who was holding on that hard.

"Susrim!" Falmer snapped, leaning forward and staring down the table at him. "You apologize, right now."

"Apologize to who?"

"To Squithy," Klay said, his voice tight.

Inside her head, Mitsy showed her the picture of Klay braving the *tobor*, all shiny, like they were telling her he was doing that now, for her.

"Apologize to Squithy for what?" Susrim asked, and stared at her, his expression pure mean. "You mad at me, Squith?" he asked.

She took a breath.

"Yes, I am," she said, and was sorry that her voice shook.

"Really?" Susrim said, looking even meaner. "Now I'm wondering—how many times you been mad at me, ever?"

Mitsy quietly produced the memory of her standing between the norbear troupe and too eager guns, but that was all right; she wasn't even *tempted* to start counting.

"A lot of times, I been mad at you, Susrim," she said. "That's how I know I'm mad at you now, it's such a familiar feeling—"

She heard Rusko make his not-laughing sound, and stopped, glancing at him.

"No, go on, Squith," Tranh said, real quiet. "Finish it out."

She took a breath, and met Susrim's eyes again. He was still looking mean, but a little puzzled, too. "You think I'm not sensible, but worse than that, you think I'm not *a person*—you think nobody's a person, except you! And that's bad thinking, Susrim, really bad thinking. It's no wonder you can't unnerstand that the norbears are people, and I tell you something—I don't want your apology, what I want is for you to change your thinking. You might think you can't, but I changed my thinking, so I can tell you it's possible, and if I did, I'm sure you can!"

There was silence around the table. Klay's grip on her hand eased off a little and when she turned her head to look at him, he was smiling, looking—pleased.

Tranh cleared his throat.

"Squith, I unnerstand you don't want Susrim's apology, but you're leaving me in a bind. Ship's rules say, if there's wrong said or done, offending party has to tender an apology. All present, and not-present, too, I'm guessing, heard Susrim say wrong. Gotta enforce the rules, don't I?"

She took a deep breath.

"Yes, you do. You're the captain." She took another breath, and looked at Susrim.

"All right," she said. "I'll hear your apology."

He considered her, his eyes still mean, glanced down at his plate, and back to her face.

"Squithen, I apologize for suggesting that maybe you aren't sensible," he said, absolutely flat-voiced.

Squithy felt Klay shift beside her, heard Rusko's boot scrape against the deck, and Falmer take a sharp breath. She held up her hand, keeping her eyes on Susrim.

"Apology accepted," she said.

There was another bit of silence before Tranh gave her a smile.

"Makes my job easier. 'Preciate it, Squith."

"You're welcome, Tranh," she said, and heard Rusko not-laugh again.

"So, where we are," Tranh said, "is we're waiting for news of Dulsey's rendezvous point. After we transfer the alt-crew we're loaning her, we'll be heading for Meldyne and the trade fair. We got some cargo, but I don't expect it to do much where we're going. We do have skills we can offer, and I want you all to review what you can do, once we dock."

Falmer's face lit at that. "Big conference and fair, they'll be wantin' cooks and prep staff. I'll offer myself to catering when we get in."

"Good idea," Tranh said, and looked around the table. "Rest of you, think on it, and when you got something, tell Klay, so he can add it to our packet.

"And, now..." He pushed back from the table and stood.

"I think we're done here. Glad we could all meet and go over these things in person."

THREE

KLAY WAS LATE, BUT SQUITHY DIDN'T WORRY THAT HE'D forgotten his promise to come talk with her when his shift was done. She didn't start counting, either. If she checked the tray of snacks and the pitcher of ice cold water she'd put in the middle of her desk three times, that was, according to the norbears who were keeping her company in her head, only a reasonable precaution. She'd brought food for sharing, and it was important to be sure that it hadn't been eaten or snuck away.

Exactly who could eat or sneak the tray away out of Squithy's own quarters while she was there, she didn't ask, just being grateful for the company.

Which reminded her that pretty soon she wasn't going to *want* norbear company.

Carefully, she formed a picture of Klay sitting against the door to the norbear area, being quiet, quiet, not listening, *quiet*.

A ripple of amusement greeted this, and a picture of two norbears snuggled in a grassy nest, lazily feeding tender leaves to each other.

Squithy felt her cheeks heat.

"We just want to talk," she said, aloud. "In private.

261

You wanted to talk in private when you were deciding who was going to go—"

She was interrupted by the wrist-patting sensation, accompanied by a feel of fur and comfortable drowsiness, before the presence of norbears inside her head was—gone.

The door buzzed, which meant that somebody—that Klay!—had put his hand over the plate and was asking if she would let him in.

She crossed the cabin to do just that.

The first thing they did was laugh, because Klay had brought snacks, too, and a bottle of the citrus juice that was her favorite.

"Just like norbears," Squithy said, delighted. "Feeding each other!"

"No higher praise," Klay said, not *quite* in the tone he used when he meant the opposite of what he said, but not quite delighted either.

"I think it's a good system," Squithy said. "I feed you, and you feed me. Nobody goes hungry."

"Something to that," Klay said, looking up from the tray where he'd found room for the things he'd brought. "Speaking of norbears, where are they?"

"They promised to let us be private," Squithy said, and met his eyes. "Though they might just have promised to be very quiet."

"Well, they're doing a good job of being quiet," he said, and she could feel him *listening* inside his head. "I don't hear a thing. You?"

She shook her head. "It feels . . . empty."

He gave her a quick look.

"You mind?"

"No," she said. "It's just—different than it's been. I like having…room. And we did want to talk, just us, didn't we?"

"We did," Klay said with a grin. "Glass of juice?"

"Yes!" she said, and he filled a glass for each of them.

Squithy looked around her cabin. Some ships had the space for an all-purpose room, where crew could meet, or play games, or talk over private things, like her and Klay were setting up to do now. *Dulcimer* didn't have that kind of room, which was why Tranh's quarters doubled as his office, and if crew wanted to be private with crew, they decided between them who would be host.

After the crew meeting, Klay had asked specifically if he could visit her in her cabin, and she'd—she'd liked that he'd given her the decision to say yes, or to say that they could talk in the galley.

The galley was less private and open to people coming through for a snack or some 'toot, not meaning to interrupt, but interrupting, anyway.

And if there was going to be more kissing, Squithy definitely didn't want to be interrupted.

It did mean that they were a little cramped, and there was only one chair, but they could sit on the bunk.

She took her glass of juice.

"Thank you."

"Glad to oblige," Klay said, sipping from his glass. Squithy sipped from hers, remembering Dulsey's lesson about social rules.

"I'm glad we trust each other," she said, and Klay looked surprised, then pleased.

"I'm glad we trust each other, too," he said. "Bunk or chair?"

"Bunk," she said, and sat down. Klay nodded, and pulled the chair closer before he sat down, their knees almost touching.

It was an awkward distance for kissing, Squithy thought. But, then, they'd want to have some snacks first, and talk, share news—oh!

"I was on clean-up after the meeting," she said, "and Uncle Rusko came in. He had the results from the aptitude tests I did, and he says I can start in studying pilot math, if I want to."

Klay smiled at her.

"Do you want to?"

"Yes!"

"That's enthusiastic," he said. "That's good, because the math gets hard, as any pilot'll tell you."

"But not *too* hard."

He frowned a little.

"For some people, it gets too hard. It's a specialization, and not everybody's head is good for it. And some other people, their heads can only hold so much."

Squithy nodded.

"That's all right," she said, sipping juice. "I want to go as far as I can. Those equations you showed me—they were so pretty and they made so much sense! I want to learn more."

"Tell Rusko that?"

"I did, and he said he'd look out a dummy board and the first level learning modules for me."

"You need help, you can come to me," Klay said. "I'm closer to Level One than Rusko is."

"Thank you, Klay," said Squithy.

"No thanks involved. I'm proud to help."

He sipped his juice, and looked at her seriously.

"Speaking of proud, I was just that to hear you give Susrim some of his own."

Squithy bit her lip.

"I thought, after, that maybe I shouldn't've spoke so hard. Susrim's been through a scary thing, and—"

"And," Klay interrupted, "he's been pushing at limits since way before that! He's been after getting rid of the norbears since first he saw one; he *don't* listen to the fact that, whatever they are, they ain't *animals*, and that's aside him shoving his work onto Falmer, and refusing to see that you're up a grade—at least a grade!—and that you're not going back to permanent Stinks, and—well, what you said. He doesn't see you as a person."

"No, he doesn't," Squithy agreed. She took a drink of juice.

"You know what made me really mad? That he tried to trick me into counting."

"I saw that," Klay said, real quiet. "Thought about reaching over and thumping his—"

He paused, but Squithy had caught it, too—the feel of norbears listening close. Or, she thought, nor*bear*.

"Mitsy," she said sternly, "you *promised*. This is *our* time—me and Klay."

The sensation she received was something like a blush—then Mitsy was gone. Or at least quiet again.

Klay tipped his head.

"Think we're alone?"

Squithy considered the inside of her head.

"I *think* so," she said.

"Good," said Klay, taking her glass out of her hands, and reaching a long arm to put both on the desk with the tray. He moved over from the chair to sit beside her on the bunk.

"Now, there was something I thought we might practice before we get to the snacks."

Squithy smiled, and leaned close, putting her lips against his.

It was, she thought, a pretty good kiss; they were both breathless when it was done, and Klay was outright grinning.

"I take it you agree. Mind if we try again?"

"No," Squithy said, and her voice was a little shaky, but that was all right, and then she didn't have to worry about that, or about anything, because Klay was kissing her again.

They were both warm with practice, but Klay had called them a rest time, and served them out some snacks and cold water. They sat on the bunk, knee pressing against knee. Squithy felt like her whole body was smiling. Klay was smiling, and she wondered if he felt that way, too.

"Don't wanna rush," he said. "Just like piloting, you go slow, and you learn the base 'quations so hard you never have to worry about getting them wrong. You move on to the next level when the foundations are firm."

Squithy nodded. "You work that out yourself?" she asked, and was willing to credit Klay with wisdom in all things.

He looked startled.

"Me? No, my cousin Vilma, she told me that." He took a bite of dried fruit bar, and chewed, frowning at a place on the bunk near his knee. "She was senior to me, and my piloting tutor, too."

He looked up.

"Listen, Squith, I just thought. We need to work out a way we're on the same shifts, mostly."

"So we can practice?"

"Definitely so we can practice, but so I'm nearby to help you with your study if you happen to need me."

He frowned at the bunk again.

"That's gonna take some finagling, on account Rusko and Tranh want to be overlapping, and we don't want the pilots stretched too thin..."

"I'm on as back-up to Susrim," Squithy said, and stopped. "That's gonna be ... tricky."

"You remember what Tranh told you—Susrim gets mad or pushy, you tell the captain, and he'll sort it out."

"Yes," said Squithy, and sighed. "Still, that's my schedule right there. Unless Falmer's study-shifts move..."

"Might be the answer right there—talking easiest and cleaner. I'm not hearing Falmer say anything about when she studies, just so she's studying." He drank some water. "I'll bring it up with Rusko."

Squithy ate the rest of her fruit bar, drank her water and sighed.

"Done?" Klay asked, and she nodded.

"I'd like to practice a little more," she said.

"That sounds like a good idea," Klay said, slow and thoughtful. He put the glasses and the plates on the desk and turned back to her. "I'm wondering though, Squith, how you might feel about this—"

He leaned over and put his lips on the edge of her ear. Squithy shivered.

"I like it," she whispered, and he did it again.

FOUR

"RENDEZVOUS POINT APPROACHING," KLAY'S VOICE WAS calm and serious over the all-ship. It made Squithy feel better even in the midst of norbear wrangling.

"Reviewing protocol." That was Tranh. "We will make rendezvous, and match. Once we're stable, Dulsey will deploy her tube. We'll connect at cargo door V6, trade air, then move the cases. How many cases is that, Squith?"

She looked up at the ceiling speaker, inclined to feel a little irritable, but, there. It was check-check-check, and that was normal. It was—not *risky*, like Klay had told her, but a *picky* maneuver, with lots of little pieces that had to fit together and *stay* together until the transfer was made. Timing was important, and the piece she was in charge of—moving the crates of feed, and the crate of norbears, to cargo door V6, into the tube and across to Dulsey—that was a big, important piece.

"We got three cases of mixed bales," she said, answering the captain's question. "An' one case of norbears. Four cases total, moving quick as we can without stretching the tube."

Susrim would be moving the three cases of bales to the tube via the minilift, and they'd go across first.

The case of norbears, that was her big problem right now. The seven bold scouts who were to transfer to Dulsey saw no reason for a case. They could walk, in fact they *would* walk. Cases were all very well and good for *food*, but a case would not do for the norbears setting off on the grandest adventure that ever any norbear had ever had...that they knew of, Bebyear admitted, in a whispered under-thought.

That thought was taken and shared excitedly, because that was *exactly* what the bold far-traveling scouts were seeking on their adventure! New contacts, wider connections, more knowledge. They would not start by being afraid!

It was all, Squithy thought, a little much, especially after Mitsy and Ditsy's rebellion when she showed them their new quarters.

Senior crew had decided that it would be a good thing to have the hold the norbears had been occupying put back to its original function. Mitsy and Ditsy being considerably less norbear than the whole pod, and there currently being no littles to care for, senior crew had decided to reassign alt-crew to the nursery cabin.

They were *not*, Ditsy and Mitsy allowed her to know, babies; they were every bit as bold and as brave as those scouts who had chosen to travel aside, and they would remain in the proper location for bold scouts.

She had countered that the new location was situated nearer to the pantry and the rest of crew quarters, which was proper for alt-crew, and nowhere casual visitors, or inspectors, were likely to venture.

Mitsy and Ditsy, came the counter, were not afraid.

This was accompanied by the picture of Klay facing the *tobor*.

"Senior crew," Squithy said then, "made the decision. You're alt-crew. Senior crew *says*, reg'lar and alt-crew *does*. That's how it is on any Looper ship I ever heard about, and the big traders, too. Neither one of you is captain yet, nor I'm not. We got our orders, is what I'm saying."

That had given them pause. While the inside of her head was still quiet, she added, "Senior crew knows you're big and you were there when Klay was brave. Senior crew knows *personal* that it's better not to have to be brave so hard all the time. There's nothing wrong with being safe, when you can be. Klay told me he still has bad dreams about being stuck to that tree."

She felt them considering that, and something under it, like the other norbears, who had been listening, but not participating in the argument, were whispering advice.

Mitsy sent a picture of the three of them sitting in the new quarters, sharing thoughts, and Squithy agreed, adding the suggestion that they go to the new quarters now, so they wouldn't get hurt during the transfer, and built up a picture of the minilift, with three cases in its claw.

More agreement, and they were gone, not offering anything like a good-bye for the norbears who were going. Well, Squithy thought; they'd done all that, when they were deciding.

With Mitsy and Ditsy gone, she had turned to explaining that norbears would cross to Dulsey in a case.

Senior crew hadn't hauled any weight in that argument like it had with Mitsy and Ditsy, and Squithy had produced the matter of timing, of norbears strolling down the tube suddenly bounced around, as if the orientation between the two ships slipped. She'd read up about tube-links and why were they done, and what could go wrong, and all the whys of doing or not, after Dulsey had sent them the coords for rendezvous, instead of the name of a port where the exchange could take place. A lot of things could go wrong with a transport tube, even when everybody was being careful. That's why timing was important.

Her image caught the norbears, who shared it among themselves, examining it from various angles. Someone—possibly Ebling—offered an image of a norbear Squithy had never seen before, with a front paw hanging at a bad angle, like it was broken.

That produced consternation, and a clear statement from Oki, backed by Holdhand and Silver, that it was hard for even the bravest scout to be bold if their paw was useless.

Squithy grabbed that opportunity, building an image of the crate she had made ready for norbears, lined with shock pads, and soft grasses, and a safety net stretched over it all, so that there would be no chance of norbears spilling out and being hurt, even if the tube did misbehave.

Oki took that image, and added in their group of seven, snugged down together among the soft grasses, sharing dreams until Dulsey pulled the safety net off, and smiled.

There was a pause as they shared this series of

images among themselves. Squithy waited, and—she felt them reach an agreement.

She smiled.

"I'm glad you're going to be safe," she said, sending feelings of approval and relief to the group.

Then, she took a breath and began to explain about timing.

"Firm connect, air pressure good, moderate flow down to *Alkovo Alvokita*." Klay's voice came over the all-ship, calm, and that not only made Squithy feel better, but it made the norbears feel better, too.

"Now, Susrim," said Rusko.

Squithy swallowed. Timing, she told herself.

The norbears were in their crate, snuggled down into the grass in a furry knot. She could feel them assuring each other that they were all brave scouts, even as the elders tucked the youngers into the center of the knot. Ebling and Holdhand were crooning out-loud, Bebyear making a thought-echo. Squithy felt Oki with her, as she checked the netting for the third time, and made sure the crate was firm on the skis, and the skis were firm in the tracks.

Everything checked; everything was good. There would, she told herself, be no problems with the transfer. Klay and Rusko were good pilots; Dulsey was a good pilot. They all three knew their numbers, and were steady at their boards. All she needed to do was to keep to the timing.

She felt a gentle pat inside her head, and smiled as she sent the same back to Oki.

"It's time, Squithy," Rusko said. "Alt-crew to the exchange tube."

"Yes," Squithy said, and pushed. The crate slid forward, slick and quick along the track in the decking, and they were on their way to cargo door V6.

The minilift was in the loading zone, half across the cargo door, ready lights blinking, but Squithy didn't see Susrim. She didn't see the three cargo boxes of norbear food, either, so he must have sent them down the tube already, and—just left the lift while *Alkovo Alvokita*'s crew cleared the tube on their end. That was all right, Squithy thought. In fact, it was better than if he'd stayed to—help, or make sure all the norbears who were going were in the crate.

Perhaps she should wait until *Alkovo Alvokita* finished moving the food and could receive, but the angle wasn't that steep, and waiting here wasn't helping her or the norbears.

And besides, she heard Klay's patient voice say "three minutes" across the all-call. She took a breath, felt another mental pat, and said, "Here we are, brave scouts, on the edge of your adventure."

"Three minutes" . . . she thought—right, Tranh had figured they'd only have to maintain the link for four or five minutes, the fewer better.

She got the crate to the edge, disengaged the skis, and pushed.

The crate slid over into the tunnel and began to slide toward the other end, which was *down*, according to local gravity. The slide didn't make much noise and if the norbears did, she didn't hear it over the ruffle air from *Dulcimer* made against her ears as it tried to equalize some change behind her.

The timing said that she should leave the area now,

but she stayed, watching the crate moving, *pushing* with her mind—pushing *good luck* and *norbears be good* and *come home soon*.

She thought she felt an echo, and then the crate reached the other end, and vanished as quick hands pulled it into Dulsey's ship. Safe.

Squithy sighed—and heard the deck ringing under rapid footsteps. She turned—and here came Susrim, carrying a large bag in one hand, his face set.

"Out of my way!" he snapped, and shoved on, slamming her against the seal. Inside her head, she saw a *tobor*, the touch familiar and—

"No! Mitsy and Ditsy are alt-crew! They're staying with us!"

"The animals have got to go—all of them!" Susrim yelled, and threw the sack into the tube.

It hit and rolled; Squithy felt pain in her leg and jumped—into the tube, down to the sack, which wasn't heavy enough to keep on rolling, though it was wriggling energetically. The sensation of danger, and the pain in her leg increased. She grabbed the bag, sending a picture of Klay and the *tobor* dead. She turned back toward *Dulcimer*, and there was Susrim filling the door using the bulk of the minilift as a deterrent to letting her back in with the bag.

"Don't you bring those things back!" he screamed, then hit a button on the lift, making it rotate and swing toward her.

Squithy ducked, rolling the bag past him, low and gentle, taking the shove on her shoulder while she was still on the tubeway, pushing with her legs, trying to move Susrim back so she could get in past the lift and the tube lock.

The lift whined briefly as he twisted a control and there was a thud, and a screech of some material tearing or straining and she pushed harder. Because the tube was shaking and that wasn't right, but her push wasn't strong enough because she was pushing *up*, and Susrim pushed back, pushing *down* with his hand while the lift rotated, knocking her off her feet, and the tube was shaking bad.

She was rolling and the tube was stretched and swinging, and she tried to grab on, to stop, to—

The tube flexed, hard. Squithy smacked against the sides, or the floor, or the ceiling.

The last thing she saw was the cargo door closing.

. . . . ❖ . . . .

Susrim spun, meaning to kick the sack back into the tube.

"Don't you even think about it!" Falmer was holding the two furry monsters against her chest, the sack crumpled on the decking at her feet.

"What in space is the matter with you?" Falmer shouted. "Captain says these ones are crew! You all about throwing crew off the ship now, Susrim? What—"

She stopped, her face going blank, her eyes distant, and that was *them*, Susrim *knew* it, them getting into her head and changing her thoughts!

He lunged; Falmer turned, and brought her knee up like she was fighting off a dock bully.

Susrim folded onto the deck.

"Emergency!" Falmer yelled. "Squithy—I dunno where Squithy is; cargo door sealed. Susrim incapable and alt-crew hurt! I think."

"Tube holding," Rusko said, sounding just as stupid

calm as he always did, Susrim thought, leaning against the wall and gasping. "Tranh's on comm with Dulsey... all received safe, says Dulsey."

"Where's Squithy?" Falmer demanded. "I—"

"Dulsey has Squithy," Rusko said. "Reports minor damage, and mad as fire. Auto-release tube; Dulsey's taking it in."

There was a pause.

"Squithy'll be traveling with Dulsey and the norbears," Tranh said. "Dulsey suggests that'll be the case until we can guarantee a safe ship for all crew."

"Better off without all of 'em," Susrim wheezed, and heaved to his feet.

"Was that Susrim?" Tranh said.

"What if it is?" he snarled. "*Captain.*"

"Falmer, get you and alt-crew to the galley, now!" Tranh said sharply. "Susrim, you're confined to quarters. You know the way, or you need an escort?"

Falmer was gone in a flurry of rapid footsteps.

Susrim sagged against the wall, then straightened. So, two of the monsters were still on-board, that was bad. But Squithy and most of the monsters were gone—and that was good. Tranh was coming the stern captain. Confined to quarters, was he? Well, the captain'd see real quick that the ship needed Susrim.

"I know the way to my own quarters," he snarled.

"Then get there. Report in to me in two minutes."

That was none-too-generous, now was it?

Susrim pushed away from the wall and shuffled into a run.

"Separation clean," Klay said, cool and firm. Rusko, sitting second board, kept his voice low and easy.

"Confirm clean separation."

"Course in. Locked. Copilot starts count and takes the board."

"Course in, confirm. Locked, confirm. Transfer, confirm. Count starting now—*one*."

"Pilot requests relief, cap'n," Klay said, calm voice given the lie by the storm on his face.

"Pilot relief granted. Take a walk, Klay."

"I'm going to kill him," Klay said, still calm.

"That you are not," Tranh said. "Straight opposed to onboard rules, killing a shipmate. I see you're mad, so I'll remind you what happens next, *after* you take a walk, or hit some exercise, and we get us into Jump. Senior crew reviews the vid from the camera on V6 to satisfy ourselves on the facts. Then, we talk to Falmer, and alt-crew—what's their names?"

"Mitsy and Ditsy," Klay said automatically.

"Right then, crewpersons Mitsy and Ditsy, we talk with them. We talk with Susrim, and then we deal out discipline. Right?"

"Right," Klay said, grimly.

"Now you're gonna go exercise, get a snack, maybe a lay-down. Squithy and the loan-crew're all with Dulsey, reported largely intact. Susrim's got a lot to answer for, I'm not saying he don't. But we're a reg'lar ship and we got protocols. Tell me yeah."

Klay sighed, and closed his eyes.

"Yeah," he said, sounding tired, which Tranh didn't blame him for that.

"Shift changes, then, Pilot. Go get yourself straightened out."

Another sigh, this one deeper than the first. Klay nodded—"Cap'n"—and left the tower.

Tranh fetched up a sigh of his own, slid into the vacant chair, made the adjustments, and opened the board.

"Got scans and comm, Pilot," he told Rusko.

"Course set in," Rusko told him. "Ten minutes to Jump." He turned his head and gave Tranh a grin. "Good job talking Klay down. I was half-inclined to let him get on it, myself."

"Me, too," said Tranh. "Reg'lar, though, Rusko. Gotta stay reg'lar."

"I agree," said Rusko, and went back to his board.

· · · ·✦· · · ·

Squithy woke up to a party in her head.

In short order, she was a bold scout who had thrust herself between norbears and a disturbing image that might have been a melding of Susrim and the *tobor*. More! She had joined the bold band of scouts on their side-trip—and here she was swamped with a host of faces—Oki, Ebling, Silver, Synbe, Bebyear, Holdhand, Rutaren—and Dulsey, who came with her own series of images, of places, and faces, and—

"Stop!" Squithy said, and sent an image of quiet norbears curled together in the sweet grasses. "I have to think."

The party got less noisy, which wasn't as much of a relief as it might've been, because in the quiet she noticed that she had a headache. There was still an undercurrent of excitement and purpose and celebration weaving between her own thoughts, which were increasingly worrisome.

Susrim had thrown Mitsy and Ditsy into the tube! He'd hurt them! And she'd run out to get them back, feeling the pain in her leg, and Susrim pushed her, and the door sealed, and the tube—the tube—

Oki sent the patting-on-the-wrist feel, and Squithy remembered to breathe.

"Ah, good," a familiar voice said nearby. "I was hoping the sudden jubilation was because you were awake again. How do you feel, Squithy?"

"I have a headache," she said, opening her eyes to Dulsey's face. "My leg—no, that was Ditsy!"

She sat up suddenly, and gasped when bruises protested.

"Susrim pushed me," she said. "I have to go back right now! He'll hurt them!"

Dulsey raised her hands.

"I have been in touch with Tranh, and he assures me that Mitsy and Ditsy are with Falmer and quite safe. Susrim is confined to quarters. Tranh particularly asked me to tell you that ship's rules would be followed, and that *Dulcimer* is a regular ship. He has agreed that you will be traveling with me and the rest of the bold scouts until it is time to return."

"But, I—I was going to be having another bold adventure," Squithy said. "I was starting to get studied on piloting, and Klay—" She foundered, not exactly sure how she could explain Klay, and the practice they'd been planning.

"Klay sent a private message," Dulsey said slowly. "I sent it to the comm in your quarters. How far along are you, on pilot study?"

Squithy felt her cheeks heat.

"Uncle Rusko got me set up with a dummy board and I had Level One loaded up to start. After we made the transfer, I had a couple hours to study before I had to back up Susrim at din—"

She stopped again and stared at Dulsey, seeing

Susrim, how mad he'd been, and he'd pushed her hard—hard enough to hurt. And Tranh said ship's rules would be followed. She felt the wrist-pat, and Oki's presence inside her head.

She looked at Dulsey.

"That was bad, what Susrim did," she said. "All of it. If Tranh's gonna follow ship's rules, Susrim—he could be expelled. From *Dulcimer*."

"Then that is Susrim's business," Dulsey said, briskly. "Are you hungry?"

Squithy considered that. "Yes," she admitted.

"And your headache?"

Squithy frowned. "A little less, I think."

Dulsey glanced over Squithy's shoulder, and she turned to see what was behind her. It was a status board of some kind; she frowned at the lights.

"This is a medical status board. The yellows here, here—and here"—She pointed to each—"suggest that your blood sugar is low, which sometimes causes headaches." She smiled. "That means we should find you a snack before I take you to your quarters so you can clean up and get settled. There will be a crew meeting a little later, where you and the norbears will be introduced. We have the complete piloting study modules, and several dummy boards, so you'll be able to continue your studies."

Squithy bit her lip.

"I—might need help," she said slowly.

Dulsey nodded.

"We all need help, from time to time. I'll see who of the piloting crew wants to sit second for you on study time."

Squithy smiled.

"You think of everything," she said, but to her surprise Dulsey didn't smile back.

"No," she said, sounding grim. "I don't."

· · ·✻· · ·

Senior crew had reviewed the vid. Senior crew was, truth said, feeling more than a little grim about what they'd seen. Just on the vid alone, it was clear what had to happen, but there was ship's rules right there on the tablet in the middle of the table, so they could refer to what had to happen next, and not rely on their own heads, hot as they might presently be.

"Now we talk to such affected crew as we have access to," Tranh said, after everybody'd gotten a refresh on their drinks. "Klay, you mind bringing the alt-crew up? You'll have to interpret for Rusko and me, but I got a couple questions I'd like to put."

"Yes, Captain," Klay said, and brought two subdued members of the alt-crew to the galley, where they sat tall on their haunches, rumps touching, facing the senior crew with, Klay had to admit, a fair show of serious dignity.

"I want to know how it came about that they were in that sack," Tranh said, and glanced at Klay. "Can you make that question clear to them?"

"No need," Klay said, as his head started to fill with images. He braced himself for an onslaught, but this—this was an orderly progression, laid out as neat and as clear as piloting 'quation. He heard Rusko make a sort of humming noise when they hit a point, though from Tranh there was nothing at all.

The sequence ended, and Klay offered the image

of quiet norbears sitting on the table, which was met with firm agreement.

Klay sighed and leaned back in his chair.

"They say Squithy told them to go to new quarters and settle in, which they did do. They had a little something to eat from supplies on hand, and curled up to dream together."

Klay picked up his mug and drank some 'toot.

"They waked up when the door come open. That quick they knew it was Susrim—" He broke off to meet Tranh's eyes. "They recognize us by our thought patterns, I'd guess you'd say. They can hear Susrim fine, even though he can't hear them."

Tranh blinked as the implications of that settled in, then he nodded.

"Good to know. What else do they say?"

"Well, they were startled out of a nice dream, and before they could gather themselves, there was the bag over them, and they were kicked in, none-too-gentle is what I've got, and then they were caught and being carried, jostling and not able to grab hold of anything, and they were afraid of the tone of Susrim's thoughts. They could tell he was running toward Squithy, and figured she'd—intervene."

He stopped again, and Rusko said, quiet-like, "Which she did."

"Yeah, they're—sorry. I'm getting that they want it on record that they should've helped, somehow, and been bolder, braver. It wasn't never in their heads to get Squithy hurt."

"Not their fault, I think," Tranh said, bending a stern look on the pair of 'em. "Everybody on this ship needs to feel safe enough to sleep on their off-shift without worrying they're gonna be snatched outta their bed and thrown off."

He looked to Klay.

"They all right? Are they hurt from rough handling, is what I mean?"

Klay felt a twinge on his leg, and looked to Tranh.

"Ditsy's got a bruised back leg, from when they hit the deck. It's being sold as minor, which I think it is."

"Right." Tranh looked at the norbears again and nodded.

"Tell 'em if that bruise gets worse, to report it, and we'll do what we can to make it right. That's their duty. We need our crew whole and able. Tell 'em, too, that I thank 'em for being open with me, and I'm set on making *Dulcimer* safe for everybody ships on her."

The norbears got that loud and clear, and Klay was able to convey their thanks for the opportunity to talk to the captain about the situation.

"Okay, there's nothing else," said Tranh. "Take 'em back to their quarters, please, Klay, and bring Falmer along when you come back."

"How's your knee?" Rusko asked, when Falmer'd come in and gotten settled across the table with a mug of 'toot to keep her company.

She blinked at Rusko. "My knee?"

"We watched the vid," Rusko explained. "Didn't look like you held back when you dropped Susrim. Want to be sure you didn't bruise yourself."

She blinked again, then grinned, halfway.

"My knee's fine, thank you. I—prolly I shouldn't've done it. Ma taught me, and she said I shouldn't never do it to anybody I knew, but Susrim—" she took a deep breath.

"He was scary, just then. I was scared, and the two of 'em were scared, and all I was doing was remembering that beast where we found 'em. The one Klay killed."

"You were effective and efficient," Tranh said. "Like Rusko said, we watched the vid, but it left us with some questions. F'rinstance—why were you at the cargo door?"

"T'say honest, I'd hit a point in the study module where wasn't none of nutrient load and balance getting through. Might as well've been pilot's math. So I decided to go for a walk, clear my brain."

She shook her head.

"Proof enough my brain needed clearing. I forgot all about how vee-six was gonna be busy with the tube transfer, and I walked right into a mess."

"It was good you happened by," Tranh told her. "Though I'm bound to tell you to pay closer attention, goin' forward."

"Will do," Falmer said, and leaned forward a little. "We hear anything from Squith? She okay? We get a port 'change for her, or do we gotta do another tube?"

"Squithy's staying with Dulsey for the foreseeable," Tranh said. "She'll be chief norbear wrangler."

"Couldn't do better," Falmer said, "she's real good with 'em. But if Susrim hit her or—"

"Some scrapes and bruises," Rusko said gently, "but willing to accept an adventure is the last report we had."

Falmer took a minute, sipped her 'toot, and finally nodded.

"Anything else?" she asked Tranh.

"There is. With Squithy off on a side-tour, and Susrim confined to quarters, we're short. I'm gonna have to pull you into full chef duties, all meals. That'll be a line adjustment, 'course."

Klay thought Tranh'd added that to ease Falmer's natural resistance to being pulled off her studies, but it looked to him like he coulda done without. Falmer grinned, wide and pleased.

"Now, wasn't I just thinkin' that I wanted to be back in the kitchen and trying out some of these notions I been studying! That'll be just fine, Tranh. Thank you."

"No problem. We'll be wanting a meal in a while, but right now I'm going to ask you to return to quarters and stay 'til all's clear. We need to talk to Susrim, now."

"Expulsion?" Susrim sneered, slouched in his chair like he didn't care about anything they'd said to him about the seriousness of his actions, and read him out the relevant parts of the ship rules. "You can't throw me off this ship, Tranh. I'm a stakeholder."

"That's right," Tranh said. "An' you got a contract. Contract can be revoked, which I'm doin' that now. You'll find a copy of the document on your screen, signed by senior crew. Stakeholder can still be set off, for violation of rules, so long's the stake's paid over at the time of separation. We'll be separating at Meldyne Station. You'll get your pay then. I'll send you an accountin' before we dock."

Susrim leaned forward, face set.

"You can't do this, Tranh."

"You're wrong," Tranh told him. "You're confined to quarters 'til we dock at Meldyne. You'll have your goods packed in good order and ready to be offloaded, along with yourself. That will be the ship's first order of bidness on Meldyne."

Susrim's face was ashy.

"You can't—" he began again, and stopped when Rusko shoved his chair back, noisily.

"Are we done here, Captain?" he asked.

Tranh nodded.

"We are."

"Then I will escort Susrim to his quarters and make sure the door is locked," Rusko said. He rose and went around the table to Susrim's side.

"You can walk or I can drag you," he said pleasantly. "And I *can* drag you, Susrim. Choose."

Susrim stared up at him, looked like he thought he was going to say something—and thought better of it.

He rose and left the galley without a backward look.

THE TRADER

＊＊＊＊＊※＊＊＊＊＊

Meldyne Exposition Central Hall
Level 15, Rim Room 44

THE TROOPER

ONE

"YES, TRADER, I APPRECIATE YOUR CONCERN. IN FACT that's why I'm here—we're trying to make sure that no one is surprised by what the Dust does. Studies and verified reports *have* shown that the larger ships have a harder time getting a perfect Jump arrival—or even *any* Jump arrival. Looks like that's the RMS graviton thing showing up when it comes to localizing—in effect there's a sphere of exclusion caused by the Dust's density.

"If your Struven units can't make the space identical, there's no way the ship can arrive, and smaller spaces—that's what happens when less energetic ships are seeking a locale—the smaller space and lower mass work—mass and energy equivalencies hold, of course—it means that this is not something the Seventeen Worlds are *imposing* on you, these are the laws of physics. If the ship can't create local identity, it can't arrive. *The Dust* makes it happen, the mass that's intruding into the systems, not trade rules."

The trader's accent argued for a down-arm upbringing, and she'd been upfront about doing most of her dealing in her family's fourteen-system Loop for the last fifteen Standards, and the family running the

Loop for sixty Standards. Fourteen systems, each no more than an eight-day Jump from next in the Loop, many of the goods pre-ordered for years ahead. A comfortable life that could be, but now—well, they'd upgraded the ship twelve Standards ago to the latest pods and power, and upgraded by two mounts, which might have to stay empty on half the runs if the mass index they were examining as the limit held true.

While Jethri could see a couple of potential ways of routing things that might work better for her, things that ought to be available in a routine scheduling program if she could see her way past Grandma's 'rangements—that wasn't what he was here for, *this* time. There were route upkeep workshops scheduled, and people with information to hand and to share. He needed to be able to concentrate on the whole story and not individuals if he could—what he needed were allies for the congress and *Envidaria,* not petitioners seeking personal relief.

This was the first day of the pre-congress, and Jethri was on the *Envidaria* table in the Small Exhibition Hall, directly across from the Main Exhibition Hall, where the trade fair was in full swing.

Jethri had thought the pre-pre-congress had been filled up and busy—and it had been, the difference being that then he had been learning everything he needed to know—or as near as possible—in order to do—this.

Sell the *Envidaria.*

It had been agreed for a long time that Jethri was the *Envidaria*'s best face; best voice. The original *Envidaria* had been his father's work, after all, and Jethri was responsible for setting it free on the trade lanes.

That had been stressful on the nerves, and building long-distance ties with the Seventeen Worlds Initiative long-distance had been a challenge. But this—

This was exhausting in a way that mere trade wasn't.

The pre-congress only lasted four days, and Jethri, at mid-shift on his first day, wasn't absolutely certain he was going to survive it.

It helped that Freza was back at the table now. She'd been absent from his orbit much of the day, busy with a series of meet-ups with TerraTrade committee members just coming in. The Seventeen Worlds Initiative ran on Freza-power, of that Jethri was convinced. Brabham might know everything and everybody, but it was Freza scheduled it all, and kept three meetings from happening at the same time.

The traffic at his table had been constant since before the exhibit hall had properly opened, and he hadn't had lunch. He'd grabbed two quick breaks, but even those had been a kind of orbital nightmare of recognition where, *his* face being familiar, the person reaching out to him acted like they'd known each other for years. The name tags helped, and he recognized some ship and company logos, but the sheer numbers of complete and semi-complete strangers surpassed anything he'd dealt with—including the receptions he'd attended during his first days as Master ven'Deelin's 'prentice.

Freza leaned forward as he managed to promise a follow up to the down-arm trader, this by giving her Bry Sen's name as a pilot who could better explain the situation to her, or to her pilot, if need be. He'd already ruthlessly given out other names, including Freza herself, and Chiv, not to mention Brabham, for similar help at the congress and soon he'd need to be reaching into the large pool of DeNobli cousins of which Chiv was only the first. Freza'd mentioned names, and now, on her suggestion, he'd begun asking the Looper arrivals for the names of their Loops and home ports...

"Did I hear you say 'Paitor' to the trio before your last?" Freza asked, low voiced, which pleased him very much since she'd had to bend in close and quiet, which showed off her ear and cheek as well as shared her scent.

He pilot-signed acknowledgment and she smiled, giving him time to relax a little before he explained. "First thing they did was claim fifth cousins with a removal, through Paitor, and expecting to see him—but I explained they'll have to catch him on the adjusted Loop the *Market*'s on—if he don't know by the time he sees him he'll get a decent answer from him or Khat, and if he does know by then he'll be all full of family about seeing me, so there's that!"

Freza glanced over her shoulder. "Looks like you got nobody in line. How 'bout a snack or a drink?"

He nodded, resisting the urge to ask for a glass of wine or a cup of coffee, both of which might be much too easy to overdo given the rush.

"How about some 'mite?" he said, remembering the stand he'd passed in the food court on his way to this room. "And some kind of a cheese crisp—I think I saw a booth. I'd love a maize button but..."

Freza nodded and straightened away from him, pointing to someone across the room, waving *come here*—

And here came Chiv, with a warm smile especially

for Freza, when he leaned in close. Maybe a little *too* close, Jethri thought, which was just proof about needing that 'mite and a minute to think his own thoughts.

"Trader's choice is maize buttons and 'mite on a quick plate," Freza told Chiv. "If Brabham's out, ask him to trip by so Jeth can have a chance to slow down."

Four Chiv signed, and was gone.

"Four?" Jethri said doubtfully, remembering the morning's crowded hallways.

"He said four, it'll be four or less," Freza said with a grin. "Man's a marvel at getting things done."

"Sounds useful to have around," Jethri said, honestly. Freza gave him a nod.

"We're all of us useful to have around, in our different ways."

She patted him on the shoulder, and might've said something else, but her comm buzzed, and she gave him a wry look before taking the call.

Jethri closed his eyes, and thought himself into one of the short-rests ter'Astin had taught him, as a student pilot. *Board rest*, he'd called that class of exercise, and for all they were so short—just a couple minutes, and not anything like sleep—they still produced beneficial effects.

He opened his eyes in time to witness Chiv's return with a cup and a covered tray.

"Row bought," he said, putting these items on the table in front of Jethri. "I've had their 'mite and it's true yeast. The buttons are basic, but I got extra slide, so that'll help."

Jethri grinned. "Thank you, cousin. I believe you're saving a life, here."

"'S'wat cousins do," Chiv answered, grin to grin.

He glanced over his shoulder, but Freza was still on the comm. "Brabham says he'll be scootin' by in a couple minutes. Best hit that 'mite while it's hot, if a cousin can advise."

"Always," Jethri told him, and took a swig from the cup.

He could feel the 'mite boosting energy even as he opened the tray, and picked up a maize button. Chiv'd been right about basic, but they were warm, and the eating of them gave him an excuse to smile and nod at people passing the table, rather than directly engaging.

He'd just finished his last sip of 'mite when Brabham arrived on a scoot, leading a swarm of young Loopers. They were fancy-dressed, excited to be "helping" the elder, though what they were in particular helping *with*, or how they were doing it, escaped Jethri's eye. Still, *he* was pleased to see Brabham, and got up on his feet to do the full greeting.

"So you just remember there, young Taber from *Lantic*," Brabham was saying as he pulled his scoot tight into the table, "this is who else you met at the South Axis Congress and Trade Fair. This right here is Jethri Gobelyn ven'Deelin, and you'll be hearing about him a long time after they forget my name, you watch!"

Taber was a slender youth, skin a little darker than Liaden gold, and already taller than most, with grey eyes and a serious mien.

"*Lantic? Lantic?*" Jethri put his finger to the side of his head like he was pushing a memory button. He grinned. "There! I think my cousin Khat flew *Lantic* one run."

Taber's mouth opened in a gasp, and they rushed

forward, daring to touch Jethri's arm before backing
away. "You're *Khat's* Jethri? She told us all about her
cousin Jeth, and—but it's *you*? I *wish* she'd come
back to us, but they say she's on full schedule now..."

Brabham laughed, and Jethri did. Clearly Khat had
a conquest on *Lantic*!

Brabham turned his scoot in a tight circle, and
his admirers did some hasty stepping so's not to be
bumped, laughter shared freely.

"Right," he said. "Now, I need to talk with my good
friend Jethri Gobelyn ven'Deelin for a little minute,
here. If you wanna hear 'bout the time I got two bad
air tanks from Dinsworld-Two and why that'll never
happen again, just wait on out there in the lobby.
I'll gather you up when I'm done here, and we'll go
down the green park."

The swarm departed, good-natured and excited,
about a dozen filtering into the lobby to wait.

Brabham sighed, and spun his scoot around 'til
he was facing Jethri again. He moved his hand in a
subtle *come here*. Jethri stepped around the table to
stand on one side of the scoot, and there was Freza on
the other. Brabham nodded to each of them, smiling.

"Well, there's someone looking for an uncle, eh,
Jethri?" Brabham said. "Khat's a dozen and half Standards on the wrong side of that one's bed, but hope
and hormones...and hope's always there, ain't it?"

Jethri nodded agreement, watching as Brabham's
smile faded, obeying a second motion that brought
them even closer, while one finger casually pointed
out a few of his followers still in the room.

"What's happening is that we got word that Terra-
Trade's being pushed hard to argue that the timing's

wrong for your *Envidaria*, that it ought to wait another twenty-five Standards so it can be researched all proper and whatnot."

Freza nodded, like this was no news to her. Jethri shook his head.

"Too little and too long," he muttered, and Brabham pulled him closer yet.

"There's word, that's what I know. I got copies of a couple circulating messages; I've got queries from old friends. We got a copy of a general message that's going around asking for ships of certain sizes that need upgrades to check in for discounted work..."

"Discounted?" Jethri said, keeping his voice down. "But the yards ought to be filling up already with refurbs!"

"Know it," the elder agreed, head bobbing up and down so hard that his ride caught a little of the motion. "Who has all that extra capacity, that's what *we* wonder. Be grand if it's out there, but if it is, why ain't we heard before now?"

"Smart yard, making a move?" Jethri offered. "Someone with capacity to build big ships looking to lock in business."

"Could be, but this whole sector's gonna be needing refits as far as we can see. So yeah, if there's someone out to the other side of Liad with the energy to do it, I'd let 'em. But it seems like the same people're offering discounts out of one keyboard, and claiming too soon out the other."

Jethri frowned. "Why would TerraTrade be—"

"In the middle for this?" Brabham flipped both palms up. "Here's my guess. Somebody's trying to break the Loops and family ships in favor of re-crewing point-to-point specials. Strip some of the big ships down as far as they go and cheap-build an outport or two, working with dregs. Take over a couple of the intermediate ports, do breakpod stuff both ways, and run the Loopers out entire. That'll take time and contracts and..."

"And misinformation," said Chiv, who'd quietly joined the circle. "Like the one says ships reporting failed Jumps are bein' paid to break Loops. That the shared broken runs are sims and not real."

Jethri looked hard at Chiv.

"That's a good way to lose ships and people, isn't it? What good..."

Freza shrugged. "If what counts is short term, there's a lot of ways to make money from confusion."

He stared at her.

"Confusion that's killing whole families?"

"That's what we're in this for, Jeth," she murmured.

"Thing is," Brabham said, dragging their attention back to him. "Thing is, there's a new generation that's got more comfortable dealing with Liadens, and the Liadens have been pushing at the edges of our Loops harder and harder. This whole thing with pirates—and I don't mean Yxtrang, but out-and-out *thieves*—they've gotta be selling what they're stealing *somewhere*, right? Who else can swallow up a ship's worth of this and that and move it in a hurry to the other side of the arm? Gotta be some big ships involved. We know your ship's not in it—"

Jethri straightened, and stared down at Brabham, not really paying attention to what his face was doing.

"*Elthoria*," he said, and his voice was so cold, he shivered, "is not a pirate."

"Said that, din't I?" Brabham countered. "Good to have a confirm, though."

"Right." Jethri sighed, glanced up and saw people moving into the room again, a good few of them on course for his table. He looked to Brabham.

"More later," he said, "I'm taking lots of notes, complaints as well as offers of help. We can only have so much strategy without knowing who else is moving on this."

"Right you are," Brabham said with a nod. "We'll talk later; lotsa talking to be done, yet; conference isn't even rightly underway. Word of advice, Jeth?"

"Be grateful," Jethri said, honestly.

Brabham grinned.

"Pace yourself," he said. "This is just the warm-up."

He turned the scoot, and sped away.

Jethri looked at Freza.

"Pace myself," he said.

"It's good advice, Jeth," she told him, half-grinning. "You figure out how to do it, just let me know."

The line had thinned out again, and Jethri was thinking longingly of calling for a shift change before it got thick again. Freza was looking at her tablet, which probably meant he *couldn't* call a halt, but maybe he could at least take a walk.

Right. He put his hands flat on the table, pushed his chair back—

The fractin in his pocket trembled, warming slightly and vibrating to a low pulse beat against his leg.

Freza glanced up, raising the tablet and waggling it lightly.

"Last scheduled person is Riben Ontaus, from the

Volanta Group, but they've sent they're running late down on the exhibit docks—that's where Brabham's talking with a bunch of folks now. Trader Ontaus asks to be granted a couple minutes' grace. Meanwhile, we got somebody else who'd like a short meeting. I think I'll go check on Ontaus in person, it's only a couple decks down. Maybe suggest he'd like to reschedule."

"Reschedule if you can," he told her. "I'm looking for a shift-end. You?"

"Sounds good," she said. "I'll reschedule. Meet you here, or—"

"Come to *Genchi*," he said. "If your boards are clear."

"If they ain't I'll find out why," she told him, and smiled. "*Genchi*, soon's I can."

She turned, looked over her shoulder, and half-grinned—she'd caught him looking. He didn't blush; she had to know by now that he liked to watch her move, but he did obey the slight inclination of her head toward the meet-line...

...where stood Minsha, *Elsvair*'s "advisor," her face serene, holding a well-used, but obviously sealed flatpack of the kind used to carry hardcopy from place to place. She nodded politely, and came to the table, allowing herself to be noted and seated, whereupon she leaned forward to offer him a hand. The edge of an easily palmable device was just visible. The Terran handshake was meant to disguise its passage from her possession into his.

He felt his fractin vibrate as he realized the device was live. He'd held such before, and had gotten easier with doing it. And his fractin, which really *did* appear to have his best interests at heart, seemed easy.

He folded his hands together momentarily, feeling

the shape—a smooth bulging ovoid, with a blunt end that had what might be controls recessed within it. The end was broad enough that the object might stand on it, but what it might actually *be*—he had no idea.

His fractin's warmth diminished slightly, but there were no loud buzzes, no signs that he recognized as warning.

He looked at Minsha and inclined his head. She extracted a sheaf of hardcopy from her pack and passed it over to him.

"A more recent listing of available ordinary trade items that might interest you, Trader. Too, a more recent inventory of our capacities in case you may be looking for trans-shipping opportunities."

With a trader's patience, Jethri looked over the very modest possibilities *Elsvair* offered, noticing that it reported more passengers and crew than one might expect with its pod-capacity. Maybe they were going to break pods by hand at some out of the way location.

He hadn't expected such a low-key presentation with a mystery device having been surreptitiously passed, but she seemed alert to moving people and when the random motions slowed, she inclined slightly from the waist in a seated bow, and tapped the hand she'd passed the object from.

"Trader. It pleases my associates Vally and Malu that I deliver to you an item which you have purchased but which was mistakenly not included in those delivered to you yesterday. They are distraught not to be able to discuss this with you in person but as the port administration has asked them to stay aboard ship for at least the next two Standard days, I myself bring it to you."

Jethri avoided raising his eyebrow, and also avoided asking the obvious question.

"It is kind of you, Trade Advisor Minsha—"

"No, Trader, please, we need no titles mentioned here in public, just Minsha."

She sounded quite firm, so he nodded acceptance.

"Minsha, then. It is kind of you to bring this . . . purchase . . . to me. Are there particulars? Instructions? Guidance? Hints? Are you in danger for bringing it to me, or I, for receiving it?"

Her mouth tightened, as if she considered on a special level, seeking the possibilities . . . and then she brushed her now-empty palm, as if removing crumbs.

"*Danger* is a strong word, Trader, but you see me here, now. You must understand that the item is exactly such as you sought last evening, and exactly such as you thought you had purchased. It is also an item that ought not to be discovered on *Elsvair*, or carried in public by—" here she played with the sounds, as if recalling the names distantly, "Vally or Malu."

Her face brightened. "If *you* carry it, or if your ship has it, it is unlikely to become an issue, since you are the *komercisto* who knows the Dust routes, and you are the man, as we understand it, who sells things to the Uncle and is applauded for it! Such a thing, to know the Uncle so well that he buys your time!"

This was portside gossip for sure, and he should have expected it to become common knowledge, but he wasn't used to being quite such a center of attention. News traveled with ships, though, and it also often grew over time, so he was well served to hear it from her.

She glanced around the room, and Jethri wondered

if she saw the things he did. She was fidgeting with more hardcopy, which was a good way for her to disguise both her expression and her careful scan of the room and doorway.

"So here, here is my card in public, Trader, and here is my thanks for buying a meal for my compatriots in the time of our need. We await a shift in fortunes, and a ship with a cargo due us, one or both. Lacking a pinbeam, and lacking connections such as you have, we are very much strangers to this place and these customs. Who expects items of interest to be contraband, I ask you? Who expects travelers to be warned by the port to stay on ship for a time when so much goes on about us?"

With a major flourish she handed over her card and the ship's card, smiling.

Rising, she nodded.

"I see Port people who may recognize me, *magiestro*; I myself have not been told to stay shipboard and would prefer to not hear it said. We will do what we can about giving directions, or if you will, warnings."

She bowed, smiled, turned and walked into the crowd. If there was someone there looking for her Jethri didn't see them; but he was seated and the crowd busy.

Alone at the table, Jethri took the opportunity to leaf through the hardcopy again, pulled a comm to make a copy of the cover, and thus disguise his own shifting of the smooth-skinned item into an inside pocket of his trade coat, just in case there was someone watching, as Minsha had suggested.

His meet-line was empty, still. He guessed Freza had been firm on that rescheduling with Riben Ontaus. Now, if ever, it was time to shut down and go home to *Genchi*.

Again, he put his hands flat on the table, and this

time gained his feet before a motion caught the side of his eye, and he turned.

Chiv was bearing down on his table with refreshments for two, Bry Sen trailing behind, face so bland that Jethri felt a twinge of concern. Of Freza there was no sign, but Chiv was clearly tense.

"I hope this will hold you for now, Trader—Freza's gone to the exhibit dock. She said your next appointment's there, so you should take a break. She said to be easy. Bry Sen needs to talk to you, so I'll go wait at the doors until things are clearer."

Jethri stared, but Chiv was already gone.

"A problem, Trader?" Bry Sen asked.

"Freza'd gone down to the exhibition deck to strongly suggest to my next appointment that postponing was better than late."

"Ah," Bry Sen said. "About that. I have information."

Jethri frowned.

"I am ready," he said in tart Liaden, "to hear information, Pilot."

"Gently, gently," Bry Sen said, in Terran. "Here, sip your 'mite, which I am told is better drunk warm. I will likewise sip mine, and we will recruit ourselves as comrades sharing a difficult shift."

"How difficult?" Jethri asked, in Terran. He picked up a cup as Bry Sen settled into the chair next to him with an extremely unLiaden, but perfectly Looper, "*whoof.*"

Jethri drank some 'mite, which really *was* better hot, and watched as Bry Sen sipped from his cup and tried not to grimace.

After another swallow, Bry Sen managed a slight smile, and leaned his head closer to Jethri as if he'd suddenly picked up the habit from the rest of Jethri's aides.

"Information?" Jethri suggested.

"Ah, information." Bry Sen leaned to put his cup on the table, and settled into the chair again.

"We have received several more deliveries of flowers, Trader, and I have arranged to have them taken to our suite, where they can occupy a room with its own airflow so that we do not suffocate from the heavy odors these blooms exude. I say odors because *fragrance* is too kind."

Jethri took another drink of 'mite, and waited.

"Yes," Bry Sen said. "Information, then. I am told that your *galandaria* Brabham has become involved in an animated discussion on the exhibit docks. This discussion has grown from one between two or three individuals to one between thirty or forty individuals, some of them much louder than is polite, while others demand the removal of yet others by the station constabulary."

Jethri sat up straight.

"Brabham? Is it a riot? Freza's there?"

"Your associate Freza did not dignify it as a riot, but she did ask me to join you here until she might bring Brabham back to *Balrog*. If necessary, Chiv and I will escort you to *Genchi*. We are prepared, even, to escort Brabham, Freza, and other *Balrog* crew members if that happens to be necessary."

Jethri put his cup on the table, and began to stand.

"I have to go there!"

Bry Sen put his hand on Jethri's sleeve.

"No, Trader. Freza, who is on-site, *particularly* asks that you not add yourself to the situation. I gather there are multiple viewpoints being expressed at volume; we are promised video."

"That's a riot you're describing, though Meldyne Station might call it different. I should—"

"You should rely on your people," Bry Sen said firmly. "Since we do not yet know the source of the problem, you should allow your people to find and bring the information to you. Also—" he reached for his cup and manfully took another drink. "Also, it is often useful in such situations to have trusted persons on the outside of trouble, in case there is a need for fines to be paid, or releases to be negotiated."

He made a soothing pilot sign with his free hand— *low jets, low jets.*

"None of the port comms I monitor has anything stronger than a call for a constable or two to move a crowd along before it becomes disruptive."

He touched his ear then, eyes going vague as he listened.

"Your comm is wanting to be turned on I gather, Trader," he said. "*Balrog* comm . . ."

Balrog comm? He thought that *was* on, in the same pocket as the device he'd just taken from Minsha.

He reached to the pocket, pulled out the comm, feeling his fractin vibrate lightly.

As soon as the comm cleared his pocket, the alert light snapped on, blinking rapidly. He brought it to his ear.

"ven'Deelin."

"Jeth, you can't put us in outer orbit while you do trade," Freza sounded breathless. "I've been signaling you—"

"Interference," he said. "The light just now started blinking."

"We'll have to look at that quick," she muttered.

"Anyhow—it's a good thing your shift's over, 'cause just about every Looper on-station's either down here arguing, or walking around looking for port officials. Go on back to *Genchi*, and I'll meet you there. I got somebody from TerraTrade you want to talk to, maybe tonight."

He blinked.

"We had plans," he said, softly.

"I know," she said with a laugh. "But this happened, and he's willing to talk to you as long as he can do it pretty quick before the first open session starts—that's two days. So sometime, but with tight meetings and tonight would be good. And he came to me to ask—that's a good sign. The crowd's starting to dither and split, so might be best if you and Chiv and Bry Sen just wander away before anybody remembers where you were sitting. I'll come to *Genchi* soon's I get Brabham back and checked."

"I can come there—" he began.

"Think not, Jeth. You'll want the meeting room ready, if we can get you together with Bory Borygard. He's not gonna be comfortable in a ship as small as *Balrog*. Trust me. I talked to him, he asked to meet you in person, and I'm gonna bring him to you if I can, or have him meet us. And yeah, I've got some video and so do some others—watch for it incoming. Be ready! Out."

Bry Sen and Chiv were both watching him. He put the comm away in another pocket, sighed, and got up.

"Let's close up, here. We're going to *Genchi*."

In his pocket, the *Balrog* comm began chattering to let him know info was coming in. By the time it stopped, he and his escort were walking back to *Genchi*.

TWO

GENCHI WASN'T ELTHORIA, A FACT THAT RESONATED WITH Jethri as he used the screen in the ship's compact conference room. While Genchi, despite being built to Liaden preferences, was far more commodious than Balrog, he'd been planning on using on-station facilities for meetings during the trade congress.

Bry Sen had convinced Chiv that the docksides were unlikely to be engulfed by rioters, and dispatched him to meet Brabham and Freza at the lifts from the exhibit docks and support them on their return to Balrog. Jethri thought about suggesting that they all make that detour—and then thought of Freza's insistence that he *be ready*, even if he didn't know what he was supposed to be ready *for*.

Jethri's quick search of congress attendee info was aided by Bry Sen's memory.

"I thought I recalled the name!" the pilot exclaimed, and thrust one of the crisp printed pre-congress handouts under Jethri's nose, pointing at something halfway down the page.

Jethri took the sheet, holding it a little further away, and focused. There, listed among the TerraTrade presenters was BOORS BORYGARD, under a flat pic of a man in trim middle age, with the bountiful side-burns and artfully styled hair of someone who was not expecting to need to don a spacesuit anytime soon. His face was broad, showing lines of experience, and his expression was grave, though both eyes and mouth hinted at more willingness to smile than would have been apparent in a pic of a senior Liaden of similar importance.

Reading the short bio, Jethri wondered why such a person was free to see him. His list of titles and letters was impressive, even though Jethri needed to cross-ref half of them. Have to get familiar with those fast, Jeth, he told himself. Boors Borygard was TerraTrade STA1—that was Senior Technical Administrator—with positions and appointments trailing away after, as if that wasn't enough, including being a trustee for a number of intertrade funds and a member of the Combine Trader Recognition Committee.

Jethri felt his pocket buzz—the *Balrog* comm unit, not his fractin this time—and connected to a breath-less Freza.

"Jeth, I'm almost there and Bory says he's ten or fifteen minutes out, soon's he's finished dealing with the port safety people that got called out anyway. Come let me in, hey?"

Jethri was pleased to have his ear kissed and nipped as the airlock closed behind them, and took advantage of the chance to hug Freza's spare frame to him for a moment. He'd have really liked to take her down the long hall to his quarters, but duty seemed otherwise. He put his hand on her back as he reluctantly guided her to the meeting room.

They'd barely arrived when Bry Sen came to the door.

"Is there a need for refreshment?" he asked, eyes flicked to Freza and back to Jethri. "There is work tea on the brew, else—"

"Work tea?" Freza asked.

"Strong and a touch sweet," Jethri said. "To keep the concentration going."

"Work tea sounds terrific," she said, and Jethri nodded at Bry Sen. "Bring a pot."

"Trader." Bry Sen was gone.

Turning, Jethri offered Freza another hug, which she stepped into, eagerly, he thought, breathing in her scent as her arms went around his waist and she hugged him back, hard.

"Tiring day," he said, and she laughed softly against his shoulder. "Forgot to pace myself, is what. Think I'd learn."

One more squeeze and she stepped back. He let her go reluctantly as Bry Sen came in with a tray bearing two mugs and a teapot—not the good set, Jethri noted. So, Bry Sen considered that Freza was a crewmate, not a visitor.

That, Jethri thought, was interesting. Even . . . pleasing.

"Thank you," he said, picking up the pot and pouring.

"Always of service," Bry Sen said. "If it can be told, do we expect visitors?"

"One," Freza said. "Big man, dressed planet-side. Name of Boors Borygard. Might trot out an 'executive director' or 'from the Commissariat' ahead of it, if he thinks you need impressin'."

Bry Sen nodded and looked to Jethri.

"Bring the director here when he arrives," Jethri said, and Bry Sen nodded again, his eyes going to the tea service. Jethri saw him weighing the *melant'i* of a commissioner against the workaday teapot shared with comrades.

"Just bring another mug," he said, and Bry Sen's eyebrows went up before he nodded a third time, and took himself off.

Jethri poured himself a mug of tea, and looked to Freza.

"So—Brabham started a riot?"

Freza snorted.

"No, Brabham did *not* start a riot."

Shaking her head, she sank down into one of the new seats that was one of pin'Aker's pre-trip upgrades. She patted the leather appreciatively, and raised her mug to take a careful sip.

Jethri propped a hip against the table and sipped from his mug, feeling his breath go as the malt hit his tongue. Tea strong enough to stand up on its own feet and shout; Bry Sen wanted them to get some work *done*, is how he read that message.

"Now, this," he said to Freza's raised eyebrows, "is *proper* work tea."

"I could get used," she admitted and had another sip.

"Who started the riot if it wasn't Brabham?" Jethri wondered, after she had settled herself deeper into the chair.

"Well, now there's the question. Could be said it was the Golds, if there was a riot, which there wasn't. Here's how it happened, Jeth—

"Brabham arrived on the deck with his escorts and lucky enough right there was Bory and a bunch of folks heading toward the exhibition docks. Couldn't miss 'em, after all, with that voice of his, but Brabham couldn't see him 'round the crowd and him on the scoot like he was, and he asked me 'Is that Bory? Do I hear Bory?'"

Her face fell into a grin again.

"Thing is, he heard the question, Bory did, and you'd have thought he'd found a free *cantra* on the floor. Let out a yip, and next thing I know there he was making me feel like a little. Brabham stood himself up and so now we had all of Brabham's escort and all of Bory's escort. Everything was good, I thought, until stupid Desty Gold and his first mate came into it, calling Bory inconsiderate for breaking off their talk to see Brabham, and then calling Brabham names for *Balrog* being pushed ahead in the docking queue, and then Desty's mate called Brabham a 'twenting backward anti-pilot' and claiming *Balrog* was broadcasting some kind of shipping interference."

Jethri'd been fascinated by Freza's face and voice, less so by the words until the last hit him.

"What? Brabham? How—"

Freza laughed, and raised her mug.

"Yes, he *did* say it!"

"But—"

"But some of Gold's friends were there, saw Brabham, o'course, and started complaining that the *Envidaria*'s an excuse for some ships to expand their Loops by taking advantage, while others'll lose 'em since they're too old or too big or..."

She broke off, with a look of distaste, shook her head and drank some more tea.

"Yeah," she sighed, looking at the mug. "I could get used."

She looked up.

"Anyhoot—it got scattered so fast, Jeth, I couldn't fairly keep track. Then Bory, well, he raised his voice, and you know what *that's* like—"

"I don't. I've never met him."

She stopped, startled, her face slowly clearing.

"I forgot, Jeth. I forgot Iza just broke off everything social when Arin died. We—I mean *Balrog*—we were still trying to rescue something from the old arrangements even after Arin broke away, and then when he died Iza never talked to nobody if Paitor could do it, wouldn't even bring the *Market* to meets that wasn't all about trade. But Bory, he stayed in and—"

The ship's annunciator told them they had a visitor. Jethri came out of his lean, and stayed on his feet, mug in hand. In moments the second largest man he'd ever seen followed Bry Sen into the room. He was *second* largest because he massed less than Jay Dorster of Balfour did, though in height he was very nearly the equal. Dorster's mass had been distributed rather carelessly about his person—he'd grown large as a child, too large to be comfortable aboard a Loop ship, too hungry to be fed as a crewman, and too serious to do much but study until his mother rescued herself and her son from an awkward situation by starting a business on Balfour.

This man lacked Dorster's beard or mane, and he lacked the sense of apology for his size that Dorster's conversation had evoked. Jethri tried to imagine him moving about in *Balrog*'s tight quarters and yes, it would have been a tight fit indeed. Here, his hair all but brushed the ceiling though the Liaden sense of proportion favored a ship interior far less tunnel-like than *Balrog*, with better lighting and—Jethri was suddenly looking at the top of the man's head, for he was bowing with some nuance, recognizably *honor to one's Line*.

Jethri returned the bow between equals, not as nuanced, but easy for even an untrained Terran to read—which, Jethri thought, Boors Borygard was. The bow had been good, but the hand position had been off, which suggested the bow had been learned in a hurry from a tape.

Straightening, Jethri glanced at Bry Sen, waiting in the doorway, and nodded. The pilot inclined slightly and stepped away into the hall, the door closing behind him.

Freza stood, standing forward to wave the man toward Jethri.

"Boors Borygard, this is Jethri Gobelyn ven'Deelin. Jethri, this is Bory, an old friend of our ship."

The voice that so impressed Freza was bold, if not booming, warm amusement suffusing the tone.

"Trader ven'Deelin, let me be pleased to meet you," he said affably. "And if I may say so, I am pleased to meet you now that you've gotten your height!" He moved from bow to handshake, graceful and clearly muscled. If this man had been speaking at volume to a crowd, Jethri could see why they might have listened.

"Sir, I'm pleased to meet you, but I think we've not met in person."

The laugh lines around Bory's mouth deepened.

"I'd have known who you are and felt like I knew you already, because I knew Arin, and from what I've seen, you're a lot like him—and not just in looks. But I guess the reality is that the last I saw *you*, you were barely walking and not awake to visitors on *Gobelyn's Market*. I gathered we woke you and you escaped from, was it Cris?"

Jethri laughed. "Cris wasn't the best baby-guard at the time, as the ship remembers. I hope I wasn't rude."

"No, sir, not at all. *Disinterested* is the word that comes to mind."

"If visitors woke me, disinterested's probably what it was. I'm told I really liked to sleep in those days! Please, be welcome, and seated. We have some working tea here, if you'd care to join us. Else I can offer—"

"I'll share a mug of tea as it's here. No reason to put the ship to extra trouble."

Jethri nodded, moved around the table and poured. Bory received the mug, took a good swallow, and sighed.

"Just the thing," he pronounced.

Jethri raised the pot toward Freza, who held out her mug for a refill, then topped off his own. Bory looked around and settled himself into a chair that was almost wide enough for him. Freza resumed her seat, and Jethri spun a third chair so he was facing both of them, and sat down.

Bory had another drink from his mug and put it on the chair's wide arm.

"Sorry I didn't see Brabham's situation coming up," he said to Freza. "I should have, the Golds and their ilk being what they are. I'll do my best to make sure it doesn't happen again, which means I'm going to have some extra security out there, to keep things calm. I'm guessing you're both good with that plan."

Freza nodded, and after a moment so did Jethri.

"Good, good." Another smile, which faded somewhat as he looked between them.

"I gotta say that I wish you might've let us know about your announcement before you made it public. We didn't get mentioned; it was all about Arin's work, and nothing from us at all. Looks like we didn't recognize it might be important!"

He paused, and shook his head sadly.

"Combine and TerraTrade both kind of took a hit is what I'm telling you. Image Management's all over me for not telling them ahead—I'm the liaison, right? Supposed to know these things. And *you* ought to know that budgets are in more-or-less chaos for us having to answer queries and the data's not in our files. I've got to hand it to you, though—hardly anybody was doing more than whispering about the Dust problem before you come on the scene with all that energy. Wouldn't have thought there was that much hold-over from Arin, but there it was... And we could have used some warning, a chance to work together—" He waved a hand. "That's all a Jump behind us, all right? Like I told Freza, we ought to be able to make this whole business run smoother, going forward. Cooperation, that's key."

The rest of his smile faded from his face and he glanced at the closed door.

"We'll want to have a quiet talk, if we can, Trader. Freza, you, me. Here. Now is a great time, so we can get on with things. Let's call it Combine to Jethri Gobelyn, or *Envidaria* to Combine, whatever."

His pause was too brief to allow comment and he moved his hand in a vague *launch this now* sign.

"Can't go too wide on it though, if you understand? I was hoping we could have Brabham in it, but with all this thing about interference and leaks going on,

I think us three can probably make a good start here and then we can do some more formal things once the congress gets a bunch of stuff out of the way."

Jethri felt his own smile ghosting away, his Liaden trade face falling into place as Freza shifted in her chair.

"If we need to talk, sure, we can talk right now," Jethri said. "Brabham can be involved, if you want him." He turned to Freza. "He's available on comm?"

"No trouble," Freza said, but Bory was shaking his head.

"No, you know what? Just us three, right here, sharing space, sharing air." He lifted his mug with a smile. "Sharing refreshment."

That was a call-out to Looper hospitality between ships, but Jethri had some doubt about whether he'd be calling Bory "cousin" anytime soon, if ever.

"Our schedule must be as crowded as yours," he said politely. "Now's good for me—Freza?"

"I'm here to learn," she assured him.

He considered her briefly. She smiled, eyes wide, and he turned back to Bory.

"Sounds to me like now's the time. Before we start, let us be clear—my recent training would have me say that we need to be certain of relative *melant'i*. If we speak as other than Loopers of long acquaintance, should we not be sure which of the masks we're wearing is feeding the oxygen to the conversation?"

A half-snort from Bory, a semi-shake of the head.

"True enough. I'll take the word of Freza and Brabham that you aren't here for the Liaden side of things. Got to admit this isn't a bad little ship you got—and lead trader, too, young as you are! Can't blame you for taking advantage where there's advantage to be took. What *I* need to know is, who's in charge, right here, right now? Do you really think just telling people a simple set of rules is going to be enough to change the patterns people're used to?"

Jethri looked to Freza; she half-closed her eyes and sighed before emulating Bory's earlier *launch this now*, raising her left hand in punctuation to indicate she was taking first turn to speak.

"Jethri made the decision to release the *Envidaria* because he was the one who *could* make the decision. All the circumstances, and Arin, too, pushed him that way, and he acted as soon as he had all the details.

"Decision's made—like you said, that's behind us. Right now, we got teams of people working on protocols, teams working on alternate routes, teams trying to pull science ships together so we can do better measuring than's been going on—"

"But *who's in charge?*" Bory demanded. "Day to day?"

Jethri frowned. Freza nodded to him, and continued.

"We're working on that, Bory. Still working. There's not one single person making all the decisions, except when one needs to be made *right now*. Even then, it's passed around and worked over, amended if it needs to be. Once this congress is over we'll have clearer lines of communication."

Bory took a deep breath and shook his head, gesturing with both hands to emphasize his words.

"Here's the thing. Arin tried to talk to me about the Dust situation back when I wasn't much more than an intern with the Combine, and he brought it up from time to time while I was working my way up.

He mentioned issues at a planet he knew about and he and his pilot—Greg, maybe his name was. They both explained to me about the Dust density and stuff, but no one was having *real* problems, so I didn't put it in the top queue when I got more involved, more invested, in the Combine.

"I wasn't happy back when Arin and his couple of friends decided that my board of trustees was off-base with the changes we were making. But the changes *needed* to be made, and commissioners who couldn't go along with it, they made things harder on us. Some of them left, some just stayed to make things harder. Sometimes decisions *need* to be made by a small group, or one person, who has all the information. Right now, are you telling me that this whole *Envidaria* scheme is a ship without a pilot? Jethri's not in charge?"

Bory looked hard at Jethri, but again Freza spoke first—

"Jethri's consulted on a lot—he has to be. But day to day, immediate action—that's coming off *Balrog*— call it me and Brabham with advice of the people and groups who pass it on. The framework's being built as we sit here; it'll be bigger next shift and bigger the shift after that. I can't be clearer: On desperate decisions Brabham and me have a consult with the best person we can get to make it three, and Jethri gets in when there's time."

"Right, so you have twenty ships or thirty in and you're disrupting trade around the whole arm? Somebody needs to make this orderly, somebody needs to ..."

"We've got close to a hundred in, official, and a bunch more coming in because they feed those ships or get fed by them. Some only need the information we've got on Dust conditions. Some want to change Loops, some want to sell, but we're way more than just three dozen ships and if someone's using that number they're off course!" Freza said sharply.

Jethri cleared his throat; the other two turned as if they'd forgotten he was there.

"We missed a portion of the agreement. I'll confess that I'm consulted on decisions being made elsewhere— there's not a 'home office' and I'm of mixed mind should there be—but we said we'd be clear who we're talking for.

"*I'm* talking for the Looper traders who identify with the *Envidaria*, the Loopers who need it, and the worlds those ships serve. Things need to happen to make sure commerce goes forth. Freza is my link, through Brabham and the *Envidaria*, to the Seventeen Worlds. Those are the worlds most affected by the Dust right now, where people need to have something like the *Envidaria* in force. In the last—call it the last quarter Standard—I've predicted route changes, discussed pod sizing, agreed and disagreed with plans for route-swapping and intershipping—and I've done it with good advice and the intent to let trade go forth."

He moved a hand.

"Freza and Brabham, they're in the same orbit as me, far as I can tell. They've lived Loop ships, they know traders, and they know what it is like to have a Jump barely go through or to have to start again and do it all over. So they're working for Loopers too; Loopers here in this arm, Loopers who've joined the *Envidaria* because they can live *with* it better than they can live *without* it."

Jethri paused. Bory's face was closed; Freza was half-smiling. She gave him a nod, and he did *not* sigh as he continued.

"What I wonder," he said, leaning in and looking straight into Bory's face, "is *what mask are you wearing?* Is your oxy free ship air or 'pressed in a suit pack?"

Bory sat up straighter—an impressive sight—and his face might have reddened slightly.

"I'm here for the Combine and through it for TerraTrade. That means all trade and all planets. *We* make trade *happen.* We make sure there's money for the exchanges, that the pinbeams get paid for, that..."

Jethri nodded, considered, heard Freza's intake of breath that meant she might speak again, held up his hand and signed a firm *launch now.*

"Let me rephrase," he said to Bory. "I've been called the ambassador for the *Envidaria.* Brabham and Freza, they're representing The Seventeen Worlds in this, as well as the Loopers. Traders, pilots, Loopers, a subset of planets with a special problem. We're at the congress to solve a big problem that's not been addressed, so far as any of us can see, by the Combine or by TerraTrade.

"You've been around Loopers if you were on the *Market,* if Arin thought enough of you to bring you on-board. But the reason *I'm* an ambassador is that this problem's been building, and TerraTrade and the Combine are so busy predicting the next big thing in galactic trade they're ignoring the fact that this small splinter of the galaxy is in trouble. Maybe a dozen and a half worlds in real trouble and another three dozen with lots of bother isn't big enough to catch the Combine's eye right now? Is that what I'm hearing?"

But this is just the start and we don't know if it'll get so bad some place that nothing can get in or out.

"And so, are you a Looper? When you breathe out, where does that air go?"

Bory sat back slowly.

"I see. Trying to be purer than the Combine is no way to work things out, Trader. You're young, so maybe you don't see that the net of wider trade is where things *have* to happen, and that warning ships away so that Loopers can run things in this arm is against the interest of wider trade—Loops are out of date, Loop ships and family ships need to be phased out so trade smooths out, and the flow of funds and goods gets steadier. Backswirls happen in any galaxy; the big framework works around the transient issues—has to. Arin had issues with that reality. He'd been good to me when I started working for the Combine fresh from The Monash, kept in touch when my work took me back to study at Otago, so it was hard when he broke with us. It was hard, and I regret it even now, sitting here talking with you and Freza."

He shook his head, slow and sad.

"Look, I wasn't born on a ship like you were—like Freza was. But I *do* want to make trade work. And what I think is that most of the ships out here talking to you, they'd be better off changing approach. Stick to a short run between two systems, back and forth on contract. Easier schedules, easier to get regular contract work from a coop or a network. Families can put down roots on a planet instead of being hauled from place to place. If a planet's got too much Dust, let the consolidated groups figure it out—or sell the Loop and let the consolidators get things together.

Decisions like these are best left to the people with the resources and the expertise, not by individual pilots risking their whole families!"

"Is this why you needed to talk to Jethri yourself? To tell him all the stuff that's in your pass-arounds and mail? I thought you were going to try to work with us."

The color was up in Freza's face, and her lips were pale, which Jethri took as signs that she was none too pleased with the man at the moment.

Bory grimaced.

"Look, you can't just run something like this with nobody in charge. That's part of what I wanted to work out with you—I wanted your people to talk to my people.

"You ought to have working people and committees that you can send to make things happen. I've spent my education learning how this side of the business works and I've learned from the people who've been running things at the top for the last four or five decades. Come to Trantor or to Altair Four, set up on our campus, and we'll see what we can do. There's room for dozens of people, hundred, *thousands* if you need 'em! We can set a schedule—say a series of study meetings over the next five Standards, with some science brought in from the ships so we can start studying it—*then* we can build a project that can start to be effective. But you shouldn't be rushing into this, and you ought to be aware that we're going to be resisting big changes all at once. There ought to be solutions to a lot of your concerns..."

Jethri looked between them for a moment, rubbing his earlobe while he thought.

"So," he said eventually, "you've got a campus, or maybe two, where you want us to send staff from working ships to meet with folks who already make their living off of them, people who are professional administrators. You want our people on planets, and that'll be hard *on them*, and you want them not to be making changes, which will be hard *on them*, and you want *them* to give you years away from what they do so that your people, who I guess live on the planets already, can make decisions that'll make life even *harder* for them? Is that what I hear? We have to have better than that: you've already got people in place across all the sectors; why can't *they* meet with the local and regional Looper teams?"

"We need consistency," Bory said, sounding stern. "Operating rules ought to be orderly; they need to be consistent."

"You may be glad," Jethri said wryly, "that Brabham's *not* here. There are local rules at most ports and for most systems. Have a small red sun with three interior gas giants and one stony and you're going to have different rules than a nine planet system with four interior stones. A system with a brown dwarf half-a-light-year out's got a lot of specials depending on local gravity anomalies—"

Jethri sat back, realizing he'd been leaning into the discussion a little too much, especially for someone with Liaden trade credentials.

"Do you have trade experience?" he asked Bory. "Have you bought and sold for a session, ever? Are you accredited anywhere as a trader?"

"I haven't—we don't want anybody to be concerned about conflict of interest. From our side. Kind of hard for your side on that point, I think, since everyone does everything. But for me—I've shadowed traders on port to watch the process, I've got the course work down..."

Jethri gave a half-nod. "Have you been in a trade ship running in on a busy port trying to get ahead by selling on the open trade net where the offers are computer matched and then you've got to overrule or make side trade at the same time you're trying to catch the whole market's mood?"

"I haven't," Bory admitted, "not on a ship. I've been on the trade floors on several worlds though, I know the pace and the necessities that way..."

"Have you been on the bridge for arrival and departure? Sat in the third seat or watched..."

"Sims, of course. When I travel for the Combine I'm usually pretty busy and..."

Jethri nodded and glanced to Freza, who took up his point seamlessly.

"I think what Jethri's getting at is that a lot of what Loopers do shakes down to split-second timing and intuition no matter that they might be on the same run their parents started forty Standards ago. The ports evolve, the trade evolves, and the locals often have special knowledge that's not gonna be covered in rules that work in ports one arm over, or even ports that run *seasonal*. If you pull four of the big station traders off of *Balrog*'s usual Loops to come to your campus, you upset standing arrangements, traditional buys, even trade forecasts. You'll need to be willing to work with small groups and let decisions come from inside, or the system's gonna favor conglomerates, cartels, and in the long run the people with the most big ships. Does TerraTrade really want to turn into an organization that basically feeds profits to Liad's big ships?"

"It isn't that simple, Freza. You've studied enough economics to know that—and the stuff I've studied does show how to keep the value flowing through trade ports, gives ships the ability to make those decisions with what we like to think of as cash-on-hand but which we all know is credit accounts and letters of account, dual transfer permissions, planetary and port tranche allowances..."

"I think," Jethri said, "we all will need to work together, and soon. We—the Seventeen Worlds, the *Envidaria* team—we need more information than what's usually been passed on from arrivals and departures; we need data all the way to mass and energy levels, we need to be told when there are Jump rejections, when there are Jump deflections, and where. TerraTrade holds that data as proprietary, but it can be life-saving, and the lives saved will be Loopers in the short run and maybe planetaries in the long. If the ships can't get in, some places are gonna be on short rations."

"But there's no sign that things will get that bad," Bory protested. "Sure, the Dust might inconvenience some shippers and a few traders. But there's no need to disrupt—"

"You told us that my father tried to talk to you about this years ago," Jethri interrupted, "and nothing got done because it wasn't bad enough, and maybe would never get bad *enough*." Jethri shook his head.

"Right now, we've got three aligned nonmember worlds that we evaluate as under extreme risk. There are several stations in worse states—places that get one or two shipments a Standard—one failure to deliver and they're on short rations for months if they're lucky, and worse if they aren't. I don't understand why—"

"But all they have to do is *sign contracts* with a reputable Combine-recognized hauler and they can get guaranteed service. We're seeing to the flow of funding throughout the arm here and a lot of other places. They can get guarantees if they have contracts, *that's* what they need!"

Jethri stared at him. "Guarantees," he said flatly, and shook his head.

"A contract's not enough, though it *ought* to be. A guarantee's not enough. What they *need* is clarity and surety. Signing a contract with a company that sees them as occasional side business doesn't give them much security, but keeping on good terms with Loopers who need them as much as they need the Loopers—that does make sense—and more sense as the Dust gets denser."

Bory crossed, then uncrossed his arms, looked to Freza.

"You go along with this? Really, Freza? Do you think Brabham does?"

She nodded.

"I agree with Jethri and Arin. Shouldn't be any surprise to you to hear that Brabham thinks this is the exact wrong time to be pushing for concentration of services—he's said it to you often enough. The Dust is gonna disrupt services—already has, which is what Jethri told you. Brabham's got a database of coincidental shipping outages and delays, like the time he was filling in for a cousin out toward . . . jeez . . . InAJam. Place throws solar storms that bounce off a couple of gassers and then they storm too—not a good place to work in a space suit if you have to and you have to be ready to do that anyplace you go. Couple of the incoming ships didn't hang around...and right there you've got that disaster sitting on a low orbit waiting to spiral in. Brabham's ship was able to get in a quick rescue run on something—I forget what—but the ships that didn't make it in just pointed to local conditions and cross-shipped a quarter Standard later. Don't even have to be Liaden to have a getaway like that in a contract..."

Freza'd been watching; Jethri saw her catch Bory's quick glance at him. Before he could figure it, she moved her hand, signing *maintain course*.

"I haven't heard the InAJam story," Jethri said. "I've heard others like it, though—and there's our point again. Before the Dust twisted toward the Seventeen Worlds, there was always something specialized happening somewhere, and there always will be. The scope of the Dust makes it different, and the *Envidaria* is special-made to address the problems that are coming for the Seventeen Worlds. The Dust moves, though— you know that—so it's likely going to visit problems to more and other locations, for a long time. Makes sense to make the *Envidaria* into the operating rules."

Bory sighed, loud, like he was a miscreant admitting defeat in a *melant'i* play. In this case, he accompanied it with a shake of the head and raised palms.

"Look, these sessions are all planned years ahead— there are sessions for the next congress that'll be locked in place before this one's half over. So what you're asking for is a special interruption to a side session unless you think there's enough interest to bring it to the committee of the whole, and that will take an official Beg of Attention."

Freza had her tablet out.

"Beg of Attention," she read. "Says here one happens 'bout every third congress. We got interest enough to do it now, if just to get it settled."

"If you're certain you want to put it up—but if it fails to go through, it'll be locked out of the rest of this congress. You get one chance."

Freza nodded, and said almost as if to herself...

"If we want to do it, we have to have the question perfect before we even broach it?"

She looked at Jethri first, then at Bory.

"Who can look at this ahead of time to let us at least get it heard—can you? Is there a person who has this as a job, to make sure the questions are right before they're put up to the body?"

"There's people, yes, people with experience. I wouldn't say *job*. If you've got the history there on your tablet, you're halfway there without any of the others."

He looked hard at both of them then, and Jethri got the impression he wasn't a happy man.

"Look, I can put you in touch with someone—maybe a couple. It might make sense for us to get this out of the way, so I can do that. I'd suggest two people, working independent, with the same information and your goals clear. I mean crystal clear. Then get them together and have them do a reconciliation of what they say—to make it clear and to be sure it is what you want to say. But beyond having that in hand when you make the request, you're going to have to have someone give the presentation. And understand there *will* be questions, and it might go on a long time. It might get loud and angry."

He paused, nibbled on his lip.

"Ten Standards ago, or even five, I'd have told you that Brabham was your man—everybody knows him. Seems like he's respected by everybody who ever dealt with him, and Loopers—well, you saw what happened with the youngers today—he's a legend. The thing is he can't do the follow-up if he's already tired, and we saw that he is."

He looked then straight at Jethri, but turned and nodded to Freza.

"See, what's happened, you got the booster in front of the jets, and I'll tell you I thought that would make my job easier here. But it's clear you're not going to let me just tuck you into an informational session like I'd been aiming for, so we might as well get you turned around."

He paused then, shaking his head, looking again at Freza.

"You put Jethri here in front of folks while you and Brabham were holding the show together. I guess you're going to have to keep on with that. Make sure he's in touch with what you're doing, him being out front, but since I gather that Jethri's face is scheduled to be everywhere for the next few days, that's a start—like I say, I'm not sure that announcement was your best course."

Freza looked at Jethri, barely avoiding a smile.

"We made the announcement—Jethri did. We needed to start and we were behind because everyone wanted secrets. We're not secret now—and since we're not, you're right, we have to get in front of it. So let the *Envidaria* grow, that's what we think ought to happen. Get us in front of the congress. Put Jethri where people will see him. Let him sell this. What do you think, Jeth?"

He swallowed—he had never personally been in front of more than a few dozen people at a time, no matter that his message was an expanding wave front at dozens, maybe even hundreds of planets and stations.

"If they need to see me, I'll talk to them. I'll work from what I know, that's what I can do; I'll work from the proposal. I'll tell them what we're building, and who's been keeping me straight."

Freza looked to the Combine official.

"Bory, if you have suggestions for folks to help with that wording, let me know who they are. I'll either tell 'em you volunteered 'em or not, as you like."

Bory bowed his head with a brief laugh.

"If you don't know the names already, I guess you can mention mine. But here, let me send that on to you."

He reached for his comm.

THREE

BRY SEN CAME BACK TO THE CONFERENCE ROOM AFTER conducting Bory to the hatch, his face stringently bland, his body language gracefully Liaden.

Jethri stood up, which was proper in a trader receiving his pilot, and waited.

Bry Sen bowed. It was a careful, well-enunciated bow in which he clearly aligned himself with Jethri in all of his necessities. Jethri figured he appreciated that, saving the part where he wasn't certain what his necessities *were*, much less what they'd demand from the pilot of the ship he was expected to provide with a commercially successful route in short order.

He bowed in return, a simple acceptance of allegiance, saw the Liaden shell melt somewhat, and took the chance to smile in full Terran.

"Our visitor is gone, Trader, and with him two of his deck watchers, leaving three more within easy visual range of *Genchi*, though they may simply be posted one to a ship, watching the three ships here in a row—*Balrog*, *Genchi*, and *Elsvair*."

Jethri bowed thanks. Freza nodded where she sat, looking less tense, as if Bory's departure was as much a relief to her as it was to Jethri.

"He did say he was going to be watching *Balrog* because of the rock-pusher and his friends," Jethri allowed, "but we don't know now if he's as much on our side of things as he wants us to feel. He admits that we're a problem..."

"We're a problem he wants to solve in a hurry," Freza said, "and we're going to have to watch out for the help he's offered. We don't want to argue by not talking to his help, but we're not going to depend on them."

She looked to Jethri, small hand movement asking a question, Jethri nodded.

"Yes, please, both of you feel free to say what you like in front of each other—I'm going to be depending on both of you. Bry Sen, you need to know that Freza's been doing this work for—I guess it must be Standards, really.

"Freza, you need to know that Bry Sen's had diplomatic training, was aimed at being culture officer on a Liaden tradeship, thought he'd got off easy, then Master Trader pin'Aker sent him to me."

"A master trader's whim, and a fortunate one, for me," Bry Sen murmured in Liaden, and Jethri shot him a sharp look.

"Humor?" he asked in Terran.

"Somewhat, Trader," Bry Sen said, following him. He bowed to Freza. "I beg pardon. I felt a need to relieve my feelings, now that the guest has departed."

Freza grinned. "Understandable."

"So, we already got people working on those motions, and other ones, too. Isn't that what I was hearing at my lessons?"

Freza grinned at him. "I like a student pays attention.

We've got five different sample statements complete with the proper motions—two were rough-written by Arin and you can work from them as you need—the names and dates are off, o'course. The others are what we drafted once we saw how the opposition was gonna try to target us. Bory showed you that—they're trying to settle us with the hint that we're being the amateurs messing with rules on short notice while they're the full-time admins who are so smooth and careful for everybody. Bory's not a bad man, Jethri, but he's so built-in to the system he can't see his own momentum."

"Do you mean we don't need his help?"

She shook her head.

"Not that. For one thing, we need help with details; what we have from Arin *is* dated—but we know what to watch out for from the helpers. They'll have stuff they'll call ordinary bill structure that'll build in delays and studies. Arin saw that coming way back when, and you heard Bory trying to force us into that orbit like it was natural. We've been watching, and there's some block language Combine admins have been adding to almost everything these last two or three congresses. Arin called 'em on it before he resigned. So we can expect Bory's helpers'll be putting that in first thing. And we're *sure* we don't want to put everything into study committees—we've gotta get this into action items, into local priority releases, get it added to piloting regulation updates. I got dozens of those things admitted to the rules committees already. Most of them ought to fly in pretty well—they've been sent to the standing committees over the last two Standards, and we're not seeing resistance—all reasonable minor changes in case of shipping and arrival issues, with cited examples. Arin left us some timelines that are usable still."

Freza glanced at her comm unit and sighed.

"And Brabham?" Jethri asked. "How's he holding, really?"

"He got himself off the deck before he got too mad, and he's prolly talked himself hoarse since he got back on board, catching as many people as he can to tell them the plan. Meanwhile, Bory thinks Brabham ran away—but, see, Bory went out *expecting* to have trouble on deck and we don't know if he set it up or if he only meant to do what he tried to do—take charge of Brabham's entry into the hall."

She sighed.

"I think the greeting got out of his range. He didn't expect Brabham to have a volunteer of young-uns with him, and that means the news is everywhere by now, that pro-Combine Loopers was pushing at Brabham and that Brabham held his own."

"Was that why Bory came to me so fast? He *did* come to me, and people will know that, too. He wants Brabham out of the way?"

Freza glanced at Bry Sen.

"What do you think? We haven't had time to go over this with Jethri—sorry, Jeth—but if we all need to know where we are, might as well go forward, right?"

Jethri saw her fingers move—a request for permission, and he nodded.

"Might as well tell everybody."

That got him a grin before she turned back to Bry Sen.

"Our plan was to set Jethri up as full special ambassador—the committee has it as 'an Extraordinary

Interworld Envoy and Plenipotentiary Ambassador for dealing with Issues arising out of Arin's *Envidaria'*—while we get the other offices into orbit."

Bry Sen blinked. Jethri gulped. When he'd first heard the basic idea just after his perhaps rash decision to release the *Envidaria*, it had sounded neat and tidy. The more he'd thought about it since, the less of that tidiness remained. Now just said out loud and matter-of-fact, it sounded lunatic, not to say terrifying.

"The basic idea'd been to really launch things here if we could, with a kind of meteor shower of motions, statements, action items, and precedents. An ambassador named, some basic rules of engagement for systems finding themselves in the worst of the clouds, getting more Jump rejection reporting in—we have it all outlined. By having Jethri up front—look, he's Looper born and bred, comes from a name family, and he's not really On Loop right now—he's investigating for something new, just like a lot of Loopers will be. And since he's *not* a Combine co-opt, not brought in from outside as an admin and then put in charge, not from a big finance group, he's purer than they *can* be, and it's got Bory worried." She glanced at Jethri. "Well, he said as much, with that crack about trying to be purer than the Combine wasn't no way to get cooperation."

Jethri nodded.

Bry Sen bowed once, and then again, a flourish in fact, bowing to the ideas of an organization and plan not his own.

"So! There are many trajectories at work, not just one, and more than one source for the calculations. I am relieved to hear this. Thank you."

Freza gave the pilot a nod.

"We need somebody young, mobile, able to be out and about. That's the plan with Jethri. Where we'll be exactly in five Standards we don't know, but by then a lot more of the frameworks we need will've been built and put out there. But we gotta start *now*—that's what Bory won't see, or can't. Truth is, he shoulda started when Arin put it to him, but that's too many Jumps behind us to even count."

She paused, apparently considering a spot of decking, or those back-Jumps, then shook her head and looked up.

"So Jethri'll be asked, formal, to be ambassador—we have that all in sealed infovids we'll distribute once things are really underway, then once we have Jethri in place officially we can see what else we can organize.

"We'll need Jethri to agree to two Standards. Once that happens it would mean that Brabham would be 'Interim Administrator of *Envidaria* Affairs for the Seventeen Worlds.' He'll give up the Combine Commissioner spot and his term will be two Standards to start. That'll give us real back-up breathing.

"There's more possible in the works, but we've come with the plans."

Freza nodded to Jethri.

"We didn't have time to go over it—was going to last night, but—well. What we really needed was for you *not* to get in a dock fight, and we needed *not* to let Combine outshine Brabham."

Bry Sen let a smile slip out for a moment as he looked questioningly toward Jethri.

"Talk," Jethri said.

Bry Sen inclined his head.

"I would that I'd had an opportunity to study this situation when I was schooled. We had in my study group a...a member of a trading family...who busily averred that Terran trade politics was a simple thing revolving around the desire to be unbothered. Unbothered to build big new ships, unbothered to expand trade routes, unbothered by the future."

He laughed then, full Terran.

"I fear me the person in question has yet to earn a ring, and will be unhappy in the profession, if they've managed to not be elevated into administrator of an orchard. Clearly, they had no understanding of what organizations do, or can do. I salute you!" He did, or at least he produced an energetic bow.

Freza produced her own bow in turn—surely she'd been practicing!—this one very close to *recognition of an ally.*

"Yes," said Bry Sen, "allies are good."

"Speaking of which," Freza said to Jethri, pulling a databar from a stealthy sleeve pocket, "Brabham sent you this. We've been working on it for a while, and the final comments just come in last night. I got 'em inserted, and compiled, so this is the latest news there is. Latest organizational charts, connections, and links to caches that have duplicates, along with our correspondents. It's not absolutely set, 'cause there's more coming in all the time, but it ought to get us through the congress."

Jethri took the bar.

"You'll want to have a safe back-up—there's some surprising names in there! Otherwise—"

Her comm beeped. She flipped it up on her belt, sighed, and let it drop.

"So, here's a note that another cousin's got to talk to me tonight, so off I go."

"Our plans?" he asked, softly.

Freza shook her head, and gave him a smile.

"You know how we was talking about how the pre-pre-congress was prep?"

"I remember."

"Well, now things are speeding up for real. I gotta get this pinned down. Straight from Tradedesk—well. Straight from Doricky . . . she 'pologizes if she didn't explain enough back when she saw you last and says I'm s'posed to pass on an extra three hugs for her since she can't get here to deliver in person!"

He shook his head, allowed a smile—

"If it comes direct from Grandma Ricky, then it's got to be attended. You'll pass on that I miss her bad?"

Freza stood, smiling now. "That's the kind of thing she likes to hear, I know— And look, we'll reschedule soonest—promise!"

He stood, the bow coming unbidden, along with the rueful smile as their hands met for the transfer, lingering for a moment before she winked at him and let go.

He saw her to the hatch, and watched her walk away. She didn't turn around this time, so she didn't see the longing he felt. Once she'd reached *Balrog*, he turned back, sealed the hatch, and stood, considering the databar in his hand.

"Necessity exists," he said to the air, and left for his office and its wall of data screens.

. . . .

FOUR

. . . .

JETHRI QUICK-READ EVERYTHING ON THE DATABAR IN TWO hours, then took a break. He put his day-clothes to be cleaned, put the fractin in the jewel-box with his necklace, his father's ring, and his South Axis Congress and Trade Fair ID tag. He paused in the act of removing pin'Aker's whimsical trader's ring, and decided to keep it. Who knew but that he might need backup when he hit the databar again, for a close-read?

A quick shower soothed him; putting on simple ship togs with flat pockets a pure relief after the hours of dealing with multiple comms, back-up comms, ID cards, business cards, info cards...

He hit the galley for a mug of 'mite, and returned to his desk, flipping back to the beginning of Freza's data. He sighed. It was dense stuff, all right, but it was well-organized, and meticulously cross-referenced. He ought to be able to finish a close reading, with note-taking, in three hours.

He opened the first file, gathered himself to read— closed his eyes, had a swallow of 'mite and sighed.

"Well," he said to the empty office. "Maybe four hours."

He'd been working steadily, taking notes, checking

the meanings of technical words and clauses, when a chance phrasing reminded him of the language Malu and Vally spoke between themselves, and he opened a side search.

After some traces and leaps of ingenuity, he thought that *magiestro* might be *Elsvair* dialect for *minister,* and he could trace *komercisto* to commissary and from there make the leap to *commissioner.* Which were at least consistent with each other and with a mistaken assumption that he was at the congress as a commissioner or deputy.

The confusing word was *kohno*, which wasn't spelled close to what it had sounded like, and, while meaning many things to many people, had no bearing on his *melant'i*, even a *melant'i* mistaken. In some places a *kohno* was a military officer, a person of some *melant'i* and import. However, in some back world locations *kohno* was an honor given, or willfully assumed—the sources weren't entirely clear—by someone who owned property or was otherwise acknowledged as being a leader. And just to confuse the docking even more, *kohno* was sometimes offered as an honorific by someone who didn't want to besmirch the *melant'i* of a worthy person. Unfortunately, as with any number of casual honorifics, the opportunity for ironic use was wide.

So! Did the crew of *Elsvair* intend *kohno* as their little joke, or were they trying to let him know that *they* understood he had a different and deeper *melant'i* than the average spacer he'd been pretending to be when he first met them? He'd need to get clear on which it was, going forward, he supposed.

He closed the side search and went back to Freza's files.

The timeline presented was ambitious; in fact portions of the various proposals had been taken from the *Envidaria* itself, though modified for new arrangements and necessities. Using current Loops and trade schedules, acknowledging the existence and growing importance of Tradedesk, suggesting that perhaps Liaden Scouts might be asked for assistance on the science side and that the Pilot's Guild certify reports of Jump anomaly as being essential sharing rather than proprietary information ...

That last was going to be difficult, Jethri thought, since it basically asked ship captains to rate the effectiveness of their drives and Struven units, the accuracy of their scans, even their tendency to purposefully offset Jump points to favor their ship's peculiar spins.

He remembered a long-ago conversation between Cris and Khat, when Cris had come back from helping some cousins who'd gotten short a pilot. Turned out the cousin's ship tumbled bad when it came out of Jump, while the *Market* only produced a modest spin that had long been corrected for in her 'quations. It hadn't meant much to him at the time; he'd only heard 'cause he'd been on Stinks, like he always was, and so usually everybody just talked like he wasn't there.

But it turned out that the tendency of some ships to leave Jump with spins or tumbles they'd not had on entering, and the fact that not all ships came into the location the 'quations aimed them for, but spread over a larger region of space—was important. *Arin* had known it was important, and the *Envidaria* emphasized the need to share info from ships and pilots, info that might have given a pilot and a trader an advantage in time and efficiency—*private* info—so it could be studied, and Dust Warnings added to the latest maps and directories.

That was going to be a hard sell. Jethri sighed. Almost all of it was a hard sell, and for a couple breaths he wished he'd decided otherwise on releasing the *Envidaria* into wide space.

And, then—there were the planets and stations that depended on their regular ships, and the ships that depended on bringing trade to those same planets and stations, not to mention the ships that would be lost for lack of good info.

Sighing, Jethri reached for his mug, and found it empty. He shook his head, frowned at the screens.

The sounds of ship-on-port were in the background, the extra vibrations, the additional notes of messages being received and sent locally, even the low *ding* of the annunciator telling the ship someone had something to deliver. Crew was taking care of that; the flowers had given way to personal cards of invitation to so many meals he'd have to eat nonstop for a Standard to do them all justice. He'd need to write notes, of course, but for this while, the cards could rest in the basket in the foyer.

He flipped back to the timeline. Two Standard Years, the *Envidaria* Team wanted from him, to stand as ambassador and do his best to save ships, planets, and lives, while finding a new and profitable route for *Genchi*, possibly finding time to take a test for master trader, and whatever else the master traders had in mind...

It was all a bit overwhelming.

"You're thinking too far out, Jeth," he muttered, and made an adjustment to the screen, so that only the

timeline for the pre-congress was visible. He pulled up
the list of committee meetings and seminars he was
scheduled to attend in order to explain the *Envidaria*,
the Dust, the need for *all* Loopers to join, not just
those who supplied the Seventeen Worlds. The Dust
would move on to threaten other systems, that was
certain. The protocols, supports, and contacts they
were building for the Seventeen Worlds were going
to be needed again and again, adjusted for each new
situation, though the framework would stay pretty
much the same.

The list of items he was obligated to attend as
speaker or presenter—that's a lot of meetings, he
thought, reading the descriptions. Along about the
third one, he realized that, though there *were* a lot
of meetings, each one was limited to thirty people.
That was good—he couldn't see himself down front
in a room that held hundreds, trying to explain the
whole business to a faceless sea.

A small group, he'd be able to see faces, adjust for
the audience. He might even know some attendees,
or at least their ships. He could make himself clear
to thirty people, even if one of them was Mac Gold.
He could make them understand *why* they needed to
do more than fly their Loops and tend their business,
and *why* the future was counting on them to join in.

He made some notes on hard copy, a habit he'd
picked up from Scout ter'Astin, who'd pointed out
that while "erased" digital notes could be recovered
or shared if someone had the proper equipment, the
same was not true of fiber products reduced to ash
and molecules in any standard recycling unit. Since
he didn't want directional notes to himself to make it

into digital formats where he might inadvertently add them to shared information, this was a good start.

He sighed, and realized that his nerves were—fizzing. It was like the feeling he got when his fractin was on alert—but his fractin was in his jewel-box, in his cabin.

"Think close in," he told himself. "Remember what Brabham said—pace yourself."

He made some more notes, sketching in some ideas. The best way to convince people to buy something was to be open and clear—or as Master ven'Deelin would occasionally say, apparently serious, though lately he'd begun to wonder about that—"A trader is made of window glass, my son, transparent to every eye."

He sighed, and looked at his mug again. It was still empty.

Things were, he reflected, speeding up for real.

And if he was going to be up to speed, he'd better get some sleep. He'd gotten used to Freza beside him, just that quick, and he had a doubt that he would sleep, without her, but a man had to try.

Sighing, he saved his files, turned off the comm, and went to bed.

. . . . . .

FIVE

. . . . . .

SURPRISINGLY ENOUGH, HE DID SLEEP, AND WOKE FEEL-
ing rested, and—somewhat optimistic about the coming day.

He showered and dressed, then sat to breakfast.

He'd started adding 'mite to his breakfast during
the relaxing days of pre-pre-congress, and it seemed
like a good idea to keep that up. He sipped, chose a
cheese muffin, and opened his screen to review his
day's schedule again.

It was somewhat more crowded than he recalled from
his review last night. A careful perusal showed him
why. In addition to his scheduled talks, presentations,
and turns at the table—and in one instance, *against*
a talk—there were several items marked as *musts*.
Opening the details, he saw that he was scheduled to
attend a large general informational meeting about the
organization of TerraTrade. A second meeting also had
him as one of a large group, gathered to be informed
about the administrative teaching campus on Trantor.

Jethri sat back, and sipped his tea, frowning, because
here was Bory's hand, writ large.

Tie him up in basic-level info-meets, keep him off
the floor and derail his presentations, was that it? Jethri

flicked through the details again, eyes narrowed. Not that the information was useless, if you didn't already have it. Which gave him an idea.

His *melant'i* as the proposed ambassador for the *Envidaria* was clear. However, it would not do to—openly—scorn the efforts a declared ally made on his behalf. And there *was* good basic information on offer. Which he didn't need, but *somebody* would.

He reached for the comm.

"You're right, Jeth—we oughta send somebody to those meetings Bory's been kind enough to arrange for us to get into. Got a couple worthwhile youngers—" Freza paused, apparently thinking.

"How about Taber, from *Lantic*?" Jethri asked suddenly. "In for the trade side, or something else?"

"Taber's all about the trade side," Freza said. "*Great* idea. I'll get Brabham to make the call personal."

She laughed, and he imagined her shaking her head.

"Bory's trying to slow you down, Jeth."

"I'm a little insulted," he said. "Did he think I wouldn't *see* that?"

"Well, he's gotta try," Freza said. "He don't know you, so it's like a test—how sharp is *this*—" she made her voice bold and deep, in imitation of Bory's, "*young trader* who's lead on his own Liaden ship?"

Jethri grinned. "He'll have to do better."

"'Spect he will. Next one's not gonna be so easy to spot."

"I got expert help," he said. "How's your schedule this evening?"

"Won't know 'til I know," Freza said. "Same might be said for you."

"I'm gonna do my best to keep the evening schedule open," he told her.

"Fair," she answered. "I'll do the same, but—no promises, Jeth. We're in it now, and we gotta work with what comes."

"Understood," he said, and added, "Until soon, Frez."

"Soon," she answered, and closed the connection.

He was reaching for his coat when he realized that he had let an important piece of information languish. He'd best be up-to-the-minute on Brabham's riot, he thought, for it would surely be a topic on the day.

He picked up *Balrog*'s comm, found the vid, and sent it to the room's large screen.

There was Brabham, on his scoot on an already crowded dock, his cluster of volunteers around him, and Freza to one side.

And on the opposite side of a crowd of Loopers catching up with each other—there came Bory, likewise the center of a cluster, walking purposeful, and maybe not paying as much attention to Desty Gold, walking and talking at his side, as the man might've supposed.

Jethri straightened his coat and smoothed the sleeves, eyes on the screen.

"Well, look at the crowd of us!" Bory boomed, stopping so sudden Desty went two paces past him. "Reminds me of when I was just first—"

"Bory!" Brabham could make some noise when he put his lungs into it, Jethri thought. "Is that Bory I hear?"

"The man himself!" Bory boomed, and people turned, startled, and then instinctively stepping out of the way of the big man bearing down on them.

Bory arrived at Brabham's scoot, the volunteers having

stepped aside in deference to such self-confidence. There was a moment, relatively silent, with Brabham and Bory gripping each other's forearms, two old friends, silently communing, before Bory broke contact, and turned to present Freza with a fulsome compliment, subtly shifting his position next to the scoot, and leaning forward slightly, possessively.

"If I'd had any idea you were coming in so early," Bory was saying, "I would've set up a proper meeting, Brabham. If you're of a mind right now, why don't we sit down together over this *Envidaria*, and—"

And *that* had been the wrong thing to say.

Jethri paused the vid, wondering if it *had* been a misstep or if it had been purposeful on Bory's part; if he'd realized he wasn't going to be able to co-opt Brabham with all his volunteers around, and had gotten creative.

If his idea had been to sow confusion, it had worked a little too well.

Jethri started the vid again and heard one of the crowd yell that the *Envidaria* was a plot to turn the Loops over to the Liadens, which actually had some sense behind it, Jethri thought, given his status as the 'prentice and adopted son of a Liaden master trader, and also the person who had released the *Envidaria* to all of space.

And here came Desty Gold, grabbing Bory's sleeve and looming over Brabham in his scoot, shouting insults and starting to look a little chancy—which was when *Lantic*'s Taber gathered some other of the taller volunteers with a look and a jerk of the head, and suddenly Desty didn't have a place to stand, on account there were three volunteers between him and Brabham.

Jethri fast-forwarded from there, saw Bory belatedly take charge of the mob he'd created, purposefully or not, booming down the loudest argumenters, while others peeled off to shout among themselves.

Sighing, Jethri admitted that Freza'd been right to not want him in that. Just a shouting-match, a mix-up to test the temper on the dock, maybe.

Jethri turned off the comm and stowed it in a right inside pocket, while *Genchi's* comm went in the left; cards in a public pocket, the small mingle of Terran and Liaden coins in another. His fractin was already in the pocket of his pants, by all signs completely disinterested in the riot.

Riot, he thought. Temper on the dock. He paused with his hand on his hideaway, considering the shouting, the angry faces, and the non-committal faces at the edge of the crowd. They'd looked sharp and rough, those faces, and he remembered Arin telling him that people wore weapons open or kept them close for reasons, and it was up to him to decide not only what was the reason, but how he wanted to be seen.

Liadens took social pressure and hideaways as their weapons of choice, though arms master Pen Rel had been known to wear his weapon openly on some ports where he insisted upon escorting the master trader.

Loopers tended toward the same thought process— open weapon, open warning, on rough ports; reputation and intimidation on ports not-so-rough.

Jethri had considered that the South Axis Congress and Trade Fair would be a place of refinement and courtesy. But he'd failed to take into account the likelihood of high tempers—especially of high tempers aimed particularly at him, as the bearer of unwelcome news. The *Envidaria* pushed change; change was hard, even for a good reason.

Right.

Jethri reached for his broader belt, with its built on holster. Then, he unlocked the weapon drawer and took out his other gun. He checked it and holstered it, then stepped to the mirror to manage the drape of his coat. After a moment, he slipped *Genchi's* comm onto the loop opposite the gun, and put his hideaway into its usual pocket.

Confronted with such a costume as this, Jethri thought Pen Rel would ask if he also carried a secret blade, in the event that the open gun invited trouble, rather than deflecting it.

He wasn't a knife fighter, Jethri thought irritably, knowing Pen Rel would openly laugh at him for saying so, and at the end of the day, the man *was* an arms master.

Jethri slipped the knife into his sleeve, as he'd been taught.

He checked the mirror again, deciding that he looked sufficiently dangerous. In fact, he looked like a man credited with the deaths of two people, even if one had technically committed suicide and the other wasn't *factually* dead.

"It's all about the rep, Jeth," he told his reflection, and turned toward the door. Time to get started on the day.

There was a sponsored reception when the table closed. Jethri's invitation had been hand-carried, and a quick consult with Brabham by comm had revealed that it was not something Jethri, as the ambassador of the *Envidaria*, could miss.

"Got something similar myself tonight," Brabham said. "Freza's got another. Between the three of us, we're just about enough to keep it all covered."

In fact, the reception had been useful. He'd made solid contacts, answered good, thoughtful questions, and had maybe even pulled a couple of waverers at the edge of the Dust zone over the line into supporting the *Envidaria*.

He got back to *Genchi* late, and full of nerves. He checked his messages—nothing from Freza—and sat down at his desk to review the next day's schedule, and sketch out some notes for tomorrow's big talk.

Distantly, he heard a ping—more flowers, he guessed, and wondered briefly where they all came from before going back to his notes.

A moment later, Bry Sen knocked on the edge of his open door, bowing apology for his interruption.

"I am at a loss, Trader. One has arrived at the hatch, bearing your card, insisting that you had desired an immediate meeting."

Jethri frowned. He'd spoken to so many people, given out not a few cards. But for most of the day, he'd had plans with Freza, and had been very careful to keep the evening clear. Nor could he remember demanding an immediate meeting with *any*one.

"At a loss in what way?" he asked Bry Sen.

"She gives a single name, as if you will know her personally. Malu?"

Jethri blinked, sighed, and rose.

"Oh," he said. "Malu. Of course."

In truth, he almost didn't recognize her. She had shaded and painted her lean face artfully so that it seemed rounder, and rosier, and subtly exotic. She had used a purple tint on her eyelids, which made her close-set brown eyes seem wider and more trusting. She had done something to her eyebrows, he thought, and her lips were fuller, looking soft, pliant. The entire effect was of a woman both fascinating and intriguing; innocent and knowledgeable.

Her clothes—a dark top cut low under a barely discernible piece of jewelry—a silvery gossamer net in which tiny jewels glittered and winked in the foyer's lights. She was wearing a rich brown skirt slashed like the sleeves of a Liaden gentleman's evening coat, the slashes lined with silver. The skirt flowed nearly to the decking on one side; the other side caught up above her knee with a silver riband. There were rings on her slender fingers. A pair of high black boots with a sensible low heel that would have had the boot makers of Seybol crying out in protest completed the outfit.

She might, Jethri thought, be going to a *shivary*, only—

"Minsha told me you and Vally were confined to *Elsvair*," he said. "So you understand my surprise at seeing you here."

"A determination has been made," she said grandly and stepped forward, her hand held out for him to shake, Terran-style, even as she swayed in a small bow he would have found too fascinating if Protocol Master tel'Ondor hadn't been determined to produce not only a person of manner from a Looper, but an adult from a callow youth.

"Minsha brought the news that you wished further instruction on some of those items you purchased from us. I am here to provide what instruction I can. I tried to send a message first, but your system is backed up, *Kohno*! It is a short enough walk from *Elsvair* to *Genchi*—and so I am here."

She gave him a large smile, and squeezed his hand strongly. This, too, might have been distracting, but Jethri's mind had caught the important detail. He slipped his hand free, and stepped back, his bow an instinct—*necessity*.

"A moment, please," he said. "I must check my info-stream!"

Nine quick steps from the foyer and he was on the bridge, where he confirmed that Bry Sen and the captain were working their way through a backlog.

"Eyes on the foyer, please," he murmured, leaning on the back of Bry Sen's chair. Captain sea'Kera obligingly opened a tile at the right side of his number two screen. There was Malu standing in the foyer, arms crossed, one hand stroking the delicate silver collar. She was frowning, but as if she was puzzled rather than angry.

"Comm lines backed up?" Jethri asked.

"Yes, Trader," Bry Sen said, his hands moving rapidly among the comm keys, sorting messages faster than Jethri could read the subject lines.

"We have been the recipients of quite a large number of portside service advertisements, and supposed informational mail, which was not. Automatic filters were overwhelmed, and the stream of legitimate messages was disrupted. Kel Bin went to *Balrog* and elder Pilot Brabham was good enough to alert port admin to the problem."

Jethri frowned. "*Balrog* was hit, too?"

"To a lesser degree, Trader. Captain sea'Kera and I

believe it is a general condition as Meldyne merchants seek advantage among the ships newly arrived for the congress, and not an attack targeting *Genchi*."

"We are," Captain sea'Kera said, "experiencing a high volume of legitimate comm traffic, Trader. There are many who wish to speak with you regarding your sponsorship of the *Envidaria;* and fewer, but not few, if you take me, Trader, who wish to renew the ties of kinship; among them are legitimate station alerts, and updates from the congress administrators." He glanced over his shoulder to Jethri. "I garner these intentions and meanings from the subject lines, Trader. Of course we do not open your mail."

"Of course not," Jethri said, inclining his head. "I am grateful for your insights and information, Captain."

"We're also in receipt of a round dozen messages originating off-station, Trader," Bry Sen continued. "Many of the names are familiar to me because of my House's connection to trade. Included among them are the Rabbit and the Star-With-Three-Rings."

Correspondence from Master ven'Deelin and Master pin'Aker might be expected, but a round dozen of other Liaden traders?

"Please forward those to my action queue," he said. He would answer those letters first, after he had found what information Malu had brought him.

He glanced again at Captain sea'Kera's screen. Malu was sitting, hands in her lap, eyes closed. She might have been asleep, or practicing board rest, or considering the most satisfying way to fillet a rude trader, *kohno* or otherwise.

"I had considered the wisdom of sending the young person to *Balrog* with her necessities, pleading the trader at study," Bry Sen said in Liaden. "My wits awoke just then, and thus I appealed to you."

Jethri blinked, for a moment considering Freza confronted by an apparent port trinket demanding to speak with the *kohno* on a matter of private business.

"I am," he answered in the same language, "in debt to your wits, Pilot."

"Never say so, Trader, for I will freely confess that your own wits astound me."

Jethri considered the top of the pilot's head, then met his eyes in the screen.

"My master trader would have judged you a silver-tongue, Pilot."

In the screen, Bry Sen blinked.

"I am properly set into my place, I believe."

"I felt the same way," Jethri assured him. "Tell me now—what might I do to assist?"

"You'll do your part, later, Trader," Captain sea'Kera said surprisingly. "Myself, I wouldn't care to read all these messages, much less answer them."

The voice he heard inside his head this time was not Master ven'Deelin's, but Dyk's. *Only so many hours in a shift, Jeth, an' that's just the flat truth.*

"Captain sea'Kera, you said some of those messages were coming in with subject lines referencing the *Envidaria*?"

"Yes, Trader, on the average of eight from every dozen."

"Send those to *Balrog*," he said, "and beg that they will answer those most urgent, as they are able."

"Yes, Trader."

Jethri frowned, staring at Malu's image on the screen.

"Also, those that seem to be requests from kin,

please direct to *Balrog*. They will have the most current listings of ships and families. It is true that I have been long away from my cousins and do not wish to make an error in my replies."

If it hadn't been *very* unLiaden, he would have said that he heard Bry Sen snort.

"It will be done as you say, Trader," Captain sea'Kera said.

"My thanks. If Kel Bin is not on some other necessary task, might he bring a light tea to the conference room? The young person from *Elsvair* and I will be conducting our business there."

"Certainly, Trader. Is there anything else?"

"Not at this present," Jethri said, and deliberately shook himself out of the Liaden mind-set to say, in Terran. "Carry on, crew."

He conducted Malu to the conference room and saw her seated with all courtesy on the leather chair Freza had occupied earlier. Like Freza, Malu touched the leather with approval, and inclined her head graciously.

"Indeed, you are a *magiestro*, are you not?"

"I'm a trader," Jethri said, hoping that bluntness would move the business along. Malu's word games were a distraction he would rather dispense with.

He was grateful for the relative roominess of *Genchi*'s conference room. Given Malu's tendency to lean toward him, and to touch, he chose the seat on the opposite side of the table for this meeting, and smiled.

Malu returned the smile, and fondled her necklet once more, rings shining against the silver netting.

Kel Bin appeared just then, bearing what Jethri thought must be the ship's former best tea service, bright with *Genchi's* name and seal, and not the service that had been used earlier, to serve Freza and Bory.

"Thank you, Kel Bin," Jethri murmured. "We will serve ourselves."

"Trader." His crewman bowed and left them, the door closing behind him.

Jethri lifted the pot and poured, feeling his face heat as the scent reached him. Not a working tea, this, but a social tea such as might be shared with a friend. A *close* friend.

He passed the cup to Malu, who held it until he had filled his own, then took a deep drink, giving no attention to the flavor or the intent, for which Jethri could only be grateful. He sipped from his cup, and set it aside.

"So this determination that was made in your favor—"

"Bah!" Malu said, and put her cup on the table, having drunk all of the tea. "In our favor it is not, *Kohno*! No, the determination is that we may leave our ship, but not together! And we are restricted to this docking level. We may not come up into the shopping district, we may not attend the festivities, nor even the business of the congress. Yet it has created so much busyness for port administration that they may not even make a true ruling regarding the complaint made against us until after the congress has ended.

"Look!"

She stood suddenly, brought her leg up, braced her boot against the table, and swept a hand downward. Jethri followed the gesture, and saw the tracking bracelet around her ankle.

"Should I leave this docking area, that device will report me and I will again be confined to the ship!"

Quickly, Jethri reviewed the Meldyne Station rules and regulations he had memorized.

"Station admin has to hear your case no later than three station-days after the complaint is filed," he said. "I'm—assuming that one of the station merchants made a complaint about your...tour the day we met?"

Annoyance crossed her face, as she flounced back into the chair.

"The station merchants make no complaint of us, *Kohno*. Why would they? No, this comes from Lufkit— off-station, you understand. Lufkit lays a complaint against Vally, with myself named a secondary, because... because we are so often on port together."

Jethri picked up his teacup, motioning for her to continue.

"Yes. Lufkit sends to Meldyne admin that Vally had been on Shaltren, which is a world that Lufkit does not approve of. Further, they say that Vally has been on Lufkit—which is perfectly true, *Elsvair's* own log attests it!—but that he had previously been on Shaltren—which *Elsvair's* log does *not* reflect— and did not report this to Lufkit admin, which is, you understand, a crime upon Lufkit, entailing fines, because we all know how much admin admires its fines, do we not, *Kohno*?"

Jethri put his cup down, wondering how to answer this, but she swept on as if she expected no answer.

"We showed the Lufkit inspectors the log. They did not believe us, and they were about to make a second duty-search, for which the ship would be obligated to pay the *fee*, which is just another word for *fine* and—and the captain decided that *Elsvair* would not remain on a port which sought to extort honest ships."

"So you lifted," Jethri murmured, in order to hold up his end of the conversation.

She smiled at him.

"So we lifted. We came, in due time, to Meldyne, and the great trade congress, which has brought so many here, yourself among them. We hoped for profit here. We hoped to make contacts, to attend the conference, and especially the festivities. But, no! What should occur but Lufkit admin contacts Meldyne admin, saying that Vally is suspected of being attached to a known criminal enterprise, and that Meldyne must send him back to Lufkit. Lufkit says that it is sending an escort, who is expected to arrive after the congress has completed itself. In the meantime, Meldyne admin confines us as I have said, until this escort arrives and *Elsvair*'s own logs can prove the lie."

Well, that did take them out of the local ordinances, Jethri thought, and leaned over to pour her another cup of tea.

She took it without thanks, drinking half in one gulp.

"Even if Vally and I are on the dock at the same time, the device will report, and we will be confined to *Elsvair* once more." She looked at him over the rim of her cup, her artfully painted eyes wide and soft. "It is very hard, *Kohno*."

She stood again, very slowly, as if she did not want him to miss an inch of her. Then she put the tea cup on the table, smiled slightly and spread her skirt between her hands, making a little unnuanced bow as she did so.

"Here I am, dressed for the *festivalia* of a mighty congress, and restricted. I ask, *Kohno*, is there not something you could do?"

"Do?" Jethri stared at her. "What do you think *I* can do?"

She moved her shoulders and the silver netting moved, the little gemstones flashing seductively.

"*I* am not a *magiestro*. It is my part to ask, and yours to oblige, or deny."

Jethri shook his head.

"I'm not a *magiestro*. I'm a trader. My father was a commissioner. He created the *Envidaria*, and I am here to represent it and the procedures it puts forward, so that worlds, stations, and Loopers can survive the incoming Dust. I don't have any—" he flailed here, as his brain wanted to provide him with the Liaden concepts so elegantly suited to the situation, and finally arrived at—"*leverage* with station admin. Lufkit has more, I'm sure."

Malu sat down, and folded her hands in her lap.

"So," she said, pressing her lips together. For a moment, she considered the decking, then looked up at him, eyes wide and soft once more.

"I thought you might call this *liaison* I hear of, between the congress and the station. You could tell them that you wish to attend the *festivalia* this evening, and that your friend you wish to bring with you, to introduce to your associates, is inconvenienced by this ankle-bracelet. You could ask that it be deactivated while I am in your company, and guarantee a time by which I will be back here on our dock, and the device reactivated."

That—Jethri felt a reluctant admiration for this plan. So simple. So innocent. Even Master ven'Deelin would have admired it, he felt, as one admires a piece of art.

He shook his head. "If you came only to ask me

to—*exercise my influence* with station admin, I'm sorry for both of us. I have no influence. I am not a *kohno*, any more than I'm a *magiestro*. A trader is what I am, that's all." Again, he recalled Master ven'Deelin, and her good friend Master pin'Aker, and shook his head.

"And not even a top-tier trader, at that."

Malu's frown was pronounced.

"You *are* a *kohno*! You are a person of power, Jethri Gobelyn and ven'Deelin. People will follow you, if you need them to, they will band together for you—already they do so, pleased with themselves that they have seen your quality so quickly! Some of course will follow your power, while others will resist it. I have heard on the comms that—"

Jethri saw her hear her own words, and stop, lips pressed tight.

He waited. She looked away.

"On the comms, Malu?" he prompted.

She brought her eyes back to his, her face still stormy.

"What else was there to do while we waited on the ship for the budsperson to make their *stupid* determination? The ships who are docked here—they are not careful, and many of the messages were in the open, anyway. Why should they hide when they are proud to stand for their own future, eh?"

It would, Jethri thought, be useful to have the names of the ships who were declaring for the *Envidaria*, and those who were against, except—it was snooped-out info, and more than that, if he asked for it, he gave Malu an advantage.

"So," she said defiantly. "I will call you *magiestro*, *kohno, and* trader, for that is what you are—all three!

They say you are taught by a Liaden trader of great substance and honor. Surely, then, you know how to be more than one thing!"

And he did, Jethri thought, know how to be more than one thing. It was figuring out which thing he *should be* at this particular point in time that was giving him some trouble.

He sipped tepid tea, thinking. Malu had come to him to provide what instruction she could on the Old Tech he had purchased. He had brought her to the conference room with the understanding that she would be providing that instruction. His *melant'i* therefore was plain.

He was a trader.

He put his cup down, and folded his hands on the table, feeling himself calm in his role.

Malu considered him, lips straight.

He nodded.

"I had hoped that you were here, as you said, to provide me with information about the devices I purchased. That's something that could benefit both of us."

She narrowed her eyes.

"I see the benefit to you," she said. "I see no benefit to me."

"That's because I haven't made my offer yet," he told her. "Don't rush the trade, Malu."

She raised her brows.

"I am instructed, *Kohno*. By all means, make your offer."

"I will bring the devices I purchased from you to this room. You will show me how you may have handled them already, especially if you can do so without activating it. I want to be sure of my purchases.

I will pay you for your time and your expertise—a consultant's fee."

She said nothing, her eyes measuring his without flinching. Finally she let her breath out in a soft hiss.

"Tell me then, *Kohno*—what is my time worth, to tell you stories about strange objects?"

"That's a good question. If you don't have a figure in mind, I'll ask the ship's copilot to come in and go over the rates posted for the congress with you. I'll retrieve the items in question, and when I come back, we can negotiate from current rates to a payment that is fair and reasonable. Does that suit?"

She pressed her lips together, saying nothing, and he added.

"Of course, if you must discuss this with your trade advisor . . ."

She looked up sharply.

"I am able to decide this. Yes, let us do this thing. Let the evening at least be profitable, if it cannot be entertaining."

"Excellent," he said, and turned his head as Kel Bin quietly asked from the open door. "More refreshment, Trader?"

Jethri glanced at Malu. He believed her story about wanting to attend the parties and meet people, though he questioned her motives. Malu, he thought, was someone who needed to be among people, a person suited to crowds and worthy of admiration. He couldn't provide a crowd of admirers, but he could offer a little festivity.

"Would you care for a light luncheon before we go to work?" he asked her. "Is there anything in particular you would like?"

Malu looked startled—genuinely so, as if either the offer of food, or being consulted on *which* food was something that did not often come her way.

"It is too early for wine, I think, when we have business ahead of us. So—tea would be good, *Kohno*. To eat—" She took a breath as if she was about to say something, glanced at Kel Bin and smiled before turning back to Jethri.

"You know your own larder best, *Kohno*. I will be happy to eat of whatever feast you provide."

"A fortifying tray for two," Jethri said to Kel Bin in Liaden, "with a fitting tea."

"Yes, Trader." Kel Bin swept a bow, and was gone.

SIX

AS BEFORE, MALU ATE WITH QUICK EFFICIENCY. SHE DID not compliment the food, or attempt to make conversation. Jethri sipped tea and watched her, from time to time taking a bite of a cheese pastry that he didn't particularly want.

In an astonishingly short time, the tray was empty, but for the dishes. Teacup in hand, Jethri sat back, and Malu did the same, leaving her empty cup on the table.

"Can you tell me," he said, "how many active fractins are in those cases I purchased?"

Malu looked up, raising a hand to the jeweled necklet, fingertips stroking the glittering points.

"No, *Kohno*," she said after a moment, "I cannot tell you. Which is to say that I do not know."

She seemed truthful, even regretful, yet Jethri felt the unmistakable fizz of fractin energy. He considered her.

"I wonder if the answer would be the same, if I asked it with the pen activated?"

She glared at him, plainly exasperated.

"The answer would remain the same. *You* may be able to see through people and find such things, but

365

I cannot." She paused, and glanced a little aside. "We did know that there *might* be Befores where we were going, when we found the dead ships. It was information passed to us by someone who has worked with the—with your—uncle in the past." She inclined her head slightly.

"Minsha advises that, while you are not the Uncle's own person, you are to be treated openly on these topics. Therefore, I tell you what I know of these matters, as I would tell the Uncle himself. I do not know how many active fractins are in the lots you purchased from us."

"And this site—the dead ships? What killed them?"

She stroked the necklet again, and shook her head. "I do not know. We found wreckage, and bodies, and stored items. Some of them were clearly not true Befores. Others were as you have seen—powers that we do not know."

"But you've been using some of these things!"

"Not all of them came from that site. Some have been with us, or with Minsha, for many Standards. I will tell you, *Kohno*, that finding out what they do—that is best accomplished a little way apart from crowded places. Some of the devices did come with notes, but most, we found their purpose ourselves, or—like the pen—not at all."

"The device that you used to steal the jewelry up at the mall," Jethri said. "Did that come with notes?"

Malu looked down her nose at him.

"I stole nothing, *Kohno*. I was testing the device, which, as you saw, pushes things. It has been useful to us on occasion. Minsha advises that if we continue to use it, we will be taken up by the *garda*, or port admin. So, it is no longer in our inventory."

Again, a fizz along his nerves. Jethri leaned forward.

"You're wearing something now, aren't you? Something from Before."

"Am I?" She stroked the necklet again. The fizz was definite this time and he leaned forward, pointing.

"That," he said. "The object you wear around your throat."

"This?" Another touch, another fizz. "We think this is not Old Tech. It was a gift, wrapped for sending, in the ship's mailroom. There was a name on it—I think...Isa—*Vally* and another found it. Clearly it is old, but not so old as to have been from Before. It is a fine thing, and we thought we might sell it, but we would first need an inspection by a jeweler, such as the one we expect to be on the ship arriving soon."

"Every time you stroke it," Jethri said carefully, "I—*feel*—it respond. I've felt this around other Befores."

She continued to stroke the net, and Jethri had the conviction that it was aware, that it was trying to do...*some*thing.

"When you move your hands like this," he said slowly, demonstrating the motion on himself, "at the top, near your neck, there's less energy. When you stroke downward—over the jewels, then there's more energy. It may have been a gift, but it's no ordinary thing you're wearing. Not contemporary. There's—This is not an ordinary thing you wear—it's Old Tech."

"We *looked*, I say to you, *Kohno*. We are not novices, though we are not so experienced as your uncle. And now, I think that I will not answer any more questions until we have settled on my fee."

That was certainly fair, he thought, and nodded, putting his cup aside as he stood.

"Excuse me while I go talk with my copilot. He'll help you find a rate that's fair to both sides. While you're doing that, I'll fetch the devices."

She inclined her head, granting him permission to attend his business, and he left her, not without a quiver of the nerves.

Happily, he met Kel Bin in the corridor.

"We have finished," he said in Liaden. "The lady ate with very good appetite. The food was flavorful and the tea well-chosen. My compliments."

Kel Bin bowed the Liaden equivalent of an ear-splitting grin.

"The lady will shortly be joined by Bry Sen," Jethri went on. "Please remain until he arrives, in the event that she should want anything. After Bry Sen has arrived, please bring a thermal pot of working tea, and some sweet crackers."

"Yes, Trader." Kel Bin bowed again and moved toward the conference room. Jethri continued on to the bridge.

"Bry Sen," he said. "A word with you in the galley, please."

"I am at your side in bare moments, Trader. Only let me mark my place."

He was exactly that quick; Jethri had barely arrived in the galley when the pilot joined him, touching the door to close it.

"Is there a problem?" he asked in Terran.

"Not—as such," Jethri said carefully. "I want to make sure we're reading the same instruments, like we used to say on my ship."

Bry Sen's face lit. "I like that one," he said enthusiastically.

"Use it often," Jethri said cordially. "This'll be the quick-form 'cause we got bidness waitin'. If you find yourself not in agreement, say it, hear?"

"I hear." Bry Sen leaned a hip against the table and crossed his arms over his chest, face serious, eyes watchful.

"Right. You know that sometimes I deal in fractins and the like—got the knack from my father, and I hear just recent from my uncle that it's in the family. Now, it's those things that aren't fractins we're dealing with, here. I bought some few items off the young person's ship, and she's here now to give me tutoring on how they work.

"Unnerstand me, these are *devices*, such like the Scouts find themselves willing to confiscate. I don't deal dark or even grey, as the thing's seen Terran-side, but we're a mixed ship and gotta consider the Liaden-side as well. I don't willingly tarnish a pilot's reputation, and I'm right in with Master pin'Aker's plans for your future on *Genchi*, but—"

Bry Sen grinned.

"Just like you to think of it! My rep's solid, my friend—Terran-side *and* Liaden-side! Can't be otherwise, didn't we agree between us? Not with Master pin'Aker in it!"

Jethri felt his face relax into a grin.

"So long's you're sure," he began, and Bry Sen clapped him on the shoulder.

"I'm sure," he said, then dropped back a step and bowed as to a comrade. "All honor to you, Jethri ven'Deelin. My *melant'i* is secure."

Jethri returned the bow, straightened and grinned.

"Thus assured, I immediately place you in peril," he said.

"Am I to attend the young person, Trader?"

"You are, indeed, but with a mission in mind. We must find a balanced fee for consulting. The young person is unsure, her advisor being absent, and also inclined to grasp ahead of herself."

"I will be pleased to assist the young person and the trader to find balance in this matter," Bry Sen said gallantly. "Do I go at once?"

"Of your goodness. I must fetch those devices for which I seek instruction, and will join you as quickly as I may."

"I go," Bry Sen said—and he did.

Grinning, Jethri left the galley, heading for the trader's personal cargo area.

Bry Sen and Malu were on good terms by the time Jethri returned.

"We have arrived at a range," Bry Sen said, turning the screen to Jethri, "by triangulation, if you will, Trader. We have compared rates from recent trade journals, rates listed on Meldyne Station's job boards, and those offered by the congress for on-site spot-work. We agreed that this is not a congress-specific project, and that a clean average of trade journal and Meldyne rates would give us our best answer."

Jethri looked at the screen, flicked through the reference links, and back to the suggested fee.

Malu had agreed on a basic fee for arriving in answer to Jethri's request, and then a per-shift rate, payable in quarter-shift increments, wholly. The per-shift was eye-opening, but Jethri didn't think the consultation would take a full quarter-shift, much less flow over into a second, which meant that Malu would receive a reasonable amount of credit in exchange for her special knowledge.

Jethri looked to her.

"You agree to these terms?"

"*Kohno*, I do."

"I agree, too," he said, and put his thumb against the screen before turning it back for her to do the same. She blinked, and slipped the rings from her right hand before fixing her thumb to the screen.

Bry Sen stepped up to affix his print as witness. When it was done, he looked up.

"Else, Trader?"

"Please send a copy of the agreement to *Elsvair*," Jethri said. "We will want privacy for the consultation."

Bry Sen bowed. "Trader." He gathered up the portable screen and left, door sealing behind him.

"He is clever, that one," Malu said, her rings now returned to her fingers.

"I think you're right," Jethri said, half-distracted.

He'd stopped in his quarters on his way back to the conference room, and had his lucky fractin in his pocket. It had been *interested* in the small crate of objects he'd been carrying, but now it was—excited. Very excited.

Jethri took a deep breath.

"That—necklace . . ." he began.

Malu drew herself up.

"Do you think this is for sale?"

"Yes," Jethri said frankly. "I think you wore it here because you wanted to sell it."

"I wore it because I was seeking a party!"

"Maybe you did. But you brought it here, to me, and it's Old Tech."

"It is *not* Old Tech!" she exclaimed. "Here—see it for yourself!"

She lifted her hand toward the plunging line of her blouse, touched something, and whirled, the necklet fluttering like silver wings before it winked out of sight.

Jethri straightened. His fractin was even *more* interested, if that was possible, but—

"Where?" he demanded.

Malu laughed and stepped closer.

"Hold out your hand, *Kohno!*"

He did so, palm up, and she brought her fisted hand close, opening the fingers one by one.

It poured into his palm, all but weightless, nearly liquid, taking his breath, and sending a rush of icy clarity into his head. The fractin in his pocket stood up and cheered, if he was any judge of the matter.

Malu stepped back.

"*Kohno?*" she said, her gaze intent.

He took a breath, looked down at the pooled silver in his palm, pinched it between thumb and forefinger, shaking it out, found edges, and spread his hands. The netting stretched, took on shape, until it became not a necklet, but a capelet, a fine metallic mesh into which the tiny gems were woven in a pattern he could almost recognize. He held it up, feeling that fizz along his nerves, tracing the path of the gems by eye.

The bulk of them went from the shoulders down to the waist, in a flared sweep of tantalizing color, leaving the inside border stone-free, except for a dozen matched pairs down the edge, that looked to be fastenings.

To test that theory, he brought his hands together until each stone found its partner with surprising strength.

"Each pair of the magnets is matched," Malu said. "If you try to put the bottom one with the top, they repel each other."

Jethri glanced at her, then back at the dainty garment, feeling his hands warming, and something else—a familiarity, a yearning...

"This is meant to *do* something," he said, and turned to put the capelet on the table, spreading it so that its shape held no more secrets.

Or did it?

He motioned Malu closer, and touched the back of its neck with light fingertips. "This here, see? Is it a frill, or something else?" He pushed with his fingers and the extra fabric, if something so fine could be said to ever be extra, unrolled, just a fraction.

"You have good sight, *Kohno*. We did not see that, and we *did* examine it, very closely. Even Minsha said it was jewelry."

Jethri listened with half an ear, tugging at the fabric a little more firmly.

"You did not tear it, did you?" Malu asked. "Such a lovely thing—it would be a shame."

"No, I didn't tear it. Look—it's a hood."

It *was* a hood, thickly woven with the small gems, and how it had remained invisible to hand and eye was something Jethri wasn't certain he wanted to know.

He met Malu's eyes.

"*Not* contemporary."

"So you say, *Kohno*, and so I now believe, as well." She sighed, then turned her hands palm up. "We had all agreed to sell it, when we thought it was jewelry. Now that it is revealed as an item in your area of interest—yes, it is for sale."

She dropped her hands.

"But do not ask me to teach it to you, *Kohno*. In minutes, you know it better than I, who held it for months."

He nodded, and turned, leaving the capelet on the table, though he felt a pang at putting it aside.

"Let's talk about the things you do know something about. We'll come back to that one when we're done with those."

"Yes," she said. "That will be best. Remember, *Kohno*, that some of these items are risky. It's often better to test them in private."

"I agree. Old Tech is risky. This—" he gestured at the walls—"is as private as we can arrange. Do you have reason to believe any of the objects I have here are life threatening?"

She turned to the box, and removed each item, one by one, putting them on the table as far away from the capelet as was possible. When they were all lined up, she considered them, frowning slightly.

It was, Jethri thought, theater, and of a kind he could appreciate. The art of hesitation was one every trader practiced occasionally.

Speaking of art—Malu's painted face, now that he really looked at it, was more art than artifice. Whatever she and the rest of *Elsvair*'s crew were about—and he didn't doubt that some of it crossed the line from merely questionable into grey—it wasn't a careless life, but practiced—and dangerous, if wrecked ships and side-salvage was a routine part of it.

Malu stirred.

"The pen, we know already—another of your discoveries, *Kohno*. This one, and this—I do not know, nor does Vally or Minsha." She put three items back into the box.

"*This* one," she touched the device Minsha had brought to him with a light fingertip. "I know very well what this one does. Let us begin here."

The item from Minsha was, as he had begun to suspect, a general jamming device. It was, Malu told him, possible to turn it off, but somewhat less possible to *keep* it turned off.

"It is as if it is so eager to perform its function that it will turn itself back on, if it has been idle too long," Malu told him, and shook her head at the device, as if it were a disappointing child. "We had it wrapped, but it was not enough. A stasis box generally is sufficient for such eager items, but we did not have one free."

Jethri deliberately did not ask what was in those implied full boxes. He did call Kel Bin, and asked him to have someone deliver a small stasis box to the corridor outside the conference room.

"This one?" he asked, pointing to another device.

"For this one, we will need cameras and comm units. It is easier to show you what it does, and it is—less risky than that one." She jerked her head toward the jamming device.

"All right," Jethri said, and made another call, this time to have two stand-alone cameras and two comm units also brought to the corridor outside the conference room.

While they waited, Jethri poured them both a short mug of work tea, and leaned against the wall sipping his.

"Does *Elsvair* only do salvage work?" he asked, since he had developed some curiosity on that point.

Malu shrugged, deliberately provocative, or so he thought.

"*Elsvair* does work of many kinds, though it is true that we are not...officially Loopers."

"Aren't you?"

Another shrug, careless rather than suggestive.

"My people do much as Loopers do. We live on the ship if born there, but we also have other arrangements. Some of my cousins have lived on planets for years, while others work as side help on the lesser ships. We stay in touch, you understand—as you and your cousins stay in touch across ships. But, no. Your TerraTrade and your Combine, they permit us, but they do not prefer us, and the Liaden masters are much the same."

The comm pinged. Jethri answered and received Kel Bin's report that the stasis box and requested equipment had been delivered to the conference room door.

They practiced with the second device first in the conference room. Jethri noted the effect in the cameras. Instead of jamming the transmission, the device suggested to the cameras that they were seeing Jethri, even when he was standing behind them, with Malu directly in their sights.

"By doing *this*—" Malu demonstrated a setting change, "you may convince them not to see you at all, even if you stand before them." She handed the device back to him and stepped away from cameras. "Try and see."

It was as she said. He was invisible to the eyes of both cameras.

"Press the blue button, and you will also not be heard," Malu continued. "The blue and the yellow together, and you may place your voice into a conversation a distance apart from your location."

"How long a distance?"

"*Kohno*, I do not know precisely. It is not the sort of test one might make on port, without more risk than Minsha allows us."

"Well, maybe we can get a range on it. You stay here, with this comm and the cameras. I'll take the device and the other comm down to cargo and run through the varies."

They'd established that the device could act across the length of *Genchi*'s interior, and Jethri was experimenting with combinations of settings. His comm pinged, and he heard Bry Sen's voice.

"Trader?"

"Pilot?"

"I am here, as you know, on the bridge with our good captain, who points out to me that we have just seen what may be your image, faded and full of static, on three of our external video feeds. Do assure me that you are not spacewalking without a suit."

Jethri blinked, then frowned at the device in his hand.

"I'm in the small hydroponics work room. Our guest is in the conference room speaking to me on the local comm video feed. Tell me about this image."

"It is superimposed on our usual feed."

Jethri switched comms.

"Malu, is it the red button and the bar to the right, to make the image disappear?"

"Yes, *Kohno.*"

He went back to Bry Sen. "My apologies, Pilot. Allow me to make an adjustment."

Jethri, who had moved the bar to the left, slid it back slightly.

"Your image is fading," Bry Sen said, not sounding comforted. "But we should not be seeing it at all!"

Jethri pushed the bar further.

"Gone," Bry Sen said after a long pause. "External camera feed returns to normal."

Jethri pressed the yellow button.

"We now have static on all external cameras. Are the pilots allowed to know if this is an effect of the trader's ongoing business?"

"I was establishing a range," Jethri said, as contritely as the Liaden comrade mode allowed. "Forgive me, Pilots. Testing is now suspended. Your input has been extremely useful."

He switched comms again.

"I'm coming back to the conference room, Malu. Please choose another device."

The quarter-shift was almost done, and there remained one last item.

Jethri sipped tea, having twice gently brushed aside Malu's offer to consider the consulting over, if he'd like to have a quieter chat somewhere more comfortable.

"Tell me about this . . . garment," he said finally. "Today was the first time you'd worn it? It hasn't been off-ship or in public before?"

"It has not been off-ship since we found it. I put it on because it is so beautiful, and felt good to wear. A thing that a person might wear to a *festivalia.*"

Jethri nodded and put his mug aside. His fractin buzzed slightly as he ran his fingers down the fine material, finding the touch of the small gems enticing, sensual.

He picked the netting up, shook it lightly, and on impulse spun it around, feeling it settle across his shoulders—Malu was right, he noted, it *did* feel good to wear.

In what seemed a natural fall the hood came over his head. His hair stood on end briefly, then the frisson faded, and the hood settled closely, smoothly. He lifted a hand and ran a negligent finger down the line of paired magnets, sealing himself into the netting.

Malu hissed, said something sharp in the language he had heard her speak with Vally. He heard the words, almost understood them, stored them away to hear again.

He felt the small device in his pocket warm and settle, pleased.

Jethri smiled. Yes.

Yes, this was *his* to wear, *his* to own, *his* to merge with and learn from.

Again Malu hissed. She made a motion, rings glowing, and around her a nimbus formed, as if she had invoked protections. That was wise, though she was sadly a foolish girl. To dare the wearing of the hood? Well, her ignorance had protected her, and he would protect her now. After all, she had done him a very great service.

The hood—the hood lay close against his head, closer than his hair, embracing his skull, comforting and welcome, as the knowledge began to flow.

The rings—*secoro* rings; small disrupters. Effective protection from the mischief of such devices as they had been toying with earlier, but nothing that could prevent *him* from doing as he pleased. At the moment, it pleased him to do her no harm; he had more important matters to tend to.

He recalled the phrase she—Malu—had spoken just now, and he knew the words and their meaning as well as he knew his own name.

"*Cieloghia, savu min de stulteco,*" he said aloud. "This what you asked? That is—" He chose Terran because the Liaden translation would have given him—no, would have *required* him!—to make demands of her loyalty . . . "Celestials, save me from stupidity."

Malu's eyes widened, and she nodded, twisting the rings 'round her fingers.

The motion drew his eye, and he spoke again.

"You wear rings that hide your touch if you wish it, rings that hide your fingerprints and that can give you extra grasp. Rings *tuned* to you."

She nodded again, her face wary.

"Which celestial would you have help you?" he asked. "They've been left behind, the celestials. We are in new space. New arrangements follow!"

If it was possible, he would have said her eyes widened more, for he had spoken in the language of her ship kin. According to their own myths the kin were bands of stragglers and opportunists brought together in the new space by the elder Uncle to insure that the strange places were fit to live in, that those living on planets did not fall into the habits of the old order.

She answered in the same language, admitting with

an odd tilt of the head that was somehow also of that language, "I have no names, we were never permitted the names, since they are gone!"

"Then tell me which stupidity are you to be saved from—mine, for donning this, or yours, for bringing it to me when I could not ignore it?"

"*Kohno*, I meant no harm." She spoke now in Terran, which made Jethri happier, this speaking in strange tongues made his head feel vaguely fuzzy, and not quite himself—no, that was wrong. As if he was *more* himself.

"Did *any* of you try this on?" he demanded.

"Only me that I know of; to me are given the little treasures we find while we wait for our heptad to form, since so many of the *gadje* buyers will deal high to make a woman smile at them. The rings were like this; it was only after I wore them for a time that we saw they had more effects than we knew. I have not tried to sell them. They are too plain, too clearly not marvelous, and so the dealers would not pay well for them."

Gadje. It came to him that *Elsvair*'s crew was *not gadje*, and everyone else was, it seemed, though he wasn't quite sure what a heptad was, it carrying overtones of clan, crew, and family all at once.

"So this—device, the one I'm wearing. It translates, or knows words." He smiled. Malu did not smile back. "I wonder what else it does."

He stroked the clasps with the flat of his hand, thinking that they might do double-duty, thinking that the netting held secrets, like the weather machine he'd fumbled with at Tarnia's vineyard—secrets, knowledge, danger—

The weather machine, he thought, recalling its feel in his hand, the dial, the symbols...

It was as if a training vid began to run inside his head. Here was the very device with which he had inadvertently created a wind twist. The vid continued, now overlaid with a stern voice explaining the system, and the meaning of the symbols. This was someone personally familiar with the device, explaining the meaning of the pictures that flashed through his head—the proper way to activate the device, though one must *never* do this— There! *That* had been his error! He'd set three controls to maximum while trying to make it do *some*thing. That was the very first error he was warned against!

He struggled briefly with his thoughts. The information on the weather machine was interesting, but not current. Trade was on the table, and he must know...

He must know, he thought deliberately, strongly, if this device—the device he was wearing—held operational files for itself. If so, how could he find and review them, quickly?

But there—in his head he heard a voice, vaguely familiar in tone and timbre, speaking on the self-storing smart-bead training assistant for humans and top-level Batchers, not to be copied or distributed.

"Batchers?" Another term that he ought to know, he thought, and another vid opened. He saw a line of seven people, or a line of the same person. A batch of clones, the voice instructed, and Jethri blinked. Who would make *batches* of clones? Who would *need* batches of clones?

Information—no! Memories!—flowed from somewhere then, somewhere not in his experience but as real as if he had himself stood in a sterile room, watching as a line of ceramic pods were opened, one by one, and people stepping out of each pod, naked and identical.

There were signs on the walls, information on the board above each pod. He'd never seen the language, knew neither alphabet nor words, yet—he knew their *meaning*, understood that this was a facility in which people were made in Batches, to order, and he suddenly *knew* that the ten identical people he was staring at were a mining team, belonging to—the name of the company rippled past his understanding, as if the memory had been deliberately smudged.

Jethri shook his head, trying to step away from the vid running in his head, the vid that was answering his question all too thoroughly. He'd heard of sleep learning modules and of the theory of that kind of learning, but this—this was something else. This, he reminded himself, was an Old Tech device in action, fully functional.

And Old Tech devices were so very risky.

Batchers were needed, the voice-over was instructing him, not only to fulfill the functions for which they were created, but their production was also necessary to shield a part of the resistance's plan to defeat the *sheriekas*, the Great Enemy bent on the destruction of life. There was another level of Batchers being manufactured beneath the superficial production of cheap labor.

The resistance was creating super soldiers, stronger and better equipped to fight the Enemy—to defeat the Enemy.

The vid shifted, the image coming in close to the

instruments and readouts screens, and there—there were frames with fractins slotted in, more frames where technicians were placing more fractins, willfully, in service of the resistance.

Jethri's attention was divided as never before: while he clearly saw Malu standing by the table, face intent, fingers entwined, the images inside his head were compelling, insistent, and he knew, *ancient*, extragalactic and extra-universal, terrifying memories recorded by Old Tech before the Great Migration.

He sat straighter, reaching for the tea, or the 'mite, or whatever drink it was he had there, he forgot, repeating to himself that despite the absolute conviction, the assumed knowledge, of this sharing, there *was no* Great Enemy destroying system after system, no need for dozens, thousands, *millions* of manufactured soldiers and countless batches of other clones to support them.

It was tea. He tasted it, knew it to be a fine tea, recalled the name, found some *other* process going on inside his head—three—four! As if his dream states had been called to attention, as if, he thought, the device—the smart-beads—had assessed him as he was assessing it, and had realized how deficient he was in basic, necessary knowledge—

And it was trying to catch him up.

He made an effort, trying to disentangle himself from the various streams of information, but *he* was only one thread, and a young one, at that.

Data thundered through his head; somehow he was able to view all of the threads simultaneously, understand—assimilate—the information without the effort of learning it.

One thread was trying to...to annotate what was wrong with the vision of the frames and clones, to correct the history, or amend it to include what was a new—a *newer*—history, that there had been a strong but ultimately hopeless resistance, followed by an escape, a Great Migration.

Another thread was doing its best to include him into the fabric of the device, to pull his experience, examine it, and record it for whoever came along next.

In the meanwhile, his idle wondering thought about tea had become an ever-widening search, expanding into general beverages, branching into beer and wine, which was a known heading somehow, and others to variations on yeast-based hot drinks and others to coffee, and then his particular knowledge of teas Liaden, and wines Liaden, and simply Liaden, because things Liaden was a *new* heading, the fact of Liad was *interesting*, the fact of tradeships doubly so...

If his eyes were not closed, it was because he was too busy to concentrate on that action while he analyzed the tea in hand, recalling bulk prices on ports he hadn't seen in two Standards, recalling the failings of it as listed by competing tea masters, and the rebuttals of dockside sellers and happy buyers, all these appearing as overlays in his mind's eye, like extra screens at the piloting board.

Malu was beside him, eyes very wide. He knew that because she'd touched his hand, the shields her rings gave her proof against this device's demands. Her approach had sparked another thread, and now he'd somehow started a file on *Elsvair* and Malu, recalled that she'd been hoping for some wine and times...

"*Kohno*? *Kohno*!"

She said something in her own language, demanding that he return her property, foolish child.

But there, while the information about tea was being compiled, there was wine!

Wine, yes, wine was a good topic. Universal. Extra-universal.

Did he know anything about Tarnia's wines? He did! He knew the feel of the leaf and vine, the smell of the grapes, the—

Yet another file opened, collating the manner of transporting and sharing wine, which led to general trade routes, styles of trading, what history he had of Looper trade, the names of his—

Malu touched his hand again, pinching the web between thumb and forefinger. It hurt; the sensation was filed, and her voice, calling for Jethri Gobelyn ven'Deelin, and there was a edge to her voice that was fear, yes, surely fear. That was . . . not good. Who knew what the child might do if she was frightened?

Truly, he should answer her, send her away, so that he could concentrate without these minor interruptions, but he had time to organize this new file before he spoke. It was important that he thought *right now* about being named Jethri Gobelyn, knowing the while that he was line kin of the Uncle, Arin's scatter.

Malu patted his hand, softly, and through the datastorms he understood her to have moved away. In a moment, he heard her speaking loudly in Terran.

"Emergency! The trader requires assistance, now!"

Well, an emergency, that was interesting. He wondered about the trader and what assistance might be required, and why Malu couldn't provide it. She had offered assistance, he remembered that, offered a

sharing, in fact, though slyly, which could also have
been interesting, though she was not someone Arin
had ever seen . . . and he needed to concentrate—so
much was clear, answers to questions he'd never known
he had . . . but wait, here was another line of inquiry
on Arin and Grig, with sidelines to Dulsey, all neatly
being plucked, considered, sorted, stored, with the
Envidaria coming complete and unabridged to his
instant recall. He remembered the game he'd played
and won as a child, a game that inspired Arin to—

"Jeth?"

Only a few people called him that, Loopers and
family; the list of the people who'd called him "Jeth"
was collected into a dataset, one with friends and
lovers—it had been hard to get Liadens to unbend
to Terran diminutives, even when one's hands were
molding . . .

"Jeth?"

So yes, this one was not Malu. This one had nibbled
his ear and stood beside him staunching his bleed-
ing. Malu, Malu called him *Kohno*. No, this one
was Freza DeNobli, she from a line of the DeNobli
and Carresens alliance, Looper bred. All of what he
thought about her and knew about her filtered into
data, information, relationship and genealogy charts
along with the secret knowledge of touches that gave
her pause, the ones that made her tremble for him.

"Jeth! Look at me! Talk to me! Tell me my name!
Jethri!"

Perhaps it was the touch of *her* hand, and her
imperative squeeze, or the volume of her voice or even
the sounds of shushing as Bry Sen discreetly ushered
Malu out of the room, and he heard the murmured

words, "I will see you to your ship, Consultant. The captain is even now calling to inform them of your quick arrival."

"Jeth," Freza said again. "Listen, right? That consultant, she says she doesn't think taking this hood off will hurt you, because you have an affinity, and there's an accord between you, whatever that might mean to you. What it means to me is that we're going to get this thing off your head, so if there's any withdrawing you can do, do it now. Tell me *yeah*."

He gathered himself.

"Yeah."

There was a split second of hesitation, a blankness that would have been terrifying if it had lasted any longer, and then—

The threads rolled up, the files in process, and those being reviewed closed, the speculations, edits, and additions folded in on themselves and vanished, each into its own bead, or cluster of beads. He knew that was what happened, though he didn't see it. The information would be waiting for their next session. Truly, he should rest now. It had been, said the shadow of the teaching voice, a vigorous and informative session.

"With me, Jeth?"

"Yeah," he said again, and opened his eyes, surprised to find that they'd been closed, after all.

Freza's face was inches from his. She smiled at him, but the corners of her eyes were tight.

"That's good," she said. "You wanna take this pretty the rest of the way off? I'd do it, but I'm not clear on how to unseal it proper, and I gather it's something you'd rather not seen torn."

There was no power that Freza could bring to bear

that would tear the capelet, that Jethri knew without any doubt. He did feel some concern though, for her, and what the thing might do, if she touched it.

"I'll take it off," he said.

"Do that," she said. "I've got Kel Bin here with a stasis box, open and ready to receive."

He raised his hands to where the hood lay 'round his neck, fought an intense, but brief battle with the urge to draw it back up, and instead folded it back and back again, his fingers tingling as it withdrew into its secret pocket. Bringing his hands to the closures, he felt a stirring, and waited as a blurry pattern formed laboriously inside his head. Ah, there was a correct order to touch the magnets, if he wished to save his recordings, and his places in the files. He touched the magnets in the order shown, the capelet fell open, and he slipped it off, holding it in one hand as it folded in on itself again, and again, becoming a slender silver necklet, adorned with small gemstones.

"Box," he said, and there was Kel Bin, box in hand, opening tipped slightly toward Jethri. He placed the netting carefully inside, feeling a pang as it slipped away from his fingers, and withdrew his hand.

"Seal it, pray, and take it to my private hold."

"Trader." Kel Bin slid the lid into place, triggered the lock and the field, bowed and left.

Jethri closed his eyes and sighed. The inside of his head felt—empty. Peaceful.

He felt cool fingers against his cheek and opened his eyes again.

"Freza."

"Still," she agreed, her smile easier this time.

"Thanks," he said.

"No problem," she said. "Feeling yourself? Nothing too wrong or too good?"

"Tired," he said, realizing that he was, absolutely. "Thirsty."

"Thirsty, we got covered."

She turned, reached, and offered him a glass, chips of ice floating in the water.

He drank thirstily, and when the glass was empty, she took it back.

"'Nother one?"

"Not just yet. Malu's gone back to her ship?"

"Bry Sen's escorting her. There was something about a consulting fee that he'd be transferring just so soon as you signed off on the time."

"I'll do that . . . in a minute. Or two. How'd you get here?"

"Malu figured out something was wrong, yelled emergency, got Bry Sen, who sent for me on the run. Brought my medkit."

She was half-sitting on the table in front of him, their knees touching.

"So, how you feeling? Pretty much yourself? Got a headache or anything else you'd like to tell me about?"

"Tired," he said again, and paused to do an inventory. "No headache, not dizzy. Been a long day-or-month."

Her mouth twitched. "Has, hasn't it? And tomorrow'll only be longer. So how 'bout I check you over with the kit, and we'll get you to bed so you can do a little something about that *tired*?"

He sighed, but she was right. He didn't think the smart-beads had hurt him; Malu's argument for affinity made a certain kind of sense, but—

"Best to be sure."

"That's how I like a man to talk." She reached behind her and brought the medkit forward, pulled out the scanner.

"This'll take a minute. If nothing turns up but *tired*, then you get yourself to bed."

"Come with me?" he asked.

"Tempting, but I've still got a year's worth of work to do before *I* go to bed this month. Good idea, by the way, to have the mail from your various cousins sent over to us. Got one of the youngers researching lines—good practice for her, and she feels like she's in the thick. So far, no kin-hits, though we're all cousins on the Loops."

Jethri grinned. The scanner beeped.

There was a short silence while Freza read the results, then she turned and slipped the scanner back into the kit.

"So that's five percent of your mass gone since last time we did this," she said conversationally. "Call your cook in here, why not?"

She turned and he heard the noises associated with pouring water into a glass. More water would be good, he thought, and raised his voice sufficiently to be heard over the all-ship.

"Kel Bin, attend me in the conference room, of your goodness."

The man must've been standing outside the door, because he was there before Jethri had taken his first drink from the refilled glass.

"Trader?"

Jethri inclined his head, and spoke in Trade. "The medic wished to consult with you, I believe."

"Indeed," Kel Bin turn to Freza and bowed as one ready to serve. "Medic. How may I assist?"

"The trader requires a restorative diet," Freza said, her Trade crisp and cool. "He has lost significant weight, suddenly, and he has demanding days before him. I don't want to overburden your kitchen—"

Kel Bin raised a hand. "Keeping the trader well-fed and healthy is the kitchen's happy burden," he said. "I have recipes; further, I am back-up medic, with a specialty in foods that heal and restore."

Freza grinned. "You've taken a big burden off of me, then, Medic. Will you provide a high-calorie, restorative meal for the trader, who will—" She fixed Jethri in her eye—"who *will* eat, and then retire?"

"It will be my great pleasure as well as my duty," Kel Bin assured her. He turned to Jethri. "I will bring this meal to your quarters, Trader, so that you may eat undisturbed before you seek your rest."

Jethri inclined his head.

"My thanks, Medic," he said meekly.

Kel Bin bowed once more to the room in general, and left at speed.

Jethri put his empty glass down, and looked around the conference room.

"I'm going to have get these things into stasis boxes before—"

"You tell Bry Sen to get it done," Freza said, and sighed gustily. "Jeth, you can't be scaring me like this. You scared all of us, including your Malu!"

He tried to disown Malu with a shake of his head. "She's not *my* Malu. I haven't—"

"Didn't ask," Freza interrupted. "Point is, she was scared for you, and not just because she brought an accident down on your head. How she got to feeling that way isn't my bidness, but she's stuck on you, or the idea of you, pretty hard. Trust me, Jeth. Even if she never sees you again, she's gonna remember you.

"Point is, you had *all* of us scared, and I don't think Bry Sen dresses up to lure you to his side, either."

She bent close and kissed his forehead. He slipped a kiss onto the edge of her ear, and sighed when she sat back.

"All right, now here's your orders, Trader. Go to quarters, eat your meal, and *go to sleep*. You gotta be up and alert and talking to people."

Jethri frowned, half-inclined to argue with this high-handedness—and didn't. He *was* tired—physically tired, just like he'd been at the board two shifts back-to-back, and both of them nothing but in-close maneuvering.

His mind, though, seemed—hyperalert. Freza's scanner—well, but mental acuity wasn't something that could be measured by a scanner. But he felt like he was thinking harder, or deeper, his attention focused just slightly somewhere else, like he was trying to be in the moment, analyze and file it at the same time.

Maybe if he got some good sleep, his brain would settle.

"All right, Medic," he said, trying to be light, "orders received."

"Good."

Freza came to her feet and held a hand down to him.

"Come on, now. I'll walk you to your quarters."

They met Bry Sen in the corridor, and Jethri paused to give orders about placing all of the equipment in the conference room into stasis boxes.

"Each in their own, absolutely, Pilot. If we lack a sufficiency—"

"Worry not, Trader. Each item in its own box is your word. It is now my task to perform." He held up a common courier envelope.

"These, too, I will place in their own box. The consultant sends her rings, with the hope that they may be returned to her, after the trader has studied them. She also wishes to assure you that you will receive an invoice from *Elsvair* for the silver cape."

"Good," Jethri said, and hesitated. There were other things, surely, to put in train? "A moment," he murmured, but Bry Sen raised a hand.

"All for the morrow, Trader. Your ship and your crew will shield you tonight. You have nothing to do but heal from your latest adventure."

Jethri felt tears rise, hot and unexpected.

"Thank you, Bry Sen."

"It is a pleasure to serve, Trader."

"C'mon, Jeth," Freza said, tugging gently on his arm. "Let's get you settled down."

SEVEN

• • • • • • • •

HE HAD A SINGLE GLASS OF WINE WITH HIS SOLITARY meal. Both wine and meal were so tasty that Jethri took leave to doubt either was restorative, though the wine was not familiar, and the sauces more liberal than customary.

After, he took himself to his bed, also solitary, fully expecting to lie awake as his brain buzzed with plans and back-up plans, and a running in-depth analysis of the meeting with Bory. Instead, he arranged himself comfortably beneath the blanket, sighed, closed his eyes—

And wakened, absolutely at his usual hour, entirely relaxed, mentally alert, and with the conviction that his sleep had been not only restorative, but *productive*. He had apparently settled Bory to his satisfaction while he slept. And, despite having several small-group presentations to give today, as well as long hours at the *Envidaria*'s regular table in the pre-congress exhibit hall, he was calm and mildly optimistic.

He had a quick shower and called up his personal screen while he was getting dressed.

The first action item was...

He blinked at the queued line of messages in

astonishment before he recalled last evening's flood of messages, and his instructions to send those which had come from traders to his action queue.

And here they were.

There was a letter from *Elthoria* mid-way down the list, and another, from *Barskalee*, toward the end. The first was from—oh, surely not!

He recalled the name. It would be many years before he forgot the Liaden trader who had propositioned him at his come-out as ven'Deelin's son, and him nothing more than a curiosity. He couldn't call to mind one thing that Trader sig'Flava would be writing him about.

He opened the letter.

To Trader Jethri ven'Deelin, I offer well-wishes and support.

May I flatter myself that you recall our first meeting as vividly as I do, and as often? It can only gratify to learn that my first impression of your worth was correct, and that you, indeed, have outstripped my expectations of you.

That you have so quickly achieved the purples, and stand as senior trader on Genchi, affiliated with the Three-Ringed Star, can only bring joy to those several who have followed your career, and wish you every success and honor.

Though there are those several, such as myself, who have no doubt of you, there are others who seek to deny you the rights and rank which you have so clearly earned.

Let me be plain, Trader Jethri: When the discussion of your accomplishments and suitability come before the Guild, mine will be a voice raised in support. It is never wise to challenge the future with unseemly surety, however, as I was so very correct in my first assessment of you, allow me to say—you will prevail, sir. I am beyond confident.

I see that Genchi's route has yet to be fixed, beyond the South Axis Congress. I therefore append a list of settled destinations for Trebloma Lyktini, across the next three Standards. If Genchi should come to a shared docking, it would be my joy to share a meal, a special vintage, and what else mutual desire might suggest.

Until that pleasant hoped-for reunion, I remain
Parvet sig'Flava, Trader, Trebloma Lyktini
via TerraTrade PassMail

Jethri closed his eyes.

How, he thought, was he to answer that?

Later, he answered himself, and scrolled down the line of messages until he found the one from *Elthoria*.

To Senior Trader Jethri Gobelyn ven'Deelin, greetings.

You will perhaps have received similar assurances from Master Trader pin'Aker, although he is very busy and as I know to my sorrow somewhat in arrears of his correspondence.

Let me therefore speak as he would, in the sincere belief that it is better to be informed twice, than to reside in ignorance.

Matters move. You may hear rumors. You may receive letters. In fact, you will surely receive

*letters. You may safely set those aside without
reply, for none are expected. You may wish to
set them aside without reading, for you have
your own business in hand, and will not wish
to be distracted by what is, after all, merely
process.*

*Be strong of heart, Trader, as I know your
will to be adamantine. Very soon, all turbulence
will flow away, leaving clarity in its wake.*

I remain,

*Norn ven'Deelin, Master at Trade, Elthoria
sent via pinbeam*

Jethri sighed. There, he told himself, all questions
answered.

He flipped to his day schedule.

The first thing was breakfast, within a generously
flexible time frame. Apparently, the medics had decided
to let him sleep as long as he cared to. Well, obviously, he had slept exactly that long. He touched the
comm, exchanged good mornings with Kel Bin and
requested breakfast in his cabin.

It arrived as he was putting on his rings. Kel Bin
disposed the dishes—rather a lot of dishes, Jethri
thought—with neat efficiency, and stood with tray in
hand, regarding Jethri with somewhat sharper interest
than he was used to receiving from the cook.

He moved a hand toward the laden table.

"Am I still in need of restoration, Kel Bin?"

"Trader, I have had time to consider Medic Freza's
lessons of last evening, and I have determined to care
for you more nearly. I had not concerned myself with
your schedule, nor taken into account the extraordinary

efforts required of you at this event. Last evening, after you retired, I sat with Pilot Bry Sen. We reviewed the intent of your work here, as well as your daily schedules, so far as they are yet known.

"In fact, you are expending much of yourself in this endeavor—I speak only of your work at the conference, Trader, assuming such adventures as you undertook last evening to be the exception. Your mind must be clear and your body able, even more than would be usual upon the trade floor. There are foods and preparations which will boost your natural resources and mitigate the toll upon your person."

He bowed, as one who is honored to serve.

"I will see to it, Trader, that the kitchen properly supports your efforts. Please, enjoy your breakfast."

And with that, he was gone, last night's tray with him, allowing Jethri no opportunity to respond properly— *because I have business to do,* Jethri thought. Kel Bin had only said what needed to be said, and got gone. That was part of supporting the trader's efforts, too.

He poured himself a cup of morning tea, uncovered his plates, and served himself. He sipped, sampled, and went back to his review of the day's schedule.

He was on the table until mid-morning, when his presentations began. Four in a row, but enough time between each to grab some food off the row, and recuperate. The meetings were in a variety of venues suitable to small groups, so he would be able to stretch his legs by walking between them. That was good.

Breakfast was good, too. He had another sip of tea, another of the dense little muffins, which weren't quite vegetable muffins, or cheese muffins, but delicious all the same.

He poured some more tea, and moved to his personal news list, pared down as much as he'd dared in the days before arriving at Meldyne. Among the items he followed were recent routings and dockings of particular ships, and news from stations he'd been on, or had dealings with. It was eclectic, even in its abridged-for-the-trade-conference form, and often produced surprises, or items of note.

In the last Standard, for instance, he'd been surprised to learn that Port Chavvy, the station where he had reconnected with Freza and Brabham, and also survived a duel with a man who'd intended to kill him, no matter what—Port Chavvy had almost entirely dodged a cometary encounter.

Today's news brought him another surprise.

The connection was again Port Chavvy, and the duel that had resulted in him killing a man dead enough, and he was still of two minds about had he done the right thing. Master ven'Deelin would have it so—*he'd* survived, after all. The duel had been forced on him, and there was very little doubt that he *wouldn't* have survived, had he taken the weapons pushed at him.

In the end, it'd been his own particular sort of hull-headedness, the fixed determination that, if he was going to take part in dockside violence, by space, it would be a real, Looper-style brawl, every bit as offensive to his self-declared opponent as Jethri himself.

So, he'd gone to a ship docked nearby—they'd been doing some interior repairs, and had rented the use of the dockside tool rack. Jethri had seen the stinks hammer, recalled his father and Grig sparring. He could still hear his own voice, shouting, "Stink hammers and starbars, seven paces and closing!"—like he'd known what he was doing, like he was the unlettered Terran brute his opponent claimed.

But, there—it was *Dulcimer*, the ship that had given him the lend of his chosen weapons. He'd never had a chance to thank them for it, after.

And here was *Dulcimer*, reported docked at Meldyne's so-called "open ring," within the last Standard Day.

Must've been a last-minute decision, to come to the conference, Jethri thought. The open ring wasn't close in, and it didn't have much in the way of comforts. Just access tubes, and transient ships locking on at bow or stern with no expectation of moving cargo. Their commerce would be in people needing access to the station, and being willing to move to another location, if they did pick up cargo, or needed maintenance.

Here was his chance to say thank you, and put at least *one* thing right out of a cargo-can of wrong.

He reached for the comm.

"Listen, Frez, got something else."

"Go."

"You remember *Dulcimer*, on Port Chavvy?"

There was a pause.

"Yeah, I do," Freza said, slowly. "Why?"

"Well, they're just in, over on the transient ring, and—I owe 'em. I would've been the one dead, if it hadn't been for them lending me from the tool box."

"But what're they doing *here*?" Freza interrupted. "Didn't *Dulcimer* do pick-up runs at the black edge o'grey? I read their back-routes after you'd left, on account they did a cousin's part, right enough. Figured they were orbiting one of the Juntavas bosses out the other side of the arm."

"Might be they were," Jethri said, "but they're here. Put a spot in the port notes. Here: 'Looking for Loop contacts and consultants, especially Dust-knowledgeable. Hiring general spacer with Loop experience and expectations. Cook-caterer looking for immediate fair or congress position for event duration.'

"Sounds like an eager working ship to me," Jethri continued. "Maybe they're changing routes."

"Happens," Freza admitted. "What do you want to do about them?"

"I owe them," Jethri said. "I don't want to send over a buncha flowers and a pretty note. I want to give them the same style and quality of help they gave me."

A long pause, this time.

"I'll start it in motion," Freza said. "Got the note right here. Look, Jeth, I gotta rush to get fed. Quick, tell me how you are."

"I'm fine," Jethri said. "More than fine. Looking forward to sharing some more time together. I've been working up some ideas."

She laughed. "I'll be looking to see those ideas, next time we're together, Trader."

"Deal," said Jethri. "Fly safe, Freza."

"You, too, Jethri. You, too."

Breakfast done, and *Dulcimer* provisionally dealt with, Jethri stood to put on his coat.

He was on the edge of leaving his quarters when he remembered that he hadn't read Master pin'Aker's letter. He hesitated, thinking that it was likely only a repeat of what Master ven'Deelin had sent him, crossed in the message streams, and he took a step toward the door.

And stopped.

"*Master trader,*" he said aloud, in case there was some other careless idiot present.

He went back to the table, brought up the message queue again, and opened the letter from *Barskalee*.

It was brief, and not at all a repeat of Norn's info.

> *Trader Jethri, a word in your ear.*
> *There will be a test.*
> *Be on your mettle.*
> *Rantel pin'Aker, Master at Trade, Barskalee*
> *sent via pinbeam*

Jethri met Kel Bin in the hall, bearing a tall covered glass.

"What's this?" he wondered.

"A fortifying elixir, Trader." He offered it and Jethri perforce took it. "I see you are wearing an expedition belt for today's work. Please, drink, and I will bring you day rations of nutritious quick-snacks that will fit in your belt. Carrying liquids is tedious, but I strongly suggest that all dockside team members—especially you, Trader—stay hydrated. Hydration assists clear thinking, and staves off the minor contagions sometimes shared in crowds like these."

The "elixir" was a thickened fruit drink, perhaps slightly more robust than Jethri usually had to end a breakfast; he closed his eyes for a moment and was tempted to savor it. He began to break out the identifiable flavors when Kel Bin returned with his packets of snacks.

Jethri sighed, handed back the empty glass, and stowed the snacks in his belt.

"Bry Sen will be with you in short order, Trader, to walk with you to the halls. Know that you may call on me if you require a meal or a fortifying drink.

"Also, you will wish to know that Pilot Brabham has traded his recipe for maize buttons for the recipes for my signature *chernubia*, so I will have samples for you to test tomorrow!"

That, Jethri thought, was downright amazing.

He bowed.

"Thank you for your care," he said.

Straightening, he heard footsteps, and turned to greet Bry Sen while Kel Bin slipped away.

"Ready for a day of adventure and daring, shipmate?" Bry Sen asked in bright Terran.

"I'm ready," Jethri said, with feeling, "for a successful day of teaching."

Bry Sen grinned, Terran wide.

"Well, and what did I just say?"

· · · ✳ · · ·

Jethri's early shift at the table had been busy, and fulfilling, as he felt like he made solid connections with most of the people who stopped by to talk, and more than half of them had signed up for informational sessions.

His first presentation had likewise gone well, the audience intent, and the question and answer period lively.

He arrived back at the table in a glow of satisfaction, more hopeful of their chances of seeing the *Envidaria* made official than he had been since the meeting with Bory last evening.

Even the sight of the long line at his table wasn't enough to dim his spirits. He stepped into his spot, and bowed to those gathered.

"I'm Jethri Gobelyn ven'Deelin, here to answer general questions about the *Envidaria* and the Dust. We've got some sign-up sheets for seminars and informational meetings, which will be more specific than I'll have time to be. I'm due to give one of those presentations in two hours, so let's get started.

"Who's first?"

First was a woman he figured for around Iza's age, dressed like a Looper, and walking like she was shipborn, and as broad a grin as a Terran could produce on her strong-featured face. He'd never seen her before, to his certain knowledge, and so was that much more surprised when she leaned right over the table, and grabbed his shoulders in a half-hug.

Jethri felt, rather than saw Bry Sen's step forward, and managed to sign *steady* on his off-hand, while extricating himself from the woman's grip.

Her grin faded, and her shoulders drooped.

"Now, Jethri, you sure recognize your cousin Corann!"

"No, ma'am, I don't," he said politely. "What ship?"

"What ship?" She laughed, shaking her head at the same time. "Well, there's the question, ain't it? Was ustabe *Toad* 'course, only then *Salimander* was short crew, and I was young, and general, so there I was traded off, anna good thing, too, right before *Toad* went down, but that meant I was outta first-kin, and when *Salimander* got restructured after the cap'n stepped aside, I was traded off to *Kitt's Kondor*, and by then I was studied up to be—"

Jethri shook his head, and she stopped, tears welling in her eyes.

"The Wildes weren't cousins," he said. "They were business associates of my father's. And, you'll excuse me sayin' it, given the lot you're trying to sell, but you don't have the Wilde look. Red hair and white skin, every one of 'em."

The tears had spilled over. Jethri bit his lip, conscious of eyes on him, and ears, and wishing she would move along before—

Bry Sen stepped round the table to Corann's side, his face showing something like sympathy, if sympathy could be said to be *stern*.

"Let's step aside, now," he said in brisk Looper. "There's folks behind who've got their bidness to speak."

Jethri braced himself for anger, but Corann looked down at Bry Sen, and nodded, shoulders slumped. She turned and left the table.

Bry Sen stepped back behind the table, and Jethri saw him touch the ear where the comm-bud rode.

He turned back to his particular business.

"Right," he said. "Who's next?"

EIGHT

. . . .

CAPTAIN, PILOTS AND CREW SAT IN THE GALLEY TOGETHER, staring with varying degrees of disbelief, anger, and worry at a modest pile of dark-grey goods in the center of the table.

"I suppose," said Rusko, "that it's not just stuff we somehow missed when we were cleaning house?"

"Where they were?" Tranh snapped. "Where they were, a blind inspector could walk in here and find 'em by smell. No, it's a set-up."

"Mitsy and Ditsy," Klay said, putting his mug o'mite by, "were dead clear. They saw Susrim put these things in the cubbies."

Klay had a headache, Mitsy and Ditsy having been that insistent. Also, he was trying not to think about how he should've strangled Susrim when he had a chance.

"So, it's a set-up. Where're the inspectors?"

"Station's a thought busy right now," Rusko pointed out. "A little matter of grey-shipping isn't near the top of their list. Now, if we're found to be trading 'em—"

"Which we won't be, which Susrim's gotta know," Tranh said. "So why make the effort?"

Klay noticed that none of them were asking where

Susrim had gotten the items, when all crew had been ordered to turn anything remotely shading to grey to the captain for a determination, with the understanding that all grey goods was forfeit, as not being in line with the ship's new policies.

"Prolly he didn't figure on it being so busy like it is," Klay said. "It'll take him some time to come up with a new plan."

He didn't add, *not one of your fast thinkers, Susrim*, but he might've thought it too hard, because he saw Rusko's lips twitch.

"Right," said Rusko. "We should put some thought onto what he's likely to do next." He paused frowning, and glanced at Tranh.

"Not likely to go after Falmer, is he?"

Tranh sighed.

"He'd have to know she'd got in with the congress catering crew, which isn't impossible, but not easy, either. Then, he'd have to find her in the dorms or the kitchens, which is even less easy. No . . . *Dulcimer*'s the obvious target. We're right here where anybody can find us with just a search on the name." He shook his head. "There's only the three of us—" he glanced at Mitsy and Ditsy "—the five of us. I was hoping to let us each work solo—get more information and contacts that way. Guess we'll do partners, though. To be safe. Two on port, alt-crew on-ship, and one with 'em as backup."

Ditsy and Mitsy showed Klay a picture of the *tobor* being faced down by themselves, the image glowing. He countered with an image of himself curled down in a pile of greenery, sleeping.

Mitsy gave the norbear equivalent of a chuckle, but Ditsy produced a sigh at him being alone, and thought

Squithy into the scene, curled beside him, head on his shoulder, which caught him right in the chest.

"Everything good there, Klay?" Rusko asked.

"Good as can be," Klay answered, which was the truth, and reminded himself that Squith was in good hands. Dulsey Omron and the seven side-traveling norbears would none of them let anything bad happen to Squithy. Hadn't Dulsey made it clear enough that none of *Dulcimer*'s travelers was coming back until it was safe for them? And hadn't Susrim been thrown out on his own, contract terminated, ship-share in his pocket, so they could show *Dulcimer* safe?

Because Squithy was a dozen or more of Susrim, and nobody sensible would make an argument against *that* proposition.

"I propose," Rusko said, "for us to sit together with the conference schedule and plan out which sessions and workshops we need to have covered. There's appointments open for private consults with trade route specialists and Dust experts, too."

"Sounds to me like we should start there," Tranh said. "Practical first, then theory."

"Sounds like a plan," said Rusko. His eye fell on the sorry pile in the center of the table.

"Any ideas what to do with those?"

"Space 'em," Klay said. Tranh shook his head.

"Not while we're at station." He frowned, then nodded. "I'll put 'em in one of the deep secret cubbies that I didn't even know about and Dulsey only found with a device I wouldn't swear wasn't an actual Before. Oughta be safe enough, even if the inspectors do get bored and come out to see us. They won't be where Susrim told 'em, and I'm betting he told them."

"Inspectors might find some other cubbies, if they're inspecting," Rusko pointed out.

"Right. And I'm willing to come clean as to how the former captain and mate were awful grey, and now deceased. Ship falling to me, we decided to get rid of anything was here. Traded 'em to Crystal. Got the receipt to show."

There was a long pause before Rusko gave a low whistle.

"The truth," he said. "I like it."

"All right. I'll get these stowed. Rusko, you want to pull the conference schedules up on the screen in here? Klay, can you put together some snacks?"

Klay had just finished putting up the snacks when the main hatch's tone sounded. He stepped to the screen, and triggered the camera.

The woman standing at their hatch was . . . familiar. Klay had the feeling he'd seen her before, and recent. Thin, tough and take-charge, that was what went through his head, and then he knew where he'd seen her.

Port Chavvy, first with that Jethri, then, later, going down the line of ships talking about the terrible "accident," and her name was . . .

Freza DeNobli, off *Balrog*.

He flipped the speaker switch.

"*Dulcimer*. What bidness, *Balrog*?"

She grinned into the camera—good grin, just crooked enough, and a pair of eyes that'd see right through you.

"Your port-notes come to my attention, Cousin. I'm working with the *Envidaria* team, and I gotta say that list of wants shows you as zackly the kind of ship and crew the *Envidaria* was written for. Trader Gobelyn saw you was in, too. Remembers *Dulcimer* kindly from Port Chavvy, where you lent him the means to not get killed, the way he has it. Asked me to come by and see if we can get you routed straight to what you need."

Klay blinked.

"Thank you," he said. "We were just sitting down to a sorting session. If you got time..."

"I got some little bit of time, right now," Freza said. "*Might* have more, later. Won't have any, once the congress starts."

"Right," Klay said, and made a senior crew decision. "I'm coming down to the hatch for you. Cousin."

Say what you liked about Freza DeNobli, Klay thought half-an-hour later, but the woman was organized and unflappable. Mitsy and Ditsy liked her, though they were being very good about not clamoring for her attention. For herself, Freza received the image of her patching up Jethri Gobelyn's head with a blink, a nod, and a calm, "Pleased to meetcha. Didn't see you at Port Chavvy, or I'd've done the pretty then."

"They were keeping low at Port Chavvy," Rusko told her. "They'd created an environmental mess."

"The flour," Freza DeNobli said, clearly not a fool, either. "I remember that." She sent a Look at the nor-bears. "Not a good thing to have all that dust clogging the vents. You know better, now, I bet."

Ditsy assured her that they did. Klay watched her face, and saw her get something, but not, he thought, the full impact.

"All right, now," she said, turning to Tranh. "Let's

talk about your port notes. Looking for contacts and consultants, right? Especially somebody has some straight data about the Dust. You got a copy of the *Envidaria*? Went out on all-band—"

"We have it," Rusko said. "We haven't studied it."

"Do that," Freza told him. "What's your current shipping look like?"

Tranh shook his head.

"Previous captain and mate, they didn't want to be tied into a Loop, and I won't lie to you, Cousin, they had some shady contacts. Current captain and mate have different views. We're in for a Loop, or to tie into a figure-eight. Those're the kind of contacts we need. And the Dust—the pilots're able, but *Dulcimer*'s old."

"Small ships in the old style are zackly what's gonna make sure the Seventeen Worlds don't starve. And the Seventeen Worlds ain't the most of it. The Dust's moving. There'll be need ongoing, is what I mean.

"Here," she pulled the bag she'd been carrying up on the table, began to unload modules and hardcopy.

"This gets you started, right? I gotta get over to the exhibition halls. I marked out some work sessions that'll be useful for you, and people for you to talk to—and here—" Another reach into the bag, and out came three badges spinning on bright green ribbons.

"Congress IDs," Freza said. "Guests of *Balrog*. They'll get you in, no questions."

She patted the bag, assuring herself that it was empty, then folded her elbows on top.

"Jethri Gobelyn ven'Deelin is gonna wanna talk to you, is what I heard, so we'll need to clear some time on his schedule for that. In the meantime—"

The main hatch chimed. Rusko got up, went to the

screen, let out a hard breath, and said, "Well," before he turned around.

"Susrim," he said to Tranh. "He's got Choody with him."

"I'll go," Tranh said, pushing himself to his feet.

"With me," Rusko answered. "Pairs on port, didn't we say? And for just this reason."

Tranh hesitated then gave a sharp, tight, nod.

"With me, then. Klay, take Cousin Freza out the side hatch, an' walk her to wherever she's gotta go."

"Right," Klay said. He walked Tranh and Rusko down to the main hatch, made sure they had their belts; that Rusko had the stun-stick, and Tranh had the override.

Then he walked back to the galley and Freza DeNobli.

Freza was standing at the screen when he got back.

"That's Choody Wharton?" she asked.

"It is." Klay sighed gustily. "Former management— Choody was their idea of a good contact."

"Well," said Freza, "*I* never heard anything good about him or his organization."

"'Cause there's nothing good to say," Klay answered, and brought up the volume on the screen.

"Tranh Smith, what've you got yourself into?" the slim man in the upscale trade clothes asked heartily. "Why, I was just talking to Captain Smith here, an—"

"*I'm* Captain Smith," Tranh said, and Choody smiled.

"That'll depend on if you can come up with a better deal, don't it?" he asked. "Though it would be awkward, being as I already promised Captain Susrim Smith this ship, for considerations."

"Susrim Smith has no claim to this ship; his contract's been bought out, and he's no longer needed nor wanted on *Dulcimer*."

"Now, that's where you're wrong," said Choody. "It happens that *I* want him on *Dulcimer*, and that's what's gonna happen—there's no other outcome possible. The only choice we have between us is—do we do this the easy way, or the hard way?"

Tranh said nothing, though he crossed his arms over his chest, which brought his hand that much closer to his hideaway.

Beside Choody, Susrim smirked.

"Better just sign over the ship, Tranh. You can prolly get a job as a pilot—big hiring fair here on-station, right now. Rusko an' Klay, too. But that ship is mine. Da meant me to have it. *I'm* willing to work with our contacts, but you? You sold everything away to Crystal! *Going reg'lar.* Ain't no money in *reg'lar.*"

"Yes," said Choody, "we will need to have a talk about your disposal of my goods, Tranh Smith, but my first priority is to get Captain Susrim here installed on *Dulcimer*, with a good crew of my cousins. You can come with us down to admin and sign over the ship's ownership now. There's law-jaws enough to do the legal. Do that, and you walk away, alive, and free to seek a berth on a *reg'lar* ship."

Klay felt Freza move beside him, and turned to see her at the table, a comm to her ear.

He cast another look at the screen, and moved toward her.

"Look, we gotta get you outta here."

"Nope," she said, and jerked her head toward the screen. "Monitor that, Pilot, right?"

Klay hesitated, then turned back to the screen. "Right."

"So, I'm hearing the easy way's of no interest," Choody was saying, with a shake of his head. "Just like your Da. Though I should be grateful; the hard way's gonna be fine on my side. We'll just get that started now. Captain Susrim?"

Choody turned and walked away, but Susrim—Susrim tarried, malice in his eyes, as he leaned in.

"Greyware report ain't enough to get through to the proctors with this fair going on, but a report of *diseased animals'll* get their attention right quick. Stations take disease serious. You'll lose the ship, your license, *and* your stake."

He grinned up into the camera.

"Shoulda done it the easy way."

"So, I'm takin' it that these are the *diseased animals*?" Freza nodded at Mitsy and Ditsy, who were crouched together on the end of the table, touching along their whole lengths, and as glum as Klay'd ever seen a norbear.

"They're not animals," he said now. "They're people."

"Got that." Freza gave him a nod, and looked around, to Rusko and Tranh. "I got somebody covering my first meeting, but I *gotta* be at the next one. Choody's right that *disease* is gonna be bringin' proctors on the run, but we can buy some time. First thing is to cut 'em off."

"Cut 'em off, how?" Tranh asked. "Can't deny a port inspection."

"That's right." Freza gave him a nod. "But you can take your own law-jaw and go on up to admin and file a harassment complaint against Choody, and demand your right to a ship inspection, and a clean bill of health from Meldyne Station."

There was a short silence, before Rusko said that still meant inspectors on the ship, and the norbears were a solid fact.

"They're people," Freza said, nodding at Klay. "He hears 'em. I do, some bit." She pointed her chin at Rusko. "*You* hear 'em."

"I get the very edges," Rusko said, "an' only sometime. Klay here's fluent, though not so much as Squithy."

"Squithy. She's the one gone to catering?"

"No, that's Falmer," Klay said. "Squithy—" he shook his head. "Long story. Profit line is that it's me right now who's most fluent in norbear."

Freza gave him an approving smile. "That's right—long stories later. First thing's to get this mess straightened out. Thinkin' on it, I agree that the best thing is for there to not be any norbears present to confuse overworked station health employees. So, we shift 'em, with Klay as translator. They ain't big, *Balrog*'s got room, and Klay can get a grounding on base Dust 'quations from our pilots."

"Not that easy," Tranh said. "Norbear food's gotta shift, too, or there'll be question why we're shipping bales of greens. We got a special 'ponics set-up—"

"Which we can use to prove Susrim was shorting his duties, to the harm of the ship," Rusko murmured, and Tranh turned to stare at him.

"Well, now, that's true," he said slowly. "I hadn't thought of it, there having been so much else 'gainst Susrim's staying."

"Which is why you need to get up to admin with

your law-jaw," Freza said, breaking into this moment of revelation.

"We ain't got a law-jaw," Tranh said.

"You can have one waiting for you at the main mall tubeway, soon's you say *yeah*. Tell 'em the whole story on the walk up to admin."

Tranh hesitated, then moved his hand. "I'm grateful, and I'm willing, but I'm not seeing my way to there's no norbears nor signs of what'll look like animals being kept on this ship."

Freza nodded. "You and Rusko get off to your appointment. I'll call in some cousins to move the necessaries, and stay here, to keep the ship. You're short-crewed, and it was pure good luck you happened on some cousins to help you out, am I right?"

Tranh blinked, and nodded slowly.

"You're right. The way life's been, *Dulcimer* crew's been cut off from cousins."

"Time to fix that. So! Time's short. The cousins're on their way. The law-jaw's on her way. Tranh and Rusko, you better be gettin' on *your* way. Klay and me and Mitsy and Ditsy'll stay here 'til the cousins arrive, and Klay'll let 'em know what's gotta get moved, and what other clean-up might be good. Then him an' me'll take Mitsy and Ditsy to *Balrog*, and I'll make a run for my next meetin'."

She put her eye on each of them, one by one.

"If there's anything else on this ship that ought not to be here, now's the time to bring it forward."

Tranh got up.

"Won't be a minute," he said.

Freza turned to Rusko. "This will be the grey goods Susrim filed with the port?"

"Right. Left 'em real obvious, but we'd cleaned, and weren't lookin'. Happens alt-crew witnessed what happened." He nodded to Mitsy and Ditsy. "They told Klay. Klay told us. Tranh moved 'em to a...more secure situation, but better if they're off the ship entire."

"Witnesses..." Freza frowned at the norbears, then shook her head. "Too complicated," she said, maybe to herself.

"If you don't mind my asking," Rusko said, "and understanding that we're grateful for the help, but—why did you start the cousins moving before you'd talked to us?"

Freza grinned at him.

"Saw your port-note, saw you were short-crewed, saw Choody's playing games. Any of that, you needed cousins. You was sensible at Port Chavvy and I was countin' you'd stayed that way."

Tranh came back, and put the greys in the center of the table.

Freza extended a hand, pulled it back, looked up at him.

"That? *That's* what he was gonna call the inspectors on?"

"Not the brightest light on the board," Rusko murmured.

"It *is* grey," Tranh added.

"There's that." Freza sighed. "All right. One of the cousins will wrap it up and get it courier'd to a safe holding. I'll write a note. Pilot Klay an' me, we can get these norbears on the move."

"Take a minute to get my gear," Klay began. She cut him off with a wave of a hand.

"Be a few minutes before—" She stopped, frowning, and Klay waited, not sure how much she'd caught.

"What's this I'm getting—family? There's more than just these two?"

"There are," Klay said, "but they're touring with Dulsey Omron, from Crystal Energy, for the next while." He turned up a hand. "Part of that longer story I owe you."

"Right." She nodded. "Like I was sayin'—we all of us gotta move. Tranh and Rusko—go meet the law-jaw. Tell her the truth and the long story, including the unclassified sentients that Crystal Energy's taken a personal innerest in. Pilot Klay an' me'll wait on the cousins. Once they're here and put abreast of the situation, we'll move these two down to *Balrog*." She stood. "Jet!"

Rusko and Tranh left. Klay went to his quarters to pack changes of clothes, and some gear. When he came back to the galley, Freza was sitting in a chair, Mitsy and Ditsy on her knees. She had the air of a woman who was listening hard, while the norbears were offering simple, clear messages, sending wide delight when she caught the whole of it.

The main hatch chimed, and Klay went to the screen.

"Freza," he said, not wanting to disturb class, but mindful of time moving on.

She got herself untangled, stood, glanced at the screen, and headed for the hatch.

"Come on and meet your cousins, Pilot Klay."

The cousins were on the job, and it was time to move. Klay considered the norbears. Freza walked over to the table, picked up her empty bag and held it open.

"In," she said to the norbears. "It's a walk, so you be patient, and quiet, and trust Klay and me to do what's right for you."

Klay waited for the inevitable argument—but it didn't come.

There was a feeling of—resignation, but nothing more as Mitsy and Ditsy marched purposefully forward, side by side and climbed into the bag.

"I'll carry," Klay said, stepping forward.

Freza nodded.

"All right, then, let's go."

. . . . . .

NINE

. . . . . .

JETHRI LEFT THE TABLE FOR HIS SECOND PRESENTATION with real relief. He liked people, he liked to talk to people, to listen to people, and to try to find accommodation between different viewpoints.

More than that, he was a trader; he'd been taught—by the best!—how to negotiate, how to subtly influence a viewpoint, how to—oh, so delicately—suggest that perhaps now was not the time to push this particular deal forward.

So, it was more than simply irritating when someone presented an overdone sales pitch, pretending it was a question worthy of his time. He'd wanted to shake the man and give him a quick lesson in how to engage with the customer—which included not irritating him.

He sighed, and shook his head as he walked. A glance at Bry Sen suggested that his pilot-escort was paying close attention to comm traffic, and Jethri left him to it, his thoughts turning again to the last session at the table.

For the most part, it had been good, he told himself. Just—he hadn't expected anybody to show up with a supposed invoice that *Gobelyn's Market* had never paid, from before Arin had married into the ship, expecting Jethri to make good on it *right now*.

And then there had been Desty Gold, who had waited patiently in line for a chance to lean in and tell Jethri in a growl that carried to the end of the line that he was a traitor to his ship and to Loopers everywhere, spying for Liadens and trafficking with pod-breakers and pirates.

"Combine's gonna revoke that key you been flaunting around, that Paitor was so daft to give you! You either trade Liaden or you trade Terran, Jethri. There ain't no both!"

He'd picked up a handout from the pile—the one that broke out the main points of the *Envidaria*—glared at it and threw it back down on the table in plain disgust.

"Making a stake by talking people into what's least good for 'em," he snarled. "It's Arin all over again, ain't it?"

And with that he stalked off, leaving Jethri shaken and shaking, whereupon Bry Sen had stepped forward and announced that the trader was required at his next presentation, very soon, and Chiv arrived from somewhere to stand behind the table.

"I got this, Cousin," he said, for Jethri's ears alone. "Take the long way 'round to the next one. Good thing to stretch your legs."

And it had been a good thing, to stretch his legs, and let his temper settle before he arrived to deliver his second presentation.

Which went well; the question and answer period was every bit as lively as the first had been.

He came out of that somewhat . . . unwilling to return to the table, and it was with some relief that he learned from Bry Sen that they had been given a special mission from Brabham.

"Representatives from New Carpathia?" he asked.

"Indeed. A personal meeting is required with someone of a sufficient *melant'i*. Brabham might do, or Freza, but Chiv will not. Brabham then offered yourself, and you were judged fitting."

"Always a relief to be found fitting," he said, "but I'd like to have more precision on that *melant'i*."

"Ah. Brabham was explicit. Your *melant'i* in this is as a child of *Gobelyn's Market*. The person you will be meeting is Chief Secretary Waznik. It is a matter of some *paperwork* that must be handled. It is, so Brabham allowed me to know, a technicality only."

Bry Sen slanted a look up at Jethri's face.

"Understand, this does not relieve *Balrog* of its necessity to likewise meet with Secretary Waznik."

"I'm the stall, am I?" Jethri smiled, briefly amused. "I can do that. Maybe I can even pry *Balrog's* *paperwork* out of Secretary Waznik. Might be worth a try."

"Indeed," Bry Sen murmured. "Perhaps Brabham is hoping you will do just that."

The parlors set aside for the world displays were through the Grand Arcade, a large, mostly empty space with a domed ceiling glowing yellow. Jethri sighed. He'd grown up shipside; he was used to close quarters and constant noise, but it was good, right now, not to have people jostling him, or the disorderly sound of people trying to out-talk each other in his ears.

New Carpathia's parlor was directly off the Arcade. The door was open and there appeared to be no guardian on duty. Jethri strode in, Bry Sen just behind, and approached the table where there were several almost casually dressed people seated with a screen they had access to, and another in the act of joining them—taking off her glittering over-jacket with the air of somebody who was relaxing from a stint on the trade floor.

She glanced up as they approached, sighed, and stepped around the table toward them.

"Oh, Traders, the main display is across the arcade. This is the administrative—"

She broke off, apparently realizing that Bry Sen was not dressed in trading clothes and that Jethri— Her eyebrow slid up as she considered Jethri and she took another step toward them.

"May I help you?"

"Yes, I hope so, or that I might help you. I'm Jethri Gobelyn ven'Deelin, formerly of *Gobelyn's Market*. I was told that there was paperwork that needed to be completed."

She blinked, then patched on a smile.

"Oh, oh! You? You're as young as you looked in your release, aren't you? Just—please, would you like a seat? I'm Chief Secretary Waznik. Redbird Waznik, that is. We weren't sure you'd be by today, but thank you so much for coming. May I offer refreshment—fizzwater, beer, juices? For both, I mean."

"Allow me to introduce Bry Sen yo'Endoth, *Genchi*'s pilot."

"I'm pleased to meet you, Pilot yo'Endoth." Secretary Waznik turned and beckoned two women from those at the table, who were introduced as her aides, Joslynn and Jordina, also Wazniks.

"Cousins," she said, smiling. "Cousins, not sisters. But we're all administrators, and I'm sure you know that talents run in families, right?"

She paused, as if she had lost her place and was hastily reviewing a script.

"This is so good of you to come, Trader. We don't get off-world often, especially not this far from home not even to see cousins, and we're really interested in—but here, Joslynn, why don't you get the packet? We can talk about it first and then have Rinkin come over from the display to do the documentation. Fleeva will be so pleased!"

"Cousins?" Jethri'd heard that go by, along with the word "packet" both of which sounded like the crew here knew a lot more than he did about something. Or maybe a lot of things.

"Cousins!" Secretary Waznik said brightly. "Yes, cousins. Because of the agreement that the crew and first one hundred Loop ships to join our registry on-world would be registered as cousins and citizens of New Carpathia. *Gobelyn's Market* is Number Eighty-Two on the list! We lost track of a few ships during the troubles decades ago, but when we saw your *Envidaria* release we found the news that you're off *Gobelyn's Market* and we knew *Balrog* would be here, which is so very exciting for us, you know."

As seemed to happen so often, Jethri's mouth went to work before his brain and he interrupted her happy narrative with a puzzled murmur.

"I've read most of *Gobelyn's Market*'s log, ma'am. I'm sure New Carpathia wasn't on the visit list up to four years ago."

"Is it not strange, then, that *Gobelyn's Market* is registered on New Carpathia?"

Well, that was certainly true, Jethri admitted. He'd never thought overmuch about the *Market*'s registry. Most of the Looper ships he knew were registered on ports they didn't fly to—and look at himself, registered as a member of Waymart's population to make sure that Iza's changeable mood couldn't leave him without an official home base at all. He supposed he might claim Liad, through his adoptive mother, Norn ven'Deelin, but he also supposed that might be—awkward.

He bowed slightly to Secretary Waznik.

"In fact ma'am, I'd never considered it, not being in ship admin. I'm pretty sure the *Market* wasn't built on New Carpathia, and I can't swear that the log was always as straight as it ought to have been, though Gobelyns try to keep the keel clean."

She smiled at that, though he hadn't been joking. Then Joslynn appeared with the packet, which was of a size that it might hold a raft of ship or pilot's hardcopy wall certificates in a fold-over case.

Secretary Waznik took the case and opened it, turning it around to show Jethri a large and ornately printed item—so ornate, in fact, that he couldn't quite make out the words before Secretary Waznik closed the case and handed it back to her aide.

"So, that is what we have for you, Trader: certification that you are a First Century citizen of New Carpathia—century means hundred for us, you know. The first one hundred registered ships earned that by supporting us in our trouble. Your ship keeps us, which we appreciate, since there are several other registration worlds these days! The packet also includes a list of our legalities—things like age of majority, marriage, birth, and death reporting.

"Also, for people who wish to see which cousins they might be—New Carpathia was settled by pre-Loopers and Loopers in the early days. There was a lot of mixing happened the first Standard century or two."

Jethri found nothing to say, which was just as well, because Secretary Waznik was sweeping on.

"Do you recall, Trader, if there was a listing in your logs for Simone, or even Dark Simone?"

Recollection was instant.

"Of course! Yes, Dark Simone. There were three visits in short order, all food runs with the cabins stuffed with extra people one way and extra food coming back."

The Chief Secretary nodded.

"*That* is why you're on the cousins list. That was the time of troubles for us, when the storms were unexpected on Simone and the food scarce. That was when the stationers got overrun by insects and the station evacuated and then rebuilt.

"Loopers kept us and helped bring things around when Simone became uninhabitable. The planet we have now was called Dark Simone, for being so dark blue when Simone had been so bright. We changed the name of the system and our world to New Carpathia to put aside the old expectations, to heal the old wounds, and to remind us to look into the future, not the past."

She smiled.

"There, in short, is how we became a data and registration center: we needed some way of earning our food."

"And now," she said conspiratorially, "we are pleased to offer you and your *Envidaria* our expertise. It appears to our data experts that some worlds will lose their crops, others their shippers, others will simply be isolated for some years . . . and we can consult for them. And you, as a Century Citizen of New Carpathia, and your family's ship—why should you not have a place to go should you need it? Since we have a planet with multiple large landing fields and support systems there's no need to be concerned there will be a lack of room for you if needed."

"And if I happen to be trading on another ship? As I am." That was a little sharper than he had intended, but Secretary Waznik was undaunted.

"If you are a principal in the operation—lead trader or master trader, then of course you and your ship would be welcome."

"Must I renounce other arrangements? Can I be a citizen of New Carpathia and still act under the laws of, say, Waymart?"

She laughed.

"So many people have gone to Waymart lately, but surely you can see we have advantages over them, and we trust they will serve us well. One of our advantages is that we are assured by physicists and astronomers that our already low-Dust location is unlikely to encounter any such problems."

She gestured toward the wall, and an ornate hanging that Jethri realized was a representation of the various locations of the registration worlds in relation to the current movement of the Dust.

"You're somewhat outside the normal trading zones," he said, after he had deciphered this.

"Yes, but that keeps us on our toes to do better. This is why we permit multiple citizenships, and our laws are often seen to be less onerous even than Waymart."

"And must I sign an acceptance now?"

She laughed and motioned. Joslynn moved forward and placed the bulky folder in his hands before stepping back.

Secretary Waznik smiled.

"You have the papers in your hands, Trader—you *are* a citizen now. We would appreciate if you would allow us to make a video showing you receiving your papers only sixty-six Standards late. It will be good for the universe to see that New Carpathia honors its promises."

Jethri looked at the folder in his hands, turned, and found Bry Sen ready to receive it. He was, he thought, as he turned back to the Chief Secretary and her aides, beginning to understand why Brabham had wanted nothing to do with this.

"You said that *Balrog* shares this honor with *Gobelyn's Market*?"

"Oh, yes! *Balrog* is Number Seven on the list. We've tried to contact them, but they are very busy and so far haven't been able to send someone to us."

Jethri nodded. "They are busy, but my ship is docked very near to *Balrog*. I'd be happy to take their papers to them."

A sad shake of the head.

"An interesting offer, Trader, but each ship must send a personal representative to receive the paperwork. Your packet includes forms for *Gobelyn's Market*'s current crew and Loop, and past crew off to other ships, like you—they can fill them out at will!—but your receipt means that our part of the original arrangements is done. Your video will be a proof that the ship knows they have been notified, and will make wonderful watching for the broadcast bands back home, where they'll see how we're coming back to being worthwhile trading partners!"

It took Jethri a few moments to process "back home" to mean New Carpathia, but once he did it was as if a well of understanding was uncovered—all of this was not so much about the crews of the "century ships" or the good of the Loopers or the *Envidaria*, as it was about influencing the politics or polities of that planet. That it might prove useful to others was a *side effect* of the offer for these people, not the goal.

It felt for a moment like he had the silver mesh enclosing his head again, as if the smart-beads were analyzing this situation, and would in just a moment produce some knowledge or insight. It was there, just under the surface of his memory. All he needed was the right key.

He felt his fractin warming in his pocket—and there! Yes. *Yes.* These people were grasping the potential disaster, even helping delay action, so that they might gain influence by changing the patterns of knowledge transfer to go through them. They wanted to be paid well—and often!—for information that ought to be free.

He could feel the database building itself in the back of his head. He needed more information, he thought, as much as he could gather, so that they could be properly documented and dealt with. He—

"Trader, I believe it is time for you to take your supplement."

The database folded in mid-build. Jethri blinked himself back into the parlor, and looked down at Bry Sen, who was offering a small container. He took it with a slight bow.

"My thanks," he murmured, and opened the small bottle, while Bry Sen turned to Secretary Waznik and her aides, drawing their eyes to him.

"The trader is on, to him, a backward schedule; this would normally be the middle of his sleep shift. We on his staff must from time to time remind him to relax between events else he will begin to fall asleep, no matter how stimulating the company."

Jethri closed the bottle and slipped it into his pocket, producing a deep and theatrical bow of no known provenance.

"My apologies, my apologies, my apologies, Chief Secretary Waznik. I was dreaming of the assistance you offer us—and, yes, it's exactly as Bry Sen says; I am a sorry case, with more meetings before me before this day is over. I'll take my leave now, bearing this honor, and please whatever other materials you have there—so that I may share them with my family and others! If there is more, please send them to *Genchi*, I will be happy to receive them."

"But the documentary—" cried Secretary Waznik.

"As time permits. I will make every effort to return for the vid, and to plan with you. I thank you so much for making New Carpathia known to me. You will not be forgotten, I guarantee!"

A bag full of materials was thrust at him by Joslynn; it was intercepted by Bry Sen, and so they departed, the pilot over-burdened and Jethri only carrying himself.

Around the curve of the arcade, Jethri stopped at a table loaded with free drinks, and said, "Tarry a moment, Pilot. I'll draw some fizzwater."

"Trader."

Bry Sen settled his load on a nearby chair, and drew a fizzwater for himself. Jethri found one of the board-rest exercises Scout ter'Astin had taught him, and after a moment stood refreshed, mind clear.

"My thanks," he said after a brief comradely bow, "I can see now that pilot's training may need to be expanded, if this is a result I can depend on!"

"Trader. I am concerned. You were concentrating so hard that..."

"Oh yes. I *was* concentrating very hard. When a difficult trading path is opened one must find a way forward, which is what I believe I have done."

He turned to pick the folder up from the chair, while Bry Sen claimed the bag.

"Let us back to the table, if you will be so kind," Jethri said, feeling almost light-hearted. "And please tell me as we travel, Pilot with diplomatic training, what did you think of the honor I have been offered?"

Bry Sen rocked his head slightly from side to side, eyes narrowed—real Looper body language there, Jethri noted. The pilot had been studying.

"To begin," Bry Sen murmured, "it concerns me that these packets and presentations are the means to bring people forward so that a video may be made which will be introduced into the political situation on New Carpathia.

"You, Brabham, distant Loopers in general, become celebrities by default, heroes, if you will. Your *melant'i* is of course your own, but it seems there's an effort to tie your *melant'i* and the *Envidaria* effort to whatever faction has brought the citizenship effort here. As we cannot know the details of the political situation on New Carpathia, this is—worrisome."

He paused and struck a pose.

"Each ship must send a personal representative to receive the paperwork," he announced in breathlessly accurate mimicry of Chief Secretary Waznik.

Jethri grinned, waiting. Bry Sen's expression turned thoughtful as he began to walk again.

"Do you know, Trader? I believe that this situation

is worthy of close study. You might even, with honor, solicit advice before returning for a formal ceremony. Indeed, I—a humble pilot—question whether there is any necessity for a formal ceremony. Did Secretary Waznik not say—" He paused, for effect, Jethri thought, and not because of any failure of memory. "Did she not say *your receipt means that our part of the original arrangements is done*? That phrase might give a qe'andra or, I expect, a trader versed in the complexities of contracts, a moment's pause."

"I caught that," Jethri said. "I was told that the thing's done, and that I can pass on papers of citizenship to my choice of *Gobelyn's Market* crew, past, present, or off-side. The phrase you cite seems to finalize the contract. I'm in Balance with New Carpathia, and New Carpathia's in Balance with *Gobelyn's Market* through me, their personal representative."

He exchanged a solemn look with Bry Sen.

"It couldn't be much clearer, could it? Though I'll take your advice, Pilot, if you think I ought to consult a law-jaw."

"No, no, I think we have together reasoned through this knot to a Balanced conclusion, supportable to a . . . law-jaw—I thank you, Trader!—should that be made necessary."

"Good," Jethri said, and sighed. "It's a good thing that they didn't have the video equipment set up."

Even as he said it, he felt his stomach clench. He looked to Bry Sen, and grimaced.

"Indeed," the pilot said softly, all trace of mischief vanished. "We have their word on that, do we not?"

TEN

THEY'D BEEN LATE GETTING BACK, AND A LINE HAD formed.

Jethri stowed the materials from New Carpathia under the table, and motioned the first person to come forward.

It quickly became apparent that most of this crowd had come directly from a presentation made by Chiv DeNobli on the origins and movement of Rostov's Dust. He'd recommended that attendees who wanted more detailed information, especially about the plans being proposed to keep trade and ships moving to the Seventeen Worlds, should stop by the table in the hall.

To Jethri, it looked as if most of them had.

He quickly pulled Bry Sen into the mix, to talk with pilots who had just started to notice Dust-induced errors.

That left Jethri with reps of planetary coops, and trade associations, who had very little understanding of the math, the Dust, or how either might cause them problems.

Jethri found himself repeatedly slipping his hand into his pocket to tap his lucky pocket fractin while wishing there was a way to hurry the visitors who'd been better off reading the signage. But the fractin was no help at all, remaining cool to the touch, and so far as Jethri could tell, entirely disinterested in the proceedings.

What did help was the two screens that a couple of clever cousins from the Carresens side had established on each end of the table. People could—and a number of them did—put themselves on a wait list to receive such information and procedures as were available, or to sign onto a class.

Jethri, who was talking with a small-time local trader from one of the Seventeen Worlds had just agreed that changes were happening now, and would probably get worse, to the extent of altering the rest of their lives, when a movement near but not of the waiting group drew his eye.

The face was familiar, the stance uncertain, as if the person was unable, quite, to commit to a course of action.

It was that wavering of posture that triggered recognition: Captain sea'Kera, who had apparently committed to something, after all, for he had a crew-duffle slung over one shoulder and carried a smaller bag in his off-hand.

He was wearing a generic uniform, lacking both *Genchi*'s logo and colors.

Jethri held up a hand to the line, requesting a pause, and stepped to the side of the table, producing a bow of puzzled welcome.

"Captain," he said in Liaden, choosing Comrade mode as the most giving. "Is there some way in which I may assist you?"

Captain sea'Kera clearly sighed, bowed a recognition

to authority, and approached. Jethri felt a movement at his elbow and was unsurprised to see that Bry Sen had arrived, his face specifically and properly bland. Captain sea'Kera bowed again, to an authority of a clan not his own. There was a fillip there Jethri didn't recognize, though Bry Sen clearly did, because he moved half a step back, putting himself just barely behind Jethri.

"Trader, may I speak here, in confidence?" Captain sea'Kera's voice was soft.

Jethri bowed his formal permission, which seemed to firm the man's resolve.

He swung the duffel to the floor at his feet, and placed the bag next to it.

"Trader, I know this is sudden, but I have only this shift received necessary permissions from my delm. I may now put forth my resignation as captain of *Genchi*, effective as of start of shift, to you, as the representative of the owner. I have here all the ship documents I normally control, and I now formally turn them over to Pilot yo'Endoth as captain pro tem."

He picked up the small bag and offered it across extended palms, as he bowed.

"Captain," he said. "You have made yourself familiar with *Genchi*, as a good pilot ought. You do not need my assurance that the ship is sound, and the crew of good heart."

Bry Sen stepped forward, took the bag. "I will do my best for her, Captain," he said firmly, and stepped back to his previous position.

Jethri took a breath.

Captain sea'Kera straightened from his bow, and met Jethri's eyes.

"Engineer eyl'Fassa holds *Genchi* and awaits your word, Trader, or that of the acting captain."

Surely, this was his place to speak, Jethri thought, but Captain sea'Kera wasn't done yet.

"I feel that you should be informed of my reasons, Trader."

He took a deep breath, paused, and exhaled lightly.

"For over a dozen Standards *Genchi* ran quiet routes with a minimum of changes, few to no visitors, on a tight, reasonable schedule.

"It has become clear to me that the mission has evolved. *Genchi* now carries a trader of acclaim. Instead of running long-term fixed routes where few adjustments were necessary, *Genchi* will be acting as a... scout for a new route concept, and will from time to time be called upon to serve as a diplomatic base. This will entail many adjustments. I have no expertise in any aspect of this new mission."

He paused, glanced down at his duffel, then back to Jethri's face.

"I have no experience with a style of trade that prefers the trader's direction to that of the captain. This is a question of my comfort and habit of command, and does not reflect upon you, Trader. You have been everything that is competent and amiable. It is clear to me that you have many new ideas, and I do not doubt that you will see them successfully implemented. In order for *Genchi* to do her best in these changed circumstances, she must have an able captain who shares your vision, and that of the new owner."

He bowed once more, in respect, as Jethri read it.

"My arrangements are fixed. I will serve as temporary third officer on a Liaden ship which will be returning to Solcintra immediately after this event is completed. I am on my way to my new berth now, with your permission and agreement. This is necessity. Acting now spares all of us awkward moments at another location."

It seemed that Captain sea'Kera had at last come to an end of all he had wished to say. He bent, picked up his duffel and placed the strap over his shoulder.

Carefully, Jethri bowed, accepting sea'Kera's actions, and acknowledging that he had heard and understood.

"Necessity is, Captain," he said. "I thank you for your cordial and prompt visit with me here, and wish you all the best going forward. Thank you for your confidence. Have you need for additional references or documentation you may apply to me directly if you so like. Allow me to assure you that we are perfectly aligned in Balance."

Relief actually showed for an instant on Captain sea'Kera's face, before he bowed once again to a recognized authority.

"Trader. Captain yo'Endoth. I leave you now."

He turned and walked away.

Jethri turned to Bry Sen.

"We must in short order allow Master Trader pin'Aker to know of this development. The port, also, must be apprised of the change of captain. I will send to the port. You will please return to *Genchi*, reassure the crew, and send a pinbeam detailing our new configuration to *Barskalee*, marked for Master pin'Aker's urgent notice."

Bry Sen bowed briefly, and glanced over his shoulder at those standing in line, faces avid, curious, and a bit impatient.

"And you? Will you hold the bridge here?"

"Yes," Jethri said, switching to Terran and raising

his voice so that he could be heard by those in line. "I promise not to overstretch myself. Go ahead and get that done for us."

"Yes," Bry Sen said. He put the bag's strap over his shoulder and turned away. Jethri let him walk six steps before he called out, "Oh, Cousin!"

Bry Sen turned, a quick, neat shifting of the feet. "Cousin?" he returned.

"Be quick, willya?" Jethri asked. "An' bring me a coffee when you come back."

"Quick as can," Bry Sen promised, and moved off at just short of a jog.

Jethri returned to the table, and spread his hands in apology to those waiting. "If it's not one thing, it's something else, am I right?"

A few chuckles and short laughs greeted that, and Jethri waved the first in line forward.

"What was all that?" she asked him, eyes wide.

Jethri shrugged. "Just some housekeeping, like we all do from time to time. Now, what have you heard about the *Envidaria*?"

He *oughtn't* feel better now that the captain situation was settled, Jethri thought. He hadn't wanted to be the one to dismiss Captain sea'Kera, even to a new berth, and he couldn't help but feel that the man had had the right of it—do it now, do it quick, do it while the ship was in port for some days yet, so that any problems that might come up with the change of command could be dealt with calmly.

He took advantage of a momentary lull in visitors to send a comm message to the Meldyne Portmaster's office, apprising them of Bry Sen's ascension to acting captain.

By the time he hit *send*, the line had formed again, and Jethri went back to work, mood still elevated.

Next up was a young pilot who had a scheme for better distribution of Dust reports to the hubs.

"Good," Jethri told him. "That's exactly the kind of thing Freza DeNobli's team wants to hear about. They'll be at this table tomorrow, or you can use one of the keypads on this table to send a message, and somebody'll contact you by comm."

The pilot smiled and moved over to the keypad, while Jethri nodded at the next in line. He was feeling a little warm in general, and wondered if the hall was that crowded.

Then, he realized that it was his fractin that was warm—not vibrating, not obviously excited, just... warming, as if it had become slightly interested in the proceedings despite itself.

The line in had gotten bunched up somehow. What he could see of the person immediately in front of him was the back—someone of about his own height and weight, wearing a tailored day suit with nothing of the uniform about it. He was speaking quietly to the people behind him. He gestured suddenly, an overdone pilot's sign—*launched to the sky*—the ring on that hand flashed, the firegem and Triluxian band combining to draw the eye.

Jethri knew that ring—knew exactly how to use its flashing gem to direct—or misdirect. Hadn't he used it for both, himself?

Laughter and nods of agreement and the slightly louder retort to someone's remark from the man with the ring came to Jethri's ears.

"We all need some time to tend our own necessities,

gentlefolk, and Dulsey is no exception. We'd not envisioned such a scheme as I'm invited to here, but here I must be, and she where she must be. Perhaps before the next congress we shall meet again on Tradedesk!"

The fractin in his pocket was actually hot, and Jethri had a vision of his pocket bursting into flames. The heat subsided somewhat, though the fractin was still warm, and he knew that ring, that hand—that voice.

Bry Sen swept in from the side at that moment, large cup in hand.

"The crowds are growing, Trader, just as you see! But I am returned in good time, with coffee and news!"

"Coffee first." Jethri took the cup, and had a sip. Hot and bitter, and definitely not 'toot.

"What news?" he asked then, keeping an eye on his uncle's back.

"Freza asks me to let you know that Bory is setting up a one-shot for you. From her expression, I deduce that this is not preferred."

"A one-shot?" Jethri blinked. "No, it's not preferred. To say it mild."

He might've spoken too loud, or it might've been that his uncle was sensitive to his voice.

Whichever, he produced another extravagant sign— *business goes forth*—before he turned.

It was the face that had taken him, when they'd first met at Tradedesk. And it was the face that took him now. *Almost* his father's face. If it came to that, almost his own, though there was that clear difference in age.

He bowed with opened arms, did Uncle Yuri, offering both professional acknowledgment and a fortunate reunion.

His conference ID badge swung out as he did, and Jethri read "Guest of the Carresens."

Jethri bowed welcome, and waved Bry Sen forward. The pilot's eyes flicked between the two faces, and his expression settled into polite blandness.

"Captain Bry Sen yo'Endoth of *Genchi*, please meet my Uncle Yuri."

Bry Sen bowed welcome, and stepped to the side, motioning for the next in line to come to him.

Uncle Yuri leaned forward, close enough to share breath.

"You and I need to talk."

Jethri's fractin *buzzed*, no blame to it. There was definitely a touch of anger in that voice so like his father's. Worse, it was as if Yuri had spoken twice; Jethri heard an echo of *Rifuzo tian enmisigan!* inside his head, which was surely the language of Malu's ship, and he felt a flicker of the bright clarity the silver cape had imparted. He shifted his stance slightly, and heard his own voice answer, sharp for sharp.

"*Ĉieloj diras, ke la petanto parolas pacience, dezirante aŭdita.*"

His fractin stopped buzzing, and this time Jethri heard the translation in his mind: *Celestials say a supplicant speaks patiently, wishing to be heard.*

Yuri's face went still. Jethri's stomach tightened in his own spurt of temper.

The tone this time was less overtly angry, and woke no echoes of cape-borne languages. It didn't do much for Jethri's temper, though, being something too close to the tone Paitor used when he was explaining how stupid you'd just been.

"Clearly, we need to speak in depth, and urgently.

Make time, and I will do the same. In the meantime, I pray you not meddle further with any objects you have from *Elsvair*. If you have any sense you'll speak no more in that tongue."

Well, that didn't do much to improve the temper, did it?

Jethri bowed, with cutting brevity.

"It was perhaps an infelicitous phrase," he said, which wasn't an apology, and wasn't going to become one, any time soon.

"For this other thing—you may have urgency, but I have business for some hours yet—two workshops to present, several meetings and a speech to prepare."

Uncle Yuri frowned, the hand bearing the Triluxian ring rose to stroke the air between them. His tone this time was more moderate.

"Do not put me off, Jethri. You are very much in danger if you use certain objects without training, and your ignorance endangers many others. I have one unbreakable meeting here at the congress, and it begins in minutes. I understand that you are busy. Nonetheless, we must meet. This evening, as late as you must, as long as you need. That would be prudent. Here!"

Jethri took the proffered card, which carried a comm code under the image of a large, single crystal.

"You are the only one on this station with that code. Use it, and I will answer immediately."

· · · · · · · · ·

ELEVEN

· · · · · · · · · ·

"WHAT IN THE WET MUD AM I SUPPOSED TO DO WITH these?"

It was late, the last workshop had been...trying, and the walk back to *Genchi* interrupted several times by people who wanted to argue about the *Envidaria* with him *right now*. It had taken all of Bry Sen's persuasiveness and all of Chiv's muscle to shift them and move on.

They'd all sighed in relief when they reached *Genchi*'s dock—until a shadow burst out from behind the ship-board, moving straight for Jethri.

He dodged, Bry Sen twisted, Chiv threw a punch, which didn't land, and the shadow spoke sharply.

"*Kohno*!"

"Stop!" Jethri gasped, lunging forward to grab Chiv's arm. "He's from *Elsvair*."

"Why ain't he there, then?" Chiv demanded, which Jethri allowed was a good question. He stepped up into a pool of light. Vally stayed inside the shadows, his eyes gleaming, dark inside darkness.

"What do you want, Vally? Be quick."

"It is this paper, *Kohno*. Malu said that you wished to have it, as soon as we found it."

A pale rectangle appeared, seeming to hover in the dark air between them. Jethri extended a hand, and the rectangle was placed on his palm. Paper. Jethri closed his fingers over it, and stuffed it into the pocket holding his fractin.

"Anything else?"

"No, *Kohno*."

"Then jet," Jethri snapped. "Give Malu my thanks."

"Yes, *Kohno*."

The blackness suddenly felt empty.

"All right," Jethri said. "Chiv—"

"I'll see you to the hatch, Cousin, then I'm for home."

"Right. Thank you, Cousin."

"No worries," Chiv answered, as the hatch opened, and Kel Bin stepped aside to let them in.

"There is a box for you in the conference room, Trader," Kel Bin said, so Jethri had gone to the conference room.

There was a box, and two envelopes. Jethri recognized Freza's hand on one of those, and opened it.

Jeth, can you take care of these so nobody finds them? We need to talk about Dulcimer, real soon. Love you, Freza.

The *love you* was almost enough to banish the dull ache between his brows. Then he opened the box.

"What in wet mud am I supposed to do with these?" His voice was sharp and too loud, and the headache flared. "Take care of 'em so nobody finds 'em?" Jethri went on, pulling the things out of the box. "Who *wants* 'em?"

"Trader, your drink," a quiet voice broke into his tirade. He turned to see Kel Bin enter, bearing restorative elixir.

Jethri took the glass gladly, and swallowed some of the thick, tasty beverage, before waving a hand at the junk on the table.

"Who brought this, please?"

"Two persons who said they were," he paused and mustered the Terran from memory: "*Freza's cousins Erl and Loozie.*" Kel Bin hesitated. "Did I err, Trader?"

Jethri shook his head, and had another swallow of elixir. It felt like the pain in his head was easing a little.

"No error on your part, comrade," he assured Kel Bin. "Merely—" He nodded at the table. "This is junk, utterly worthless, which I am asked to place where it cannot be found, and I am confounded."

"Captain Bry Sen allowed me to know that the day was long and trying," Kel Bin said. "Your reserves are low. The elixir will help you regain energy and clarity. A moment and I will bring *chernubia*, as well."

Left alone, Jethri surveyed the junk on the table, muttering to himself.

"Knock-off roll coins, imitation energy blades, a stasis box with a broken seal, two fake Before *pistols*—" He shook his head. "It's *all* junk."

His eye fell on the second envelope. He opened it and drew out a single sheet—an inventory list of the items received, with *destroy this* written hastily across the top in Freza's hand.

"Trader," Kel Bin set a plate of *chernubia* on the table by the glass and vanished again.

Jethri frowned at the list, picked up the glass and sipped elixir.

Where had this stuff come from? he wondered. Freza had been going out to *Dulcimer*—had they been carrying it? If so, why? And did he really want to know the answer to either question?

Destroy was actually a good idea, he thought, for the list and the listed.

He finished the elixir and put the glass aside. The *chernubia* failed to tempt him, which was a measure of just how bad his temper was.

Destroy, now—he shook his head. Junk though it was, it would still require energy to destroy it, and he didn't want *Genchi* to show a spike at dockside. Prolly best thing was to—

The hatch gong sounded. Jethri sighed. Prolly more flowers. Well, the crew could deal.

"Trader, your guest has arrived," Bry Sen stated on closed call to the conference room.

Jethri frowned.

"Am I expecting a guest?"

"So the guest claims. It is your Uncle Yuri, Trader."

Of course it was.

Well, it wasn't as if he could pretend not to be at home. Jethri glared at the wall speaker.

"Is my Uncle Yuri alone?"

"Yes, Trader."

"Then bring him to me," Jethri said, bowing to the inevitable. "Please ask Kel Bin for tea."

He thought of asking for more elixir, then lost the thought as his fractin warmed appreciably in his pocket. He slipped his hand inside—and felt paper.

Right, he thought, and pulled it out.

It was not nearly so clean as it had seemed against the darkness, and Jethri very much feared that the stain on the upper right corner was blood. But despite the dirt, a portion of the address was clear: *Veeoni, Crystal Rezonics, Freebar City*—

The door opened.

Jethri turned.

Bry Sen stepped into the room, a Bry Sen re-visioned, in a sharp uniform in *Genchi*'s colors, and the captain's ring on his finger, his collar a-glitter with multiple pins, rather than the simple pilots guild pin that had previously adorned him.

He bowed.

"Trader, here is Yuri Tomas for you."

"Uncle Yuri," Jethri said, without warmth. "Come in, please."

"I am wanted on the bridge, Trader," Bry Sen murmured. "The communications difficulty again."

"Go," Jethri told him. "Uncle Yuri and I will do very well together."

Possibly.

Bry Sen bowed and left. The door closed, and Jethri looked at his uncle, who was staring at the pile of junk on the table.

"Really, Jethri? Surely you know better than these."

"I do, but somebody don't," Jethri said with a sigh. "I'm charged with hiding them so they won't be found."

"By whom?"

"A friend," Jethri said, and sighed for being snappish. "I'm thinking she wanted me to hide them 'mong my stock, but these things put honest tech to shame. Not to say that anybody with half-an-eye could tell they weren't the same at all."

"What will you do with them?"

Jethri shrugged. "Prolly hide 'em among my stock. In a stasis box, maybe. In a back corner."

The speaker clicked.

"Tea, Trader," Kel Bin said.

"Enter," Jethri said.

Kel Bin did, bearing the everyday tea service, which he placed on the table, taking the empty glass onto the tray.

"Else, Trader?"

"Thank you, no," Jethri told him, and he was alone with his Uncle Yuri.

Who was still gazing in offended horror at the junk in the middle of the table.

"Let me put them back in the box," Jethri said.

"They are distracting," his uncle admitted, stepping back to allow Jethri past him.

"Here," Jethri said, handing over the address label. "Thought you might know who that is."

His fractin warmed as he was repacking the box, but Jethri thought it was interest in Uncle Yuri, and not the other items.

He closed the top of the box, bent and slid it under the conference table.

Straightening, he found himself quite close to his uncle, who was still holding the label in his hand.

"May I ask where you found this?"

Jethri shook his head. "Vally brought it. Malu said the silver net had been wrapped up in the mailroom of a dead ship. She thought Vally might've kept the label and said she'd send it, if he had."

He moved his shoulders in a Liaden shrug.

"It's been in my possession less than an hour."

"Thank you." Uncle Yuri inclined his head. "In fact, I do know this person. What came of the silver net?"

"I have it," Jethri said. "It's in a stasis box."

"Excellent. I will take it."

Jethri sighed and moved down-table. "Tea?"

"Thank you."

He poured, noting the amber color, and the floral scent. Kel Bin had rolled out the Jasimun Flo'at, the best tea on-board, and not so many tins of it, either.

Uncle Yuri received his cup and drank, pausing to savor the leaf with eyes closed.

"Excellent," he murmured.

Jethri sipped respectfully, then, still holding the cup, he accessed the pilot's renewing exercise.

As always, the exercise offered a moment of peace, then, as the muscles and mind relaxed, clarity and a renewed energy bloomed, until of a sudden, the exercise ended, leaving the pilot awake and refreshed, as if from a comfortable nap.

"I wonder, Nephew, what has occurred? The tea is fine, but not as resuscitating as that!"

Jethri smiled lightly, feeling the start of a trade session gambit . . . and recalled he was not dealing with a Liaden this time, nor a Terran as such.

"I accessed a pilot's exercise, sir. That's all."

A nod. "I understand. Early in a career such events as these can be quite wearying. So much opportunity, so many ways to make the wrong move. It can be useful to acknowledge and prepare yourself."

Jethri had another sip of tea and put the cup down. Uncle Yuri did the same. He looked at Jethri and spread his hands, the firegem flashing on his finger.

"We must now arrive at my topics, though the tea

is still on the table. First, you have interfered with arrangements of mine. This is not entirely your fault. *Elsvair* has been collecting for me for some time and your appearance—your *knowledgeable* appearance here in the midst of so much activity, has disrupted the delivery of items that were—*that are*—necessary to projects I've been involved in for some...time."

"The goods were offered, and I purchased them in good faith," Jethri said.

Yuri sighed.

"Yes, I understand from *Elsvair* that you conducted yourself well, and gave good prices. As your uncle, I have no complaint of your comportment. However, that sidesteps the fact that those items were not yours to purchase, and that *Elsvair* was not to have sold them to anyone but me."

Jethri nodded. "The actual you," he said, "and not an instance of you."

His uncle eyed him. "Someone was...casual."

"Confused, I think," Jethri said. "We settled it out that I was neither, but I don't think it took. Also, they were running out of room."

"I see. Still, the goods should not have been offered, and I will have them."

"I paid for them," Jethri said.

"And I will reimburse your out-of-pocket and reasonable expenses. I'm not a fool."

Jethri had recourse to his tea cup.

"What about the fractins?"

Yuri frowned. "Fractins."

"I bought crates full of fractins, mostly imitation. But the ones that are real, aren't just real—they're special. At least as special as my own."

"Have you held these...specials in your hand, counted them?"

"I have not. This isn't a good place to dump fractins out on a deck and go through them one-by-one, asking my fractin to find the specials. It's busy here, and people might get a funny idea or two."

"So they might. Let me save both of us time. I will buy back all of the items you purchased from *Elsvair*, including the cases of fractins. I will pay you this evening, and take the memory veil with me. Tomorrow, I will send a team for the rest of the items.

"I learn that *Elsvair* crew used some of the devices, and while they have had some training, they are not by any means expert. I am told that they showed you how several operated. I hope that you haven't damaged yourself by this activity. Some of these devices are very dangerous, as I think you know. In particular, I must have the memory veil." He paused, then asked, softly, "Did you use the memory veil, Jethri?"

"I did," he said, there being no reason to lie, not after his bungle with the language. "Malu thought it was a necklace. My fractin and I thought otherwise, and when I had it in my hands, it was clearly something else, though I didn't know what, until I had it on, with the hood over my head."

"That was—forgive me—a very foolish thing to have done," Uncle Yuri said. "There is a whole course of training that...ought to be mastered before attempting to use the veil. It provides a highly immersive experience, and without the training, a user could be...absorbed entirely into the beads."

"It was startling," Jethri admitted. "I think it was recording; it kept asking what I knew, and building databases. I learned some things—that language, for instance—history—old history. Batchers . . ."

He looked up.

"Are we made in batches?"

"No," Uncle Yuri said firmly. "*We* were *never* made in batches." He sighed.

"We cannot undo what is done," he said. "We can only resolve not to do it again. Where is the veil?"

"In a stasis box, in the safe room."

"And the other devices?"

"Each in their own stasis box, in the safe room."

"Well done. One more question, if you allow it. The phrase 'my fractin and I.' This is one of the so-called special fractins?"

"Yes. My fractin is active, it knows Old Tech. It likes some, and doesn't like others." He paused, considering, and then added. "It liked the memory veil. It didn't like—"

He stopped, remembering.

"There were some things I didn't buy," he said. Uncle moved a hand, inviting him to go on.

"On *Elsvair*—there's a partial—I think it's partial—arms mount. There are things—I don't know what they are, but they're *hungry*, and if it were me, I'd drop them into the nearest sun."

"Ah." Uncle Yuri failed to look horrified. "I will examine those, thank you. Once our business here is done, I will be returning to *Elsvair*."

He paused, apparently considering, then looked up.

"You may not wish to hear this, but I feel that I must say it. Jethri, there is no *we* with a fractin. Fractins are machines—tools—even the special ones, saving that those hold more potential for mayhem than the genuine worker fractins. The specials, as you call them, are linking fractins. That's why it may feel to you as if it is reacting to various devices. Very possibly it *is* reacting—to timonium levels. It is not sentient. It is not your friend. I would counsel—strongly counsel— that you allow me to take your special fractin with me when I go."

Jethri shook his head.

"There is a *we*. Throw my fractin into a crate of fractins—even special ones—and mine will come to my hand. When the Scouts impounded it, they tried to fob me off with a fake, but mine called to me from across the room."

Yuri looked grim. Jethri shrugged.

"The fractin's in my pocket. It reacts to *you*. I haven't asked it what it does. I should've asked the memory veil, I guess." He smiled briefly. "Hindsight."

"Indeed." Uncle Yuri sighed.

"It is late. Have the memory veil in its stasis box brought to me, and produce me a list of your expenses, which I will pay. We can arrange pick up of the other devices and the fractins—"

Jethri blinked. A framework was building in his mind, a multi-dimensional wire diagram with himself at the center with the fractin, as a unit, and shaded points of light beyond. He knew the veil was the net of fine bright points within that diagram, and there were other points of active light, quite nearby, a dozen or more of them.

The wire frame diagram in his head shuddered and now there were eerie smudges, too, some of them close, so close they might have been in *Elsvair*, where, after all, he'd left those things he wanted nothing to do with.

Jethri opened his eyes, saw Uncle clearly and saw multiple concerns clouding his expression.

"Uncle Yuri, the *we* I see is your fault."

"Mine?"

"You told me that you and Arin between you had settled on how I wouldn't be you and how I wouldn't be Arin. I recall this.

"You told me yourself that you'd done something to modify who I'd be so that I could be more in tune to Old Tech. Well, it *worked*, Uncle Yuri." He paused, smiling into his uncle's eyes.

"We can't undo what is done," he said. "We can only resolve not to do it again."

Uncle Yuri—laughed.

"You are yourself, Jethri Gobelyn ven'Deelin," he said. "But you are also plainly family."

He bowed slightly.

"At some point we will have a discussion that Arin was to have had with you. In the meantime, I will ask you to be careful in your experimentation. What you do with your legacy and what you must do for the *Envidaria* is important work, work you are uniquely qualified to perform. Do not remove yourself from the center of this!"

Rising, Uncle extended a hand.

"Please, bring me the veil. Keep your fractin if you must."

Jethri sighed, and for a moment he thought he'd refuse to part with any of the devices, most especially the veil.

But, no. Uncle Yuri was right. The *Envidaria* and all it meant, *that* had to come first.

He reached for the comm.

"Trader," Bry Sen said over the system.

"Trader, there is an individual at the lock loudly demanding to speak with your guest. He tells me that *the Uncle* will be pleased to speak with Choody, and sooner is better for all!"

TWELVE

UNCLE YURI SIGHED, AND SMOOTHED HIS COAT IN A PAT-
tern that Jethri recognized as a weapon check. He
bowed.

"Pray keep the devices we have been discussing
safe for me, Nephew. I will send for them later. Most
especially, the veil. And Jethri—"

Jethri held up his hand. "I know—leave the veil
alone."

A brief smile.

"A quick student. So." He raised his voice slightly,
addressing the comm.

"Captain, please convey to Choody that I am on
my way out, and—"

"Forgive, Ser Tomas," Bry Sen interrupted. "I am
told that the business Choody carries is best discussed
in private, and that . . . *Lord ven'Deelin* will also be
interested in what he has to say."

Jethri moved to the screen and brought up the
image from the lock cameras.

There was one man standing as close as he might
to the main camera, perhaps not having noticed the
second and third. Those cameras showed several
plain-dressed individuals standing at a distance. He

457

pulled the images closer, confirming that they were none of the usual dock-strollers, and therefore could be assumed to have escorted this . . . Choody.

Jethri gave his attention to the man at the lock.

He appeared to be Terran, with longish hair by Looper standards, combed straight back. He was not tall by the breed but taller than an average Liaden. His clothing was well-made but not worn well, rings glittered, several to each finger, and the visible wrist displayed several mismatched bracelets. He wore a wide belt, half concealed by his coat. He was carrying weapons, then, Jethri assumed, more than one.

He felt a whisper of movement at his shoulder.

"Who is he?" he asked, without turning around.

"A contractor," Uncle Yuri replied, sounding somewhere between resigned and sorrowful. "I will deal with him, Jethri. You need not be in it."

"Assuming *Lord ven'Deelin* is meant to be me, I'm *already* in it."

He turned his head. His uncle sighed.

"As you say."

Jethri cleared the screen, locked it, and touched the comm.

"Captain, please allow Choody to know that we will see him directly. First, I will wish Kel Bin to remove the tea service from the conference room. We will not be offering this person refreshment. All crew, save yourself, are to become invisible."

"Trader, it shall be done as you say."

Choody shouldered Bry Sen out of the way, and stepped into the conference room with energy, a smile on his face, and his hand extended as if to shake hands.

Neither Jethri nor his uncle offered a return hand, or any bow. Choody shrugged and turned to Bry Sen, who remained in the doorway.

"You can go, big guy," he said, waving his left hand dismissively. "Not wanted here, get it? No introductions needed. Uncle and me have worked together a long time, and I'm sure he'll introduce me to his ... family."

Bry Sen's expression did not change, but his posture did, and Jethri was abruptly looking at a dangerous man, one heartbeat from drawing a weapon.

"Captain, please leave us," Jethri said, in cool Liaden. "My kinsman and I shall deal with this person appropriately."

That gained him a sharp look, but his face must have been reassuring. Bry Sen bowed, "Trader," and left them, the door closing shut behind.

Choody turned back to them, still grinning, and tucked his hands into his belt as he made a show of surveying them.

"Well, now, just look at the pair of you, so much alike you could be brothers! That's the word I want, isn't it, Uncle? *Brothers*?"

"In fact, the word is nephew," Uncle Yuri said coolly. "What do you want, Ser Wharton?"

Choody raised his hands, palms out, grin still on display.

"Is that so? Well, have it your way. Now that I see the two of you together, a whole lot of things are coming together for me. Famous Jethri ven'Deelin who-was-Gobelyn, eh? And his uncle, too. Collectors of stuff so grey nobody wants to talk about it, or even admit it exists! Us three, we got bidness to do."

Little man, Jethri thought, though Choody wasn't

short nor small. But large as he was, his air and lack of manner made him small. This, he thought, *this* is what it means when a Liaden says, "that person has no *melant'i.*"

"Not gonna introduce me?" Choody asked.

Uncle Yuri raised his eyebrows, and said nothing.

"That's fine, I'll do it myself," Choody said, with unimpaired humor. He turned to Jethri, and put his hand on his chest.

"Choody Wharton. Remember that name, Trader; it's gonna be real important to you. Uncle and me, we been working together, and pretty soon, you and me will be working together, too.

"So, how it began is that Uncle hears about me from somebody else that I do good work of a kind he needs. So, he asks me to retrieve some things for him, and I do that. He pays me. Then, a while later, comes another commission to find something else, which I do, and he pays me. After a time of this, I start to see what his thing is—these Befores, these things the Scouts don't like, that do crazy stuff, or else they just blow up in your face.

"I'm innerested, so I find a couple of these things on my own, having gotten a feel for where to look. I let Uncle know they're available and does he want them? He does, he pays me, and I go on the lookout for more of this stuff.

"Some of the things, he don't want, but that's all right, somebody else in my network usually bought those. And all the while Uncle's giving me lessons in what to look for, what's good, what's bad, what's dangerous."

"And you start to branch out," Jethri said, hoping to hurry this along.

Choody brought his palms together sharply, producing an explosive sound that did nothing for Jethri's head.

"Right you are! I branch out. Had a network already, small, you unnerstand. We all start small. Got a big network now, people working for me, and that's where you come in, Trader Jethri."

Jethri shook his head.

"Not interested."

"Oh, but you will be," Choody told him. "You gotta listen the thing out to the end. But, hey, it's late; you're tired, I can see it. I'll make the rest of it short, so you can sign on and go to bed."

Jethri stared at him, wondering how he was going to rid *Genchi* of Choody, and an image of the inventory list of junk items leapt into memory, with the note *destroy this too!*

"Real quick, now—there was a downturn in bidness. One of my contracts got in a gun-fight, got dead. Next thing I hear, there's a new captain, he drops the route, and sells the stuff that was due to be delivered to me, direct to Crystal, and I got no profit.

"Back-checking that ship, I find it at Port Chavvy just in time to loan some Jethri ven'Deelin the tools for a port-scrap he takes straight to a Liaden trader. I'm innerested in the Liaden big-ships, like everybody doing bidness, so I look a little deeper, and here's Jethri ven'Deelin was ustabe Jethri Gobelyn off *Gobelyn's Market*, and he's involved with this *Envidaria*, which, looking at it, has some angles for my network."

Jethri shifted. Choody held up his hand.

"Right, right. Bottom line—here it is. It don't take much to see Uncle's got himself a tight network. His—nephew, is it?—right there on Port Chavvy to make contact with the ship who direct-sells my stuff to Uncle, and cutting me right outta the loop."

He shook his head at Uncle Yuri.

"Won't do, Uncle, you gotta see that. You got a rep, you gotta tend it, 'cause what do you have if you don't have honor?"

He glanced at Jethri. "Am I right, Trader?"

"I don't see a bottom line," Jethri gritted through clenched teeth.

"All right, here it is. I know who you are. I got *Gobelyn's Market*'s route, so I know where they are. It doesn't matter if they're part of Uncle's network, what matters is I can get to them, any time I want. And this is why you'll come to work for me, Trader, and you'll be happy to do it."

Jethri's hand twitched toward his hideaway in the instant that he felt strong fingers close around his wrist.

"What do you want, Ser Wharton?" Uncle Yuri said wearily. "In short, please."

The grin vanished, and Choody's expression turned ugly. He thrust a finger toward Uncle, but didn't, Jethri noted, connect.

"From you, I want my money. That's the money you cut me out of when you bought *Dulcimer*'s cargo, and the money you been underpaying me all along. Going forward, we're gonna be *partners*, you and me, Yuri Tomas."

He spun, finger stabbing toward Jethri.

"And from you, *nephew*, I want connections on Liaden big ships. I want master traders taking my comm calls, and following my say-so."

Jethri didn't laugh.

"And I'll do this because . . . ?"

Choody shook his head.

"Not as bright as your uncle? You'll do it because I know *Gobelyn's Market*'s route, nephew. I still got my network, and I'll tell you from experience that it's no trouble at all to make a ship disappear into the Dust. And if you and your ship folks broke up, like some of the stories go, we know who you talk to now, nephew, and we know who that sweet redhead is, too. *Balrog*, isn't it? One ship or two, trouble's easy enough to deliver when you know the ways of it."

He stepped back.

"So there you are—bottom line. I've told you both what I want. It's your job to deliver." He glanced at Jethri.

"Before somebody gets hurt."

Jethri took a breath—

"I understand your wishes, Ser Wharton," Uncle Yuri said smoothly. "Let us go now, and leave my nephew to his rest."

Choody shook his head.

"Yuri, I'm worried. I'm worried you think you got nothing to lose. So, I'm just going to mention that I know *Elsvair*'s on port—I've already been and talked to that Minsha."

Uncle inclined his head.

Choody sighed.

"So, yeah, it's late. I know where your ship's docked, too. You'll hear from me tomorrow, and we'll work out the partnership terms after you pay me what's in arrears."

He turned.

"I'm gone, now. Sleep sound, nephew."

The door snatched open, and there was Bry Sen, grim, and a weapon in full view on his belt.

Choody grinned at him.

"Sure, big guy, show me out."

The door closed.

Uncle Yuri let go of Jethri's wrist.

"That person cannot be allowed to continue," Jethri said in cold Liaden.

"I agree," his Uncle said in the same language. "I have created this problem and I will solve it. This, I swear to you."

"Choody has left the ship," Bry Sen's voice came over the comm. "He and his escort have departed our dock."

Uncle Yuri sighed.

"I, too, will take my leave. *Elsvair* will want me, I think."

"I'll see you out," Jethri said.

"Do you want an escort?" he asked when they had reached the hatch.

Uncle Yuri shook his head.

"I'm safe so long as it is understood that I have secrets," he said, and put a hand on Jethri's shoulder, the firegem sparkling on his finger.

"Be careful, young Jethri, and, also—be bold! Understand that your actions will bring change. I would also ask you to understand that we are not in opposition, no matter what you may hear. Do not worry that you are acting against me, but act as you must."

His fingers tightened, and then he was gone, out the hatch, and away.

Jethri went down the hall to the bridge, where Bry Sen sat in the pilot's chair, watching the screens.

"We need to warn *Balrog*," Jethri said. "Choody Wharton threatens ship, crew, and in particular Freza."

Bry Sen spun the chair around, his face absolutely without expression, and used his chin to point at the open intercom.

"I took the liberty of listening to Ser Wharton's conversation," he said, his voice cold in Liaden. "I have alerted *Balrog* and *Elsvair*. Will you wish to send a pinbeam to *Gobelyn's Market*, Trader?"

Jethri stepped further into the bridge and collapsed into the second chair, spinning it to face Bry Sen.

"And tell them what, I wonder?" he said, accepting the pilot's choice of language. After Choody's "conversation," Liaden was downright soothing. "Shall I say that the universe is dangerous? They are aware, I believe. I might send the name, I suppose, but are they put more at risk for knowing it?"

"*Balrog* knew the name," Bry Sen said, his tone thawing somewhat. "Perhaps a mention that the name is presently exercising malice, and mentioned the ship in passing?"

"That's prudent," Jethri allowed. "And a recommendation that they contact DeNobli for updated information."

He spun the chair, reaching to the board.

"I'll send that now."

Some while later, Jethri stepped out of the shower and put on his dressing gown, taking pleasure in the sheen of the silk, and the embroidery flowing down the front placket and then 'round the hem. To a Looper's eye, it was a ridiculous garment, overdone and picky, but tonight it soothed and brought back welcome memories.

Maybe, he thought, I'm homesick.

He sighed and looked around his quarters. It was

late, he thought, and he ought to go to bed. Which he would, except that he expected he wouldn't sleep.

Well. Might as well put waiting to work, as Master ven'Deelin had it. Take another look at his speech, or—

A sharp buzz interrupted his thought—*Balrog*'s comm.

His heart squeezed in his chest. Choody and his threats leapt to mind, and Freza!

He snatched up the comm.

"ven'Deelin."

"Jeth," Freza's voice was soft. "I'm at the hatch. Come let me in so Chiv can go back to bed?"

Relief made him dizzy even as he smiled.

"Sure," he said. "Won't be a sec."

Jethri carefully poured the wine into a pair of crystal glasses. He handed Freza one with a bow before taking a seat next to her welcome warmth on the bed.

"So," he said, raising the glass, "tell me."

She raised her glass to match his, took an appreciative sip, and sighed.

"Long or short?"

He thought a moment, having her beside him making him contemplative, and allowed, "Give the day its due, I s'pose. Don't skip anything I should know, but leave the numbers and their decimals for tomorrow."

She smiled, took another sip, leaned back so her arm was brushing his.

"I can do that—an' you'll share, too, right, same terms? Fair trade?"

He sipped, added weight to their touch and sighed.

"Fair trade," he agreed.

Freza sipped and sighed.

"Bory's still workin' against us, that was part of

the day. He's tried to schedule us against each other on a couple of things tomorrow. Been fine-tuning the agenda for the congress, while he's at it. Trying to bring allocations and funding up before new bidness. *Envidaria's* new bidness, o'course, so any approvals would have to be in principle only—funding held over for when there's money to allocate."

She sighed, and sipped her wine.

"This is good, Jeth."

"It is," he admitted. "Want something to go with it?"

"Could enjoy that," she said.

He got up to call the kitchen. The door chimed before he'd turned away.

"Thank you, Kel Bin," he said, as the tray was placed on the table. "That was—remarkably quick."

Kel Bin bowed. "Will there be anything else, Trader?"

Jethri inclined his head. "This is sufficient, I thank you. Rest yourself, please."

"Trader."

The door shut after him.

Freza got up and walked over to the tray.

"Expecting a call, was he?"

"He's been trying to be make sure I have access to those *healthful foods* the two of you want me to be eating," he said, joining her, and eyeing the tray.

He supposed the *chernubia*, wine biscuits, candied fruits, and cheese weren't *un*healthful. He met Freza's eyes.

"He was expecting a call."

She grinned, and helped herself to cheese.

"So, Bory's still trying to stall the *Envidaria*," Jethri said, choosing a biscuit. "Can we stop him changing the agenda?"

"Not us, particularly," Freza said. "But the seated commissioners can object to last minute changes. Brabham's on that. Agenda's finalized in advance for a reason—not every commissioner and every ship can stay the whole congress. They 'range it to come in on the items they're needed for. Even the Combine folk rotated in an' out. So, the last minute agenda changes're gonna be tough for Bory to get through."

She looked thoughtful.

"Guess it says something 'bout how desperate he is, that he's even tryin' that."

"So," Jethri said. "Good news: Bory's scared of us."

She laughed.

"'Bout time, I guess."

She choose a *chernubia*, and Jethri another, neither one speaking as they enjoyed the treat.

"What else?" he asked when he had refreshed their wine, and they were side-by-side on the bed again.

"Well, we'd talked about Brabham handing off his commissioner's seat to you, if it got to being tight," Freza said. "Only, with all this maneuverin' Bory's doing, Brabham's gotta stay right where he is. He knows everybody. Everybody knows him. I could maybe call, and maybe most of 'em would give me a listen, on account of I've been Brabham's assistant since forever. So, we're gonna hafta to get the Ambassador for the *Envidaria* through, which means getting the whole business through, right now. And that's gonna be harder. We were wantin' to get the infrastructure set up this congress, show we're reasonable folks, and we can work with people. Can't risk it now."

She swallowed some wine.

"A commissioner can name his own successor, right?" Jethri asked.

"Right. But—tellin' the truth, now, Jeth—what we need isn't another person in Brabham's chair. We need more chairs filled with commissioners who're with us. *And*, we need somebody out there for the *Envidaria*—that's you. Gotta be you. *Balrog*'s been carrying the flag, but the routes're set. You already had more flexibility, and now you're trade lead on your own ship—"

"Which doesn't presently have a route, so I can go pretty much where I'm needed," Jethri finished. "Got that. Agree with it. Getting more chairs, though—that would be good, too."

"Got cousins who want to do the work," Freza said. "Just gotta get 'em in place."

There didn't seem to be anything to say to that, so Jethri sipped his wine, and Freza sipped hers, leaning comfortably against each other.

"So," she said eventually. "You sent me out to talk to *Dulcimer*, remember that?"

"Yeah, I do. How'd that go? Easy meeting between cousins?"

Freza laughed.

"Now, see, I figured it'd be quick 'n easy, too. Right up 'til when Choody Wharton showed up to try to extort the ship out from under existing crew."

He sat up straighter.

"Busy man, that Choody."

"Been that way from a boy, is how I heard it."

"What was his bidness with *Dulcimer*?"

"'Parently he needs a ship. Was using an ejected crew member with a grudge to make *Dulcimer* his. Told the captain to sign over the ship so this not-a-pilot kid could be named captain. That's why you got all that grey-stuff. The kid with the grudge'd seeded the ship with it before he was turned off, an' Choody was threatening to get the proctors in it, if they didn't cooperate."

"They didn't cooperate," Jethri guessed. Freza snorted.

"Well, would you? Second move was going to the Port Authority claiming *Dulcimer* was carrying 'diseased animals.' Figured *that'd* pull the proctors right out, see?"

Jethri choked, and Freza patted him on the back, grinning.

Recovering, he waved his hand around, encompassing the station. "With all this going on?" he asked.

"Yeah, not long on thought. Still, something had to be done. Pulled cousins from all over, 'cluding a law-jaw third cousin! *Dulcimer* filed harassment against the ex-crew and the cousins moved that junk I sent you, and *Balrog's* got the . . . the . . ."

She sighed, staring hard into her glass, as if ordering her thoughts.

"Right," she said. "*Balrog's* got this guy Klay—he's second pilot on *Dulcimer*—and he's officially studying Dust-lore and piloting with us right now. Good guy, good guy . . ."

She raised her glass and sipped.

"Brought some duffel with him, so he can spend part of the next couple days right where he is . . ."

Jethri looked up, feeling a pressure in his chest.

"Good guy?" he repeated, soft.

She laughed, patted his knee.

"He might be, but near as I can tell he's only got eyes for his Squithy. See, it isn't a straight story. I'll tell the main line right now and fill you in on the curves, later. Klay came to us with the so-called 'diseased animals,' who're called Mitsy and Ditsy. They had to be somewhere else if and when the proctors showed up. Klay brought 'em and he's gotta stay as long as they do, to translate."

"Translate? For animals?"

Freza shrugged.

"Not animals. Thinkers. Not human, though, and when you see 'em, you do think 'animals.' It's the fur, I 'spect."

Freza peered into the ether, or so it looked like to Jethri, because she was looking so hard at some spot on the wall where there wasn't much to see but a well-sealed seam.

She turned suddenly to look hard at Jethri.

"Have you ever had pictures put in your head? Like someone was able to reach in and put this picture or idea right here into your head?"

"Very recently!" he said, with feeling, but she was talking on, paying as much attention to her own thoughts as to him it seemed.

She put her glass on the side table and touched her fingers to her temples.

"Like right here. Choody and the ex-crew say animals and for all I know the ex-crew believes. Choody wouldn't care one way or 'nother, s'long as he could use them to get what he wanted. But I met 'em—they know who you are, and who Dulsey is. Your Scout's a favorite, and Squithy and Klay are special family to them, really crew and alt-crew."

"If they can make that much sense, why *animals*? How could they know *me*? Have they *met* me?"

"See, that's the thing. You've gotta meet them

yourself. It's like they collect people and connections. So they saw you on the vid on Port Chavvy, or maybe they could read your mind, I don't know. They don't talk like you and me, but they do a good job of following talk, and they know what a joke is. They're *people*, I'd say, but they look like...creatures, furry creatures with four legs and paws that are pretty much hands."

"Like a cat?"

"Nothing like a cat, not the ones I've met, but they're pretty much people anyway."

"So, when do I meet them?"

"I was thinking tomorrow morning you could walk me back to *Balrog* and meet 'em then. But if Choody's widening his circle o'trouble, maybe best not."

"Maybe best not," Jethri agreed. "You tell me when. Meantime, give 'em my regards."

Freza grinned, "I'll do that."

She nudged his arm with hers.

"Looks to me like that bottle's not empty yet, Trader, but the night's moving on and I have plans—"

"Ah, lady, forgive me."

He bowed where he sat, rubbed his hand down her leg from thigh to knee, and rose to retrieve the bottle.

THIRTEEN

"LOOKIN' GOOD, JETH." FREZA GRINNED AS HE ENTERED the Event Hall's reception room, Bry Sen beside him.

Freza came forward, flanked by Chiv and a skinny Looper Jethri couldn't quite place but was sure he'd seen somewhere before.

"Dressed for success," he said, with a grin, nodding to Freza. For the Big Reception, he had decided on evening clothes, such as a Liaden gentleman might wear to the theater, or to dine with a group of friends and allies. It was plainly not business-wear, being somewhat frivolous in the matters of lace and embroidery. The pants were tighter than might be considered modest in Looper terms, and unsuitable for any exercise more taxing than taking a turn at dancing down the room. By rights, he ought to have been wearing soft shoes, but he'd compromised, there, with low-heeled black ankle boots.

Bry Sen was dressed in similar splendor, which would, Jethri thought, make it easy to find them both in the crowded hall he could glimpse through the half-opened door.

Freza was wearing new, he thought—a high-necked, form-fitting black shirt under a knee-length deep blue

473

vest shot with silver threads. Her pants were snug, though not so tight as his, and her boots were deep blue with short red heels, close enough both to be in *Balrog*'s own colors. It was an elegant echo of Looper port-clothes. Her cropped red hair blazed above the dark colors, the blue ear cuff gleaming like it had been buffed. The spiral tattoo was in less evidence, covered, he thought, by a layer of makeup.

"Looking *fine* yourself," he said, and bowed full Liaden pleasure at beholding a valued and valuable associate, making the lace work for him.

He straightened into Freza's smile. She raised a hand and waggled her fingers near her cheek, as if fanning herself. "Careful with that. This is s'posed to be a no-weapons room."

He grinned. "I'll be careful, promise."

She turned her head to the right and left, glancing at each escort over her shoulder.

"Here's Cousin Chiv," she said, like he didn't know Chiv's face better than his own by now. "And Cousin Klay. Last time you two saw each other—it musta been Port Chavvy."

"I think it was," Jethri said, looking at the man with renewed interest and sudden recall. Cleaned up for display he was older than Jethri'd thought on Port Chavvy, and nearly pretty, with gold-green eyes, and the planes of his face set with good-humored determination.

"Cousin Klay, it's good to see you again. In all that mess at Port Chavvy, I never got a chance to say a proper thanks for your help."

Klay grinned. "Always happy to help a cousin. Glad to see you standing upright." He jerked his head toward the reception room. "My seniors Tranh and Rusko are inside already. They'd be glad of a sight of you, too."

"Let's not keep them waiting," Jethri said, and stepped forward to offer Freza his arm.

She hesitated a moment, head bent as if she was inspecting the embroidery on his sleeve, then slipped her arm through his, hand resting on his wrist.

Raising her head, she looked across him and nodded at Bry Sen.

"I know you'll forgive me for having a preference, Cap'n Bry Sen. But, I'd be behind in truth *and* politeness if I didn't let you know that you're looking *real* fine."

Bry Sen produced a very pretty bow of no mode Jethri had been taught, and straightened with a wide, Terran smile.

"In fact, we are *all* beautiful," he proclaimed. "The room is ours to rule."

"That's the ticket," Freza said. She grinned, nodded at the cousins, and looked up at Jethri. "Let's go conquer."

Tranh and Rusko were dressed in portside clothes, not new, but sober and respectable. Rusko took advantage of his flawless eyebrows, pale skin, and light hair to show off a couple slender silver rod-earrings tipped with tiny deep blue crystals—Jethri guessed at a vanadium component to get that!—while Tranh went with simpler studs of a red laserite, setting off his darker skin without emphasizing his skinny height.

Klay did the intros, while Freza stepped back with Chiv and Bry Sen.

"Now you're looking well set up," Rusko said jovially. "Last time I saw you, there was a head wound involved. Worried me that you might not've got over that."

Jethri nodded, touched the barely visible spot a fragment of bullet or metal had left behind.

"I was just telling Klay I'd've likely *lost* my head, hadn't been for *Dulcimer*'s help. Good you could make it. Freza'd been telling me you were looking for a new route—anything come up, yet?"

Tranh shook his head. "Got here late for the fair, which was me not thinkin' how this could help us. Then got some time took up for us by a former crewmate and an associate of the previous captain."

"I heard you was takin' it to Admin with a law-jaw," Jethri said.

"Did that, and I gotta tell you we'd still be tied up in red tape and paying a fine or three if it'd just been us, no matter Rusko being able to talk the paint off a hull—"

The two exchanged an affectionate grin, and Rusko took up the story.

"The law-jaw cut through the tape, showed a pattern of mischief and bad intent, and for a minute there I thought she was going to get the fine turned back on the accusers, with an upgrade!"

"They did have to pay the costs of the paperwork and the proctor's time," Tranh said.

"That's so. And the woman who earned her fee— wouldn't take one," Rusko added, and shook his head. "I don't feel right about that. Must be somethin' we can do to put us square."

"Might be something'll turn up," Jethri said, admiring the impulse toward Balance. "You been to the job fair at all?"

"Today." Tranh nodded. "Picked up some info, made a few contacts, but nothing firm—we'll keep at it. *Dulcimer*'s an older style; we thought there'd be room for her to work edge o'Dust."

Jethri leaned forward. "You got experience?"

There was a brief silence. It was Rusko who answered.

"The previous captain and trader worked grey—no secrets there. Now they're previous, Captain Tranh and me're lookin' to do better. No secret there, too. *Dulcimer*'s played with the Dust's skirts, back before it was big news. Ducked in an' out more'n once. We know it can be done. We got the way of doin' it, and we're willing."

"But no more grey markets," Tranh said. "I promised the crew." He took a swallow of his beer.

"I promised me."

"Hey, Jeth," Freza's voice was in his ear. He turned with a smile.

"I'm gonna go circulate, if you're okay here with our cousins?"

"I'm fine," Jethri told her. "You're taking—"

"I got Chiv right here—swear to the man you won't leave me, cousin."

"She's not gonna get away from me, Cousin Jethri, and nobody she don't want is gonna get close. You can trust me."

"That I do," Jethri said honestly.

He turned back to the pair off *Dulcimer*.

"The *Envidaria*'s gonna be adjusting some routes, making new ones. We'll be needing able ships, Dust-wise pilots. Can't pull a route outta my pocket just yet, but if you're innerested, you're on the list."

Another quick glance between the two, dark and pale, tall and solid.

"We're innerested," Tranh said.

"Absolutely," added Rusko.

An hour later, Jethri stood as part of a group surrounding the nucleus of Bory and Brabham. They were talking about supply chains and scarcity accelerations in time-sensitive foodstuffs—courteous enough, between the two of 'em, though Desty Gold had managed to bring some acrimony in by pointing out that the new 'rangements being brought in by the Combine would have small ships shifting from a Loop made up of multiple worlds and systems, to a Loop that served one big ship.

"How's that gonna work with the payouts?" Desty asked, which was, Jethri thought, a good question, better'n Desty was usually known for.

Bory made a show of leaning toward Brabham.

"Always watching the payouts, the Golds," he said, like it was just between them. A couple people in the crowd tittered. Desty's face colored up, and Brabham shook his head.

"Nothing wrong with keepin' an eye on the payouts," he said, looking around at his volunteers—only four tonight, dressed respectful, with Taber from *Lantic* looking particularly fine with a lacy scarf thrown 'round their neck.

"Payouts're what keeps the ship. 'Course there's gotta be payouts, and on time, too. It's not a bad question Desty's asking, Bory, and I'm innerested in hearing your answer right along with him."

Bory swept his hand out, including the whole circle in his answer.

"The payouts will be put down in the contracts right where everybody can see them. Each family ship supplying to a big transport will be writing contract with that ship. Combine's got a fee schedule all set to present at the opening session, so those interested in payouts will want to be there. *When's* going to be particular to each contract, just like *how*."

"*How*?" said somebody Jethri couldn't quite see. "A payout's a payout."

"No, now that's where you're not seeing the advantages of this new system," Bory said, chidingly. "Some folks might want their payout to go into some account other than ship ops. Those who decide to settle family planet-side might want the payout split, see, or—"

Jethri couldn't have said what alerted him—he might've just caught the bow out of the corner of his eye.

Whatever it was, he turned just in time to see one of the ushers moving purposefully toward their little knot of arguers, closely followed by three people shorter than most present, and dressed in a style that was not even remotely Looper.

He took a step toward them, and another as he saw the relief on the usher's face.

"Here he is, now, gentles," he said in crisp Trade. "Trader ven'Deelin, I am pleased to bring you Trader Izeel jen'Vornin of the Roella Route. Trader jen'Vornin, here is Trader Jethri Gobelyn ven'Deelin."

The trader was diminutive, even for a Liaden, yet she managed to give the impression of addressing the usher from a height.

"My thanks for your service. Trader ven'Deelin and I are well-met." Her voice was light, and her Trade bore an accent, though not one he had previously encountered.

"Thank you," Jethri said in Terran, and added the proper Liaden phrase as near as Trade would let him: "The trader and I will do very well with each other."

The usher faded, and Trader jen'Vornin folded into a bow—supplicant to expert, as Jethri read it—with the hand motion that indicated one who was cognizant of receiving an extraordinary honor.

That seemed—a little much. Jethri answered with a bow of trader to trader, which was to his mind much more balanced.

"You are gracious," Trader jen'Vornin murmured, when he had straightened from this salute. Her accent in Liaden was also unfamiliar—it was crisper, the vowels less rounded; the consonants harder.

She moved a hand. "Allow me to bring my associates to your attention, Trader. Here are *Qe'andra* Elys val'Tildin and Captain Jas Kin ern'Keylir."

Apparently taking their cue from him, they bowed as to an honored colleague, which Jethri was pleased to allow.

"Gentles," he murmured.

It came to him that the trader and her associates were dressed not for a reception but for trade. *Qe'andra* val'Tildin's tunic and loose slacks were unexceptional, as was Captain ern'Keylir's jacket and rings. Trader jen'Vornin's jacket was clearly meant for the markets, though it was of a style that had either gone out of date before Jethri Gobelyn became aware of Liaden fashion—or was considered the first stare in a location far distant from the homeworld.

"Gentles, please tell me how may I serve you," he said, suddenly aware that his silence had perhaps stretched long. "May I call for refreshments? Perform introductions?"

"Yours was the introduction I most desired," Trader jen'Vornin said. "I fear I am precipitate, Trader. My excuse is that we are in need of just such assistance as the *Envidaria* you have published would offer us. In short, I am here to join your effort, hoping thereby to rescue the route and our clans."

"I fear I must display my ignorance, Trader. Where, precisely, is the Roella Route?"

"A question not unheard when we speak to main-line traders." She allowed herself a small smile, followed with a graceful sweep of arm, an extension of a spacer's *beyond the beyond* exaggeration. "We are the main tradeway for the small cluster with Roella at its core and an arm of Dust has come twixt the rest of the arm."

"This is why we are come," Captain ern'Keylir murmured. "But, indeed, Trader, to importune you in the midst of a gaiety—Even we edge-runners are not so rag-mannered."

"Indeed, indeed," said the trader, moving her hand soothingly. "We are only just in, Trader ven'Deelin, and behind our own schedule. I had hoped to find you at the pre-conference, but the navigation—well! In anywise, dare I hope for a meeting with you? I would lay out our situation, which you will not, I think, find unique, and I would ask for introductions to those who may help us. jen'Vornin would be in—"

"Well, Trader Jethri," a big voice boomed in his ear. "Who are our guests?"

Bory loomed at Jethri's shoulder and performed a

bow that might, if the Liaden party squinted, have been recognizable as host to guest. Which was, Jethri thought, riding close to an actual untruth.

He turned his head to stare at the bigger man. From the side of his eye, he spied Bry Sen and Brabham, arm in arm and moving in their direction.

"Trader Jethri," Bory said, at somewhat less volume, "an introduction, please?"

Jethri turned back to Trader jen'Vornin.

"Trader, this my colleague desires to be made known to you. He is not...fluent in Liaden. Might you allow Terran? Or Trade?"

He caught the trader's smile before she inclined her head.

"It must be Trade, sir, for my abilities in Terran are a match for your colleague's, in Liaden."

Jethri inclined slightly, and moved his hand.

"Trader jen'Vornin, allow me to bring to your attention the Executive Director of the Commisserat, Boors Borygard. He facilitates the operation of the Commission's day-to-day and long-range goals.

"Bory, here are Trader Izeel jen'Vornin, *Qe'andra* Elys val'Tildin, and Captain Jas Kin ern'Keylir of the Roella Route."

"Sir," the trader murmured, and the three of them bowed acknowledgment of the introduction.

"Pleased to meet you all. What brings you to—"

Brabham and Bry Sen had arrived; Jethri turned smoothly, bringing them forward with a sweep of the hand.

"It is also my pleasure to introduce Commissioner and Pilot Brabham DeNobli, and Captain Bry Sen yo'Endoth. Sirs, here is the delegation from the

Roella Route—Trader Izeel jen'Vornin, *Qe'andra* Elys val'Tildin, Captain Jas Kin ern'Keylir."

Bry Sen's bow was everything that was courteous and smooth. Brabham produced a slight incline and a murmured, "Welcome, all."

"Commissioner Brabham has decades of piloting experience, and is of course very knowledgeable; he is a key member of the *Envidaria* work group. He will be able to guide you to other knowledgeable people.

"Brabham," he continued without pausing to give Bory a space to jump into. "The Roella Delegation is here because their routes are already experiencing disruption from the movement of the Dust. They've come to join the *Envidaria*."

"You're exactly the folks we've been looking for," Brabham said. "You're already dealing with the problem—we got a lot to talk about, information to share. Now, Trader ven'Deelin here, he's our ambassador, and as such, he's your first point of contact."

"Indeed," murmured Trader jen'Vornin, "we had understood this, and came a-purpose to find him. We very much wish to share information. There are systems at risk, as we stand here together and—" She flung a hand up, and inclined slightly.

"There, my concern erodes my manners. Please, as Captain ern'Keylir has said, it is not our intention to disrupt anyone at their pleasure. If the trader will give us a time when we may all meet together, we shall excuse ourselves."

"You've come a little late for the exploratory meetings," Bory began. Jethri took one step forward and bowed slightly, his lead shoulder leaning toward the trader and his trailing nearly a blockade against the larger man.

"From my side, I'm willing to meet now," Jethri said, making a show of looking to the right and left. "It seems the gaiety is moving along without any need of my personal oversight. I don't insist. You're fresh in and fatigued—"

"We are not fatigued, Trader," the *qe'andra* murmured. "A meeting sooner rather than later would be a great kindness."

"I agree," Brabham said. "You don't even need to leave the hall. There's private meeting nooks right over there—" He nodded to the wall at the left. "Trader ven'Deelin can escort you. I'll arrange for some refreshments to be sent on in. Jethri, will you be wanting Freza?"

"Yes, sir, if she's able to assist." He turned back to the Roella Delegation. "This would be Commissioner Brabham's special assistant, Freza DeNobli. She's been running day-to-day ops for us, and organizing our people."

"A knowledgeable and welcome addition to our group," Trader jen'Vornin murmured.

"Yes," Jethri said, turning to Bry Sen. "Would you honor me by escorting Assistant Commissioner DeNobli to us, Captain?" he asked in Liaden.

Bry Sen inclined his head. "It would be my very great pleasure, Trader."

He bowed to the rest of the group and departed.

Bory's face was showing a little flush. Jethri ignored him, and turned to Brabham.

"Elder?" he said in Trade. "Will you join us?"

"I've got some meetings to attend to myself," Brabham

said. "I'm on-call if you hit a knot. Between you and Freza, though, you've got everything I know."

"Your escort?" Jethri asked, and Brabham turned, motioning Taber from *Lantic* to him.

"Make your bow to the Roella Delegation, young Taber," he said, and a bow was produced—not a Liaden bow by any means, but well intentioned and respectful. The trader returned a bow to a willing student, and Brabham put his hand on the younger's shoulder.

"All right now, my friend," he said jovially, in Terran, "take me back to Trader Gold and the others. Then, I'll be wantin' you to go over to the freshments table and arrange for a tray to be sent to Trader Jethri's group."

They went a few steps, before Brabham turned and spoke again, "Comin', Bory?"

The flush was distinct now, and Jethri could see the big man struggle for a second before he gave a stiff, unnuanced bow in the general direction of the Roella Delegation and turned to join Brabham.

Jethri swept a hand out toward the far wall. "Gentles?" he said, back in Liaden. "Shall we?"

Freza arrived on Bry Sen's arm, and shortly after, refreshments and general-use tablets, delivered by Taber and another of Brabham's volunteers, who kept her eyes modestly lowered.

Freza was introduced, the tea sampled, and the discussions began. In large part, the story told by the Roella Delegation *was* familiar, and left Jethri thinking unworthy thoughts about large organizations.

"The Trade Guild declares the Dust a piloting problem. The Pilot's Guild accepts this responsibility and has been gathering data. The Scouts have taken an interest because—"

Trader jen'Vornin paused.

"I have," Jethri murmured, "personal acquaintance of Scouts, Trader."

"Then you understand! One does not wish to denigrate their efforts, but it is almost a game to them."

"Not a game, Trader," Captain ern'Keylir objected. "Not—quite—a game. It is only that Scout ships may go wherever they please, or so it seems, unimpeded by those difficulties that beset tradeships. The Dust is therefore a curiosity to them, without, perhaps the urgency..."

"Yes, yes," the trader interrupted. "But the case *is* urgent to trade! That is the core." She turned to Jethri and Freza. "You understand this."

"We understand," Freza said. "We've been struggling with data sharing, and hoped that the Scouts might be willing to help."

"I've written to my contact, Scout ter'Astin," Jethri added. "My mother gives me to know that he is—somewhat less playful in these matters. I found him very sensible during the mission he and I recently undertook. I asked for an introduction to the particular Scout overseeing the collection and analysis of data pertaining to the Dust, as if there must be one. I am hopeful of a quick answer."

"Hah." Trader jen'Vornin gave a half-smile. "It is true that we all want more data. The unfortunate truth is that we must all work with what is in-hand." She glanced to Captain ern'Keylir, who inclined his head.

"We have the data that we have ourselves collected, which we will share for the group good."

"The more we know, the more we *can* know," Freza said, which was one of Brabham's sayings. Trader jen'Vornin inclined her head.

"I think it would be useful," Jethri said, "for Captains ern'Keylir and yo'Endoth to meet together over the piloting data. Freza, can you put *Qe'andra* val'Tildin in touch with the *Envidaria*'s law-jaw?"

"Already sent her a message," Freza said, tapping the tablet on the table before her. She looked at the *qe'andra*. "Realistically, that'll happen tomorrow, not tonight."

"I am astonished and gratified that it may happen so quickly," the *qe'andra* assured her.

Jethri looked to Trader jen'Vornin. "You and I, Trader, should go over routes, supply lines, ships, and other such matters familiar to both of us."

"I stand at your convenience, Trader."

Jethri tapped up the tablet, accessed his calendar. The next day was more than full, but there must be an hour somewhere—

"Here," he said, looking to Freza. "Can Chiv and Klay cover the table in the hour between my talk with the Junior Piloting Committee and before the presentation to the League of Independent Ports Steering Committee—that's at the SeventeenW suite, and not *Genchi*'s, right?"

"I think—" She glanced down at the tablet, fingers tapping. "I can make that work," she said. "Might have Tranh or Rusko standing by, too—"

"Wait." Jethri held up a hand and turned to the pilots. "Captain Tranh Smith of *Dulcimer* has practical experience navigating the Dust. Would his expertise be useful to your meeting?"

"Yes," Captain ern'Keylir said definitively.

"Yes," Bry Sen confirmed. "More data in-hand can only aid all."

"Right, then."

"I'll let him know to stand by for Bry Sen's call," Freza said, fingers busy again on the tablet.

Jethri turned back to Trader jen'Vornin, automatically pulling his own Liaden-language business card and one of the triple lingo suite cards.

"Tomorrow, meet me at this suite at—Freza will give you the time. I will leave word that you should be admitted and that we will be utilizing the conference area privately. It will be a quick meeting, but an hour's work between determined traders—"

Trader jen'Vornin laughed.

"What can we not accomplish!" she said. "It is good, Trader."

She stood, and the rest of the room as well. Bows were exchanged, and Bry Sen opened the door to allow the Roella Delegation to leave.

"The Roella Route," Bry Sen exclaimed. "The very jen'Vornin—and she seeks out Jethri Gobelyn ven'Deelin!"

Jethri eyed him. "That's something special, is it?"

"Special!" Bry Sen flung his hands out, palm up.

"The Roella Route—understand, they are outworld—"

"Pirates?" Freza asked sharply.

"Never say so! Merely, they do not look to Liad for—anything. That they speak the language can be thought an accident by this time in their career. They *are* respectable," he insisted to Freza's continuing glare. "They are even honorable, though the Council of Clans chooses to think otherwise. They can occasionally be found at stations where Midys might rarely stop. They are traders, but more—they are a Council among themselves. Those who left Liad to settle thus far out—those names are in the Book of Clans. Indeed, jen'Vornin is old in honor on Liad. Neither ern'Keylir nor val'Tildin are names known to me. From which we learn that the Departees have continued to expand, and to make their own way in their own way."

"And they came to Terrans for help," Freza said, and suddenly grinned. "No. They came to *Jethri* for help."

"Exactly," said Bry Sen, collapsing at last into a chair. "Your name will be a legend, Trader ven'Deelin."

Jethri snorted. "She came to the *Envidaria*," he said. "And only after the Guild failed them." He frowned. "That's the Trader's Guild? The Liaden Trader's Guild?"

"Pilots guild and the trade guild," Bry Sen said. "Those outlying stations of which I spoke—there are guild offices available, on a rotating schedule. You will understand that the concerns of those who use such offices are not, perhaps, the top guild priorities."

"Sounds like she's closer to Loopers than Liaden big ships," Freza said.

Bry Sen sighed. "Yes. Precisely."

Freza looked down at her tablet.

"Got an ack from Tranh, Bry Sen. Sent the info to your pilot account."

"Thank you. I will contact him when we get back to *Genchi*. Speaking of which, Trader, are you for home, or more reception?"

"I did what I came to do at the reception, and a bit more," Jethri said. "Frez?"

She tapped the tablet off.

"By this time, Brabham will have done everything we wanted. If I go back now, I might trip over something I shouldn't."

"Back to *Genchi*, then," Jethri said, standing, and sweeping a bow in her direction. "May I escort you, beautiful lady?"

Freza laughed, and came to her feet.

"Sure can."

Bry Sen had opened the door and stepped outside. Jethri offered his arm, and Freza took it, her fingers cool against his wrist.

"To *Balrog*, or *Genchi*?" he asked.

"Good question," she answered, and sent a searching look into his face.

"Freza—"

She patted his hand. "I'm thinking *Genchi*," she said, "since you asked."

"*Genchi*, it is, then," Jethri said, with a calm he didn't completely feel, and turned them toward the door.

FOURTEEN

·············

TRADER JEN'VORNIN WAS BEFORE HIM IN THE SUITE, though he'd cut the question and answer session ruthlessly short, and excused himself with scant courtesy from those who had tried to buttonhole him after the presentation was done.

"Urgent bidness," was his excuse, and it was sufficient, as it would have been at a gathering of Liaden traders. He arrived at the SeventeenW suite barely breathless, and only five minutes past the hour.

Stepping into the private parlor, he made certain the door was locked and showed the "in use" flag before he bowed contrition.

"Trader, pray forgive my tardiness."

She considered him, head tipped to one side, as if he were a particularly interesting length of cloth. Then, with great precision, she bowed, trader-to-trader, and straightened, frowning.

"We should perhaps," she said, "take a moment to learn each other a little better, if you will indulge me, Trader."

"Certainly, Trader. Familiarity can only improve trade, so my master taught me."

"Ah, did she so? Well, it was never said that the

Rabbit bred fools." She brought her hands together in a sharp clap, and smiled when Jethri did not start, but merely turned upon her a look of grave inquiry.

"Truly, you are a work, Trader ven'Deelin—and here we arrive at my topic. Understand, I beg, that I am not High House Liaden. Indeed, I have been given to know that we who Departed are no longer Liaden. That is a question for the scholars of the Code, as would be the question, should your master be so maladroit as to ever allow it to be asked, of your precise standing within Ixin. These are not matters that need concern us. We meet as traders. We may, if you deem it useful, proceed upon our business in Trade. If you prefer to continue in Liaden, please know that my mode diverges considerably from that which is taught to the children of Ixin and Midys. I am plain-spoken—painfully so—and I do not play *melant'i* games for either advantage or blood."

She paused. Jethri waited. She inclined, very slightly, from the waist.

"To be clear, I take no offense, that a trader deep in his own business has made time to see only one of the many who desire the gift of his time and expertise."

Jethri barely stopped himself from bowing. Instead, he produced an incline to match hers, and a smile broader than Liaden, more subtle than Looper.

"I understand, Trader. Thank you for your frankness and clarity. I would choose to go forward in Liaden, as the mercantile mode is more nimble than Trade."

"I agree," said Trader jen'Vornin, and waved at the table, set up for a meeting, with tea, tablets and screens. "Let us begin."

✳   ✳   ✳

"Already, the Dust limits our ability to trade. Ships come out of Jump half a system distant from their calculated entry points. Worse—*Rose of Roella* Jumped for a system that is well-known to us, and—bounced back. Understand me, Trader, she could not enter the system *at all*."

Trader jen'Vornin paused to sip tea.

"At another of our usual ports, we were unable to navigate the currents well enough to gain a parking orbit. There, we dropped the cargo in nets for the in-system ships to fetch down to the planet. These disruptions have been introduced by the leading edges of Dust. How will we serve our worlds once we are truly engulfed?"

Trader jen'Vornin took a hard breath and bowed her head, visibly calming herself.

"Your pardon, Trader."

"I would be frantic myself, in such a situation," Jethri said. "In fact, we've had other reports of the hazards of navigation. Yours is the first I've heard of a ship being thrown back to the original Jump point, but at this gathering alone, I've heard numerous accounts of ships falling out of Jump well short of their destination."

He paused, frowning down into his tea.

"There have been reports for some time of Looper ships arriving at the correct system, but somewhat distant from the expected point of entry. The thought had been—because Looper ships are of varying condition, many quite old, their Struven units in need of tuning or replacement, their navigation computers—idiosyncratic, if not actively argumentative..."

Trader jen'Vornin laughed softly, and Jethri smiled.

"Yes. In any case, it was the wisdom of our pilots and navigators to place the burden of error upon ship systems, and ways were found to route around known glitches. In some cases, ship systems are surely to blame, but in others—we were perhaps seeing a forerunner of Dust effect."

He sipped tea.

"We have found that the larger ships are experiencing more navigation problems even in low-Dust situations. *Elthoria* and *Barskalee* have experienced entry errors and early departure from Jump, while the small tradeships report no such difficulties."

He tipped his head.

"I suppose I should say *yet*. These effects you report—do they consistently trouble large ships and small?"

"There you hit the crux, Trader. Our tradeships are of a size, the routes designed to accommodate both ships and ports served. Understand that the ancestors removed, perhaps not wisely, to an—*interesting*—area of space. They planned very well for conditions as they were, and when they Departed, they did so in ships of a particular structure and capacity. Our shipyards build to a template, and in truth, we build few, being more focused on maintaining the fleet we have."

She raised a hand.

"It is a static system, and a master trader would chide us. Indeed, *I* have seen the need for expansion, and have designed several small side routes, as a base for what I dreamed might become a larger route, in future. But that is a mere diversion. First, we must feed our worlds and keep our people—the tradeships are necessary to survival on some of our worlds, while merely feeding comfort on others."

"I understand," Jethri said. He frowned, hearing Bory in memory's ear, maybe not so patiently explaining the Combine's new scheme to Desty Gold: "Each family ship will be writing contract with their big ship connection . . ."

He blinked.

"Trader?" murmured Trader jen'Vornin. "Have you thought of something?"

Jethri smiled at her. "As obvious as that? My master would hide her face. But yes. I have thought of something."

He glanced at the clock, and shook his head.

"Very quickly, for our time is almost spent—how if your ships had smaller ships, less distressed by the Dust, to take your cargo on the final leg to the port?"

The trader leaned forward. "That would be a boon, for now. As the Dust increases—"

"We can't know that the solution will hold in the face of changing conditions," Jethri agreed. "But as a beginning?"

"As a beginning, it sounds very well. However, I must point out that the Scouts will not turn their hands to such work."

It was humor, Jethri thought, and grinned.

"We need not trouble the Scouts. There are Looper ships which will be in need of work, given the Combine's new arrangements, and the movement of the Dust. There is opportunity for alliance, and mutual benefit."

"I like this in principle," Trader jen'Vornin said slowly. "Can it be made to work, practically? I speak of cultural differences now, Trader."

"I understand, and here I apply the wisdom of my cousin Khat, a pilot. She has it as a life certainty that one cannot know, until one tries."

"Hah."

Jethri pushed his chair back.

"Trader, time presses on me. Let us meet again, after the Replenishment. In fact, let *all* of us meet together then, to share our progress."

"I will arrange it," Trader jen'Vornin said, rising also. She bowed.

"Trader ven'Deelin. It has been a pleasure to sit at work with you. I have hope, now, and for that, I thank you."

Jethri slid into the aisle seat next to Freza.

"What'd I miss?"

"Intros and warm-up speeches," she whispered back. "How'd it go with Trader jen'Vornin?"

"Trader's got a real problem, but I think we're seeing a route forward. After this, all three work groups are meeting back at the SeventeenW suite. Working lunch—" He squinted. "Dinner? You got time? We'll be wanting you."

"I'll come. You want Brabham?"

"More heads we got on this, the better, is what I'm thinking," Jethri answered.

She nodded and pulled out her tablet. "He's down over there, sitting with the rest of the commissioners. I'll send a message."

While she worked with the tablet, Jethri looked for "down over there," locating Brabham's spare form between a taller bald man dressed like a dirt-sider, and a shorter woman wearing what looked like a ship-jacket, her dark hair in a Looper buzz, and a gold hoop in one ear.

Brabham raised his hand without looking around, and Freza made a satisfied sound.

"He'll be coming along, after."

"Good," Jethri said. "How was—"

"Hold it," Freza interrupted. "Here comes the big show."

In fact, there was some rustling and shifting "down over there," and then a big man got out into the aisle and headed for the stage. He was dressed for portside, with a jacket open over a sweater and a scarf wrapped loose around his throat. His boots were shiny, which was one giveaway that he was only dressing the part— the luxurious hair was another, and the Combine logo on the jacket was a third.

Still, Jethri thought, it was a good effort.

A woman dressed in dirt-side bidness clothes stepped up to the front of the stage, and touched the button on her collar.

"Gentlefolks, we've come to what past congresses have called Replenishment. That's when we fill vacancies in the Commissariat, and replenish our guiding body. We have a tradition of having Commissioners name their replacements, and it is a fine thing, worked for a long time. But as you know and I know, sometimes events sneak up on us and folks don't get to name their follow-on. In those cases, we have to arrange that ourselves.

"This time we'll combine Replenishment with Initiation, so everything can go smoother and faster for us all. In this time and place the pre-congress will end and the congress will simultaneously open. And here's Commissariat Executive Director Bory Borygard, a veteran of a half dozen congresses, at least, come to guide us to safe docking!"

She turned to watch Bory stride across the stage, both hands raised over his head, acknowledging cheers and clapping from the audience.

Freza was clapping, so Jethri did, not hard, and not long, just enough, so he judged, to show goodwill.

Bory reached the woman, and leaned down, so she could fix a button onto his sweater. They shook hands, and she walked to the back of the stage. Bory walked to the front of the stage, grinned into the ongoing noise, raised his hands, and moved them—*cool jets. Cool jets.*

That only got him more noise, with whistles joining the general racket.

Up on the stage, Bory shook his head, raised a hand to touch the button on his sweater, and boomed with a bravado and working port accent he didn't come by honestly.

"Finish it up on your own time! We got some serious bidness to deal with, here, and soon's it's done, we can call end o'shift and have ourselfs a beer!"

A renewed shout went up. Jethri took a breath. Cool fingers closed around his wrist, and warm breath moved against his ear as Freza whispered.

"Hey, now, Jeth, you wouldn't wanna ruin the party, would you?"

"Might be inneresting," he answered and smiled when she laughed soft.

"It'll finish soon," she promised. "I wonder who he's got—Yeah—there. Over on the right side, 'bout a quarter way up the rows. There's his cheer-on, right on cue!"

Jethri looked over to the right just as a woman in battered port clothes leapt to her feet and shouted.

"Hey! I dunno about you lot, but I want my beer! Everybody just cool jets, and let the man talk!"

That got some laughter, and a round of hoots,

and then, amazingly, the noise did die down. Jethri looked around, trying to see if there were proctors going down the rows, but didn't spot any. By the time he looked back to where the woman had risen, she was gone, and Bory was standing on stage, hands in pockets, grinning, until it was so quiet you could've heard a micrometeor tick a scratch in a windscreen.

"All part o'the show," Freza whispered.

"Show." Jethri turned his head, distaste for the proceedings plain on his face, but she briefly put her fingers across his lips before settling back into her chair with a hint of smile.

Jethri sighed and did the same, his smile for hers.

"All right, now. Like you just heard Director Mauriline say, we're here and official at Replenishment, which is some couple of things all at the same time.

"Firstly, it's closing ceremonies for the pre-congress. Tomorrow morning, we'll have opening ceremonies for the South Axis Congress. You could say that the pre-congress is where we all talk to each other about what we want the Combine and TerraTrade to be doing for the next four standards, and maybe for four or eight after that.

"The congress is where we get to work, and line everything up formal so that the work we've decided to be most important gets done."

He paused, looking out over the room, and nodded like he'd just heard a question.

"Now, you heard me say *we*. That's because we're a representative body. Commissioners are drawn from the membership, from us. It's not them and you. It's us. We're doing this work, for the good of us all.

"And that brings me to the second thing this meeting

is: We don't want to leave ourselves a mess to clean up before we can get to work. We want to be sure that we can get right to bidness when our congress opens for work tomorrow. We don't want to waste time getting set up. We want to sit down at the board, and get right on the route."

There was a brief cheer here. Bory shook his head, and the noise subsided.

"So, what we gotta do for ourselves, is we gotta make sure that there's enough of us to do the work that's gotta get done. That means putting some of us into empty seats. Just like you replenish supplies in hydroponics, and we gotta do that with what makes us work, and that's people! It comes to happen that this time, we're six short of a good working congress."

A mutter ran through the room at that, and Jethri sighed. Six seats to fill? He remembered his father talking to Grig about procedures and voting, nominations and cross-nominations. Such things commonly took hours, if not whole days.

"Now, I know what you're thinking," Bory said. "You're thinking that to do this right is gonna take some serious time. Maybe you heard stories about procedural voting that covered days. In that case, you'll be glad to hear that the seating of commissioners has been streamlined."

He flashed a grin around the room.

"I want my beer, too, don't I?"

Laughter. Jethri shot a look to Freza, eyebrows up, but she was watching the stage.

"So, here's what we do, to make sure there's enough of us tomorrow to do the work, and we don't die of thirst. Me and the other commissioners on the nomination committee have had our ears open during the pre-conference, and whenever we heard that this one or that one of us would make a fine commissioner, or had ideas worth looking at, we took note. We met just today and compared our notes, and we got the names of six hard workers who want to make a difference for us going forward."

He paused to take a breath.

"So, how this goes is that I'll call out the names, one by one, and those people will come up here to join me. Anybody who objects has until they get up onto this stage with me to shout out. If there's no objections, then we got a commissioner, right then, with full rights to do what a commissioner does. We do this six times, and then we get our reward. We'll be Replenished and Initiated!"

Another pause to look around the room.

"Anybody not clear on this?"

The room was as quiet as vacuum.

Jethri sat, riveted.

"All right! Let's get this done, shipmates!"

The room roared, and under cover of the noise, Jethri leaned to Freza. "They're going to let the Combine choose six commissioners."

Freza nodded. "Been moving toward that way for a while now. Brabham remembers when it changed—it'd've been after Arin resigned."

"I don't see any questions," Bory said from the stage. "There's one more thing you need to do, and that's to be quiet. We gotta be able to hear if anybody objects, so save your applause until all the commissioners are standing up here with me! Last call for questions—anybody?"

The room was silent. Bory nodded.

"Looks like we all understand each other!" Bory called. "First name! Gert Dare of *Dare's Challenge*!"

There was a shocked flutter from the left side, back, as a stocky woman with grey hair got down the row, and into the aisle. She walked to the stage in utter silence, climbed the ramp and came to stand next to Bory.

"Congratulations, Gert," Bory said. "You're a commissioner. See that you do good work for us."

Gert grinned and bobbed, and at Bory's direction went a few steps to the rear so as not to block the path of the next commissioner, who was—

"Desty Gold of *Gold Digger*!"

Jethri twitched. Freza put her hand on his arm, pressing hard.

"Shhh... Take it easy, Jeth."

He swallowed, closed his eyes, and accessed one of the exercises Scout ter'Astin had taught him that imposed calm.

When he opened his eyes again, there were four new commissioners standing on the stage with Bory, and the fifth walking down the aisle. He'd missed their names and their ships, but Freza would know, and she'd make sure he knew.

Bory congratulated the fifth commissioner, and asked her to step back with the others. He paused for a heartbeat, then, looking down at the stage, like a man considering what he should do next. Slowly, he came forward to the very edge of the stage and looked soberly out over the room.

"I know I said we were going to get to our beers quick," he said, his voice quieter now, "but I'm going to ask you to be patient with me, because this next commissioner—it's a . . . special . . . honor to be able to name this next commissioner to work for us, and I'd like you to know why."

He looked out over the room.

"Some of you here might remember Arin Tomas, who married onto *Gobelyn's Market*. Arin worked for us for a lot of years—good work, far-seeing work. It was my good fortune to work with him, to learn from him. I considered him a friend."

Bory paused again, head bent. Nobody in the room breathed. Jethri didn't, though he stiffened in his chair, and Freza's hand pressed harder on his arm.

"I'm not going to bore you with ancient history. Just say that Arin found a difference of opinion with us, and he quit working with us and for us. That hurt. It hurts still. I blame myself, thinking I should have come up with some way to make it right, to bring him back working for us, but I never did. Then, there was an emergency, and Arin was right there with the rescue team—you see, right? He was helping us, still! Well, that was where he took his final Jump, and there wasn't any making it up from there. I'd failed us, and him, and me."

"Jeth?" Freza whispered.

"Right here," he answered, easing forward in his chair. Commissioner. Bory was about to name him a commissioner, fulfill his dreams of following his father. He looked down at his hands, his trade ring on one hand; his father's commissioner ring on the other. It was—overwhelming.

He sought calm, heard the words in his head.

Commissioner Jethri!

He twisted the ring on his hand, knowing he wanted to hear that said, even as doubt washed out from his backbrain.

It would be so good to hear.

But did it serve trade?

He blinked, and through the roaring in his ears heard Bory's voice ring out.

"So, that's why—why I'm honored to call out the name of new commissioner Jethri Gobelyn ven'Deelin, off of *Genchi*!"

Jethri got to his feet, stepped out into the aisle, turned, and held his hand out to Freza.

She stared, eyes narrowed, rose slowly, stepped out beside him and took his hand.

Somebody whistled. Somebody else stamped their feet. Somebody else said, "Quiet, please. The floor is open only for objections."

There were no objections.

Jethri and Freza went up the ramp, and walked across the stage. Freza let go of his hand before he reached Bory, who snatched him into a show-off hug, and then set him back.

"Commissioner," the big man said, his voice sounding choked. "I'm proud."

Jethri resisted the temptation to smooth his coat, and produced a modest smile as he peered out into the crowd, recruiting himself with the ghost of the bow accepting honor, the ghost of a nod of acknowledgment.

"I wonder if I could say a few words," he said. "If the people can wait another minute for their beers."

Bory smiled, and turned around.

"Commissioner Gobelyn would like to talk to you. Are there any objection?"

Silence.

Bory nodded, reached to his sweater and detached the button. He leaned forward and attached it to the lapel of Jethri's trade coat.

He stepped back and bowed, just slightly, and moved his hand, showing Jethri the way to the front of the stage.

"Commissioner," he said. "You've got the floor."

Jethri looked out over the room. Hundreds of people, here and there a face that looked generally familiar. Right in the center was a cluster of Golds, grinning and elbowing each other. Over to the left, another cluster—Wildes, he thought, by the hair. Right in front, he looked down at the rows of commissioners, faces as neutral as any Liaden, and Brabham looking almost sleepy. Over to the right, sitting with a chair empty on either side, a very familiar face. Might've been his father, except his father was dead. Back, and up toward the top of the room, he saw Bry Sen sitting in a row with the Roella Delegation, Chiv, Tranh, and Law-Jaw Pocono Ventrella.

The room—rustled, which was people wanting their beers.

Jethri smiled, and he bowed, as one honored. He straightened with both arms outstretched, letting everybody get a good look at him: the Terran standing tall in a good Liaden trade coat, made especially to fit him.

"I want to say particular thanks to all of you, new commissioners and old, the Combine directors, and the nomination committee," he said. "I'll be keeping this short. We've all been workin' hard these last couple days, and we deserve a down-shift. I just want to say that—like Bory told you, my father was a commissioner. Put a lot of his life, and his passion into the job. He believed in trade going forth, he believed in routes, and Loops, and families; he believed in us serving our ports, and keeping the trust on both sides."

He paused in absolute silence. The air in the room— tingled, and Jethri thought he felt the hair on his head stir.

"For most of my life, I wanted to be like my father. Work the Loop, improve the trade." He took a breath. "Serve as a commissioner."

That got a spatter of applause from the commissioners down front, and Jethri smiled.

"Yeah, I dreamed of being a commissioner like Arin," he said, raising his hand. "And I got his ring right here on my hand, to remind me of that dream."

The applause was louder this time, more widespread. Jethri ducked his head, and waited for the noise to subside. Uncle Yuri, he saw from the side of his eye, was leaning forward slightly; Brabham's head was cocked to one side.

"Now, dreams—sometimes you grow out of them, sometimes they grow out of you—and sometimes a new dream rises up and says, you're the one—work with me, serve trade, and honor, the Loops and the families, ship-side and dirt-side. And that's what happened to me.

"I still want to be a commissioner—sure I do!—and work for all of us, like Bory said. But there's this new way of working for us all—the *Envidaria*—seeing it in place and working for all of us—that's my priority in a way that it can't be a commissioner's priority, nor the Combine's or even TerraTrade."

Jethri felt the air shift behind him, glanced down at the front row, and saw Brabham lift a shoulder.

Finish it up, he told himself, and leaned forward, like he was talking personally to every person in the hall.

"So, here's my first dream fulfilled. I'm a commissioner, with all the rights of a commissioner, including that traditional right to name the replacement to my chair—which is what I'm doing right now."

He turned and beckoned. Freza stepped up to join him at the front of the stage, and he took her hand to raise it high.

"Freza DeNobli of *Balrog*! She's been workin' for us near all her life. She learned at Commissioner Brabham DeNobli's knee, stood as his assistant. Every Looper here knows the DeNoblis, and you know she'll work for all of us!"

The room exploded into cheers and shouts, clapping, whistles, and stamping.

Jethri released Freza, pulled off his father's ring, and held it high.

The noise abated—slightly.

"Commissioner DeNobli," Jethri said, taking Freza's hand again. "Do us proud!"

He slipped the ring onto her finger.

FIFTEEN

· · · · · · · · · ·

"I CAN'T BELIEVE YOU DID THAT, RIGHT UNDER BORY'S nose!" Freza collapsed into the nearest chair and closed her eyes. "My nerves, Jethri!"

"You've got the steadiest nerves of anybody I know," he told her, continuing across the room to the buffet.

"And seriously, what did he *expect* me to do? It was a challenge, wasn't it? You can't just ignore the challenge, especially one so in the public eye! And he thought it was a way for him to be better than Arin—like he was forgiving Arin for splitting with them! There's a trade trick that works like that, where a trader makes it seem like they are publicly fixing an error you made, in your favor, and so you're stuck with what they do."

Jethri shook his head, recalling Bory's obsequious introduction, and went on at pace.

"The *only* way to deal with that kind of challenge is by using the momentum, and the momentum I have is that *Arin was right*, and now look—Bory's got to smile and be pleased. I'm glad you're up to it but I didn't have time to do anything else and have it be clean! Arin's ring, and you wearing it—was the best way out!"

The others filed in as Freza peered at the ring, somewhat too large for her, that she still wore.

They'd arrived en masse back at the SeventeenW

party suite—him, Freza, Brabham, Taber from *Lantic*, Chiv, Bry Sen, the entire Roella Delegation, plus Tranh Smith. Jethri'd worried that they might get caught in the general congratulations at the end of the seating of new commissioners, but Brabham had snatched them both away on "official bidness," got them through a side door, and there was the rest of their party, held firmly in hand by Bry Sen and Chiv.

They'd gone by back halls, hurrying and not talking, until they were safe behind doors.

"Beer?" Jethri asked over his shoulder.

"Wine!" Freza said positively.

"Of a certainty, wine," said Trader jen'Vornin. "We must toast a coup, if we have understood Captain yo'Endoth correctly."

Jethri turned and caught Bry Sen's eye.

"I thought it would be instructive," he murmured, "for the delegation to see the congress at its business."

"He kindly translated for us," said *Qe'andra* val'Tildin, and bowed in Jethri's general direction. "A neater turning of villainy back upon the villain I have very seldom witnessed, sir."

"Villain," Jethri said, shaking his head. "No villains. Just Terran dirty tricks aimed at me and my father."

He stared at the bottles on the bar, suddenly not able to tell one from the other.

"Allow me, Trader," Bry Sen said, appearing next to him. "Recruit yourself. I took the liberty of ordering in food, and will set out the trays as soon as the wine is poured."

"Taber," Brabham said, from his chair next to Freza, "you find out from Cap'n Bry Sen what needs done, after the wine, and see to it, right?"

"Right!" said Taber, moving forward with energy.

"A likely youth," Trader jen'Vornin said in Trade, as Jethri took the seat between her and Freza.

"Eager and then some," Brabham agreed. "Been a big help to me, these last few days. Thinking about asking *Lantic* to give us Taber on lend, Frezzie, what d'you think?"

"I think I'm going to need a clerk, just like you did when I was Taber-high," Freza answered. "If *Lantic* allows it—"

"I'll talk to the captain. Thank you."

That last was to Bry Sen, who had arrived with a tray of drinks. As elder, Brabham was served first, then Trader jen'Vornin, Jethri, and Freza. It was, Jethri thought, holding his glass, a non-standard order. Usually the guests were served first, but, then, it had been a non-standard day—and beside that, the guests were busy.

Chiv was moving more chairs into the parlor. Elys val'Tildin was opening up the original conversational grouping, and Tranh Smith was fitting the extra chairs into the spaces she made.

Captain ern'Keylir and Taber entered, carrying trays to the buffet.

"I don't see how you could have done anything else, Jeth," Brabham said, quiet, but keeping to Trade. "Like Ms. val'Tildin said—prettiest reversal I've seen in many a year. Problem being, you made a powerful enemy."

Jethri sighed.

"I'm collecting the whole set, seems," he said, and paused as the rest of their company found chairs, wine glasses already in hand. Taber was still at the buffet, uncovering the trays, and laying out the plates and cutlery.

"Honor will always find enemies among the honor-less," Trader jen'Vornin said, surprisingly, and suddenly rose, holding her glass high.

"If a guest may make so bold—Well-played, Trader ven'Deelin! It was a pleasure to watch you at work."

Face heating, Jethri drank with the rest, then got to his feet.

"Commissioner DeNobli," he said, raising his glass. "You're going to turn them upside down."

Freza blushed interestingly. "Only when they need it," she said to general laughter, and they all drank again.

"That's fine," Brabham said, "well-done, all. Now, I got time-in-grade, so what I suggest is that we get something to eat, then get to work. The congress starts tomorrow, early, and there won't be any downtime for any of us 'til the gavel falls for done. Whatever problems we have should be en route to a solution before that."

"Agreed," said Trader jen'Vornin, on her feet again. "May I have the honor of bringing you a plate, Elder?"

Jethri was standing a little back from the buffet, not at all sure he was hungry, but sure he'd better eat something if only to keep the wine out of his head. There were teapots set at ready, but he did know better than to go from wine straight to tea while riding a crest of adrenaline.

"Hey, Jeth," Freza said in his ear. He turned and smiled.

"Hey," he answered.

"It was good tactics and a good show, too, but, Jeth—about Arin's ring. You'll be letting me give that back to you."

"You do that," he said cordially. "After you get

done, you give the ring back to me. Before that—you wear it. If you want to, that is. If you'd rather not—"

Freza bit her lip.

"Thing is—I do want to—" She straightened and wrinkled her nose, somehow managing to evoke Bory perfectly. "I do want to borrow it for use during my tenure, Jethri."

He laughed.

"Good. Then you do that." He reached out and took her hand.

"Thanks for going along with my play, Frez. I know it was a surprise."

"Surprises all around," she said, grinning. "It turned out all right, I think."

"I think—"

Somewhere, a comm chimed. Bry Sen stepped to the small screen at the far end of the room. Jethri saw his shoulders stiffen.

"*Genchi* requests permission to forward a message. It is a pinbeam for Trader ven'Deelin from the Trade Guild," he said.

Jethri blinked.

He'd already gotten his turn-down letter, so this must be—

The test notification.

"That was *quick*," he muttered to Freza and crossed the room to put his finger against the screen.

Bry Sen stepped back, ceding Jethri privacy.

The letter was brief. Trader Jethri Gobelyn ven'Deelin was to report for testing at the Traders Administrative Guild Hall on Pommier, between the fifth and sixth hour of Askop Firstday of the next *relumma*. He was reminded that a failure to be on time for this testing would result in a fail, after which he would be required to wait six Standards to re-test.

He tried to do the day-math, having to retreat from the Terran reckonings of Meldyne Station to the Trade and thence to the High Liaden mode employed by the Guild in this message of import.

He blinked, and read it again, more slowly, checking the date at the top of the screen, frowning at the planet designation code. Finally, he called up the Terran translation, put it side by side with the original Liaden on the screen, but that didn't improve the math, nor his mood.

"Bry Sen," he said.

"Trader?"

"I need you to check my numbers. Third class and doing it in my head—I think I bobbled some decimals and multiplied by zero. *Can* we make this port by the time specified?"

He looked around, realized his guests were an informed audience if there ever was one, and rose to the moment.

"Gentles, a matter of trade and piloting for you to consider, too, as long as you promise a confidential glance."

He touched a few keys, sending the contents of the small screen to the larger one high on the wall, so that it could be seen by all and stepped back, waving Bry Sen and his conversational partners forward together to look at it, showing merely the location and time, though not the letter entire.

Bry Sen's face was—perfectly calm, which Jethri had learned was no good sign, but it was Tranh Smith who spoke first.

"*Some*body's math's off, Trader . . . but it ain't yours."

"Indeed," Bry Sen said calmly. "We *could* make that port, in that time frame, Trader, if we left within the next hour."

"What's this?" Brabham asked from his chair across the room. "You leaving, Jeth? In an hour?"

"It's his master trader's test," Freza said, and met his eyes. "That's what it is, right, Jeth?"

He nodded.

Brabham stood. His hand on Taber's shoulder, he tried not to shuffle as he joined the growing cluster of squint-eyed calculation near the screen.

"Dump pods," he said. "You need provisions, we can send over from *Balrog* while you're on the way. You've got to clear it with—"

"I know that world," Captain ern'Keylir said, abruptly. "I assume that Captain yo'Endoth would indeed dump pods, and take a high acceleration run to Jump short of the usual point. For a pilot of skill—it is possible to make the Jump—from this end. But on the other end? That is crowded space. Even ships that are scheduled and expected are often turned back to a day or even a *relumma's* holding orbit for lack of docking, and that's assuming you weren't on the wrong side of the traffic control station by not being on an expected-soon list."

"In fact," said Trader jen'Vornin, "this is a *Liaden* dirty trick, Trader, of a particularly pernicious sort. It pretends to be a good-faith offer, but it is nothing of the kind."

"It's a set-up," Freza said in Terran, and Tranh Smith nodded.

"For the trader's information," Bry Sen said carefully, "even were we able to arrive on such short notice, this is not properly done. The Guild knows that it will be addressing a trader who is busy at his work. They know that it will take time to rearrange appointments, deliveries, to find another trader, perhaps, to cover the route. An appointment for a master's test would be reasonably set at least two full *relumma* in the future."

"That is so," *Qe'andra* val'Tildin said, and inclined her head when Jethri looked to her with surprise. She added, "My area of expertise is trade law."

Jethri bowed. "Of course it is. Forgive me, *qe'andra*."

"I take no offense," she assured him.

"I assume that a copy of this message has been sent to the master who has sponsored me?" Jethri asked. "I do not see a copy specified. That ought to have happened, right?"

Trader jen'Vornin snorted lightly; the *qe'andra* looked like she wanted to do the same.

"In the usual way of things, Trader . . ."

"One—" Trader jen'Vornin spoke with emphasis as she waved her hands in the pilot sign for *repeating information*—"dirty trick does not preclude another." She peered upward, and looked back to Jethri.

"If they can also ruin you with your sponsor, why would they not do so?"

"Yes," he said. "I see."

He looked around the room, hearing pilots throwing unworkable what-if solutions at the time-and-distance problem on the screen, while traders and lawyer shook their collective heads at the assumptions the guild had made—

Freza stood near, looking at what she could see of the letter and equations, wine glass wrapped in her ringed hand.

"What're you gonna do, Jeth?"

He smiled, reached for her free hand and gently kissed her knuckles before weaving their fingers together, and turning them to face the room.

"Gentles," he said, raising his glass and his voice. "Gentles, let us all understand what we have here. We have received another challenge. In effect, the Guild wishes to know if I value a ring above my duties as a trader. It is an interesting question, and at another time, when I am at leisure, perhaps I will answer it for them.

"For now, I am needed here, to serve trade, to preserve it, and expand it. I intend to continue here."

Beside him, he heard Freza draw a breath. Across the room, Brabham nodded, and Trader jen'Vornin bowed as between equals, hands forming the sign for *pathbreaker*.

He smiled and inclined his head.

"Apt," he murmured, and gestured again with his glass.

"I will ask you to refresh yourselves and recruit your strength while I step aside to inform my sponsor of this turn in events. When I return, I will be ready to work."

Freza dropped his hand, and stepped aside, raising her glass with a flourish.

"All of us—to accepting the challenge!"

The toast was met with acclaim, and when they had all drunk as comrades, Trader jen'Vornin raised her glass.

"To working for the good of trade!"